"O... ...,

... ."

He raised his foot, drew back, and with all his strength, kicked the latch. It burst apart under the force of his blow. The door crashed open, and he was in the cabin, striding angrily across the tiny space.

She stood with her back to the wall, her breasts thrusting against her shirt and her face white with rage. She was holding a pistol, pointing it at him. He walked up to her, seized her collar and yanked her forward, drawing her up to within an inch of his face.

"I have one thing to say to you," he shouted, holding her so close that her breath touched his cheeks, "and one thing only."

"Say it!" she screamed.

He smiled, his teeth flashing white in his swarthy face. "I love you."

And then his head bent and he claimed her lips with his own . . .

MY LADY PIRATE

DANELLE HARMON

AVON BOOKS ◆ NEW YORK

For his romantic embodiment of courage,
For the inspiration of his life,
For bringing me to England,
and all that I found there—
This book is dedicated to Horatio,
Lord Nelson ...
with love, reverence, and enduring admiration.

MY LADY PIRATE is an original publication of Avon Books. This work has never before appeared in book form. This is a work of fiction, and while some portions of this novel deal with actual events and real people, it should in no way be construed as being factual.

AVON BOOKS
A division of
The Hearst Corporation
1350 Avenue of the Americas
New York, New York 10019

Copyright © 1994 by Danelle F. Colson
Inside cover author photo by Thomas F. Keegan
Published by arrangement with the author
Library of Congress Catalog Card Number: 94-94065
ISBN: 0-380-77228-0

First Avon Books Printing: August 1994

AVON TRADEMARK REG. U.S. PAT. OFF. AND IN OTHER COUNTRIES, MARCA REGISTRADA, HECHO EN U.S.A.

Printed in the U.S.A.

RA   10 9 8 7 6 5 4 3 2 1

"It is your sex that makes us go forth, and seems to tell us, 'None but the brave deserve the fair,' and if we fall we still live in the hearts of those females who are dear to us. It is your sex that rewards us; it is your sex who cherish our memories; and you, my dear honoured friend, are believe me, the first, the best of your sex."

Lord Nelson,
in a letter to Emma, Lady Hamilton

Acknowledgments

Special thanks to Helene Chadwick, Trena Haroutunian, Karen Hayes, and Leone Laferriere for dockyard attention; Pesha Rubinstein, Marjorie Braman, and Christine Zika for navigational assistance; John Shissler, Gary "Mo" Morgan, and Bill Pilon for tactical advice; the crew of the GEnie RomEx's *She-Wolf* for their unfailing loyalty and support; and finally, all of the wonderful folks I met "across the pond" while I was researching this book in England—the people of the Norfolk Burnhams, the historians in both Portsmouth and Greenwich, and especially, Peter and Andy in Portsmouth, who not only personified the meaning of British hospitality, but went out of their way to fill my "Nelson pilgrimage" with memories I shall always treasure.

To all of you, my most heartfelt thanks.

Chapter 1

He was the scourge of the Spanish Main.

Nearly a century before, the pirate Blackbeard had taken some sixteen lovers in New Providence alone, and Gray, not to be outdone, was determined to best that score in the Caribbean that *he* now ruled.

Tonight, the lucky lady was one of his particular favorites—the delightfully wicked, carnally creative, Lady Catherine Fairfield, daughter of the richest sugar merchant on Barbados.

No pirate who'd ever swung a cutlass in these lawless waters ever looked more formidable. A hoop of gold pierced his ear and a patch covered one eye, though there was nothing amiss with the dark orb it concealed. To his other eye, Gray held his night glass, a heavy, brass and leather-bound instrument that he steadied against his arm and now, trained on the blaze of distant light that marked the palatial residence of Lord Fairfield. . . .

And—the pirate smiled wolfishly and closed the glass with a snap—his beauteous and willing daughter.

The breeze, as warm as the bedmate who awaited him, as sultry as the charms of that lovely lady herself, frisked over the dark Caribbean and pushed the little pinnace hard over on her beam. Waves crested white in the darkness, and the pirate's long hair rode in the wind like a wild, untamed banner, black as the night itself.

"Fetch her up a point to starboard, Bones," Gray

commanded, and the cadaverous man at the tiller did as he was bid, hiding a smirk as did his mates. Tolerant and loyal tars, they were well used to their leader's nightly sojourns. This raid on Lady Catherine's bedroom would be the pirate's last before duty called them all home and the Caribbean was once again safe from his roguish appetites.

Now, the pinnace skated across the dancing waves, aligning its nose on that distant mansion of light. The pirate hooked an elbow around a shroud, propped a foot atop the gunwale, and, thus ensconced in this lordly pose, leaned far out over the waves that licked greedily at the toe of his big jackboot. "Ah," he murmured, seeing the single light glowing in an upstairs bedroom, "the prize awaits me. . . ."

"Boarding in darkness is never honorable," grumbled Bones at the tiller.

"And rousing my temper is never wise," he said with a chuckle. "Hold your course, helmsman, or I shall seize you up to the mainyard 'pon our return and dangle you like a puppet on a string. *Then* you may talk to me of honor!"

The boat crew laughed, right along with him. Their leader was in good spirits, and why not? Soon they would be heading home, tonight he was going ashore to live his favorite pirate fantasy and . . . the most wanton lady in the Windwards was standing a secret watch in that upstairs bedroom.

But Fate has a way of upsetting even the most carefully laid plans, and on this late spring night in the Year of Our Lord, 1805, it did just that.

Gray the pirate would never know what spilled him into the warm embrace of the Caribbean and thus changed his life forever. A freak wave? A slip of his booted foot atop the gunwale? A shove from a mischievous spirit? One moment he was the proud commander of a pirate ship embarked on a dangerous raid; the next, he was the sorry victim of shipwreck, floundering in heavy seas that threatened to drag him down and lock him in the hold of Davy Jones forever.

Gray quickly recovered from this odd mishap. He surfaced, cleared the salt from his eyes, and trod water for a moment, unafraid of the depths beneath his booted feet nor the embarrassment a lesser man might've felt after being so disgracefully dumped in the sea in full view of his subordinates. He heard them calling for him, saw the muted shape of the pinnace's sail as a dim glow in the windy darkness. For a fleeting moment he considered striking off in its direction, but his blood was up, his appetites lusty, and damn him if he wouldn't make the raid after all!

But his jackboots—his prized, precious jackboots—they would have to come off.

The pirate took a deep breath, reached down, and allowed himself to sink while he tugged furiously at the boots with heel and toe and, then, frantic hands. One came off. His breath burst out in a spray of hissing bubbles and he clawed upward, clutching the boot like a prize and damning it for its weight; a similar maneuver and he made a prize of the other, too, while his bare feet thrust him back up to the dark surface.

His head broke water and he blew air out of his bursting lungs. The breeze was warm, sultry, skimming over the salty chop and carrying with it the distant, island scents of roasting meat and blossoming flora. He couldn't be far from his destination.

But the problem of the boots still remained.

Sweet Neptune.

He trod water as best he could with his free hand and strong, powerful legs. His breeches, wicked and daring and far more boastful of his masculine attributes than his usual attire, fit him like a second skin. But damn him, he would not part with the boots, even if they were fouling his progress!

So what if that old London shoemaker had eyed him quizzically when he'd brought the print of Henry Morgan to him; he'd certainly paid the man well enough to fashion a pair of boots after those the long-dead buccaneer had been portrayed in. After the trouble he'd gone through to get them, he'd be damned if he'd surrender them to the fish. Ingenious as always, he tore the knife from its scabbard, slashed a hole in the fine leather at the top of each boot, dragged off his knotted, sopping sash, and wove it through the holes, effectively snaring both boots before once more tying the sash around his waist to anchor them.

Now, he was ready to make his raid, and the devil take any who dared try to stop him!

Grinning heartily, he struck off with powerful strokes of his muscled arms that drew him closer and closer to the island, where the twinkling lights of Fairfield's mansion stabbed the darkness. Already, he could smell the aromas of roasted pork and beef drifting toward him on the breeze; already, he could envision the more succulent delights of the flesh that awaited him in that upstairs chamber. Aaah, the pleasures of working in the Caribbean! Balmy weather year-round, and free rein to live his life as he damn well pleased. Savory meals by day, and erotic pleasures by night ... the Lady Catherine being his fairest, and most recent, conquest.

The Lady Catherine.... She too would be in proper dress, in deference to his fantasy of taking a lady pirate to his bed. Catherine, of course, was only a nobleman's bored and beautiful daughter, but her carnal appetites were as insatiable and imaginative as Gray's own and she was willing to go along with any sexual games he sought to play with her. He grinned in anticipation. While her papa moved his corpulent bulk among the revelers at his grand banquet this evening, toasting the king and damning the emperor, *she* would be upstairs and waiting in her bed, her decks scrubbed down and damp, her rigging strung tight, and her entry port ready and willing to receive him. . . .

He couldn't wait to drop anchor in *that* harbor.

And thus encouraged, he put his mind to the swimming, the current washing his skin, the waves buffeting his face. The water was obscenely warm; salt stung his eyes and with a curse, he finally tore the eye patch loose, allowing it to trail from around his neck and lose itself in the sodden, floating folds of his shirt.

Fatigue, however, was catching up with him. He paused, treading water while he gave himself time to catch his breath. Unlike most sailors, he was a good swimmer, and a strong one at that . . . but surely, he had swum far enough that the shallows should be near at hand.

Blinking, Gray wiped the sopping hair off his brow, knuckled the salt from his eyes—and saw that the lights of the island were not growing closer, but moving *away* from him at an alarming speed.

God's teeth and blood.

He was no fool. He was a powerful man, a good commander—but first and foremost he was a sailor, and as such, he respected the laws of the sea. To try to swim against the current and toward the island would only be folly, for his strength, great as it was, could not hold out forever.

He allowed himself a brief moment to lament the forfeited rendezvous with the Lady Catherine. Then, motionless in the water, his keen mind began to plot a strategy, while the receding tide and swift ocean current bore him away to God-only-knew where.

And still the jackboots trailed from his waist, heavy, sodden, dragging behind him like a foul-weather anchor.

He did not cut the sash.

The lights of the island dimmed, faded. The riding lights of his great ship, mounting eighty guns and flying a Jolly Roger from her masthead, dropped toward the horizon, then under it, as the current bore him farther and farther away.

He was alone.

But still, he did not panic—nor did he consider loosing the jackboots.

There was nothing to worry about, really. At dawn, Colin would bring the mighty *Triton* in search of him. There would be a few thumps on the back from some of his men, a few snide and obscene comments, but nothing more—

Something splashed in the darkness off to starboard.

Gray froze, all thoughts of the Lady Catherine instantly vanishing from his mind.

Above, a ceiling of stars. Below, blackened fathoms. And around him, nothing but the soft wash of tumbling waves, and a sigh of the wind combing them into foaming peaks of white that glittered, diamondlike, in the night.

He began to relax.

And then, the splash again.

Shark.

His hand groped for his knife, yanking it free of its swollen scabbard. Something passed beneath him, pushing him upward on a great swell of current; he felt its size, its power, its total adaptation to a sea on which mankind was only an ill-equipped visitor.

And Gray, in his loose linen shirt, tight black breeches, kerchief, eye patch, and yes, jackboots—was ill-equipped indeed.

The creature plunged beneath him again, and he was dragged downward for a brief instant by the rush of water that went with it. Flailing to say afloat, he raised the knife, his feet kicking savagely at the threatening depths.

"Sheer off, you blighty devil, you!"

A fin, glistening in the starlight, cleaved the surface, circled him, and was gone.

Steady as you go, man, he told himself, fighting to control his rising panic. *Wait 'til it comes close and then fire as you bear.*

The fin broke the water.

It came toward him, the sea parting from it like the bow wave of a man-of-war.

Closer . . .

He gripped the knife, determined not to go down without a fight, and shook it at that approaching wedge of death.

"Come on, you bastard!"

Closer . . .

"Come on, damn you!"

He drew back his fist, and then the great sea creature burst from the surface, expelling a fountain of misted breath and water straight up to the stars before plunging gracefully back into the warm embrace of the sea.

"Bloody *hell,*" Gray swore, on a shaky breath.

And then the animal's wake smashed him in the face and sent him into spasms of coughing.

Cursing, he grabbed the dolphin's offered fin when it came to him again and, shoving the knife back into its scabbard, allowed the animal to drag him forward through the night.

From around his waist, the jackboots still trailed.

She liked sword-fighting, ships, and a stout mug of ale. She was suntanned and lean and not above ruthlessness when it came to getting what she wanted. She loved sharks, fancied herself a monarch, and now, stood as an unwilling witness to Celtic magic after a recent prize had yielded an old book of spells that keenly intrigued the lot of ex-prostitutes, barmaids, refugees, and slaves-turned-pirate-women who stood with her.

Her hair, caught in a thong of tough leather at her

nape, was heavy and straight and of the darkest shade of red, a shimmering fall of polished chestnut threaded with strands of ruby. Her temper was fiery and her stance warlike as only a gleaming dagger, a set of pistols, and a necklace of sharks' teeth could make it. Two large hoops of gold hung from her ears and kissed the bare tops of bronzy shoulders. Her clothes were garish, her manner belligerent, her face clever, hardened, and, after seven years in the Caribbean sun, Maeve Merrick, the Pirate Queen, was as dark as the hide of a coconut. But when she smiled, her teeth made a startling contrast to such darkness of skin, and her laughter was full-blown and hearty, as blustery as a reefing wind.

But the Pirate Queen was not laughing now. A quick-running tropical storm shook the palms and slashed against the roof of the abandoned planter's mansion that was now home to her jolly crew of the schooner *Kestrel*. It was not the gale that annoyed her, for she loved storms and could sail her ship through the eye of a needle, if necessary; the dangerous passage between the coral reefs that guarded her private lagoon would not have stopped her if she had wanted to go a-raiding. But the wishes of her crew did, for she was a pirate captain, supreme in battle but otherwise subject to the rules of Majority, and Majority ruled that this cynical Damsel should have her Gallant Knight.

Maeve, eyes flashing, mouth set in a line of annoyance, bare foot tapping out a drumroll of impatience upon the cool hardwood floor, stood now before the hastily built altar and what would have to pass as their cauldron—a pot, borrowed from the kitchen and framed on the right and left by twin pink candles that sputtered and spit in the drafts as though they, too, held this Exercise in Idiocy in high contempt. She took the opened book of spells, turned up her nose at the pungent scent of mold that issued from it, and wished she was anyplace but here.

"Ready, Majesty?" chirped sixteen-year-old Sorcha, aglow with the innocent enthusiasm of a child who still believed in fairy tales.

Maeve, however, was no child, and hard experience had robbed her of the belief in fairy tales.

"This is *bilge rot,* all of it!" she snapped, slamming the book shut and raising a cloud of dust. Glittering gold eyes issued a blatant challenge to anyone who dared disagree with her. "There *are* no Gallant Knights. For you, maybe, but not for me!"

Sorcha's younger sister, Aisling, caught Maeve's arm as she tried to storm away. "Oh, Majesty, *everyone* has a Gallant Knight, somewhere! Even you!"

"Especially you!" echoed Sorcha.

"And you shall marry him and live happily ever after!"

The two Irish girls—orphaned after their parents' ship had gone down in a storm a year ago and rescued by the scavenging crew of the schooner *Kestrel*—dragged their reluctant captain back toward the cauldron, encouraged by their hooting, laughing shipmates who had nothing better to do on this miserable day than conjure up a lover for their beloved leader. Wet wind drove through the tall, open windows, shaking the gilt-framed portraits on the walls, which looked down at them as though they, too, were waiting. Orla, the Pirate Queen's quartermaster, stood apart from the rest and, without a word, took the spell book from Maeve's hand, found the proper page, and silently handed it back to her.

The crew exchanged glances. They all knew the story . . . of how their captain, seven years before, had stolen her father's schooner-of-war *Kestrel* and run away with Renaud, the French sailor her parents had forbidden her to see. Enthralled by his charm, lured by his promises of marriage, Maeve had fled her New England home with him and come to the Caribbean. Naive, trusting, and only sixteen years old, she had given her-self to this man who professed to love her—and in the morning, had awakened to find him gone.

Luckily, he had not been able to scrounge up a crew to take her schooner as he had her heart. Maeve's maid Orla, and the small crew they had gathered for their journey south, disliked Renaud. *Kestrel* had remained in her possession.

For a woman who'd been left with nothing but her schooner, her wits, and too much pride to go running back to parents who had never bothered to come look-ing for her, Maeve Merrick had not only survived, she had flourished. It was no wonder she saw men as a threat to all she had worked for, planned for, fought for. She had forfeited a safe and loving home for a man and she would never do so again.

But her crew was not as cynical, and they still had high hopes that their leader would someday find her Gallant Knight. Now, they pressed close, and Maeve, trapped, had no recourse but to behave like the cornered animal she now felt herself to be. "Why would you want me to marry, anyhow?" she snarled, hurling a handful of black gunpowder into the cauldron. Some of it missed the pot and trickled down the sides, causing the crew to cringe at the sight of the flicking flames be-neath. "It would mean the end of our life together. I have fought hard to gain respect and independence and a name for myself in these lawless waters, and I've no wish to give it up, or share it with some sneaking, skulking, enterprising *blackguard* who'd only want what I *have* and not what I *am!* Marriage? Bah! We have everything we could need or want, right here on our island. I've no wish to trade any of it for a life of hell and sacrifice and anguish! There is no need for me to marry! *None!*"

"You should marry because we want you to be

happy," the innocent Sorcha said, without missing a beat.

"Aye," her sister chirped, "we want you to have a Gallant Knight!"

Mottling with anger, Maeve turned on her young tormenters. "There *are* no Gallant Knights, Aisling, and when you get some age under your keel you'll know the truth of what I speak! Men are all rascally blackguards, every damned one of them, all intent on one thing and *one thing only,* and that's satisfying the itch between their legs! Love? Bah!" She dismissed the idea wholly with an angry slash of her arm. "Love is nothing but a cruel hoax played by nature to entice two people to rut like dogs and so continue the miserable existence of this species! I do not believe in Gallant Knights, I do not believe in spells, and I *damn* well do not believe in wasting time in fruitless nonsense when we could be out *stealing* something!"

Again, she tried to storm away, and again, they dragged her back.

"Come, Majesty, it's just a game. You must play!"

"This is balderdash, all of it!"

"No, it's all right here, in the book!" Sorcha cried, thumping her palm on the moldy, yellowing page. "But it says here that if the spell is to work, you must first tell us what manner of man you would wish—"

"I wish *none,* do you hear me?" she lied. *"None!"*

But the two sisters clutched her arms expectantly, their eyes bright and determined, their wheaten hair glimmering in the light from the altar candles. Behind them, the others gathered closer, but it was these two, the youngest of the bunch and not yet tainted by the realities of life, who were dearest to the Pirate Queen's heart.

"Pleeeeaaase, Majesty?" they whined, in chorus.

Escape, obviously, was useless. Maeve lifted imploring eyes to her crew but there was no help from that quarter and, indeed, she'd expected none. Her pleading gaze turned hard and sullen as she tried to stare each of them down; Enolia, her lieutenant, ebony-skinned and exotic, her tall, lithe form banded with muscle and flattered by African jewelry; pretty Karena, blond and blue-eyed, the finest gunner this side of Jamaica and now, offering Maeve's cutlass on a tasseled pillow of red velvet; Tia, the boatswain, dark-eyed, sultry, and mischievous; Jenny, the sailing master, unsurpassed as navigatress; her loyal Orla; and there, at the forefront of this mettlesome pack, the two grinning Irish sisters.

Tight-lipped, Maeve snatched up the cutlass—a wicked curving length of steel won in combat from a Spanish pirate whose misfortune it had been to cross her bows two years past—and gripping this savage weapon that would have to act as the Magic Wand, turned her reluctant attention to the cauldron.

She shoved the spell book into Sorcha's hands. "All right, tell me what I'm supposed to do so we can put an end to this lunacy!"

"You're supposed to tell us what sort of man you want for your Gallant Knight," Sorcha said, pushing her hair behind her ear as she peered earnestly down at the page. Everyone's heads bobbed forward, their bodies throwing shadows over the ancient text. "Then"—she frowned, trying to decipher the words—"then, you're supposed to tap the Magic Wand against the cauldron three times and—ta da!—your Knight will appear, just like that!"

"Ta da, just like that," Maeve grumbled, her temper rising.

"Yes, just like that."

Fuming darkly, Maeve ground her back teeth together. Then she turned away to stare out the window, her hard eyes momentarily unguarded as she allowed herself to dream of something she would never have. She sensed their anxiousness, felt their eager eyes upon her back. At last she sighed, and still gazing off over the horizon, gave in to their demands. "Well . . . He would be a sailor," she mused, blushing a bit, "tall and lion-hearted, and strong as an oak. He would be a prince of the sea, a fearless warrior with courage to rule his every deed. . . ."

"Yes? Go on!"

She tapped a ragged fingernail against her chin, her eyes beginning to gleam as she warmed to the fantasy. "He would be dark and handsome, masterful and brave. And of course," she added with a fleeting smile, "he would be an officer . . . a courageous officer, a worthy man of purpose and honor and decency—"

"A man like your papa, then?"

Abruptly, her smile vanished and a cloud as dark as the one outside passed over the Pirate Queen's face. "Aye," she said bitterly. "Like my *father.*"

An uncomfortable silence ensued. Swift glances were exchanged, and Aisling flushed crimson at her ill-chosen words as the Pirate Queen turned to stare out the window, her eyes hard, her mouth an unbending slash of pain. Orla, who seldom spoke, made as if to do so now, but Maeve quickly recovered. Prideful as ever, and forcing aside the pain of the second, and most savage, betrayal of her life, she snatched up the spell book and affected an air of humor that fooled no one.

"Bah," she spat, forcing a smile to belie the sudden pain in her eyes, "why do I stand here wasting time? My deeds are too black, my heart too hard, for such a worthy man to ever take notice of me. Besides," she added, in the haughty tone of the All-Knowing, "I had one of my Visions last night. I already know what manner of man I shall have, and he is no better than I am—a *pirate,* a thieving blackguard worthy of the gallows and nothing more!" Her voice rose with suppressed hurt. *"That* is what the Sight has shown me, and it is never wrong!"

"It is *sometimes*," Aisling taunted.

"Well, it's not this time!" Maeve shouted. "Enough of this madness, *Kestrel* has not been out in three days and my palm grows itchy for want of good, stolen coin—"

"Oh, no, Majesty. We can't leave without first completing the spell!"

"Damn the spell!"

"But there are other things that must be added to the cauldron!"

"I'll tell you what I'll add!" Snatching up a gold drinking cup, Maeve stormed outside and returned, her hair wet from the rain, her eyes blazing, and flung the contents into the steaming cauldron. "Gull *shit!* Add this to your damned spell and see what you conjure up! And when you gain nothing, you'll see just what I think of this stinking nonsense! There *are* no Gallant Knights in this world, there is no magic, and *there is no man who will ever love me!"*

And with that, the Pirate Queen's arm savagely scythed down and cutlass met cauldron with a ringing crash, once, twice, three times—

The explosion rocked the room. It may have been a resulting spark and the black gunpowder that caused it; or maybe it was the spell itself. The cauldron went up in a burst of pink-and-orange flame, exploding outward with the force of a warship's broadside. The crew dived for cover, their captain was slammed backward against a wall, furniture went flying, and windows blew apart. A piece of metal ripped the spell book from Orla's hands and missed hitting her by an inch. Thick slime blasted against the white walls and trickled down in unholy torrents. And somewhere amidst this shattering melee of noise and slime and fear, a commotion filled the doorway and a man was hauled unceremoniously forward by two pirates who contained him with pistols held at either side of his set and stubbled jaw.

Too stunned to notice, the Pirate Queen lurched to her feet, her eyes still on the spot where the cauldron had been, where the two pink candles had stood, where there was now nothing but a blackened spot of singed flooring and an ugly mess of iron and sludge and stench. Her hands shaking, she reached up and touched her cheek.

"Orla? Aisling? Sorcha? You . . . all right?"

But they were all frozen in place and staring fixedly toward the door, their eyes as round as shot, their faces pale with fear.

Maeve knew, even before she took a deep breath and slowly turned to follow their gazes, what she would find.

A man. Not just any man, but a gloriously handsome one whose black hair streamed in rampant disarray past mighty shoulders and down a broad back; a man whose great hands were bunched into fists, a man with the devil's own fury blazing from eyes as darkly blue as an empty midnight.

Not the gallant officer she pined for . . .

but a pirate.

Queen Maeve stepped forward, and gathered herself for a question that needed no answer.

"Who the *hell* are you?!"

His gaze bored into hers. Furious, he reached up and flung off an offending clot of slime that stained his dripping brow. Then, he shoved the women aside and stepped forward, over six feet of towering male purpose, muscle, and rage.

"Your gallant-bloody-knight!"

Chapter 2

Gray's advance was halted by the Pirate Queen's pointed cutlass against his chest.

Bronzed by the sun, his shirt gaping, his bare skin smeared with sugary beach sand, through which little rivulets of seawater ran down, his wet and mighty body was like an impregnable fortress—but even so, he could not walk through a sword.

"Stand aside, woman." His voice was steely and hard, its tone dark, dangerous, and commanding.

The slender arm holding the cutlass did not lower. Neither did the regal nose, nor the glittering gold eyes that clashed with his. "I am the Pirate Queen of the Caribbean," she said, her voice quivering with rage, "and *you* will address me as *Majesty.*"

"I," he retorted, "will address you as I damn well please." His gaze insolently drifted down her open vest and blousy shirt.

"*You,*" she snarled, "are on *my* island, in *my* house, and barging in on *my* spell. Therefore, I'd just as soon skewer you to the wall and feed you your entrails for breakfast as toss you to the sharks. *Do I make myself clear?*"

A thick silence followed, the air crackling with tension.

"I said, *Do I make myself clear?*"

Gray stared into the golden depths of her eyes, matching her in fury, matching her in a struggle for

16

power, matching her in silent, savage combat. *This* young brat was the Pirate Queen of the Caribbean, a renowned figure he'd dismissed as an overinflated legend made large by the same superstitious sort who professed to have seen mermaids, sea monsters, and the ghost of Blackbeard?

Don't vex me, little girl, he thought, darkly; and then something tickled his temple and, reflexively, he swiped at the last of the slime that still dripped down his face. At that moment the absurdity of the situation struck him with sudden force and the corners of his mouth began to twitch in helpless amusement, even as his gaze slid down the graceful arch of her throat, the swell of breasts beneath the loose shirt, the bare legs and shapely ankles below the baggy, cutoff trousers. He liked what he saw, and his mouth curved in a slanted, wolfish grin of appreciation and amusement. But this formidable Amazon was anything but amused. She glared at him, eyes blazing—and Gray, undaunted, loosened his sash, let the dripping jackboots fall to the polished floor, and swept her a courtly bow.

"Your every wish," he drawled, coming up and making an elaborate, all-encompassing gesture with his arm, "is my *command.*"

She was still not amused. Her cohorts were not amused. Even the parrot that swung on a perch near the window did not seem amused. The Pirate Queen's mouth went white with fury and the cutlass kissed his chest, drawing a bead of blood.

"Kneel," she commanded, in the imperious tone of a monarch.

"I beg your pardon?"

"I said *kneel,* damn you!"

Deliberately, Gray let his gaze travel the length of that heavy sword and the arm that held it, until it once again met her angry gold eyes. He gave a faint smile. She posed him no particular threat. He could disarm her in a moment, of course; she was only a woman, and a young one at that. But mercifully, he decided to spare her dignity in front of this malevolent pack of she-wolves. Pushing the sword away with casual nonchalance he said, "Dear lady, I kneel to no one." He then turned on his bare heel to leave.

A knife hissed past his ear and impaled itself in the mahogany frame of the door, two inches away from his nose. And in that moment, he realized that the situation called for a definite—and immediate—reassessment.

His amusement faded abruptly and he reached toward the dagger.

"*Don't*," came the Pirate Queen's voice. "Unless you place no value on your life."

Yes, a most definite *reassessment of the situation.*

The room grew deathly quiet. Somewhere, some-place, he heard his own thundering heartbeat and, in that moment, became desperately aware of everything: the greenery, shiny with rain and thrashing in the storm just outside; the angry bay with its cruising whitecaps beyond; the warm breath of wind and rain; the sudden sweat on his brow; the chill of the floor beneath his feet. Then someone jabbed a pistol against his skull, another into his back, and he was acutely aware of *her,* coming up behind him.

Slow, measured, footsteps. The soft rustle of her clothing. The hot force of her anger as *she*—the woman whose existence he now wished he *hadn't* discounted, the woman who, so the tales went, was as likely to slice off an errant manroot as cut out a tongue that wagged too much for her liking—came up behind him.

"Imperious *dog,*" she seethed in a black whisper, standing on tiptoe to better hiss into his ear. And then that hiss changed to the roar of an angry lioness: *"How dare you come here and insult me!"*

It seemed that even the wind hushed, not daring to intrude upon the Pirate Queen's fury.

"Gallant Knight, my *ass,*" she snarled. "So much, *ladies,* for your stupid spell! I told you the Sight foresaw what manner of man I'd have, and it has proved true!"

" 'Twas the gull shit that ruined the spell, Majesty," a girlish voice murmured.

"Silence!"

The pistol thrust against the back of his skull. "Shall I kill him now, Majesty?"

"Nay, Enolia, *that* honor will be *mine,*" the Pirate Queen spit, her breath blasting Gray's neck like the hot wind of a close broadside. He could feel her stare burning a hole between his shoulders, the heat of her lissome body blazing through his damp and clinging shirt. "Lucia! Jan! Tell me where you found this . . . this *dog!"*

"Turlough brought him, Majesty."

"Turlough. I shall have to speak to that damned dolphin! This time, his penchant for rescuing people has gone too far."

Speak to a dolphin? This woman was not only bloodthirsty, but crazy as well. But Gray's snort of derision ended in an abrupt grunt of pain as the pistol was again thrust against his skull with force enough to make him see stars.

"No one laughs at Her Royal Highness!"

"Nay, let him be," the Pirate Queen commanded on a haughty note of disdain. "He'll learn soon enough. Lower your weapons, ladies. I've no wish to address this *vermin* by the back of his head! Let him turn and face me as a man, and prove to me he can *die* as one, too!"

The pistols were withdrawn with obvious reluctance, but not before the one pressed to Gray's spine was driven hard against his vertebrae for good measure. He set his teeth and bit back a curse.

The cutlass slammed against the doorjamb, two inches from his face. "I said turn around, damn you!"

Slowly, he turned to face his tormentor. The cutlass was clenched in her fist as she stared up at him, bare feet spread in the stance of a warrior, her mouth hard, and her complexion hot with anger. Fire flashed in her eyes—*tiger eyes,* he thought—and he saw her gaze dip, as though she could not help herself, to take in the expanse of his chest, and follow the spearhead of dark hair that disappeared beneath his breeches. He didn't say a word, only letting a little smile play about his mouth in recognition of and response to her obvious interest.

"Damn you, *kneel!*" she raged, and lashing out, drove her hand savagely against his shoulder.

Her action did nothing to budge a man who had some eighty pounds of solid muscle and sinew on this spitting cat of a woman. But it shook Her Majesty to the very core. She staggered, dropped the cutlass, and fell back against the wall, her eyes dazed and glassy, her face draining of blood, her lips going white and falling open. Instantly, two of her evil consorts—one a dark-haired sprite with a Celtic look about her, the other wheaten-haired and garbed in canvas trousers and a shirt of bright paisley, rushed to her aid.

"Majesty!"

"The Sight . . ." she murmured, staring at him with dawning horror and yes, fear.

They were mad, the whole damned lot of them, as mad as a compass with the needle pointing south! Shaking his head, Gray thought of leaving, but something stopped him. It was not the threat of pistol, cutlass, nor knife. It was not the imperious command of a woman he could've disarmed in the beat of a moment, nor the horde of female savages hovering protectively around her.

It was the woman herself.

Supported by her crew, she was still staring at him, her bosom rising and falling, a pulse beating wildly at her throat, her lips—lovely lips, of the sort to drive a man to madness—parted and trembling.

"You . . ." she whispered, in a tremulous voice.

And then, without warning, she shot to her feet, visibly shaken but in command of herself once more. *"Who the hell are you?"* she demanded, seizing her cutlass and storming forward.

"Gray."

"Gray *what?*"

"Just . . . Gray."

Twin stains of scarlet flared to life beneath her high cheekbones. "You'll be *gray* and *dead* if you persist in this deliberate taunting of me! Don't think I won't run you through and enjoy every moment of it! I asked your name, damn you!"

He shrugged, leaned negligently against the doorframe, and, with studied nonchalance, plucked the dagger from the wood and gallantly offered it—hilt first—to her. "And so I have told you." He gave a faint smile as she grabbed the knife. "Gray."

Her eyes narrowing with vicious cunning, she thrust the dagger into the scabbard at her belt. "Your ship, then."

"Tri-"

He caught himself just in time.

"Try-*what?*" she demanded, raising the cutlass threateningly.

He pushed it away. "Tri . . . *umphant.*"

"Bah! I've never heard of her, and *I* know every ship that plies the waters between these islands. You lie!"

"I do not lie."

"I do not lie, *Majesty!*" she roared.

He smirked. "Aye, you're right, I do not."

The cutlass slashed down three inches from where his shoulder rested lazily against the doorframe. "Dare you anger me? You shall regret the day you crossed my bows, damn you! Orla! Enolia! Seize this dog and throw him in the dungeon! A few days of starvation in company with the *rats* will soon teach him to show manners to a lady and respect to a *sovereign.*"

"*Lady?*" he murmured, with a dubious grin.

This time the flat of the cutlass slammed against the side of his head, and when Gray awoke, it was to pitch-darkness . . .

. . . and chains.

The Pirate Queen lay in her bed, the sheets flung back as she stared up into the shadowy darkness. Her hands were crossed behind her head, her naked body sweating from the island heat. Outside, she could hear the roar of the sea, the soft, eternal rustle of breezes moving through the palms.

"Gallant Knight, ha!" she snarled.

But there was the Sight. The Vision she'd had fore-telling his arrival. And despite what Aisling had said, she knew the Sight was seldom wrong. . . .

Maeve shuddered, suddenly afraid that this might be Renaud all over again.

Bah! She was not *afraid!* She sat up and in sudden fury, picked up a vase from her night table and flung it across the room. *I am not afraid!*

But she was.

He was The One. Her Gallant Knight. She knew it in her bones, knew it in the way she'd responded to his confident virility, even as she denied it with all her heart. She who had wished for a gallant leader just like her father, Captain Brendan Jay Merrick. She who idol-ized the brave English Admiral Lord Nelson had yearned for a sea officer cut from the same mold. But what had she been given? *A pirate.* A disreputable rogue with bad manners, a tattoo on his arm, and an in-solence she had yet to see matched. No gallant knight was this man; his scruples were no better than her own. Oh, she knew his kind; far too handsome for his own good, disdainful of any and all, and likely to break a woman's heart.

"He'll not break mine!" she cried suddenly, and threw another glass object across the room, hearing it shatter in a thousand pieces. "No man shall *ever* break my heart again!"

And *Gray.* What the hell sort of name was *that?*
Don't think about him!

Cursing, she flung herself onto her side and stared out her window and into the night, her gaze on the star-lit horizon, her heart twisting and turning and remind-ing her that the object of her thoughts, and, unfortunately, her desire, was not several hundred feet away.

Don't think about him. She turned her face into the pillow, pounded it with her fist.

Don't think about him.

Her heart slowed, became regular again, and closing her eyes, she forced herself to breathe deep and hard, finally putting that wickedly handsome face out of her mind and replacing it with older, gentler memories, un-til at last her anger cooled and her spirit began to drift. . . .

Home. It would be late spring now. Robins on the lawns, birds' nests in the trees, lilacs and apple blos-soms bursting with color, and the ice long gone from the river. Fishing boats being scraped down, blackflies on the beach, a fresh crop of kittens following Mama from the house to the barn to the pasture. . . .

Her eyes shot open.

"No," she whispered into the darkness. "Don't think about *that,* either. . . ."

But it was no use.

Daddy at the shipyard with Uncle Matt, working on plans for a new brig or a fine schooner, while her brothers and sisters and cousins played atop the logs that floated in the mast pond; Mama trying desperately to make a fruit pie and wondering why everyone had an excuse for skipping dessert . . . ornery old Grandpa Ephraim, surrounded by his beloved clocks and still fighting with his short-tempered daughter. . . .

It had been seven years since she'd allowed herself to cry over all she had lost, and now the tears spilled over, running silently down her face to soak the hot pillow beneath her cheek. Fury rose in her heart at her inability to quell this womanly weakness, but she had no more control over the wretched tears than she did the memories that had brought them.

Seven long years. Of watching the horizon for authorities who would never find her. Of watching the horizon for rival pirates over whom she must continue to triumph.

Of watching the horizon for a daddy who had never come.

It was the cruelest betrayal of all.

Maeve Merrick—daughter of the most famous privateer in the American Revolution and now, the undisputed Pirate Queen of the Caribbean—rolled over in bed and cried for all she was worth, for she didn't need the Sight to know that the handsome rake chained in the old storehouse just outside was no Gallant Knight—but the next in a line of men who would only break her heart.

Chapter 3

In the dark gloom of the dungeon it took Gray exactly forty-five minutes to work himself free of his bonds, and another ten minutes to assess the walls that enclosed him. It was no dungeon at all, but a simple chamber of stone. In other days, it had probably been used to keep foodstuffs cool; now, it was as empty as the hold of a warship too long at sea, and smelled no better. Mildew, moss, stone . . . well, perhaps a *little* better, he thought wryly.

He'd cursed those rough walls when he'd awakened—and blessed them when he discovered that, by rubbing his wrists up and down against the cool stone, he could steadily chafe away the hemp that bound him. Whoever had tied him up was either kind, stupid, or both, for his bonds were not so tight that they'd cut off his circulation to leave him numb. But after an hour of this steady chafing, he wished they *had* been.

Now, his hands were free, his wrists scraped and bleeding. His clothes—especially the snug-tight breeches—were still damp and now, itchy with salt against his skin. That discomfort, however, paled in comparison to the loss he felt for his precious jackboots. They were finally gone for good. And while Gray was not one to admit defeat by any means, he was certainly ready to call a cease-fire, and the rusty manacles around his ankles demanded he do just that.

And so he waited.

He looked outside, past a rusty, iron-spiked door entangled with vines bursting with pink and scarlet flowers. Sunset blazed on the horizon like a rim of molten flame, turning the serene waters of the bay orange, the beach pink, and casting the palm trees in silhouette. His eyes narrowed. In that sheltered harbor lay the finest schooner he'd ever seen in all his thirty-six years, waiting quietly for whatever lawless endeavors her piratical crew sought to engage her in.

By the rakishly cunning design of that schooner, she looked very well suited for such endeavors—and, in that moment, Gray vowed before heaven and earth that the trim little craft would assist in getting him out of this predicament.

When—he amended, with a rogue's grin—he was ready to leave.

His stomach growled with the ferocity of a tiger on the hunt, and he realized he hadn't eaten for nearly a day. Did Queen Maeve—he chuckled at the absurdity of the title—think to starve him into submission? Submission to *what?*

Her?

He threw back his head in laughter. *Majesty* indeed! She was naught but a she-wolf, an unscrupulous thug who deserved no more than the loop end of a rope. When he got free, he'd damn well consider giving her just that for the way she'd treated him!

Escape would not be difficult. However, *wanting* to be free was another matter. Gray considered the lush beauty of his captor's body, enough of which had been revealed to whet his appetite to see, touch, and yes, enjoy, more.

He vowed first to escape and then, he thought, with a wolfish grin—to *conquer.*

He had just sat down on the single item of comfort the room offered—a filthy straw pallet—when he heard the soft crunch of sand outside, growing louder and louder as the footsteps approached.

"On your feet, dog."

Gray yawned, hid his hands behind his back, and did not bother to rise.

"I said, *on your feet!*"

"I prefer to sit, thank you," he drawled. "Especially since you've anchored me to the floor. You understand, don't you?"

Sure enough, he heard the angry clang of a key in the old lock, and a moment later the rusty hinges squealed in protest as the door swung outward. Gray waited, his hands behind his back so his captor would not see that they were loose and, therefore, quite capable of strangling her.

But the Pirate Queen was taking no chances. In one hand she held a lantern, in the other a flintlock pistol. Both the lantern and the pistol were raised; the one to blind him, the other, if need be, to kill him.

"Get up."

He shrugged and got to his feet.

"Make one move and I'll blow your damned head off."

Gray had a whole vocabulary of smiles. Smiles to tease, smiles to charm, smiles to frighten, smiles to bode ill . . . smiles to win a female heart.

This last he flashed at her and was rewarded by a burst of angry color across his captor's face.

"Blast your eyes, have you no brain in your head? Are you not afraid of me? I could have you shot! I could have you nailed to a tree and gutted! I could—"

"Why don't you, then?" He regarded her with studied insouciance, his gaze raking appreciatively over her lush bosom.

For a long, terrible moment she said nothing, her face a pale oval of anger and disgust. She finally set the lantern down, flung her hair over her shoulder and spit,

"Because you might be *worth* something to me." She turned away to hide her bitter expression, began picking at her sleeve, and in a sullen voice, added, "Because . . . you're my Gallant Knight."

"Your *what?*"

"*My Gallant Knight!*"

He shouldn't have smirked. He shouldn't have laughed. But unable to help himself, Gray did both, and the resultant blow across the side of his face stunned him to silence.

"Do *not,*" she shouted, "ever laugh at me again!"

It was all he could do not to reach up and touch his throbbing cheek, but Gray could not, would not, allow her to see that he was far from being totally at her mercy. Instead, he drew himself up and, still clenching his hands behind his back, summoned another smile: this one reserved for Ladies Who Have Just Been Insulted and Must Be Placated.

"Forgive me, your most *Royal Highness*"—bending deeply at the waist, he gave a chivalrous bow—"but I merely found the idea of a Gallant Knight . . . amusing."

"You laugh at me again and I'll give you nothing to be amused about!"

He bit his lip to prevent such a possibility, for this spitting cat—armed, thinking herself dangerous, and setting more than his cheek afire—was amusing him highly. And, if he had his way, she would *amuse* him even more before the night was out.

But his silence, and perhaps the gleam in his roving eye, did Maeve in. She waited for him to say something more, to further fuel her wrath, but he did not. Instead, he merely looked at her, his dark gaze wandering suggestively down her bosom in a way that set her cheeks afire with anger and her body aflame with erotic longings which had been long dormant. His eyes met hers; one side of his mouth was turned up in a rogue's grin, and there was a boyish dimple beneath it. Maeve didn't care for that smile. She didn't care for what it did to her heart nor the temperature of her blood.

"Don't look at me like that," she snapped.

"I cannot help it. You are quite beautiful."

She chose to ignore his remark. "Why did you laugh just now?"

" 'Tis my secret."

"Share it, or I'll blow your privates off and leave you squeaking like a field mouse!"

Gray happened to value his privates. And right now, they were beginning to throb with the familiarity of arousal. "Well, here you are, so lovely, so serious—and you speak of talking dolphins, spells, and now, Gallant Knights. Forgive me, Majesty, but I am utterly charmed and thoroughly taken aback."

"Charmed? By *what?*"

"Why, by you, of course."

Her cheeks went scarlet, as though his words embarrassed her and made her uncomfortable. She looked trapped; scared, even. Couldn't she accept a compliment? Then she turned away, her jaw hard and angry once more. "There is *nothing* about me that is charming, and you'd best remember it!"

"Aye, you're not of the ordinary sort, to be sure. But, a delightful change from the plump, peach-skinned, and ripe."

"Are you talking about females or *fruit?!*"

He grinned wolfishly. "One and the same. I happen to enjoy both."

She flushed, her eyes challenging. "And what about me?"

"Oh, I should dearly love to enjoy you. And I intend to, before the night is out."

She jerked the pistol up and pointed it at his heart.

"But please," he continued smoothly, "not here. What do you say to trysting on the beach outside? Surely, the water lapping around our flesh will only heighten the pleasure . . ."

"You *dog,* how dare you speak to me like that!"

"What, is the notorious Pirate Queen a mewing virgin and not the spitting tiger she pretends to be?"

"What I *am* is something you'll not find out in a devil's decade!"

"I beg to differ"—he grinned rakishly—*"madam."*

They stood locked in silent eye-to-eye combat; finally, his gaze lowered and roamed over every ripe curve, every hidden hollow that graced her lovely body, the way a sailor might assess a ship he found particularly striking. Tanned by the Caribbean sun and wearing a necklace of sharks' teeth, a blouse with the sleeves ripped off, and trousers hacked off at the knee to show equally tanned calves and ankles, Queen Maeve was not his idea of femininity.

Nor, he thought wryly, of boredom.

He wondered how much *more* of her was tanned, besides what he could see—

—and made the mistake of asking.

Her hand came up to deal him another stinging blow, but this time his own flashed out from behind his back and caught it, neatly, effectively, smartly, his fingers closing around bones he could've snapped with one jerk of his wrist.

Their gazes clashed. She smiled cunningly. And then he felt the prodding nudge of the pistol against those private parts he would go to any lengths to protect.

"Unhand me."

With a dramatic, reluctant sigh, he let her go.

She stared at him, her eyes glittering, haughty, assessing. He stared back, refusing to be cowed. For a long moment she said nothing, the very picture of the affronted monarch. And then, surprisingly, she threw back her head and rich, billowing laughter burst from her throat. "Ah, pirate, you do not disappoint me after all! Do you think I'd wish an insipid pup with the blood of a jellyfish for my Gallant Knight? Bah! Perhaps there's hope for you after all. A brute you may be, and a wolf-hearted rascal besides, but you have managed to work yourself free, stand your ground in the face of my fury, and prove yourself more clever than I had given you credit for. Huzzah for you."

"*What?*"

"Do you think us incompetent, that we'd leave your wrists so tightly bound that you could not possibly escape?"

He stared at her, gaping in shock and severely wounded male pride. "You mean, you *purposely* left my bonds loose?"

"No need to look so downcast," she said prettily, her eyes taunting, a playful smile flitting about her hard mouth. She tossed her head and turned to go. "You may be worthy of me, yet!"

Gray lost his temper. "Like hell!" he thundered, and in a lightning-fast movement knocked the pistol aside, grabbed her by the shirt, slammed her up against his body, and crushed her in his arms.

And then, he kissed her.

Long and hard and deep and devastatingly.

He had meant only to prove his mastery over her.

What it was, and what it became, was much, much more.

Chapter 4

In that moment, Gray was done in.

It was only natural that he—born one hundred years too late and obsessed with all things piratical—should find himself totally undone by the unconscious charm of the most legendary she-wolf to rule the waves since Anne Bonney herself.

Just as it was also only natural that Maeve—cruelly used by that long-ago French lover, forgotten by a family that had never forgiven her, and distrustful of any and all males old enough to sprout hair on their chins—should find herself helpless beneath the masterful demands of a corsair's kiss.

The pirate's lips drove against hers, first with anger, then intent, then . . . then, only sweet rapture that robbed her legs of bone, her body of will, her hand of the knife that had reflexively swung up to plunge into his back and now fell to the floor on a clatter of defeat. A moan escaped her throat; Maeve felt her heart pounding against her ribs, her pulse echoing in her ears, the silky slide of her hair tumbling down her back.

Let me go. . . .

But his arm was a stout bulwark behind her shoulders, his chest a pressing wall of heat and strength, and her heart was trapped mercilessly between them.

She tried to twist away, but his arms only tightened, crushing her. Feebly, her palm came up to press against his chest, and in that moment his tongue plunged into her mouth—ah, delicious torment, heady glory!

She fainted, and lay like a wilted flower in his arms.

Gray felt her go limp, her mouth falling slack from his, her arm tumbling off his shoulder to swing like a pendulum above the stone floor. At first he thought it was a ploy, and expected a savage explosion of pain in parts of his body that were now burning with fever; but then he saw that this formidable woman was dead to the world, at his mercy, and truly, totally, out.

The gate to freedom was open.

Beyond, the schooner stood waiting.

And in his arms, the Pirate Queen lay senseless.

"God's *blood,*" he swore, as though he lived back in time along with Morgan and his murderous crew.

Gently, carefully, he set her down on the floor, spreading limp limbs over cold stone, arranging shiny chestnut tresses around a face fairer than any that had ever graced a governor's daughter, a dignitary's wife, a willing noblewoman, a skilled courtesan with the charms of Venus at her beck and call—all of which he'd bedded at one time or another during the span of his illustrious career. For a moment he stood looking down at the unguarded beauty of her face and the sheen of her hair, aflame in the warm, molten glow of the lantern; then, with deft fingers he plucked the key ring from her waist and unlocked his leg shackles. As he did so, he glanced once more toward the sleek little ship anchored out in the bay . . . but even he, skilled mariner that he was, could not sail her to freedom all by himself.

Patience, good fellow.

There was little recourse for him, really. And so he did what any red-blooded sailor in his advantageous position might do; he crouched down, slid one arm beneath the Pirate Queen's body and the other behind her neck, seated himself on the floor, and pulled her up against his chest, cradling her in his arms and positioning her so that her gaping shirt revealed parts of her that made his prison seem like paradise.

She was beautiful.

She was warm and soft and perfect.

And, she elicited a rush of tenderness in his breast that was as unfamiliar and alien to him as the idea of falling in love.

Love?

It was suddenly hot and stuffy in the little room, and he tore at the lacings of his shirt, loosening it at the throat and exposing his flushed skin to the breeze whispering through the doorway.

Love at first sight. . . .

A ludicrous notion, that! But even as his mind rejected it, his heart didn't, and his head jerked up as the idea seeded itself firmly in his brain. He stared blankly at the wall, hearing nothing but the sudden, tumultuous thundering of his heart.

"God help me," he said softly.

Why not? She was, after all . . . a pirate. His fantasy in the flesh.

"Dear *God,* help me!"

Out in the darkness, the tide swung the schooner toward him, and he had the unsettling feeling that the little vessel was laughing.

The Pirate Queen stirred. Her arm jerked against his chest, then her fingers curled, childlike, in the soft hair there, pulling hard enough to make him gasp even as she raised herself up and her cheek fell against his shirt and the tight, brown bud of his nipple beneath.

"Damn you," she murmured, and then, with pure fury, "bloody *bastard!*"

"I beg your pardon, madam—"

She raised her head and roared, *"Majesty!"*

"I beg your pardon—*Majesty*—but women don't

usually swoon when I kiss them," he said gallantly. "I wonder if I should take offense?"

" 'Twas the Sight," she muttered.

"The Sight," he said flatly. *Of course.*

"What, you think I jest?" She pushed herself away from him, her eyes bright and angry. "I have the Sight, the Irish gift to predict the future, to read meaning into Signs and Events, to ... to ... sometimes even communicate with the Dead. At least I *think* they're dead; I've never met these people before and they come to me in dreams and such. . . ."

"I see."

"Do you? *Do you?*" She leaned back and stared boldly up at him, the end of her ponytail caressing his forearm. Then she frowned as belatedly, she realized she was in his arms. "I doubt that you do, pirate," she said sharply, and let her gaze rake him from chin to chest as though she could, just by that imperious look, command him to release Her Royal Person. "Suffice it to say that I have Visions, and the really strong ones render me helpless, where I see the most *vivid* things."

He would've given his precious jackboots in wager that two minutes ago she hadn't seen a damned thing.

"And what causes these ... visions?" he asked, with the fond grin of a man who finds himself thoroughly entranced by a woman. His gaze roved over the enchanting view of upthrust breasts beneath her gaping shirt and a dark valley whose paths he wanted to explore with his hands, his mouth, his tongue ...

She caught the gaping fabric and yanked it up to the base of her throat. "A touch. A written word. A particular object. Spiced food and going to bed on a full stomach."

"And ... what did this, er, *vision* that you've just had tell you, hmm?"

"Stop leering, you vile pig."

"What did it tell you?" he persisted.

She released her collar and stared hard at him, as though daring him to insult her by looking down Her Royal Shirt once more. "That *you* are my Gallant Knight, whether I want you to be or not, and that makes no sense at all because in the Spell I asked for something entirely different!"

Gray's lashes lowered once more, and he made no pretense of looking anywhere but where his manly appetites led him. She did not move, though her breathing grew heavy, and her body tensed with wariness. His hand came up, touched the closure of her shirt, and pulled the fabric there together, as though he was a chivalrous gentleman intent on preserving her modesty—when in fact his strategic mind was plotting the defeat of her haughty defenses, and his sole intent was merely to get his hand on her skin. Under the guise of closing her shirt, he now had only to let his fingers stray innocently to the base of her throat, her collarbone, and then, of course, to the dark valley between those lovely breasts. . . .

His heart began to pound in anticipation, and he wondered just how far he'd get before she'd come to her senses and put a violent stop to his intentions. "And what, Majesty, *did* you ask for?"

"A noble and gallant sea officer," she said, hesitantly. ". . . An honorable warrior."

"Well then, allow me to pretend," he murmured, his fingers inches from those tempting breasts.

"But you're a *pirate!*"

"And a good one, too," he added, grinning wolfishly and letting his fingertips slide beneath her shirt. He leaned forward, kissed her brow, felt the flames beginning to lick at his groin. *Control, Gray,* he thought, *don't rush her.* . . . Already she was going rigid in his arms.

Knocking aside his hand, she lunged to her feet, glaring at him.

Gray rested his hands over his knees and cocked his head. "A kiss then, Majesty, for your Gallant Knight?" he asked, looking up at her through his lashes in the manner that had devastated many a heart before hers. "Surely, you can grant me that. Or will such an act put you in irons once again?"

She stepped backward, her eyes flashing, frightened, one fist bunching the fabric at her throat into a knot of strangulation. "Damn you, try it and I'll topple your mainmast and shove it up your—"

"Madam," he interrupted, allowing his eyes to widen with feigned affront, "although I am a sailor, I *must* take offense at your harsh language! Such foulness is better suited to rough tars, or the wastes of a bilge, or both. Surely a lady of *royal blood* does not demean her person by indulging in such ... *coarseness.*"

In the glow of the spitting lantern, he saw her face turn a brilliant scarlet beneath the hard tan. Her mouth opened, shut, went hard with indignation. She glared down at him, her hands fisted at her sides. "I am *queen* here," she said sharply. "This is *my* island and I'll conduct my speech in the manner I damn well wish!"

"Aye, I'm sure you will," he returned, offhandedly. "But as this is *my* prison cell, I'll thank you to talk like a lady while you're a guest here"—he flashed another roguish smile—"though I beg of you, not to *behave* like one."

"Guest! This is *my* island, and as such this prison is *mine!*"

"Very well, then. If it is yours, perhaps you should like to inhabit it? With me, of course." He winked lewdly. "We can always engage in some *royal* encounters in the palatial comfort of yon lousy pallet ... It grows lonely, don't you think?"

"Shut up!" she raged. "I don't have to stand here and listen to your sly innuendos!"

"Sly? Forgive me. I thought I was being quite articulate, Majesty. Allow me to steer a more . . . *candid* course." He rose to his feet, towering over her, and, with a mocking sweep of his arm around the dark cell, the stone floor, the filthy mat said, "Perhaps you will join me for a bout of lusty coupling upon the forgiving comfort of—"

"Silence, damn you! You make yourself very clear indeed! And now I wish you to make something *else* very clear, because if you do not, I'll cut out your tongue and use it to stir my drink!"

Gray threw back his head in rich peals of hearty laughter.

"Why didn't you tell me you're in the Royal Navy?!"

—and abruptly froze.

"I asked you a question," she said with dangerous coldness, displaying a dagger that appeared in her hand as though by divine Magic.

"How did you . . ."

Her hand lashed out, ripping apart the lacings at his throat and tearing the shirt down and apart with one angry jerk of her hand. There, proudly tattooed into the bronzed flesh of one shoulder, was the unmistakable anchor insignia of the Royal Navy, and beneath it, the name of his ship.

"You lied to me," she hissed with savage menace. "You told me your ship was *Triumphant*. I knew there was no such vessel in *my* waters! Your ship is *Triton*, the flagship of the commander in chief of the West Indies Fleet, Admiral Falconer!"

Gray's heart missed a beat and, casually, he pulled the torn shirt up to cover the damning evidence. She must've discovered the tattoo while he'd lain senseless in her clutches. "So I was in the navy once," he drawled, leaning his weight on one hip and crossing his arms over his chest. "What of it? Most pirates *have* been, at one time or another."

"And what are you up to now, eh? Admiral Falconer's ship has only been in these seas for two years! Which means *your* departure from the navy must've been a damned *recent* one!"

"What, is the navy after your hide, Majesty?"

"I'm asking the questions here," she said coldly, thrusting the knife under his chin and holding it against his throat. *"And I want to know why you left the Royal Navy!"*

"What makes you think I've left it?"

She shoved herself away from him. "Look at you!" she cried, pointing to his pirate clothes, his earring, the eye patch around his neck.

"Well, I was . . ." He bit his lip; he could not trust her with the truth, of course, could not disclose anything for fear of what she could do with the information. "I was—"

"You were *what?!"*

"I was on leave," he finished, lamely.

She stared at him; he saw the corner of her mouth trembling, jerking, then splitting apart in a wide, raucous howl of pure laughter the likes of which old Morgan himself could never have matched for gusto and glee. "Liar!" she cried, flinging her ponytail over her shoulder. "Do you think to bluff me into letting you go? Ha! You're a pirate, nothing more, nothing less. You can't fool *me* with such a sorry claim as *that!"*

Gray's mouth tightened in semblance of black fury. "I do not bluff!"

"And I do not release my captives unless I have a damned good reason to do so, especially a *deserter* who might be worth something to me! That's what you are, aren't you? A *deserter!* Vile, dishonorable *snake*. Admiral Falconer would pay *dearly* to have you back, and believe you me, I won't think twice of collecting the highest price he'll pay for you if only to see you swing from his flagship's yardarm!"

"You wouldn't!"

He was rewarded with the smile of a barracuda. "Oh, I just might!"

Gray, desperate, raked a hand through his hair, spun on his heels, and whirled to face her. "Very well then, belay that! You want the truth, I'll ram it down your pretty throat! Yes, I jumped ship, and if the navy finds me here, my life is *ruined.*"

Humor flickered in her eyes. She studied him, trying to fathom a lie. Then she raised the knife, proceeded to trim a broken fingernail, and looking up, gestured with the savage little weapon for him to continue.

"You spin a fine tale, pirate. Too bad I don't believe you for one moment. Explain to me why someone like *you* even *went* into the navy."

"You have the Sight," he shot back. "You tell me."

She swung the dagger toward his throat. "I'm warning you, pirate!"

Holding her gaze, Gray reached up, grabbed her wrist, and held the knife away from his neck. "I entered the navy because of a *lady,*" he said acidly.

"Of course."

"Aye"—still holding her wrist, his gaze flickered down to her bosom, as though he could strip the shirt away with his eyes—"of *course.*"

She glared up at him, her eyes spitting sparks. "And?" she demanded, jerking her arm free.

He shrugged, smiling faintly at the distant memory. "Like all youths, I had a natural curiosity about the female anatomy . . . in this case, the curiosity extended to Lord Rathfield's daughter, who, I'm afraid, was as curious about my person as I was about hers. During one of our, er, *voyages of exploration* we fell afoul of her father, who took the matter to mine, and, well, here I am!"

She ignored the blitheness of his tone, the smile playing about his lips. "And how old were you?"

"Twelve." Again, that challenging, wolfish grin.

"A mere brat! Well this time your *falling afoul* of the wrong person is about to land you *back* in the navy! I may be a pirate, but I come from an honorable family and I have no stomach for deserters. Nor do I have the stomach for men who insult me, force themselves upon me, and pretend to be something that doesn't exist, a *Gallant Knight!"* She spit the words with disgust. "To-morrow, I take you back to Admiral Falconer and Lord Nelson!"

He threw back his head in laughter. "Lord Nelson? Lady, you have the wrong ocean! Lord Nelson is in the Mediterranean, not the Indies."

"Lord Nelson is on his way to the Caribbean, pirate, and in a day or two you'll see the masts of his fleet as it approaches Barbados!"

Gray couldn't have been more stunned if he'd been hit by a falling block in the heat of battle. Nelson? *In the Caribbean?* He stared at her, feeling the blood draining from his face in a rush of sickish dread that left his skin cold and damp and prickly.

"L-Lord Nelson?"

"Aye, Lord Nelson! Where the hell have *you* been, eh? Trysting with a *lady?* Bah, you *are* a waste of my time, of my words, of my hopes!" She tossed her head, sending her glorious tumble of hair flying over one shoulder. "Nelson is indeed nearing the Indies, and heading for Barbados as we speak!"

"What?"

"Aye, Lord Nelson. Don't tell me you haven't heard? What England has been dreading since the war began has finally happened—a huge fleet of French and Span-ish warships under the command of the French Vice-Admiral Pierre Villeneuve escaped Lord Nelson's blockade of Toulon, and he has chased them clear across the Atlantic and into *our* waters in hopes of bringing them to battle here. I don't know much about naval strategy—I am, after all, a mere pirate—but from what *I've* heard, if enough of Napoleon's squadrons manage to escape the British blockade of Europe's ports, and rendezvous in some far-off place—in this case, our own lovely Caribbean!—the French will be able to sail back across the ocean as a mighty force, crush the Royal Navy's defenses of the Channel—and invade and conquer England."

Gray was staring at her, thunderstruck and speechless.

"So you really *haven't* heard, have you? Well, the news is quite fresh; I heard it just three hours ago." She grinned and folded her arms, her eyes taking on a distant, dreamy look. "Yes, Lord Nelson, pride of the Royal Navy, upon whom Britain has pinned her hopes of salvation from that monster, Napoleon Bonaparte, is on his way to Barbados. He has the Mediterranean Fleet with him, consisting of nine heavy ships-of-the-line and three frigates. Oh, what I wouldn't give to meet the brave Lord Nelson, who destroyed the French at the Nile—on the same day I ran away from home, mind you!—and smashed the Dutch into submission at Copenhagen. When he catches up to Villeneuve, we shall see a battle that the world will never forget."

"Dear God," Gray murmured. It was suddenly impossible to stand, and he leaned heavily against the stone wall, trying to collect his thoughts. How could he not have known? The wind. Damn it, the wind, blowing contrary as usual; that, and the pressing business he'd been attending to in Jamaica, as well.

The Pirate Queen narrowed her eyes, grabbed her lantern, and shoved it toward him. "What's the matter, pirate?"

But Gray was quiet, his mind awhirl with the incredible news he had just heard.

"Damn you, I asked—"

"Aye, I'm fine!" he hurled back, and drove a shaky

hand through his hair, even as cold sweat broke out the length of his spine.

Nelson was in the Indies.

He swallowed once to moisten his throat, twice because he couldn't, and then spilled out a string of curses so blue they made the Pirate Queen's harsh talk sound like the first words of a babe.

"Pirate?"

He had to get out of here!

"Don't you up and die on me," she commanded in her imperious tone. "The Sight said that you are my Gallant Knight and I can't have you dying when you just *might* be my only chance at happiness—"

He grabbed her shoulders, his eyes maniacal, and in a black fury spawned by dread and anger with himself, roared, "How do you know Nelson is in the Indies? He has no reason to be here! Where did you come by such information and how the bloody hell do I know you're telling the—"

"Now, see here!" she stormed, drawing herself up with regal hauteur. "I am *royalty,* and you must first request permission to touch me—"

Gray grabbed her by the throat, cut his hand on her necklace of shark's teeth, and cursing, hauled her up to within an inch of his face. "Answer me!"

Maeve looked up into that dark visage, those fathomless eyes just two inches from her own—and smiled, for her pirate was turning out to be a dangerous man. She *liked* dangerous men. *Respected* them. A thrill of excitement shot through her blood.

"I know everything," she said haughtily, with a lofty turn of her chin. "I have the Sight, remember?"

"Answer me!"

He jerked her forward. Glittering gold eyes clashed with wicked indigo ones. She felt his knuckles pressing against the rapid pulse beating at her throat, the heat of his breath against her face, the merciless pressure of the sharks' teeth driving into her nape. He glared down at her. She glared back. Then her gaze went, deliberately, to the angry slash of his lips, and with a preoccupied smile, she reached up to touch his mouth.

This time, there was no flash of insight, no Vision, *nothing,* and she felt vaguely disappointed. "No, pirate, you will answer *me.* You see, I want to know why you're in such a damned hurry, all of a sudden, to leave," she said silkily. "Do you fear the mighty Nelson as the French Admiral Villeneuve does?"

Gray released her abruptly and stood staring as she reached up to massage the spot where the necklace had pricked her throat. "What, do you think I lie?" she said prettily. "I have my own *personal* reasons for hating the French. And as for Nelson . . . the French are *not* at Tobago, as he will be led to believe. What a pity, that the noble Admiral will go chasing after wild geese when the real *fowl* are nesting at Martinique—"

"How do you know this?!" he thundered.

She shrugged, smiled, and reached up to play with the swinging hoop of gold at her ear. "Why, the Sight, of course."

"What!"

"You needn't roar, pirate. I can hear you just fine. But since you are so keen on knowing . . . Tavern talk. Swifter than the wind, it is, and far more dependable. I heard the news from some of my most-trusted crew members who had visited a tavern on a neighboring island."

"Bloody *hell.*" Gray slammed a fist against the stone wall so hard he nearly broke every bone in his hand. The French were in the Caribbean. The zealous Nelson had come chasing after them. And he—regardless of the Pirate Queen's charms, regardless of his vow to have her—had to get out of here. Duty came first, and the fate of his nation could very well rest upon whether or not he escaped her clutches! But could he tell her who he was? Could he trust her? For God's sake, she was a *pirate!*

He turned, faced her, and said desperately, "You must release me."

"Why should I?" Again, she fell to paring her nails with the knife, slanting an amused look at him from beneath her long lashes. "You have an excessive amount of fear of Nelson ... it makes me ponder the *real* reason you jumped ship and deserted your navy. . . ."

A cold chill seized Gray's heart.

The Pirate Queen gave him another sidelong glance. "Makes me wonder, perhaps, if you're not merely a deserter, but a traitor ... You see, I loathe traitors even more than I do deserters." The knife's motion stopped and she raised her head, staring hard at him. "You're not a traitor ... are you?"

He swallowed thickly.

"Are you?"

"Now Majesty—"

"That's it, isn't it?" she cried suddenly, slamming the knife into the scabbard with violent fury. "You were selling out to the French! To *Villeneuve!* Spying for them! No wonder such fear of Nelson! No wonder such sudden desperation to leave here, so you can go off and tell Villeneuve everything I just told you about Nelson!" Her eyes blazed, as though he had betrayed not his country, but *her.* "You are despicable, you know that? *Despicable!"*

"Please," Gray said, dropping to his knees before her, bowing his head and showing her the respect her self-proclaimed sovereignty demanded. The French, the English ... either navy would pay handsomely for him, but if he ended up in the hands of the wrong one ... But how to play this hellcat. Which would serve him better—the truth, or a lie?

He made an instant decision.

"For the love of God," he said shakily, and looked up

at her, "I implore you, Majesty, please, *do not bring me to Nelson!*"

"I will bring you to whoever pays the most for you!"

"The English will not pay you! They'll merely seize me and hang me from the yardarm without benefit, even, of trial!" He got himself under control, knowing he was playing a dangerous game indeed. "I beg of you, Majesty . . . please, don't turn me in! Don't bring me to Nelson, he will certainly hang me—"

"Traitor, you *deserve* to hang!"

"But I am your Gallant Knight, remember?!"

"I never said I *wanted* a Gallant Knight! And such an idea is naught but rubbish, anyhow! *There are no Gallant Knights,* at least not for me, and as for *you,* you'll do nothing but break my heart! I wanted an honorable man, someone I could *admire,* a handsome, decorated *officer,* but there's not a heroic bone in your body! *Not one!*" She was scarlet with rage, her eyes bright with unshed tears. "You hear me? Not one! You're nothing but bilge rot, a vile, wretched *traitor* with as much honor as a slinking eel! *Tomorrow I bring you to Nelson!*"

And with that, she spun on her heel, stormed across the room, and damning him to hell and beyond, slammed the gate in his face.

Chapter 5

He was forty-six years old and going blind. He loved little children. He'd lost an arm at Tenerife, the sight of an eye at Calvi, and had his brow laid open to the bone at the Nile, where the destruction of Napoleon's fleet had earned him a barony and the love and adoration of his nation. Constant anxiety had taken its toll on his body, two years of blockading the French off Toulon had left him haggard and ill, and now, fears of failing the England that entrusted *him* to save it brought him nothing but anxiety and distress.

Mighty Britannia's confidence rested on small shoulders that seemed barely wide or strong enough to support the glittering gold epaulets that rode atop them. He was a little man, with a pale and sensitive face, a pointed chin, a compassionate mouth, and once-brown hair that had faded to gray. His good eye shone with fervor and intelligence, his nose was strong and bold. Slight in stature, kind of heart, irascible in temper, and suffering from all manner of illnesses both real and imagined, he did not evoke the image of a national hero, for the Right Honourable Lord Viscount Nelson— Knight of the Bath, Duke of Brönte in Sicily, Knight of the Great Cross of St. Ferdinand and of Merit, Knight of the Order of the Crescent, and of the Illustrious Order of St. Joachim, Vice Admiral of the White and Commander in Chief of His Majesty's Ships and Vessels in the Mediterranean Station—was no bigger than a schoolboy. Yet there, beneath the empty sleeve pinned so carefully across a chest ablaze with the decorations of valor, lay the heart of a lion, the fierceness of a tiger—and a burning hatred of the French.

But Horatio Nelson did not look fierce at all this morning, as H.M.S. *Victory* drove toward Barbados with the might of the Mediterranean Fleet spread in glorious array behind her. He had invited his little midshipmen to breakfast with him after they'd come off their watch, and on this bright morning in June, he was sharing in their childish, giggling jokes and behaving with youthful abandon, when calls from the masthead—and moments later, the appearance of his flag-captain, Thomas Masterman Hardy—brought him news that the returning frigate *Amphion* was hull up on the horizon and closing fast.

Nelson, ecstatic, set down his tea and leapt to his feet. "Now, my young gentlemen, we shall learn what Captain Sutton has found out about our friend *Villeneuve"*—he pronounced it *Veal-noove,* for Nelson may have won mastery over the French fleet but never their language—"and whether or not he is indeed here in the Indies! *May we bring the French to battle at last!"*

Cheers, all around the polished mahogany table, from a circle of children and a grinning Admiral whose height could not rival the shortest of them.

He saw the wild eagerness in their eyes. "Dismissed!"

They fled topside, but a sharp reprimand from Captain Hardy reminded them to walk like young officers and not undisciplined children.

It was all Nelson could do not to go charging up after them. He began to pace, and by the time the frigate was hove to under *Victory*'s lee and her grave-faced captain, soaked with spray and flushed with news, piped aboard

and brought to his cabin, the Admiral had worked himself up into a state of high excitement and agitation.

"News, Captain Sutton!" Nelson said anxiously, seiz-
ing the officer's arm and pulling him into the cabin.
"You have news of the Combined Fleet, of
Villeneuve?"

Sutton looked at Hardy, and then at his Admiral, and
swallowed tightly. "I spoke with the governor of Barbados, milord, and delivered your dispatches to him."

"And?!"

"Our pursuit has not been in vain, sir."

"See, Hardy!" Nelson exclaimed, flushed with triumph. He pounded his single fist down on the table for
emphasis. "By God, the French are here and I shall
have them yet, you may *depend on it!*" He swung anxiously to the somber-faced captain. "And Admiral
Falconer—he is prepared to assist me, I hope?"

Sutton looked away, suddenly uncomfortable. He
glanced at Hardy, as though for reassurance, but caught
Nelson's sharp and questioning look. Slowly, he said,
"Admiral Falconer has a squadron at Barbados, sir, as
well as a sugar convoy assembled there that is ready to
sail for England. He has a frigate patrolling the Windwards, another stationed off Antigua, several seventy-
fours at Jamaica—"

"Thank God Falconer has the safety of *that* island in
mind!"

"Indeed, milord. Admiral Falconer had the safety of
all his islands in mind."

Had?

Nelson's keen mind did not miss the implication of
that single word. He saw the grave look on Sutton's
face, and felt the blood going cold in his heart. "What
do you mean, *had?*" he demanded.

The unhappy captain shuffled his feet and looked up.
"I'm sorry, sir. Admiral Falconer is ... dead. I went
aboard one of his ships at Barbados and spoke to a

Captain Warner, who confessed it was the result of a duel, sir." Sutton paused, as he saw the look of shock and horror washing over his beloved leader's face. "Falconer's flag-captain has been assuming the admiral's duties until a new commander in chief can be appointed in his place. He—he sends his regards, sir."

The words hit Nelson with lethal devastation. For a full minute, maybe two, the little Admiral stood staring at the hapless Sutton as he tried to absorb the shock. His single hand reached for the back of a chair, gripping it as though it was all that kept him on his feet. Without speaking, he turned toward the window, his slight body looking very frail in its glittering uniform, his face in profile, his lips pursed in visible pain, and only his throat moving, up and down, up and down.

The cabin grew deathly silent. Hardy glanced worriedly at his admiral, and Sutton developed a sudden, embarrassed interest in his coat sleeve. "Captain Warner said the duel had something to do with . . . um—with a woman . . . sir," he added, lamely.

Nelson took a deep, shuddering breath, his excitement about the French fleet suddenly forgotten. Turning from the window, he bent his brow to his hand and collapsed in a chair. He was aware of Hardy and Sutton moving protectively toward him; darkness swam before his eyes and he took a deep, shaky breath to ward it off. "Damn you, Falconer," he cried suddenly. "Damn you and your confounded philandering; I *warned* you it would come to this!"

"Sir?"

"I suppose the duel was fought with *cutlasses,* wasn't it, Sutton?!"

"Captain Warner did not say, sir."

Nelson raised his head, his cheeks streaked with tears he made no effort to control. "Leave me," he said hoarsely. "I wish to be alone."

Sutton beat a hasty exit, but Hardy lingered a moment. He reached out, tried to lay a comforting hand upon the Admiral's shoulder; but Nelson got to his feet once more, moving to the great, panoramic windows and staring out at the bleak expanse of the endless sea. He remained there for a long time. Then he turned, his face melancholy. "Forgive me, Thomas. You would think that after having so many friends fall in battle, such things would grow easier to bear, but they never do. . . ."

"I'm sorry, sir," Hardy said. "I know he was a friend to you."

"He was a friend to *England*. What a shame. What a goddamned, bloody *waste.*"

"Such is war, sir."

"Aye, such is war. You lose your arm, you lose your life, you pray God someone remembers you back home. But do they, Thomas? *Do they?* Or does anyone really care?"

Hardy looked down at his big hands, at a loss for words. "I am confident, sir, that when you catch up to Villeneuve you will give him the thrashing he—and Napoleon—deserve. And," he added solemnly, "a victory for England that will *never* be forgotten."

Shouts, cheers, and dancing figures on a lantern-lit deck; curses, harsh breathing, steel ringing against steel, and the singing *whoosh* of thrusting, slashing cutlasses. The sounds cleaved the night as Enolia—once a planter's concubine until her master's ship had fallen afoul of the Pirate Queen's—practiced her fencing skills with her formidable liberator.

The two were well matched, both honed with muscle and sleek with sweat, and while rapiers would have been far more manageable than heavy cutlasses, neither captain nor lieutenant was willing to make the trade. Slash and parry, thrust and pivot and slash again: fencing with cutlasses was an exercise in strength and endurance, essential qualities for lady pirates wishing to hold their own on a lawless sea ruled by men.

"Captain, I know he angers you"—Enolia swung her blade, had it deflected upward as the Pirate Queen expertly parried her attack—"I know he's a deserter, a traitor, a spy, but before you go rushing off to Nelson with him, think about what you're doing!"

Cheers erupted from the pirate crew at their captain's expert defense.

"I *know* what I'm doing!" Maeve cried, the sweat sheening her brow. She swung for Enolia's unprotected ribs and, at the last moment, the other woman danced away, the tip of Maeve's cutlass catching her shirt and tearing it from waist to shoulder. The hit decided the match, and Maeve, her lungs heaving, tossed her damp ponytail over her shoulder, saluted her lieutenant, and then clashed her cutlass against Enolia's in a handshake between steel. "Besides, he's no Gallant Knight; he proved *that* to me when I visited his cell!"

Breathing hard, she tore the kerchief from her brow, mopped her face with it, and strode to the rum barrel, her shadow long and black in the orange glow cast by the flickering lanterns. She filled her tankard, downed it. Filled it again. Drank the sweet fire more slowly this time, letting it filter down and out into every cell in her body. Her pounding heartbeat begin to steady, and she felt the trades kissing her hot and sweaty skin, drying her face and arms and torso beneath the loose shirt she wore.

"Good match, Captain. I thought she had ye there," Karena remarked, drawing her knife and paring a mango.

"And here I had my money on Enolia tonight." Tia flung a coin into a wooden bucket. "Should've known better!"

Maeve's lips curved in a harsh grin. "What, you think I've lost my touch, Tia?"

"Nay, captain, merely your heart to that handsome rake. I *knew* we should've shot him the moment he crawled onto our beach!"

Tia's observation hit too close to the bone. "Have a care for what you're saying," the Pirate Queen growled, "or you'll be the next one I challenge to a sword fight!"

"Well then, in that case—"

"Belay it, Tia," Maeve said, waving her off. "I've had enough for one night."

Tia, her eyes dancing, gave an elaborate sigh, for she, like her crewmates, considered it a privilege to duel with their formidable leader. After all, the Pirate Queen had learned to fence under the tutelage of her father, and seven years in the Caribbean had only honed her natural aptitude for the skill into one that few men dared challenge—let alone survived.

But sword fighting was the last thing on Maeve's mind. She sat down on the deck and leaned against the truck of a cannon, feeling her little ship rising on a swell, settling, rising again beneath her. Even the fierce energy she'd put into her match with Enolia had failed to drive the image of the pirate's face from her mind, or drive the memory of his kisses from her soul. She quaffed the rum in fierce, angry swallows, seeking to drown her torment in tipple instead.

"That black-haired devil again?" Orla asked quietly, discerning the reason for her captain's sour mood.

Maeve stared mutely out into the darkness without answering.

"So, he tried to take some liberties with you," Karena said. She stabbed the mango peelings with her dagger and flung them over the side. "What man hasn't?"

"Aye, you've got to give 'im credit for trying," Jenny pointed out.

"He's your Gallant Knight," young Sorcha cried, from her seat atop one of the guns. "I'm sure of it!"

"Aye, Majesty," her sister echoed, "your Gallant Knight!"

"He is *not* my Gallant Knight!" Maeve retorted, slamming her mug onto the varnished deck and staring down each lantern-lit face in turn. "My Knight—God, how I *loathe* that word—will be a brave, noble officer, someone honorable and upstanding and good. This 'Gray' is naught but a traitor and a spy, the both of which *I* have no use for! Besides," she added, glaring sullenly off into the night, "he'll only break my heart. Already, he stirs my blood, already I find myself wanting the feel of his arms around me, his lips against mine! I cannot, *will not,* fall in love with this man, for to be in love is to be exposed, vulnerable, open to abuse and *ABANDONMENT!"*

"But Majesty, he's not like those other men who've tried to court you, can't you see? None of them were worthy of you!"

"He's a *spy!"* Maeve cried, in frustration. "He's a traitor! *He deserted his navy!"*

Only Enolia, leaning calmly against the rail and backhanding the sweat from her brow, seemed to be on her side. "And if he could desert his navy," she said pointedly, "he could desert *you."*

No one spoke. They all knew their captain had been deserted *enough.* She was not to be blamed if she didn't trust men. She was not to be blamed for not trusting *this* man, with his wicked smile and dangerous charm. And she *did* have the Sight—who could know what it had shown her?

Enolia stalked to the barrel, drew a hefty measure of rum, and, lifting it to her lips, faced the crew. "I'm with the captain," she said. "Let's bring him to Nelson. The British'll pay a hefty sum for him, if only to keep him from spilling his guts to Villeneuve."

"And we can do *far* more with British money than with a British deserter!" Maeve cried, in triumph. But it was an empty triumph, for, deep down inside, she did not want to relinquish her captive. Despite his treatment of her, despite the fact he knew just how to raise her ire and seemed to delight in doing it, he had made her feel like a woman again, not the hardened pirate she was. He had made her feel beautiful and desirable.

But no. She had learned her lessons too well. He would only break her heart, and it was better to get rid of him now.

Gaining her feet, she left her mug on the binnacle and went to the rail, there to stare down at the waves curling against *Kestrel*'s black hull. Turlough was down there, drifting on the surface. She could see the dolphin's pale belly as he floated on his side, one flipper free of the water as though waving at her. Then he dived beneath the schooner and emerged on the other side, blowing out his breath on a rush of sound that was melancholy in the darkness.

She gazed across the water, the beach, and toward the old storehouse, barely discernible in the gloom— where *he* was.

Then she shut her eyes, and, as her father had once done in another time and place, quietly placed her hands on the rail of her ship, listening. But *Kestrel* was unusually silent, and instead, it was her father's presence that Maeve sensed. She could almost feel the warmth left by his hands, as though he had stood here just moments before and not all those years ago; she could almost hear his voice again, his laughter, as he'd taught her to sail this little schooner. Her father, a dashing privateer captain who'd become legendary in the American Revolution . . .

"Point her up into the wind, lass, a bit more! Faith, she's no square-rigger, you know! Let her fly!"

"But Daddy," she'd cried, in her eight-year-old voice, "she's already pointed as high as she'll go! She'll be in irons!"

"Faith, lass, I designed her; d'you think I don't know what she can do?" His laughter—rich, merry, Irish laughter—had mingled with the wind before he'd come aft to wrap his hands around hers, steadying them upon the tiller, teaching her about ships and sailing, wind and waves and weather. . . . *"Now, listen to your ship, and she will speak! Always listen, daughter, for she owns the wisdom of the sea, and the day you forget to listen is the day the sea will do you in. . . ."*

The memory dimmed, faded, was lost to the silence of the night. Maeve bit her lip and swallowed hard against the sudden lump in the back of her throat. High above, a million stars twinkled and winked in celestial abandon; she gazed up at them, wondering if those same stars stood watch over her father now, more than a thousand miles away in New England . . .

Then, as she had done every day these past seven years, she lifted her gaze to the dark horizon. But there were no lights out there from any incoming ship. It was empty, just as she'd known it would be. Her father was not coming for her. Her mother was not coming for her.

No one was coming for her, because no one cared.

"Captain?"

Quickly, she swallowed the hot lump in her throat. At least she had *Kestrel,* and all the memories that could never be taken away.

"Captain? You all right?"

"Aye, of course I'm all right!" She spun to face them, affecting a hard smile that forbade further comment. "I'm just thinking, 'tis all. My mind is made up. We'll go find Nelson, but *without* our prisoner, so that we may bargain. If this man Gray is so blasted valuable to both the British and French navies, I intend to play one off against the other so we'll get the most money for him."

"Oh, Majesty, that is brilliant!"

She shrugged and turned away, her heart aching.

"But what if the Admiral doesn't believe we even *have* such a man in our possession?" Sorcha asked, swinging her legs to and fro as she sat astride the big gun. "He may think we're bluffing!"

"I cannot risk bringing him along," Maeve said firmly, refilling her mug from the rum barrel. "Not *yet,* anyhow. Lord Nelson is supposed to be a decent man, but he may view our captive as Royal Navy property and therefore refuse to negotiate. Our captive is *our* property, and as such, we should get paid for him. And believe me, if the British want this traitor so much, they'll pay grandly to get him back. Especially if I let it be known I have no qualms about selling him to Villeneuve!"

"*I* think we should bring the prisoner to Admiral Falconer instead," Sorcha said, with wisdom beyond her sixteen years. "He may pay us more than Nelson. After all, it was from *his* flagship that our pirate escaped."

Maeve expelled her breath on a hoot of jeering laughter. "What, *that* scoundrel? Graham Falconer's naught but a rake, with his brains firmly entrenched in his breeches and standing ever at attention! He's too busy ruining female reputations to give *us* the time of day!"

"Harsh words, Majesty. You've never even met Sir Graham."

"I've no need to. His amorous exploits are no secret, and the stories about him are richer than Morgan's gold."

"Well, he *has* turned a blind eye to *our* activities."

"That's because I have never attacked an English ship! Nor do I intend to!" Maeve tossed down her ale, gave a very unladylike belch, and grabbed up her cutlass once more. "Invitation or not, we will find and board the *Victory,*" she declared, "where I shall personally confront the celebrated Lord Nelson! Now, who's coming and who's not?"

A chorus of excited "ayes" rose on the night. Moments later, the windlass was cranking, provisions were brought aboard, the anchor was coming up, sails were dropping, and the schooner *Kestrel* was turning her face toward a future that was hidden from even her mystical captain.

The pirate crew saw the lights of the British fleet as a rim of scattered stars hull up on the horizon and rising as *Kestrel* slid through the night. It had rained earlier, and now the air was fresh-washed and clean, tangy with the smell of salt and wind. She might have been a ghost ship, the rakish little schooner; the Pirate Queen had ordered all lanterns doused, all pipes out, and all commands spoken in a whisper. She was not taking any chances on losing her element of surprise. *Kestrel* was a formidable little vessel but she was no ship-of-the-line, and one ball from *Victory*'s massive cannon would be enough to send her on a quick journey to the bottom.

Maeve took the tiller herself as they drew closer. "Bring in the main!" she hissed, watching the lights of the fleet rising higher and higher. She drew her night glass and put it to her eye, feeling her hair tickling her cheeks as the gentle breeze tossed it about her face. It was hard to make out much in the darkness, but the starlight favored her situation, and she was soon able to pick out the mighty flagship of the famous English admiral as *Victory* led the fleet on a southerly course toward Tobago.

Excitement tingling through her blood, she snapped the glass shut and handed it to Orla. "Ha! The Admiral must be in one hell of a hurry to reach Tobago!" She crossed her arms, threw her head back, and planted her feet on the deck, looking every inch the Pirate Queen she was. "Well, I'll just have to tell him his search of *those* islands will be a fruitless one! Now, we cannot risk sailing in any closer. Dark as it is, all sailors have good night vision and I'll not risk having *Victory* blow us out of the water. Let's get far ahead of the fleet, then heave to."

"What do you plan to do, Captain?" Orla asked.

"The only thing I can do," she returned. "Swim."

"What?!"

"I'm a *pirate*, do you think they'll just *allow* me aboard? No, what we must do is get well ahead of the fleet—where you and I will leap overboard and wait in the water. We'll let the current carry us toward *Victory* while *she* drifts down toward *us*. There's barely any wind, those ships are barely moving—'twill not be so difficult to haul ourselves up onto *Victory*'s rudder chains, gain the quarterdeck, hide on the mizzen chains, then sneak through a gunport and down into the Admiral's cabin. Now let's go. We haven't got all night."

Nelson was usually in bed by nine, but tonight he was up later than usual, concluding his interview with Sir Graham Falconer's flag-captain, Colin Lord, while *Victory* plowed an unerring course toward Tobago, Trinidad, and—Nelson hoped—a glorious battle with the French fleet that would immortalize him forever in the eyes of England, Lady Hamilton, and of course, posterity.

The Fleet had found nothing in Barbados except Falconer's handsome flagship, the sugar convoy he was to have escorted back to England, and information from a brigadier general named Brereton, who'd sighted Villeneuve's mighty fleet off of St. Lucia. General consensus on Barbados held that the enemy had gone to attack Tobago and Trinidad, though why Villeneuve would bother with coal when the diamonds of Jamaica and Antigua were at hand was a puzzle that Nelson could not solve. His every instinct told him the information rang false, but an officer on Barbados, assuring him Brereton's word was sound, had lent him some two thousand of his own troops in support of it, and now, less than twenty-four hours after anchoring in Carlisle Bay, the Mediterranean Fleet was headed south in hot pursuit of the enemy.

Dinner had long since ended, and now Nelson and Colin Lord sat in the quiet splendor of the cabin, sipping champagne and indulging in a fine white cake while Nelson's beloved Emma Hamilton looked down at them from her portrait on the bulkhead.

Nelson, of course, had positioned himself so that the portrait was in direct line with his eye; he had only to look above the top of Captain Lord's fair head to see it.

In his mid-twenties, the young officer was tall, spare, and steady as a first rate in a gale. His cheeks were round in the English way, his brow intelligent, his eyes sensitive and of the clearest shade of purple-gray. The barrage of questions Nelson had fired at him was enough to shake even the stoutest of hearts—but the captain, son of an admiral himself, seemed well used to the demands of authority and did not quail beneath Nelson's penetrating eye, answering his queries in a frank, forthright way that brought a twisted smile of approval to his lordship's tired little face.

"I'm grateful for the truth, Colin," Nelson said, shrewdly watching the man across from him. "I did question Captain Ben Warner upon reaching Barbados yesterday, but had a feeling that he, in his eagerness to protect Falconer's name, was not being quite *honest* with me."

Carefully, Captain Lord said, "Admiral Falconer created his own Band of . . . uh, *Brethren,* sir. We were all very loyal. Warner is not to be blamed for trying to protect our admiral's reputation, if I may be so bold as to voice my opinion."

Nelson looked at him sharply. *Brethren,* the captain had said, not *brothers.* The significance of *that* fact did not escape him.

He smiled wryly. "Any commander who earns the love and loyalty of his men is to be praised. Your Admiral Falconer, eccentric as he was, was a fine sailor and a fierce fighter, and that is all that matters to *me*. I care not what he did in his spare time, but should the gossips in England get wind of this, they'll have a fine day of sport indeed. Damn them all to hell. Damn them all to hell and *beyond!*" The solitary little fist crashed down on the table. "Upon my life, Captain, this shall go no farther than this cabin!"

The younger man flushed beneath the sudden outburst and gazed down into his glass.

"Besides," Nelson snapped, petulantly tightening his mouth, "my own conduct has given the gossips enough fuel for their damned fires. D'you think I intend to give them any more? By God, I shall see that your admiral's name suffers no tarnish, and that he will be remembered for his achievements, his duty to his country, and, of course, his bravery under my command during the Battle of the Nile! Furthermore—"

He paused, the color high in his face, his fist poised above the table.

"Milord?"

Nelson was frowning, cocking his head and listening intently. "Did you hear something, Captain?"

"No, sir."

"Age. It must be age, then, what else could it be? I cannot sleep, I cannot eat, and now I'm hearing things that go bump in the night! By God, I sometimes think I am losing my mind, as indeed I shall if I do not find that damned *Veal-noove* and bring him to battle! How I long for peace! How I long for battle! How I long for my dear Lady Hamil—oh, never mind! Instead, let us discuss *you*, Colin, and the convoy you shall be escorting home to England—"

He never finished.

At that moment, a window imploded in a shatter of

glass, a figure fell sprawling to the deck, and the Admiral—darling of the British Navy, Victor of the Nile, and nemesis of the dreaded Napoleon—shot to his feet.

"Great *God!*"

The intruder picked herself up, brushed off the bits of glass, and dripping seawater, flung a long tail of wet auburn hair off her shoulder. In her hand was a dagger, and this she touched to her brow in a jaunty salute.

"Allow me to introduce myself," she said brightly, as another, smaller figure crawled through the window after her. "I am Captain Maeve Merrick, and this, my quartermaster, Orla O'Shaughnessy."

Nelson stared, his mouth falling open.

"I'm sorry," the woman said with a mischievous grin. "Perhaps you've not heard of me? I am the Pirate Queen of the Caribbean." She swept a jaunty, ludicrous bow. "Welcome to the Indies, milord!"

Chapter 6

"Sentry!" Nelson roared, recovering. *"Sentry!"*
Colin Lord dived protectively in front of the Admiral as the door crashed open and a surprised Royal Marine charged in.

Maeve's sudden shout pierced the air.

"No, milord! *I bring you news of Villeneuve!*"

Stepping impatiently around Colin, Nelson raised his hand to stay the marine. He stared at Maeve with an expression of fury and disbelief.

"What did you say?"

"I said, *I bring you news of Villeneuve!*"

Tense silence. The sigh of wind around the stern. The stamp of feet as more marines came running, an outcry of voices, shouts ... and the slow, stealthy movement of Captain Lord's hand toward his sword before Orla's dagger impaled the carpet two inches from his foot.

The Admiral gave an agitated jerk of his head. "Leave us," he snapped. "I am sure that Captain Lord and I can handle this situation!"

One by one, the marines filed out, leaving the two to assess each other; the stiff little Admiral and the savage pirate queen, each taking the other's measure like two fleets squaring off before a battle.

Nelson saw a wild, wet, untamed beauty with gold earrings tangled in hair the color of fire; a face tanned to bronze, glittering gold eyes of sunlight and sin, a graceful neck ringed by a choker of sharks' teeth; he

63

saw elegant hands, long coltish legs, bare feet, frayed and soaked trousers cut off at the knee, and a purple blouse tucked into a leather belt.

And Maeve, looking at this schoolboy-sized admiral whose height rivaled that of her chin, saw the total antithesis of what she had expected—and the smile faded from her lips as raw disappointment swept in to take its place.

So much for heroes, she thought sadly. These days they must've gone the way of gallant knights. This one stood fiercely erect which did nothing to accentuate his height, and had a pale, sickly little face unremarkable in aspect, save for the bold nose and penetrating eye, out of which glowed a fire that even approaching blindness could not dim. The Admiral's features were open, honest, earnest, energetic, vulnerable, anxious, and melancholy all at once. She saw suffering in his eyes, in the lines of his cheeks, in the rough scar that cleaved his right brow. The armless sleeve was pinned carefully over a chest bedecked with enough medals, stars, and orders to make the heavens look dim and deprived in comparison.

Surely, *this* small fellow could not be the hero proclaimed in broadside and ballad? Surely, this little gamecock was not the sailor who was the subject of newspaper jibes and huzzahs alike, paintings, poems, and sculpture, with everything from flowers to plants to streets named after him? Surely, *this* little man could not be the dread of the French, the pride of the British Navy?

Another fairy tale, blown to hell.

"Captain Lord! Do you know this woman?!"

Maeve's attention swept to the handsome, fair-haired officer held at bay by Orla's sword. His face was carefully schooled into calmness, but his color was pale and she guessed he had indeed heard of her. "Aye, sir," he answered, staring at her as though she was something out of his darkest nightmares. "Or shall I say, I know *of* her. . . . She's a pirate operating out of the Windwards—"

Nelson roared, "Ever prey upon an English ship?"

"Not to my knowledge, sir—"

"Ever plague English shipping? Annoy English convoys?"

"No, sir—"

"Ever irritate His Majesty's vessels, officers, or seamen in and around the Indies?"

"No, sir, but—"

The Admiral swung fiercely on Maeve. "Sit down!"

"Thank you," she said archly, "but I prefer to—"

"I said, sit down!" roared the little lion, and Maeve, her belief in heroes happily restored, did so with a huge smile curving her lips.

He came right up to her, the stump of his arm jerking beneath his sleeve in agitation, his eyes fierce and angry. *"You,"* he said sharply, slamming his hand on the table and leaning down to glare into her face, "have just damaged Crown property and your reason for doing so had better be a damned good one, so help me God!"

She laughed, her heart singing. *This* was the Nelson of song and legend, *this* was the hero she'd long dreamed of meeting, *this* was—

"Answer me!"

Still smiling, Maeve leaned over the table, plucked an apple from the silver bowl there, and bit into it with a loud *crunch* that shattered the strained silence of the cabin. The Admiral bristled. The handsome officer went a shade whiter and found a sudden interest in a small cut on his knuckle.

Another man, wearing a captain's uniform, stormed into the cabin, pistol primed and ready and pointed directly at Maeve's heart.

"For *God*'s sake," Nelson said curtly, "I do believe I

have the situation under control! Pray, sit down, Hardy, this beauteous *female* is about to reveal to us the whereabouts of *Veal-noove.*"

She took another bite of her apple and looked up. "Ah, Nelson's famous flag-captain." Maeve munched, swallowed, and grinned. "Don't doubt me, milord. I have the Sight."

"The *what?*"

"The Sight." She took another bite and, with the point of her knife, pried a sliver of apple out from between her front teeth. Nelson narrowed his eyes. Hardy, now seated, looked shocked. The fair-haired Captain Lord—still staring intently, unnervingly, at her—flushed with embarrassment, his cheeks pinkening in a way that was almost endearing. "It's the Irish gift of being able to see the future," she said casually. "Predict events. Interpret meaning in signs and symbols. You see, I was born with the caul over my head and I am all-knowing."

"Balderdash!" Hardy exclaimed. "You don't even *sound* Irish!"

"I'm American."

"You're *mad.*" Hardy stood and pivoted on his heel. "I shall call the guards!"

"No, Hardy, I wish to hear what she has to say about *Veal-noove.*"

"Surely, sir, you would not believe the word of this—this *pirate?!*"

"My mind is an open one, Hardy. I shall hear her out. Captain Lord? For God's sake, do sit down, you look fair to fainting!"

"I er, cannot, sir—"

The tip of Orla's sword was pointed at his groin, and held so close to the stainless white breeches that the captain could not move without risk of injury.

Maeve plucked the folds of her wet shirt from her body, smiled, and took another bite of her apple. "Be easy, Orla." *Crunch.* "Let the poor man sit down, as His Lordship says." She watched in high amusement as Captain Lord, who was still staring at her, moved warily to a chair. "Now that we are all happily seated, let me state my business."

"Yes, please *do,*" Hardy growled, clearly annoyed.

"Damn your business," Nelson said anxiously, *"just give me news of Veal-noove!"*

"Villeneuve," Maeve said, casually motioning with her apple, "has been at Martinique, where he joined forces with the Spanish admiral, Gravina. I knew that already, of course, thanks to tavern talk, and had it confirmed while speaking a ship on my way to find you. As we sit here talking, the Combined Fleet is passing Dominica on a northerly course. You'd do well to come about and steer after them, milord. There is nothing for you at Tobago, nor Trinidad."

Nelson looked thunderstruck. He glanced up at Hardy.

"Folly, sir!" the burly captain exclaimed. "General Brereton *insists* the French are at Tobago! I urge you to think carefully before considering the words of a *pirate.*"

"But Hardy, her words are in keeping with my own hunches!" Nelson cried, thumping his fist against his chest. "And when have they ever steered me wrong? What if she is right and the French are indeed heading—oh, dear God,—toward Antigua?"

"What if she is lying, sir, and we come about, steer north, and find afterward that Brereton's information was right? You will be the laughingstock of the Fleet, of *England,* for heeding the advice of a soothsayer."

" 'Twould not be the first time I believed such advice, Hardy, indeed it would not!" But then Nelson looked at Maeve, and the wisdom of Hardy's words sank in. Could he risk his career, indeed, England's safety, on the word of a pirate?

Maeve held out her apple and perused it for a moment, then took another bite. "Funny thing about apples," she soliloquized. Then she turned the half-eaten fruit toward them, exposing its pale flesh, the pocket of seeds. "Did you ever stop to consider, when you eat an apple—or an orange, or any other fruit, for that matter—that what you're looking at is something no other person on earth has ever looked upon before?"

They stared at her, each and every one of them.

"Think about it," Maeve continued, still holding the apple up. *"No one else* has ever seen the inside of this particular piece of fruit. Therefore, it is a blessing, and a gift, given from God just for us." *Crunch.* "Think about it next time you peel a banana, or bite into an apple."

"Get her out of here," Hardy said, in disgust.

"No, no, that is quite an extraordinary observation! My own father was of the clergy, Captain Merrick, and I'm sure he would have appreciated your wit and insight, as do I. Now tell me"—Nelson's voice grew a shade harder, and she realized that the mind working behind those penetrating eyes was a sharp one, indeed— "you must have a reason for bringing me this information about *Veal-noove* in person."

"I wanted to meet the Hero of the Nile," she said mildly.

"And how do I know you are not betraying me?"

"I hate the French as much as you do, milord—and wish to see you destroy them. Which you *will* do, of course."

"She has the Sight," Hardy drawled, by way of explanation.

"Yes, yes, of course!" Nelson said excitedly.

"However, the primary reason for my visit is of a slightly different nature." Still chewing her apple, Maeve looked up at him through her lashes, her eyes bright with playfulness. "I came to demand payment."

"Payment? For *what?!*"

"You see"—*crunch*—"I have in my possession a certain English sailor who has professed to be a deserter and a traitor, now spying for the French. I thought you might like to have him back."

"A deserter?" Nelson cried, in sudden disappointment. "By God, I care *more* for news of *Veal-noove!*"

"Milord, I've told you all I *know* of Villeneuve. He's off Dominica and headed north. What more can I say? Believe me, I'd like to see you give the French the drubbing they deserve, but this English sailor, this deserter, well"—*crunch*—"he has really been a burden to me, and I would like to be rid of him. However, I can't let him go for free; I *am* a pirate, you know, and even pirates have to eat. . . ."

"Guards! Remove this woman!" Hardy yelled.

Maeve held up her hand. "Oh, don't be so hasty to dismiss my offer, gentlemen. He really is a fine-looking prisoner, and shall make a fine-looking corpse at the yardarm of your *Victory*. In fact, I would've strung him up from my own little *Kestrel* but I thought he'd be worth more to you than to me—"

"I said, *remove this woman!*" Hardy shouted.

"Sit down, Thomas," Nelson said. *"Please."*

Maeve ignored both Hardy and the very discomfited Captain Lord—funny, she thought she had an English cousin whose surname was Lord. She twirled the apple by the stem, looked at Nelson, and smiled playfully. "Ah, milord . . . you don't realize what you're passing up! I mean, what use do *I* have for a roguish devil with a pierced ear, a roving eye, and the audacity to wash up on *my* island, only to insult me, attack me, and then try to pass off a foolhardy name like *Gray*—oh, never mind." She rose to her feet, a regal queen despite her wet and bedraggled state. "If you don't want him, I'll just offer him to Villeneuve instead. . . ."

But the Admiral had gone stiff, and Captain Lord as white as his breeches.

Maeve tossed the apple core out the shattered window with a haughty flick of her wrist. "It really *has* been a pleasure to meet you, milord. It's not every day that a person gets to meet a real hero! May you find Villeneuve and give him the thrashing he deserves. I hear you prefer the word, *annihilate?* Oh, and please accept my sincerest apologies about your window . . . I would send payment for it, but I do believe my information regarding Villeneuve should take care of *that—*"

"*Wait!*"

Maeve smiled, a slow, cunning smile, and turned to face him.

Nelson shot a glance at the very pale Captain Lord, then looked at her, his eye sharper than an eagle's and just as piercing. "Captain Lord . . . I seem to recall you recently had a *deserter* from your *Triton* . . . did you not?"

"Aye, sir," the young captain murmured, as he glanced from Nelson to Maeve and back again to Nelson, "I did."

"A tall, knavish sort—black-haired, I believe, with rather unusual . . . *obsessions?*"

"Uh . . . yes, sir. Indeed, that describes him perfectly."

Nelson narrowed his eyes. "Does your prisoner answer this description, madam?"

"Aye, milord," she said, grinning in triumph, "that he does."

Nelson's full mouth curved ever so slightly, and that was all that he would allow in terms of a smile; but it was enough, and Maeve was hard-pressed not to rub her hands together in glee. She saw him glance at the fair-haired Captain Lord, and the silent words that passed between them. How valuable this deserter, this *traitor,* must be, to warrant such interest! And how proud her father would be of her, if he could see that she'd outmaneuvered an English admiral!

Nelson drew himself up, his shoulders stiff and erect beneath his epaulets. He was smiling, faintly, and the tense lines about his mouth had relaxed, lending him a look of boyish good humor. He put out his hand toward her.

"Ah, dear lady . . . you have indeed done our navy a great service," he murmured, eloquently. "And I wouldn't *dream* of allowing you to sell this deserter to the French! I must, of course, heed my prior intelligence that *Veal-noove* is at Tobago, you do understand, don't you? But if you do indeed have this *Sight,* you will know where to find me. Bring me your pirate, this vile *deserter,* and by God, I shall see that you are paid *twice* what *Veal-noove* or any damned Frenchman would offer you!"

Maeve smiled back, quite proud of herself. "Indeed, milord. I shall have him for you when you return from Tobago, for you will not find the French there." She saw a shadow pass over his face, and remembering that she was the Pirate Queen of the Caribbean, put out her hand for him to kiss its Royal Knuckles.

But as Nelson took her hand and raised it to his lips, she faltered and nearly fell, her face stiffening in shock.

The Admiral straightened up, frowning. "Madam?"

She was staring at his coat, that glittering, decorated, medal-festooned coat, encrusted with lace, stars, orders, and glory—

Horrified, Maeve backed away.

"That—that coat, milord. . . ." She looked up at him, her eyes huge and full of fear. "It shall be the death of you."

And with that, the shaken Pirate Queen moved to the window, and, with Orla behind her, disappeared into the night.

Chapter 7

The pirate was justifiably proud of himself for the clever way he had tricked Queen Maeve—but then, he hadn't reached his current position of authority and respect by being stupid.

The little ship had no sooner weighed anchor than Gray had stepped out of the shackles and, using the key he'd stolen from the Pirate Queen, calmly let himself out of his prison. He'd spent the night sitting on a rock and looking out to sea, damning the winds that had prevented his knowledge of both Nelson and Villeneuve in the Caribbean, thinking about the pirates who had once sailed these waters—and comparing his captor to the inestimable Anne Bonney. Making love to Anne Bonney was, of course, an impossibility—that formidable sea-queen had been dead for nearly a century—but the she-wolf who captained *Kestrel* was surely a worthy substitute.

Gray smiled, already envisioning that smooth, hard body writhing in delight beneath him. He'd always had a fantasy of taking a lady pirate to his bed, and if he had *his* way—which he would, of course—that fantasy would become reality before his little sojourn on this island came to its necessary end. As for Maeve's meeting with Nelson—he exhaled slowly and dug at the sand with his toe—he could only hope it had gone as he predicted it would. After all, he *had* taken one hell of a gamble. . . .

He looked out to sea. The stars were setting, the eastern horizon glowing above the palms, the sea beginning to turn from black to dove gray. Soon, it would be dawn. But what would this day bring?

Nelson was in the Indies.

The pirate stared off into the dawn, his smile fond as he remembered those long-ago days when he, as a young midshipman, had first served under the cocky, overzealous Captain Nelson of the twenty-eight-gun frigate, *Albemarle.* And who else but the intrepid little admiral could've taken the British fleet right up to the anchored French one at the mouth of the Nile, pounded the stuffing out of it, and left Napoleon Bonaparte and his army stranded in Egypt? The victory had earned him a barony, the love of Emma Hamilton, the status of hero, and the mainmast of the French flagship, *L'Orient,* after that ship had blown up at the climax of the spectacular night battle; now, what remained of the mainmast was carved into a coffin which Nelson vowed he would someday inhabit.

Gray picked up an old conch shell and, tracing its smooth whorls with his thumb, watched the sun coming up as a giant ball of red-orange brilliance. The Pirate Queen had said the Admiral was here in search of an enemy squadron that had escaped his blockade of the French port of Toulon. Nelson was the commander in chief of the Mediterranean Station, three thousand miles away. Under whose authority had he deserted his post and chased the French all the way across the Atlantic?

More than likely, Gray thought with a wry smile, no one's but his own. And—he swore and tossed the conch shell into the breaking waves—the Admiral would be looking for *him.*

Well, he was stuck here, with nothing to do but await the return of his savage captor. He might have escaped his restraints, but without a boat there was no way off the island. He rubbed at his stubbled chin, first with thoughtful detachment, then with awareness of the chin's state itself. His mouth curved in a rakish grin. Another few days without a razor and he'd be well on his way to looking like Blackbeard, and the thought so filled him with boyish delight that he got down on his hands and knees beside a tide pool and, using it as a mirror, surveyed his appearance with anxious hope.

The smile faded somewhat. Well, maybe he'd need more than a few days. . . .

The sun climbed higher, painting the bay in bright, luscious tones of pink and gold. He rose, letting the tide lap around his ankles and his imagination wander where it might. *Pirates.* Had Morgan ever visited this island? Had Blackbeard ever careened his sloop on this very beach? Had Bellamy ever marooned some poor traitor on this forgotten shore? Gray smiled faintly, wishing he could go back in time and lift a mug or two with his long-dead idols. If only he hadn't been born seventy years too late. . . .

He stretched and yawned. It was growing hot now, the morning sun toasting the air and making the water sparkle out on the silvery bay. He pulled his shirt off, reveling in the feel of the breeze kissing his skin, the sand squishing between his toes. Then he stepped out of his breeches and tossed them away. For a moment, he stood glorying in the morning, his naked body bared to the sun and gilded with light, the incarnation of some Greek sea-god of classic proportions. With easy, natural grace, he strode along the frothy edge of the sea, moved into the surf, and dived beneath the waves.

He swam with strong, powerful strokes, as comfortable in the water as any creature born and bred to it. Surfacing, he filled his lungs with air, dived again, scraped his skin clean with handfuls of sand until it was raw and tingling, and then whiled away his time exploring. He saw a vivid, orange starfish nestled within the waving vegetation carpeting the seafloor, and rippled globes of coral, peppered with little fish of every color. Strangely, the dolphin that had brought him here was absent. No doubt, it had gone with the little schooner . . . or in search of another hapless sailor pretending to be a pirate.

Pirates.

He dived again, swimming through the patterns of sunlight that slanted through the depths and shimmered upon the sand, the coral, the fish themselves. But there were no pieces of eight left by some long-dead buccaneer, no bejeweled daggers gleaming from behind a burst of pink coral, no bleached skulls, no treasure chests, and no ancient ribs that had once shaped the hull of a long-wrecked pirate brig. But it was fun to pretend, and when he finally grew bored he surfaced, floating on his back, blinking in the sunlight, and lazily propelling himself with gentle kicks. He dived once more and then, naked as a babe and feeling vigorously refreshed, strode out of the water and onto the beach.

He dried himself with his shirt, slung it and his breeches over his shoulder, and, wearing nothing but the piratical hoop of gold in his ear, sauntered up the beach and toward the house, his stomach growling.

"Captain Lord here to see you, *sir!*" the marine standing guard just outside Lord Nelson's great cabin aboard H.M.S. *Victory* announced.

The door was opened by the Admiral himself. "Ah, Colin!" he said, smiling warmly and ushering him into his richly furnished quarters. "Do come in—I trust you have recovered from our unexpected visitor last night?"

"Indeed, sir, that is what I've come to talk to you about."

Tucking his hat under his elbow, Captain Colin Nicholas Lord stepped into the huge, sunlit dining cabin that stretched from port to starboard and, together with the adjoining day cabin just aft of it, took up the entire stern of *Victory*'s upper deck and made up the Admiral's private domain.

"Please, have a seat, Colin. Some wine?" Nelson offered, closing the door behind them. "Cheese?"

"No, thank you," Colin said, but Nelson was already waving him toward a small, roundtop table beneath the panoramic stern windows, where a tray of refreshments waited. Colin was not hungry, but to be polite, he pulled out a chair and took a glass of port.

"So," Nelson said, seating himself comfortably in a heavy, padded leather chair. He smiled and regarded Colin patiently. "What is it you wish to talk to me about, Captain?"

Nelson's gray eyes were kind, his smile genuine, and Colin suddenly felt ashamed that he'd been dreading this interview. "I'm sorry that I didn't come to you earlier about this, sir," he said, lamely. "In fact, I feel rather foolish coming to you even now, but I thought you should know—"

"Nonsense, Colin," Nelson said, leaning over to take a bit of fruit. "I would be much aggrieved if you did *not* come to me with a problem. Pray, what troubles you?"

"It concerns the Pirate Queen, sir."

Nelson could not prevent an involuntary glance at his newly repaired window. "Yes?"

"After she crashed in here last night, sir, I got to thinking. Though I had my suspicions, I didn't want to say anything at the time—but now, in the light of day and after much thought, I have come to the conclusion that Maeve Merrick is . . . well, someone who is, uh . . ."

"Yes?" the Admiral prompted, kindly.

"Related to me."

Lord Nelson raised a brow and leaned back in his chair.

"You see, sir," Colin continued, feeling an unpleasant wash of heat crawling up his neck and out into his cheeks, "my mother has a cousin named Brendan Merrick. He moved to New England some thirty years ago, and made quite a name for himself in the American War—on *their* side, I'm sorry to say—with a little schooner named *Kestrel.*"

Both of the Admiral's brows were raised now. "*Kestrel* ... wasn't that the name of the Pirate Queen's vessel?"

"Yes, sir, it is. And *Merrick* is the surname of the Pirate Queen."

"Aha!"

"At first, I didn't put two and two together when she came to us last night," Colin went on. "It wasn't until she mentioned the name of her schooner, sir, that I realized just who she is. By God—this is most embarrassing, sir. . . ."

"No, no, do go on!" Nelson's eyes were gleaming; obviously, he was getting far more enjoyment out of this extraordinary tale than Colin was in telling it.

"Well, my mother and her American cousin, Brendan, write to each other quite frequently, sir, and while I have never been to New England, and never met her relations over there, I do remember her saying something about how one of Brendan's children, a girl, had some uncanny ability to predict the future and see visions of what was to come. My mother—she's Irish, you know—called it the Sight.

"They had a lot of trouble with the girl," Colin continued. "Apparently she was quite willful and uncontrollable, a real handful. Then she fell in love with a French sailor, stole her father's schooner, and disappeared. Her father chased her all the way to Florida, where he found a bit of wreckage from a vessel that, according to those who'd seen it go down, answered

Kestrel's description. The girl hasn't been seen since, and her family has since given her up for dead."

"By God! That *is* quite a tale, Captain Lord!"

"Yes. I'd forgotten the incident—at the time it happened, I was a young commander and, being at sea, was not around my own family enough to have it more firmly ingrained on my mind; indeed, I learned of the girl's disappearance and death via letters from my parents. Thus, it did not occur to me that the girl who ran away from home, and the woman who crashed into this cabin last night, are one and the same."

"So, the Pirate Queen is your cousin."

The young captain looked at the freshly repaired window, and nodded with embarrassment. "Yes sir," he said slowly. "I'm afraid so."

Gray had reached the Pirate Queen's house. On the veranda, he found wicker chairs strewn amidst pots of flowering hibiscus. He stood there for a moment, his hair hanging down his back and streaming water down his spine, his backside, his legs, while he watched the sun dance across the cool stone steps in lazy patterns of shadow and light. A bird sang in a nearby tree, and butterflies flitted over a little garden just beyond the lawn. Gray yawned, stretched, and smiled. Beauty certainly existed in the most savage of places.

A thought that could certainly be applied to Her Royal Highness herself.

He grinned and stepped inside. The house was quiet, still—and apparently, empty. Sea breezes wafted through open, louvered windows, playing with gauzy curtains and sweeping the rooms with the fresh scent of flowers, vegetation, and the ocean. Gilt-framed portraits hung upon the walls, and pots of bright red bougainvillea were set in the corners. The ceilings were high, the floors of polished hardwood, the furnishings rich and elegant and gleaming. Obviously, whoever had once lived here had been more than affluent, and he wondered what had happened to drive the former owner away; but then, ruined finances, fever, and a host of other misfortunes could well break a man.

Ah, well, it was not worth his speculation. Dismissing the thought, he continued on, and his growling stomach led him to the dining room. It was dominated by a mahogany table set with silver candelabra, a vase of flowers—and a bowl of fruit. His mouth watering, Gray sat down and proceeded to help himself.

Outside, the sun rose higher and the heat came with it.

He ate until he was full, happy, lazy, and content. Fruit juice was sticky between his fingers, and he licked each one in turn as he rose and, taking one last orange padded through the house, poking into a corner here, peeking into a room there, nonchalantly tossing the orange up and down as he explored. A grand, Turkish-carpeted stairway led to a second floor, and this he climbed with all the spirit of Captain Cook on an exploration into the unknown.

The unknown turned out to be a long, airy hall and a host of bedrooms.

Gray grinned, wolfishly, and began to push open each door. There was one room decorated like a ship's cabin, complete with swinging hammock . . . another, with the lace and frills and ribbon trimmings a young girl might favor . . . another, in deep shades of gold and bloodred crimson, another with clothing thrown over chairs and chests, on and on until he came to the last, set far down the hall and apart from the others.

There was a toothless shark's skull mounted on the door, and he knew without question that this room belonged to the Pirate Queen.

Still holding the orange in one hand, Gray pushed open the door and stepped inside.

It was an immense, airy room, dominated by a huge

bed with four mahogany posts, over which was draped a gossamer, lavender netting of gently swaying gauze. Thick pillows of dark purple satin were piled at the headboard, and a tasseled, cream-colored spread made a delicious expanse of softness over the high mattress.

He pictured the Pirate Queen's lithe body spread invitingly on that spread and felt a quick stab of heat in his loins.

He stepped forward, put the orange on a bedside table, and trailed his hand over a sea chest of lignum vitae. It was carved with figures of sharks, and upon closer examination, he realized that the shark theme was carried throughout the room; there were china sharks on the dresser, wooden sharks guarding the door, paintings of sharks on the wall; and yes, upon closer inspection, even the finials of that huge bed were carved with open-jawed sharks.

Gray stood for a moment, his lashes sweeping down to lazily hooded, wicked, roguish eyes. He reached out and moved his palm over a pillow, feeling the silky satin catching in the calluses of his palm. He smiled, a slow, conniving smile. His belly was full. The play of sunlight and sea breeze against his bare skin was making him drowsy. He heard a bird chirping just outside the open window, the soft hiss of the trades through the palms, the distant, soothing music of the sea.

What the hell.

Yawning, he tossed his clothes over a chair, peeled back those luxurious spreads, and, naked as the day he was born, promptly fell asleep in the Pirate Queen's bed.

"Majesty!" Aisling and Sorcha came running from the abandoned storehouse, their hair flying behind them. "Majesty, come quick! The prisoner's escaped!"

Maeve had left her crew to see to *Kestrel* and was

halfway up the beach when the two girls, who had run ahead, nearly collided with her. "What?!"

"He's gone! We just checked the storehouse and he's *gone!*"

"Bloody hell!" Drawing her pistol, Maeve raced up the beach after them. Sure enough, their makeshift gaol was empty, the pirate gone. Only loose shackles and the pallet rested on the floor. Fuming, she kicked at the old bedding, then leaned against the cold stone and passed the back of her hand over her brow.

"Now what, Majesty?" Aisling cried, tugging at her arm.

Maeve kneaded her aching brow. "He cannot have gone far," she muttered, wishing for nothing more than a dark room and an hour's rest. Of all the times to have to face a problem like *this*. "There's no way off this island, and if he's fool enough to wander into the forest, then I should think him smart enough to come out."

"What if he's armed!"

"And dangerous?!"

"And waiting to ambush us?!"

Maeve gave a hoot of laughter and slammed out of the gaol. "For *his* sake, he'd better be *armed*. Now come on, we have work to do. When Nelson finds he's been duped by this General What's-his-name, he's going to come hightailing it back here in a fine rage, looking for me, because *I* was right. And as for our traitor . . . he'll show, have no fear of *that*. He no doubt fled because he knows I'm going to turn him in, but when his stomach gets hungry he'll come slinking out of wherever he's hiding, the blasted *coward.*" She spat the word with all the vileness she could command. "And then—"

"And then, Lord Nelson will annihilate *him!*" Sorcha cried.

"Aye, he'll string him up from the *Victory*'s fore-yard!"

"Can we stay and watch, Majesty? Can we?"

Young Aisling, echoing her sister, began jumping up and down in the hot sand. "Can we? Can we? Can we?"

They didn't notice the shadow that passed over Maeve's face. "By God, you two make Grace O'Malley look *tame*," she muttered, referring to the notorious sixteenth-century Irish pirate queen from whom she was supposedly descended. "Go help the others secure the boat, and when you're through we'll wash down *Kestrel*'s decks."

"Majesty, you look pale. Are you all right?"

"My head is killing me," she admitted, apologetically, as indeed it had been since Lord Nelson's lips had touched her hand and the Vision—God, she didn't want to think of what it had revealed—had hit her with the force of a broadside.

That coat will be the death of you.

She should never have spoken the thought aloud, for she'd had the most uncanny feeling he'd been able to look inside her mind and see what she had seen; battle with the French at last. Victory! And the little Admiral, falling to his quarterdeck with a bullet in his spine, there to lie drowning, dying, in his own blood—

"Well, you go rest then, Majesty," Aisling said, steering her toward the house. "We'll see to *Kestrel*, all right? Maybe tonight we can have a bonfire and a pig roast, and tap into the wine we stole from that Spaniard off Guadeloupe!"

"*That* should draw our pirate out," Sorcha sniffed.

Maeve, pressing her fingers to her throbbing temples, was in no mood to argue. "Very well, then. Maybe I *will* go lie down for a few minutes. . . . The devil take this blasted sun, this heat—"

"What about the prisoner?" Sorcha called, as Maeve trudged up the beach.

"I'll find him, damn his scurvy hide, and when I do . . ."

Leaving the rest unsaid, she walked toward the house, drooping like a flower in the heat and wanting nothing but the blessed sleep of oblivion.

Chapter 8

Maeve pushed open the door to her room, tossed her scabbard into a chair, and saw the pirate sprawled on her bed, fast asleep and naked as a new-born babe.

She froze.

Then, holding her breath, she slunk backward, flattened herself against the wall outside, and, shutting her eyes, leaned her head back against the wall, the image of that virile man stamped indelibly on her brain.

Fury at his insolence; shock at discovering him in her bed—*her* bed! rapture that he *hadn't* fled like the coward she'd thought him to be; excitement at the sight of that handsome body; and terror of the broken heart she knew he would give her—

Maeve's first instinct was to kill him. Her second was to slip into bed with him and have her way with that splendid male body. She decided instead to creep back into the room and stare at him until she decided between the first and the second.

She found him awake and sitting up, reposing against the pillows heaped at the headboard with his hands linked behind his head and his black hair in disarray across his brow, his arms, her pillows. His shoulders were dark against the lavender satin, his chest a formidable expanse of darkly tanned muscle. His manhood was bared to the world, his amused gaze challenged hers, and there wasn't the least shred of modesty in those wicked indigo depths—only ripe humor and bold, blatant invitation.

"Care to drop anchor beside me, lass?" He grinned, devilishly, wolfishly. "Morning is the fairest time for a tryst, you know."

For the first time in her life Maeve Merrick was at a loss over what to say, do, think. She stared at him, unable to tear her eyes from that magnificent male body that lay so dark against the creamy sheets and violet pillows, *her* creamy sheets and *her* violet pillows—

Then she grabbed up her cutlass and pointed it at him, accusingly. "You—" Her hand was trembling, and she saw humor dancing in his eyes as he looked at the jiggling sword tip. "You *escaped. . . .*"

"Aye." He gave a lewd, suggestive wink. "Proud of me?"

"Proud?"

"Aye. Your pirate here is smarter than you give him credit for." He tapped his temple and grinned. "I merely plucked the key from you when you lay senseless in my arms. You really didn't expect me to berth on that filthy pallet, now, did you?"

She could only stare. The rogue! Her skin flushed hot and feverish, flushed hotter still as she noticed his manhood beginning to swell and rise and stiffen. She tightened her now-sweaty grip on the sword hilt and forced herself to meet his eyes, admiring his courage and yes, even his insolence. No coward, *this* man! His actions were those of a warrior. They were something a Gallant Knight might have done—

"So," he drawled, taking advantage of her stunned silence. "Did you have a nice meeting with the little Admiral?"

His words jolted Maeve out of her shock. "My meeting with *Lord Nelson* is none of your blasted business! And if you think to change my mind about handing you over to him"—she stormed to the window

to escape the temptation his virile body offered—
"you're wasting your bloody breath!"

"Ah . . . so you *did* meet him," he murmured from
behind her. "Quite a remarkable little fellow, isn't he?"

"In spirit," she allowed, "but not stature. I make two
of him."

She was staring out at the blue, frothy sea, gripping
the cutlass so fiercely the wire-bound hilt drove itself
into her palm. Then she swung back, not liking the feel
of that amused gaze nailing her between the shoulder
blades, of having her back to an enemy, of knowing his
eyes were sliding heatedly over every inch of her spine,
her rump, her legs, her bare calves. . . .

"So, you failed to convince him of your mystical
powers, eh? Is his lordship's course a southerly one, after all? Hmmm?"

"I will not answer that! You're a *spy* and therefore I
shall disclose *no* information about the British Navy to
you!"

"Why this apparent loyalty to the British Navy, eh?
By your speech, I'd have thought you an American."

"I *am* an American. But I detest the French as much
as the British do. And as for Nelson, he's not only a
hero, but the finest sea officer in the world and I happen to admire him, all right? Now shut your damned
mouth before I lose my temper and flay that tongue of
yours into ribbons!"

His lips twitched, and she bristled at the thought that
he was inwardly laughing at her. "Well, you can't
blame a body for trying," he said mildly, his gaze sliding down the front of her shirt with enough heat to burn
the fabric right off her skin. Maeve slapped the flat of
the cutlass across her chest, but the action only drew
that penetrating gaze and called further attention to that
part of her anatomy. "And Villeneuve? Surely you can
tell me about *him.* . . ."

"Villeneuve is north, and that's all *you* need to know."

"Aah, but does *Nelson* know that?"

"Aye, I told him!"

He smirked. "And did his lordship believe you?"

"No," she admitted, her mouth tightening in an angry line. Unbidden, her gaze flickered to his masculinity before she glared angrily into his smug, amused face. "Damn you, do you have to lie there, all exposed?"

"It's . . . hot."

"There's a fine breeze blowing!"

He gave a lewd grin. "I wasn't referring to the weather."

In one quick motion, Maeve drew her dagger and flung it at his head, satisfied to see him jerk away so that the vicious blade impaled the wall just above and behind him. "You are disgusting, despicable, and totally without pride!"

"On the contrary, madam." Without blinking an eye, he reached up, pulled the dagger from the wall, and plucking an orange from the nightstand, began to use it to peel the fruit. "I am quite proud of it, thank you."

Still holding her gaze, he popped a section of the orange into his mouth, eating it with slow, suggestive motions that shortened the breath in Maeve's lungs and made her realize that he was not the only one who was *hot*. Her temper and her temperature were rising as well. Had she had her pistol, she probably would've shot him. Probably. Maybe. Maybe . . . not. Her gaze darted from him to the window. From the window to him. From him to the window . . . and each time she looked at him, she saw that he was watching her, fully enjoying her discomfort.

He grinned, and suggestively licked at the juices trailing from the sweet fruit, letting his tongue wrap around each section and making sure she saw him doing it. His eyes were dark, challenging, and half-veiled by heavy, thick lashes that did nothing to conceal the wicked expression that lit them.

The suckling noises increased.

"Stop it!" she hissed.

He dropped the orange section into his mouth, licked his lips with a slow, languorous, circular motion, and slowly peeled off another.

The heat rose in Maeve's blood.

"Would you like . . . a *taste,* madam?"

She raised her cutlass. "I'll give you a *taste—*"

"No decisive battle was ever fought from afar," he interrupted on a low murmur, still grinning. "Nay, two vessels must *lie* alongside of each other in order to best bring their guns to bear." He bit into the orange, making lewd, evocative noises as the juice trailed from the succulent flesh and dribbled down his chin. There was a dimple in that chin, and Maeve felt her heart skipping, staggering, faltering. "We have a signal for such an engagement in the navy. 'Tis called *close action.*"

"You are no longer in the navy, and I am *not* a ship!"

"Nay, you are not. . . ." His voice grew low, dangerously seductive. "But I like the cut of your jib, the taut trim of your sails"—the dark gaze slid over her breasts, the gentle flare of her hips—"the shape of your hull."

"Get out of my bed."

"Why? I really am most comfortable. Not as comfortable, of course, as I would be if you were to drop anchor beside me . . ."

Her skin tingled and flushed crimson. "I said, *Get out of my bed!"*

He suckled the juice from his fingers. "What, would you prefer to do it on the floor?"

"I'd prefer that you shut your filthy mouth before I shut it for you!"

"Now *that,"* he said, wickedly, "could be interesting. . . ."

"Damn you, I've had it with your sly innuendos!"

"Now, *Majesty,*" he murmured, affecting a pout. Putting the dagger down, he sat up, swung his handsomely muscled legs off the bed, and sat looking at her, charmingly boyish, alarmingly dangerous, and shamelessly naked. "Don't go getting your guns all primed. I am just a sailor . . . and what sailor doesn't lust and pant after a beautiful woman? I find *you* beautiful, and"—he let his gaze rake over her breasts, her hips, her bare ankles—"I want you."

She felt her blood sing and her skin tingle.

"Come, now, dear lady." His hand, a broad, and callused hand, graceful yet strong,—a *man*'s hand—slid over her silky sheets in a way that was calculated to suggest that same masterful hand roving over her equally silky flesh. He gave a slow, heated grin that sent the temperature of her blood soaring to new heights. "Don't make me come over there and get you. . . ."

His body seemed relaxed, but she sensed the raw power underneath, the ability to spring, wolflike, and bring her down like a helpless hare.

The Pirate Queen took a step backward.

"You fear me," he murmured, his eyes glinting. He spread his hands, as though in truce, and again she was struck by the power, the strength, in those broad palms, those beautiful, tapered fingers. Shivers coursed through her. She had no trouble imagining them around her throat. No trouble imagining them crushing the life out of her.

And no trouble imagining them caressing her heated flesh.

"I fear *nothing!*" she raged, defiantly. "D'you hear me? *Nothing!*"

"No? Your lie is thoroughly unconvincing, I'm afraid. I think you fear me very *much.*" Rising to his feet, he took a step forward. Another. "You see, Majesty, I have waited all night and half the morning for

you. I have waited . . . all my life. Now, be a good lass,
and let me pleasure you. . . . Love you. . . . Stroke your
sweet flesh into flame and fire. . . . After all"—again,
he flashed that disarming grin—"we have so *little* time
left together. . . ."

He took another step forward but Maeve stood her
ground, gripping the raised cutlass, her gaze locked
with his and every muscle in her body strung shroud-
tight—

"I'm warning you, pirate!"

Sweat ran down her spine as he moved closer.

"Stay away from me!"

"So *little* time," he said again—and reached for her.

With all her strength she swung the cutlass, and he
expertly ducked the blow that would've taken off his
head. The momentum spun her around, the sword
smashed into the bedpost and fell out of her hands.
Gray was on her before she could even think to go for
the dagger on the nightstand, seizing her wrists, jerking
them above her head, and slamming her belly up
against the doorjamb so hard the breath exploded from
her lungs.

"Back *off,*" she snarled, through clenched teeth.

"Nay. You, madam, should have had the sense to do
that when you first entered this hallowed chamber."
The silkiness was gone from his voice, the playful teasing replaced by a hot, sexual carnality that made her
tremble. His chest drove against her back, his manhood
against her backside, and she felt totally helpless. And
with her body crushed against the doorframe, she could
do nothing but shut her eyes and steel herself against
the ripples of desire he trailed with a finger down the
curve of her neck.

"All my life, I've entertained a fantasy of making
love to a lady pirate," he murmured, his hot breath stir-
ring the hair at the back of her neck, his deep voice

sending tremors down her spine. "At last, that fantasy is about to become reality. . . ."

"Over my dead *body!*"

"Oh, I hardly think so, *Majesty.* In fact, I shall take great delight in making that *body* of yours come *alive.*"

His hand slid up her forearm, over her shoulders, caught the thick fall of her hair and lifted it off her neck. She felt his lips touching her nape, his breath fanning the damp skin there, and still, his big body pinned her breasts, her ribs, her stomach against the doorjamb.

"I've heard the tales about you, but they do not pay tribute, nor do justice, to such a fair and fiery maiden . . . I think I am in love . . . Do you believe in love at first sight, Maeve? I never did, but I do now. . . . Ah, Majesty, you are the woman of my dreams . . . my fantasies . . ."

"I'll fight you, pirate! Damn your eyes, you won't touch me and live to tell about it!"

"Ah, such pluck, such fire! Indeed, madam, I *will* touch you . . . but were you to go down without a fight, I should be sadly disappointed. . . . So, indulge yourself, my lady, and"—his fingers caught her collar and pulled it downward, exposing her neck and shoulders to his mouth—"fight."

She felt his lips moving against the back of her neck, nibbling, kissing, feathering, his tongue tasting the hot skin and drawing little circles in the downy hair at her nape. Her senses swam and she pressed her brow against the doorjamb. She tried to struggle, but he only pushed himself against her all the harder, crushing her, pinning her, rendering her more helpless than she already was.

"Do you know your body is already answering mine, Majesty?" His hand caught in her hair and pulled off the leather thong, and she felt his fingers trailing through the long, silky tresses, smoothing them, stroking them, separating them. "Don't deny me, sweetheart.

Don't deny *yourself,* for your body proclaims your desires when your words do not. Let me take you in my arms, carry you to your bed, and make delicious, savage love to you. . . ."

She waited for his lips to touch the soft hollow between her shoulders; then, catching him off guard, she jerked her arm down and out of his grip, and drove her elbow brutally into his chest. But he was quicker than she, and far stronger, spinning her around and backing her spine against the wall so fast the room twirled around her. He caught her wrists, dragging them up over her head; furious, she looked up into his face, met his eyes, and drew her lips back in a feral, savage snarl.

"Let—me—*go.*"

"I can't," he said simply. "I want you too much to let you go."

Then he smiled. Disarmingly. Devastatingly. Knowingly. Something melted inside her. Her knees went weak and her breathing quickened. He moved back, ever so slightly, pressing his bare leg against her thigh and allowing her to feel his heat, his power. He dragged his foot up the side of her calf, his knee trailed toward the junction of her legs with agonizing slowness. There it pressed, burning through the loose trousers and making her long to thrust herself shamelessly against that sweet pressure.

"When I get free," she managed to say weakly, "I swear to God I'll stab you so full of holes you'll look like a damned fishing net."

"My dear madam," he murmured, still holding her arms high while he nuzzled her ear and branded her neck with warm, searing kisses, "any *stabbing* to be done is *my* delightful calling, not yours. Relax, Majesty, and give in to your deepest desire."

"My deepest desire . . . is to sink my dagger into your heart and watch you . . . die."

"And mine is to sink *my* dagger into your sweet

woman's flesh and watch you writhe with pleasure."
His lips were moving lower, toward that creamy swell
of flesh above the closure of her shirt. Maeve's heart
began to pound, and the room was suddenly too hot, far
too hot. . . . "Shall we have a contest to see who wins?"

His knee continued to press, to rub, against her
throbbing junction. Then his hand followed, touching
her, stroking her, caressing her through the thin barrier
of fabric. She felt a rush of pleasure and dampness, and
sank against his hand, knowing, even as a sob caught in
her throat, that he would win, indeed.

There was no fight left in her. None at all.

"Kiss me," she murmured, faintly.

His dark face loomed above, his eyes wicked with
challenge and desire, the dimple in his chin the last
thing she saw before her eyes drifted shut.

"I'm going to kiss you . . . everywhere. I'm going to
kiss you until you swoon with pleasure, until you melt
like sugar beneath my lips, until you cry out my name
in the throes of passion. I will make you *mine.* . . . " She
turned her head, and her cheek came up against the
hard bar of his arm, smelling of salt and warmth and
power. His fingers captured her jaw and he brought her
head around and gazed hungrily into her eyes. She
caught the scent of herself on his hand and trembled.

God, help me, she thought, faintly—

And was aware of his mouth lowering to hers . . . an
inch away . . . a hairbreadth . . .

Touching.

Sinking, sweeping abandon . . . joy . . . *surrender.* She
tasted the sweetness of oranges on his lips, on his
tongue, felt the rough press of his thumb against her
jaw, and sank beneath a feeling of being swept away,
carried away, overpowered, *ravished.* Her legs buckled
and with his strategically positioned knee he held her
up against the wall. She moaned deep in her throat and
his lips ground against hers. Her head swam and she

felt his hand pushing up the loose fabric of one pant leg
until it was bunched around her upper thigh and her
thigh was bared to the harshness of his palm.

No God, I take that back. . . . Don't help me. . . .

The kiss deepened. Her nipples hardened, ignited,
tingled against her shirt. She sighed deeply and pressed
into him, even as he slid his fingers up her arm and
brought her wrists down with them.

"Love me, Maeve."

She needed no urging. Her hand pushed into the
thick waves of his hair; the crook of her arm cradled
the back of his neck, drawing him even closer, and she
felt his kiss become savage, plundering demanding. . . .

A pirate's kiss.

Hard male muscle imprinted her body. His hands
were dragging up her leg now, leaving a trail of burning
flesh in their wake. He moved back, holding her waist,
the other hand against her leg, her inner thigh, her
damp and burning womanhood. She sank into the pressure, sobbing quietly as his fingers found the bud of her
desire and gently kneaded it through the flimsy, dampening trousers.

She twisted away, gasping. "Damn you. . . . Damn
you to hell and beyond. . . ."

But he caught her jaw once more and forced her
mouth against his. She drove upward to meet it, panting
hard and greedily taking his tongue into her mouth.
Again, the tangy sweetness of citrus; again, the wash of
feeling through every nerve in her body. Her legs went
limp, her mind reeled. She felt herself growing hot,
growing wet, growing . . . impatient.

Maeve squirmed helplessly against his palm, near to
fainting.

And then he drew back, breaking the kiss. Her eyes
opened to regard him dazedly.

"I may take a prize," he said huskily, his thumb
clearing the hair from her damp cheek, "but I never

plunder it unless invited aboard." Hot fingers dragged down her throat, circled a proud breast. "I can let you go now, dear lady, to continue on your set course . . . or you can indulge your wish to be . . . *plundered.*"

She closed, then opened her glazed eyes, her heart beating wildly in her breast.

"What shall it be?"

Did she have a choice? *Let him,* her mind pleaded. *What ill can come of it? When will you ever have such a dangerously handsome man as this in your bed, ever again?*

As long as she did not let herself fall in love with him, she was safe. Unable to be hurt, deserted, *abandoned*—

Her silence was answer enough. She collapsed even as his strong arms scooped her up and carried her to the bed.

He held her for a long moment, relishing the feel of her in his arms before lowering her to the soft expanse of silky sheets and tasseled pillows and feather-down mattress. She lay on her back, staring up at him; then he stood, tall and strong and virile, his gaze raking over her body and making her flush hotly. She swallowed thickly; their eyes met, and he smiled a long, slow, smile before easing himself down beside her.

Melting inside, Maeve trembled as he slowly began to undress her, carefully, skillfully, expertly. Masterful hands skimmed over her belly, heating her to flame. She allowed him to lift her shoulders so he could draw the shirt over her head. The warm trades kissed her . . . *he* kissed her, with lips burning against her neck, her collarbone, trailing lower to claim one hard, aching nipple, then the other. She moaned as his tongue circled the soft pink areola, the tightened bud, sucking at it greedily, even as his hand found her belt and slowly slid the leather through the buckle. Instinctively, her thighs clamped together before his hand gently coaxed them apart.

"Maeve, my Queen," he murmured, dropping kisses between her breasts as his hand slid beneath the waistband of the cottony trousers and dragged them down her hips. She felt every acute sensation; the hair of his arm grazing her legs, the warmth of his skin against her own, his lips brushing her dusky nipples. "You are truly a gift from God. I have lived for this moment all my life."

"You . . . you probably say that to every woman," she whispered, faintly.

"Aye, but I have never *meant* it as I do now," he murmured, his breath warm against her breasts. His hand moved lower, pressing against the junction of her thighs. "Open for me, Majesty. . . . Please. . . . Let me explore you . . . cherish you . . . *love* you."

All her fears fled in the face of what he was doing to her, and she couldn't have disobeyed him even if she wanted to. Sighing, Maeve opened to him, shivering with delight, anticipation, longing. His hands were everywhere, cupping each breast into a full and luscious mound as an offering to his eager mouth, coaxing fire from every inch of her skin, sweeping lazily through the chestnut curls at her inner thighs and stroking her until she was arching shamelessly against his hand. His head moved downward, his lips skimming over her belly, his breathing hot against her navel . . . her thighs . . . her—

"No!" she cried, bolting up, but his hand was there against her chest, his thumb circling one nipple as he pushed her gently back down to the thick stack of pillows.

"Enjoy our desire, Maeve. Let me savor every blessed inch of you."

She lay back, trembling, seeing the ceiling, the top of his head, through half-closed eyes. He was easy with her. His hand moved against her, inflaming her further and coaxing her legs open. She moaned and felt herself sinking down into the pillows, down into the mattress, down into . . . into . . . into *him*. . . .

"Oh, sweet heaven—" she cried, feeling that first stabbing thrust of tongue against hot flesh.

Her hands fisted at her side, then drove against his hard shoulders.

He raised his head, his grin soft and tender. "Relax, my sweet. I'll never hurt you. Trust me."

Relax. It was a command, and dazedly, it came to her that he was a man who was well used to issuing them. A dangerous man . . . a man of power, a man of authority.

She gave herself up to the pleasure, and when it became unbearable, she pushed him away, rolled onto her side, and, clamping her thighs against the throbbing in her womanhood, drove him onto his back. His eyes gleamed as he guessed her intent. Wantonly, she moved atop him, straddling him, her palms flat against his rough chest to brace herself as she began to ease herself down atop his rigid staff.

It had been a long time since Maeve had last known a man, and the years had rendered her tight and narrow. But she welcomed the pain, gazing down at him and relishing every delicious moment, every scraping slide of wet sensation, every stab of heat that radiated into her blood and melded her tight confines around his manhood. He grinned confidently up at her. His eyes were glowing, drifting shut with desire, then open, the thick lashes half concealing irises of a shade mirroring the deepest blue of the sea. Again, that wolfish smile; again, the dimple in his chin; again, that quiet amusement. He was a man in control, a man who was dangerous no matter how disarming that smile. Her heart fluttered and she bent down, heatedly kissing his lashes, his nose, his mouth. His arm circled her nape, holding her mouth to his; then he released her and Maeve, sighing deep in her throat, sat back and took the final inch of him into herself.

Sweet, savage impalement.

"Ah, love," he said gently, reaching up to stroke her cheeks with his thumbs. She felt the fires banking in her blood, and the force of them made her tremble with longing and need. "Ah, dear, sweet, love ... I have lived for this moment with you all of my life."

He cleared away a tumble of hair that had fallen over her shoulder, then pulled her down and kissed her. Deep and long and hard, even as his hands strayed down her body, finally clasping her hips and moving her against himself.

"God, you're so tight." The kiss deepened. She felt his hard palms pressing against her hips, guiding her movements. Sweat began to trickle down her back. The bed rocked beneath them. The motions came faster. Their breaths mingled, hot and damp.

"Hurry," she moaned, into his mouth. "Oh, God, pirate, *hurry.* . . . Take, me, please, take me!"

"I will *take you,* dearest, to the stars and back, as many times as you'll let me."

Dampness sheened their straining bodies. Her senses reeled, climbed, peaked—

"Oh ... Oh, *yes!*" she cried.

And then he drove savagely upward into her. She felt the warm spill of his pulsing seed, excruciating sweetness, burning climax. Her head fell back and she cried out in sweet agony, her senses exploding in a shower of glittering light. Sobbing, she collapsed atop him, her lips falling against hot, salty skin, her heart slamming against her ribs.

She lay there, tears of joy and happy defeat rolling down her cheeks. At that moment her heart filled with something huge and warm and inexplicable.

His arms came up to wrap protectively around her

shoulders, clasping her hot body to his. She heard his pounding heart just beneath her ear, heard its beat begin to steady and slow. It was a long time before she could speak.

"Pirate?"

"Aye, Majesty?"

His fingers drifted through her hair, and she kissed his damp chest. "I . . . I don't believe I'll kill you, after all."

She felt him smile against her forehead.

My Gallant Knight, she thought as she drifted off to sleep.

Chapter 9

The fate of England was of little consequence to Maeve Merrick as she lay dozing in the arms of her handsome lover. She may have the Sight—present at times, absent at most—but even such a Gift could not have foretold her how important she and her prisoner were to Lord Nelson's hopes for saving England.

And at the moment, Maeve would not have cared.

Outside, the sounds of her crew's laughter could be heard as they built up the bonfire and cracked open what was surely their third barrel of Jamaican rum. At any other time, she would be down there with them, the first to hold her cup beneath the spigot, the first to partake of the excessive revelry, the first to damn the world and everything it contained to hell and beyond.

But not this time.

Young Aisling had come earlier, knocking urgently at the door to report that the captive was still missing and her shrieking retreat when Gray himself had answered her summons had brought the rest of the crew charging into Maeve's bedroom with knives, pistols, blunderbusses, and swords drawn. But her pirate had handled this life-threatening situation with fearless, unruffled aplomb.

"Why don't you ask Her Majesty if she wishes to send me away, eh?" he'd asked, calmly pushing Enolia's dagger away from his throat and turning with an elaborate, encompassing, sweep of his arm to indicate Maeve—lying in bed with the sheets pulled up to her chin and a guilty blush spreading over her face.

It had been an embarrassing scene, to say the least. Now, Maeve sighed contentedly and forcing open her sleepy eyes, rested her head in the hollow between his shoulder and chest. His heart beat steadily beneath her ear, slow and rhythmic in sleep, and his black hair was tangled and wild, soft beneath her cheek and smelling faintly of salt water. Stretching, she let her palm rove over his broad pectorals, touching the hard little nipple, absorbing his heartbeat through the flat of her palm. Then she moved her head and kissed the warm, salty skin.

What on earth are you doing, *Maeve?*

Taking advantage of a gift from the sea, she answered herself. *Allowing myself to experience the thrill of having a dangerously handsome man tell me he wants me, and then proving it to me in the deepest, most meaningful sense of the word.* But Maeve did not believe in love at first sight. True, she had lain with, admired, and enjoyed her pirate's body, but she had held back a good part of her mind, a good part of her heart, and certainly *all* of her wary soul. She had been hurt before. She would not be hurt again.

Never!

Yet her heart, wretched organ that it was, could not remain still, and like currents beneath the surface of a calm sea, stirred and ached and pulsed restlessly. She felt wantonly reckless for allowing this stranger to make love to her when there was nothing between them except carnal lust. She felt ashamed that she had used his body for the sole sake of physical enjoyment, and that she had let him use hers. And then she felt guilty that she wasn't as ashamed as she *ought* to feel. But no, she was the Pirate Queen, and there was nothing wrong with taking a lover! After all, it was a sovereign's *right!* But deeper down lurked feelings of unsettlement, fear, anxiety, and foreboding, for this man had an enigmatic air of intrigue about him, of authority and command that both drew and fascinated her; he was dark, he was dangerous, and she had no doubts whatsoever that it would be perfectly possible—if not likely—that she *could* fall in love with him.

Damn your eyes and blast your hide, I don't want to love you! You will hurt, forget, abandon *me, and I shall never let myself be hurt, forgotten, or abandoned, ever, ever again!*

Yet, she had certainly loved him with her body. She'd lost count of the number of times they'd come together, the number of positions they'd tried. Whoever her mysterious lover was, he knew things about pleasuring a woman she had never dreamed about. She ached in places she didn't know existed. Every muscle in her body felt drained and lax . . . and sated.

Propping herself up on one elbow, she gazed down at his face, studying the pulse beating at the base of his throat, the gentle flare of his nostrils as he drew breath, released it. He was achingly handsome, and, even asleep, far too dangerous to the barrier that protected her fortitude, her femininity, her heart.

Fear and doubt began to assail her.

I shouldn't have lain with him, she thought. *I should have kept fighting him, as I had been wont to do. Then, at least, my heart would be safe.*

My heart is *safe.*

She touched the anchor tattooed on his big shoulder, her hungry gaze moving over his contoured chest, the flat slabs of his ribs, the taut indentation of his belly, the trail of dark hair leading to his manhood, now lying in repose within its pelted bed of soft, black hair. The sight of it, and the pleasure it had brought her, caused her to flush and squeeze her legs together against the sudden burning there. God, he was a handsome devil. Perfect. Bold, charming, and *magnificent.* He was all she had ever dreamed about, all she had ever prayed for, and despite the fact he wasn't an officer, he was her Gallant Knight.

Hers.

Yet who was he? What did she know about him, except that he was a skilled, imaginative, and attentive lover, that he'd once been in the Royal Navy—and that Lord Nelson would pay anything to get him back?

She shuddered with delight. His crimes against that navy must've been unspeakable indeed, and the thought thrilled and excited her. No wonder he had claimed to find her equally appealing, for her own deeds and doings were as dark as his must surely be. Yet, even as she considered this, apprehension tingled in her heart. She was hard-bitten, hard-used, the antithesis of femininity, softness, and charm. She fought with swords, stole from ships, commanded a crew of women plucked from slavery, indenture, prostitution, and the tyranny of abusive mates. She was cynical, tough—certainly no fitting Cinderella for this darkly handsome Prince.

Would he, too, desert her, as her long-ago lover had, as the world had—as her *family* had?

The brief joy fled her heart like sunlight behind a cloud, turning chill and cold and damp. Mama might've found her roguish lover *charming,* but her fine, upstanding father would never have approved of this piratical spy who had ravished her so relentlessly. But then, he hadn't approved of his errant daughter herself, nor her wicked, wanton ways, either.

He'd sure as hell proved *that* when he never even bothered to search for her after she'd run away.

Maeve's chin came up and her eyes stung with sudden tears. She was not the impulsive sixteen-year-old she'd once been, who'd fallen in love with a man her parents disapproved of and run off to the Caribbean just so she could be with him. No, she was a woman now, a Pirate Queen, and she would do what she damned well pleased! Who cared what they would've thought; it damn well didn't matter anyhow!

A tear leaked from her eye and she slashed at it angrily. To hell with her family! To hell with them, with all of them! They had deserted her, and what did she care whether or not they approved of her new lover? Their opinions, their wishes, had ceased to matter long ago.

A sob lodged in her throat, and she slammed her palm over her mouth to stifle it, feeling the hateful tears running warmly over her fingers, down her arm. Grown women didn't cry; tough, hardened, *pirate queens* didn't cry. Damn her eyes, what the hell was *wrong* with her?

Her Knight stirred—and Maeve froze.

Dark azure eyes opened, and he looked lazily up at her through his lashes.

She drove backward, upset, and it was then that Gray saw the tears on her cheeks. Instantly alarmed, he sat up and gathered her gently in his arms. It was an action of tenderness, of love, and he surprised himself with the realization that he truly *did* care about her distress, truly wanted to comfort her for a reason that had everything to do with his own blossoming feelings for her—and nothing at all to do with using her tears as an excuse to make love to her once again.

"There now, what's this? Did I do something wrong?" he said. "*Say* something wrong?" His hand caught in her hair, smoothing the glossy chestnut tresses.

Abruptly, she leapt out of his embrace as though he'd burned her and walked toward the window, putting several feet between herself and him. He swung his legs off the bed and stared at her, confused and feeling rather hurt that she wouldn't allow him to comfort her. Her color was high, her eyes wild, her bosom rising and falling rapidly, and her feet planted in a warrior's stance. He thought she looked frightened. Angry. *Beautiful*. "It's not *you*, damn it!" she shouted. "Can't you understand that? It's *not you!*"

She spun away from him and faced the window, her hair streaming in rampant glory down her slim back, her harsh breathing echoing through the room, her body trembling violently. He saw the scar of a knife high on her hip, the tautness of hard muscle beneath her golden skin. He saw pain and anger and betrayal in her stance, and found his own heart aching for her as he wondered at the cause of it.

"It's my parents," she said on a hard, steely note.

"Your parents?"

"Aye, my parents! They deserted me, left me to die in this God-forsaken hellhole, and blast you, I don't know why I brought them up but I don't want to talk about them, not now, not *ever!*"

She continued to stare out the window at the distant horizon. Very calmly, Gray let out his breath. He started to get up, wanting to gather that proud, stiffened body in his arms and comfort her in the best way he knew, but something warned him against it. Those furious, angry words—*it's my parents*—had cost her enough pride as it was.

He looked at her slim, curving back. "You miss them, I take it," he said softly.

Her shoulders rose, fell, and when she spoke, her voice was hard and sullen. "Hell no. Why should I?" She turned and faced him, her eyes blazing defiance. "They don't give a damn about *me*. Why the hell should I care about them, huh?"

Her eyes were unnaturally bright, glassy, and gold. "Yes, well, of course," he said, watching her. "They must have been brutal, awful, unfeeling people indeed," he said calculatingly, and was rewarded with a burst of defensive anger.

"They weren't awful, just . . ."

"Just, what?"

"Damn you, I told you I don't want to talk about them!"

He nodded soberly, vowing to himself that he'd get the story one way or another; if not from the Pirate Queen, then from one of her pack of she-wolves. After all, his position in life required that he be a master at extracting information. Obviously, there was more here than the Pirate Queen was willing to admit, and by God and the devil, he would get to the bottom of it before his business on this island was up.

Why should you even care, *man?*

He looked at her, standing there with such hurt in her eyes, a courageous little pirate queen who wasn't quite brave enough to allow herself to be vulnerable—and felt a rush of warmth for her. It was more than lust; it was more than admiration for a woman who was proving to be the embodiment of his every fantasy; it was affection and concern, protectiveness and caring for another person, and Gray—raised in a gentle, loving, family—was not afraid to allow himself such feelings.

For he, unlike the formidable woman at the window, was not afraid to let go of his heart.

"I will not desert you," he said.

"No, of course not," she said sarcastically. "As you are my Gallant Knight, I am your Faerie Princess."

At the window, Maeve drove her fingers into the sill and stared hard out over the sea, where a black squall loomed far out above the horizon. She ached inside, wishing, fearing, hoping, dreading, that he would come to her and comfort her. That's what a real Gallant Knight would do ... Then she heard the bed squeak as he rose to his feet ... heard the soft sounds of his bare feet crossing the room. ... felt the nearness of his body, then its heat, as he came up behind her and put his arms around her, locking them beneath her breasts and holding her ... just holding her. She trembled inside.

"No Faerie Princess. But you are *my* Pirate Queen."

She leaned back against him and swallowed the lump in her throat, wishing she had courage enough to let down her guard and trust him with her pain and fears.

I will not desert you.

Oh, but he would, whether she wanted him to or not—for she had struck a bargain with Lord Nelson, a bargain she now regretted with all her heart, and there was no way out of it that was honorable and decent.

"Are you sure you would not like to talk about it?" he murmured, gently. "About your family?"

She pulled away, and through clenched teeth, gritted, "I am *dead* sure. There is nothing to talk about. That part of my life is over, and there is no going back. *Ever.*"

Sighing, Gray stood looking down at her and feeling strangely helpless—an emotion he was not accustomed to feeling. Well, before she sent him off to Nelson, he'd get the story from her if it was the last thing he did.

So help me God, he vowed to himself.

"Very well, then," he murmured. "I shall not press you about your family. But you fear me, Maeve. Despite all we have shared, I sense that you are holding back, that there is something you will *not* share. I really wish you would trust me enough to open your heart and let me help heal whatever makes you ache so."

"Why should you care?"

"That's a hell of an attitude."

"Well, why *should* you? I mean nothing to you."

"If you meant nothing to me, would I even bother asking?"

"You just want to get me back in bed with you."

"Trust me, madam, I could get you back in bed with me very easily. But I want more than just your body—I'm beginning to realize I may want your heart."

"What, to conquer?" she spat, nastily.

"No, to love."

She was very stiff in his arms, poised for flight.

"I sense," he said softly, leaning his chin against the top of her head, "that someone has treated you very cruelly, done you a grave dishonor or injustice. Correct me if I'm wrong, but I'd stake my last breath that it was a man."

He heard her swallow hard. Felt her heartbeat quickening beneath his arm.

He turned her around to face him, caught her chin in his hand and gently forced her to look up at him. Her eyes were huge and tragic.

"Wasn't it?"

She pulled herself out of his embrace and went back to looking out the window.

"Aye. 'Twas a man."

"Tell me."

"That's unwise. My mother once told me never to talk about other men with the one you're with—"

"I am *asking,* dearest," he said, putting his hands on her shoulders. "How can I help you if you don't trust me?"

She stood with her back to him, her head bent, her shoulders hunched, and her fists clenched at her sides. He could see the inner battle she was fighting, wanted more than anything to help her overcome her fears. To show her that not *all* men were vile, wretched beings.

"I *want* to trust you, Gray . . . I just—Oh, how to explain this—it's—it's as if my heart is a castle, and there's this deep moat around it with no bridges to get across."

"I'll bet a determined and *gallant knight* could cross that moat, love."

"I can't let the drawbridge down, Gray, I just can't! Besides, you're no knight. You're a *pirate.*"

He grinned, secretively, to himself.

"So therefore you cannot cross the moat," she said

stubbornly, but he could see it in her eyes that she very much wished that he would try.

"Can't I?" He pulled her stiff body into his arms and hugged her. This time, she did not step away. "Tell me about this scoundrel that hurt you so. . . ."

A long moment passed—and as he stroked her back, threaded his hands through her hair, and held her protectively clasped against his body, he felt the tension, the wariness, the fear, beginning to ebb out of her like a tide going out to sea.

Come on, sweetheart.

And then it turned.

"His name," she whispered against his chest, in a voice so low he had to strain his ears to hear it, "was Renaud. He was French. I met him when I was sixteen, and fell in love with him."

Gray, finally understanding her strong dislike for the French, tightened his arms around her, silently urging her on.

"I grew up in a small New England seaport. We were a close community and Newburyport neither welcomed, liked, nor trusted strangers. So when Renaud sailed into town—he was a boatswain on a French merchantman—my parents were instantly disapproving of him, and of the interest he took in me. Not . . . that I didn't encourage him. He was a handsome rake, charming, had been all over the world—he used to tell me stories about exotic places, and promise to take me anyplace I wanted to go if only I'd run away with him. . . .

"I wonder now if Mama and Daddy's dislike of Renaud only caused me to love him all the more. How blind I was, how stubborn, how *stupid*. I spent too much time damning *them* for being unfair, and not enough time trying to see Renaud for what he *really* was—a deceitful, lying vagrant, who saw in me enough innocence and naivety to get him just what he wanted."

"Which was, I imagine, getting you into bed with him."

"Aye. That, and more. I was young and foolish; I *believed* his promises of marriage, his vows to love me forever. I thought that I'd find eternal bliss if only I would run away with him to a tropical isle. . . . Ha. I went away with him, and he showed me what he was *really* like. What *all* men are like."

"Let me guess," Gray muttered, feeling an inexplicable urge to find this *Renaud* and run him through with his sword. "The bastard left you."

"Aye, he left me after he realized that it was not so easy to take my schooner."

From over the top of her head, Gray stared out to sea, his jaw set and his eyes hard and angry.

"Anyhow, I was a ruined woman. I was too ashamed to go running back to my parents after what I had done. Not only did I steal my father's schooner—he designed and sailed her himself, you know, made her famous during the American War of Independence—but I also took the money that Mama used to keep hidden in a big jar in the kitchen. I was too ashamed, Gray . . . and so I stayed here. I had my schooner, and my maid, Orla. I was young and clever and could fight my way out of any scuffle—my father had taught me fencing, and my brothers, how to use my fists. I learned early in life how to take care of myself, and those skills stood me well in those first years; they stand me well now. I built a crew for myself, and now, *they* are my family."

"Are you so very sure your parents would not have taken you back, Maeve?"

"Oh, I'm sure. They damn well *proved* that they'd washed their hands of me. Seven years I've been down here, Gray, left to chance without ever hearing a word from either of them. You'd think they would've come searching, that my own *father* would've come looking for me, but no, he didn't care, no one cared, damn them all, I hate them, *hate them* ... Oh, God. ..."

And as she clung to him like a little child, he wrapped his strong arms around her, soothing her and holding her against his heart until long after her trembling ceased.

Then he lifted his gaze and looked out to sea—where the wind raced, where the horizon stretched empty, and where somewhere, a grieving father was surely missing his capricious daughter.

Chapter 10

S he lay beside him, wrapped in his arms, their en-twined bodies sheathed by a shaft of faint silver starlight.

The crew had long since ceased their revelry and gone to bed. Exhaustion tugged at Maeve's eyelids, but she was not ready for sleep. She snuggled closer to the man in whose arms she lay, feeling safe, protected, *cherished*. These long-forgotten feelings were vaguely uncomfortable, frightening, even, for they demanded trusting another person, and risking being *hurt* by an-other person. But how nice it was to lie beside him, their bodies as one, her head resting on his shoulder, her hair fanning out over his chest as he stroked the shining tresses. And how *right* it felt to savor the warmth of his leg alongside hers, to count each pre-cious beat of his heart, to think and plan and wonder about the future.

I could lie alongside this man forever.

She cuddled closer to him and felt the muscles of his arm tighten beneath her shoulders as he obligingly pulled her over against his ribs.

"Dear, sweet Maeve," he murmured. She moved her head up and looked into his face. In the dark shadows of the room his eyes looked very black. Fathomless. She caressed his chest, traced the honed muscle and ribs with the flat of her palm, drew little circles in the valley of his sternum with her fingertips.

"That took a lot of courage, telling me about your past."

She shrugged. "Yes, well . . . I rather wish I hadn't. You, too, will probably desert and abandon me."

His deep chuckle rumbled up from his chest. "Desert and abandon? Sweet lady, you make a man so drunk with wanting you that I can't even walk. Indeed, look what state you have put me in once again."

His hand came up, caught her fingers, and gently slid them down below his stomach. She felt the soft, wiry curls there, the rigid evidence of his desire, already thick and rock-hard in testimony to his words.

She smiled shyly and touched him, dabbing her fingers against the velvety tip and relishing each soft gasp he made; slowly, she stroked that hard flesh, feeling it grow and swell within her hand. Beneath her ear, his heartbeat quickened and she sensed, felt, heard, the blood beginning to rush through his body, saw, as he must, the colors and lights swirling behind his now-closed eyes.

"I promise, Gray. Just one more time, then I'll let you go to sleep."

He laughed softly, and opened his eyes. "Sleep? Those who crave sleep miss out on too much in life." He rose up on his elbow and touched his nose to hers. "Besides, this is much more enjoyable."

She fell onto her back, allowing him to rise up and thrust his hard and throbbing length into her body. Squeezing her inner muscles, she was able to give him the utmost sensation and pleasure. He groaned and pulled himself almost completely out of her; she wrapped her arms around his back and drove upward to meet him. His head lowered and she felt his breath against her neck, felt his mouth suckling her breasts, felt his hand reaching down to further enflame her moist womanhood even as he continued the tormentingly slow rhythm of his lovemaking.

He brought her to the peak of climax, slowed, and hung poised within her just before she would've found release, brought her up once again, and finally sent her soaring out into the skies of ecstasy. Her nails digging into his back, she cried his name against the salty skin of his shoulder, and a moment later he, unable to contain his own release any longer, drove himself into her with a last, savage thrust that left him gasping and exhausted.

He collapsed beside her, breathing hard. They lay quietly together, listening to the wind sighing through the palm trees outside, the ceaseless roar of the ocean.

"Gray," she murmured. "You frighten me. Would to God you had not washed up on my island. You—do things to my heart."

He rolled onto his side, propped himself up on an elbow, and smiled at her in the darkness. She reached out and cleared the dark locks of hair from his brow, her touch gentle, smooth, worshipful.

"You do things to mine, too." He closed his eyes, still smiling. "Ah, but that feels good, Maeve."

"Does it?"

"Mmmm. Makes me sleepy."

Her gaze was gentle and fond. "I thought you said sleeping was a waste of time."

"Sleeping *alone* is a waste of time." He sighed, made a contented noise deep in his throat, nuzzled her hand and kissed the back of her knuckles. "I think I would enjoy waking up with you, Maeve. Falling asleep with you. Dreaming with you."

"Really?"

"Aye. That's not much to ask, is it?"

She sat up, scooching backward until she rested against the pillows piled at the headboard. Gray smiled drowsily and pulled himself up beside her. He kissed her knee, then eased himself down until his dark head lay pillowed against the softness of her thigh, his hair tangled within her womanly curls. The sensation was wildly erotic, and was made even more so by the flutter of his lashes against her sensitive skin, the feel of his lips gently kissing her knee, the warmth of his palm roving up and down her leg.

"What a devilishly nice pillow your thigh makes, Pirate Queen."

She smiled to herself and lightly stroked his forehead. Her heart felt at peace, her soul, and body, satisfied and well loved. She felt a rush of tenderness for him as his breathing deepened and the weight of his head grew heavy against her thigh.

"Thank you, Gray."

"Hmmmh?"

"For being a friend, as well as a magnificent lover."

"Thank *you,* Majesty . . . for confiding in this loyal servant."

She trailed her fingers through his long hair, felt his lips resting against her knee, moving drowsily in a gentle kiss. Outside, the wind sang a lullaby through the trees and the waves broke timelessly along the beach.

Thank you, God, for sending me this wonderful man. I'm beginning to think that maybe he really is my Gallant Knight.

"G'night, sweetness," he murmured thickly, and she felt his body relax as he finally gave himself up to slumber. She slid down beside him, felt his arm go possessively around her shoulder, and closed her eyes. She drowned in the rhythmic sounds of his breathing.

"Good night, Gallant Knight," she whispered.

Then she, too, slept.

"Mama! Mama, help! *Ma-maaaaa!*"

The bloodcurdling scream woke Gray out of a sound sleep. He bolted upright in the bed, blinking and confused, momentarily disoriented and wondering where he was.

"Mama, help me-e-e-e-e-e-e!"

He reached out in the darkness and found a still-warm empty spot beside him. "Maeve?"

He heard her quick footsteps, pounding out of her room and down the hall. "Aisling, honey, I'm coming!"

Gray swung his legs out of bed and knuckled his eyes. He shook his head to clear it, and heard the distant sound of the Irish girl's weeping. His brain foggy with sleep, he stood up, holding on to the bedpost and trying to collect his thoughts. His breeches lay on the floor; numbly, he picked them up, stumbled into them, and made his way silently down the hall to a door standing partly open.

He stood for a moment just outside, glancing guiltily at the other doors and fearing discovery; but there was no sound in the house except the young girl's soft weeping and another voice—gentle, comforting, motherly—soothing her.

Maeve's.

"It's alright, Aisling. Shhhh, sweetie. I'm here. It's alright, 'twas just a nightmare . . . I get them too, when I go to bed on a full stomach. It's alright, now. Nothing's going to happen to you. I promise. . . ."

Holding his breath, Gray slowly pushed open the door.

His breath caught in his throat. For there, sitting cross-legged on the bed with the sobbing girl in her arms, was Maeve. Her back was to him, and all he could see was her bent head, that glorious dark red hair tumbling down her back over the whiteness of the shirt she must've hurriedly donned.

"Really, Maeve?" the girl was whispering, her voice catching on a sob. "It's because I went to bed on a full stomach?"

"Oh, yes, honey. That's why. And you had that greasy roast pork, didn't you?"

"Aye, Majesty. I did."

"That'll do it. But it was only a nightmare, Ash, and it's all over now. I'm here. I won't let anything happen to you . . ."

Gray stood leaning against the doorjamb, awed. Not daring to make a sound. A slow smile curved his lips, and in that moment he saw the woman beneath the harsh Pirate Queen, a side of her he might not have known existed if it hadn't been for the young girl's nightmare. Something huge and wonderful filled his heart, made it swell painfully against his ribs, and he felt a searing tenderness that he had never felt with any other woman.

Maeve as a mother.

The thought struck him with swift and lethal intensity, and he felt that sudden something in his heart spreading out through his breast to encompass his entire being. For a long time, he stood there in the darkness, leaning against the doorjamb watching her, as she told Aisling the story about the original Maeve, warrior-queen of Connacht, after whom she'd been named, every so often lapsing into a strange, unfamiliar language he thought must've been the old Irish Gaelic.

He watched them until the young girl fell asleep once more, and then, his heart full to bursting, he crept back to their bedroom, shed his breeches, and slipped beneath the covers.

When the Pirate Queen returned, her lover—to all appearances—was sound asleep.

But in the darkness, she never saw his tender smile.

A half hour later the Pirate Queen and her lover rose, dressed quietly, and pushed open the door of Maeve's room.

Three in the morning, and the house was dark and quiet.

Her lusty captive in tow, the Pirate Queen peered out into the darkened hall. Soft snores emanated from

Enolia's room; a balmy breeze, still wet with rain, danced through the long corridor, sending the gauzy curtains at the far window reaching out like the fingers of a ghost.

Feeling her way in the darkness, Maeve took a few steps forward and stopped. Behind her, Gray's chest bumped against her back, slamming the breath from her lungs.

"Clod!"

He laughed. Then she laughed and she slapped her hand over his mouth and shivered as his tongue tickled the sensitive palm. Strong fingers closed around hers, enveloping them in warmth and male strength; then he pulled her arm high and began to nibble its underside. She had already been caught once that evening in a compromising position and she did not want to be caught again.

"Stop it!" she tried to say in a serious tone but could not prevent the chuckle that escaped her lips. At this rate, they'd never get downstairs!

"Stop what, Majesty? Loving you? Mmmm, but you do taste good—"

"Shhh!"

"How I would enjoy ravishing you right here in this hall—"

"Gray!"

"How I would enjoy plunging my sword to the hilt—"

She grabbed his hand and ignoring his soft laughter, proceeded cautiously through the gloom toward the stairs. They were halfway down when Gray missed a step and fell heavily against her. She gasped and grabbed for the banister, but he caught her before she could fall.

The thumping racket was enough to wake the dead.

"Shhh!"

In response, the pirate's stomach let out a splitting, raucous growl that echoed in the darkness.

She couldn't help it; she laughed.

He kissed the laughter from her lips, bending her backward over his arm and seemingly ignorant of the twenty more stairs still beneath them. Then he pulled away, traced her lips with one finger, and scooped her up into his arms.

"Put me down!" she gasped, terrified that he'd miss a step and send them both plunging to their deaths. But he merely clasped her to him and carried her easily down through the choking darkness to the bottom of the stairs.

Maeve didn't realize she'd been holding her breath until he set her down on the cool, polished floor.

"You're insufferable," she snapped playfully, and when she gazed up at him, felt a strange softening of the heart.

He swept an elaborate, gallant bow. "At your service, Majesty."

She saw something in his eyes—not lust, as she'd noted upon their first encounters, but something unguarded and fond ... something ... else.

Barefoot and holding hands—he clad in his snug black breeches, she in a gauzy shirt and cottony trousers—they padded across the cool floor. All was quiet, save for the ticking of the shelf clock, the distant roar of the sea. He squeezed her fingers, his thumb playing over the sensitive underside of her wrist. She heard him breathing, felt the heat of his body just behind hers, and again, thought of how good it had felt to confide in him, to open the old wounds, to *trust* him.

Her blood tingled, and she felt a swift surge of giddy desire. Was he a dream, this handsome, piratical man? He, who had "crossed the moat" like some gallant, handsome knight? Turning, she reached up, found the contours of his face in the darkness, and pulled his head down to hers.

No. No dream at all.

Their soft moans mingled with the whisper of the trades rustling through the palms outside.

"You need a shave," she murmured, breaking free.

"I need *you.*"

But his stomach growled again, proclaiming which need was paramount, and, stifling a bark of laughter, Maeve pulled him into the dining room, sat him down at the table, and fumbling for a flint, lit a small candle.

She turned. The golden flame cast his body in a magnificent study of contoured muscle and strength. Setting the candle atop the table, she bent over him and shamelessly kissed his neck, his throat, his stubbled jaw.

"Maybe I *do* care about you," she admitted, recklessly. "But just a little bit."

"Ah, victory at last! The lady admits she has a jot of feeling for me! Well, I *care* about you too, Pirate Queen." He thought of how he'd felt when he'd seen her comforting the Irish girl after her nightmare. "But, I think, more than just a *little bit.* And as soon as we eat I'm going to prove it to you by carrying you out to the beach and ravishing you upon the warm sand—Ho now, what's this?"

There was a piece of paper on the table. He picked it up, scanning it by the flickering light. "Why, it looks like a letter to Her Majesty from two of her loyal subjects."

"What does it say?" she murmured, playfully burying her lips against the warm curve of his neck.

"It says, 'Dear Majesty. We hope you're having fun trysting with your Gallant Knight. We know you're trysting 'cause we listened at the door to make sure he wasn't holding you against your will. Don't be mad at us. There's some food on the sideboard, hopefully still warm by the time you read this. Enjoy, Aisling and

Sorcha.'" He paused, and brought the paper closer. "'P.S. Don't let him get you pregnant.'"

Her breath came out in a burst of laughter against his neck.

"It seems they take good care of you, these pirate girls."

"We all take care of *each other,*" she said, snatching up a jug of spiced wine and the tray from the sideboard. She set both before him. "And as for Aisling and Sorcha, they haven't been with us long enough to have lost their innocence and become the hardened wretches the rest of us are. I should like to keep them that way, if I could."

"Twould seem, Majesty, it is too late for *that,*" he murmured, tossing the note aside and grinning at her. "Now, what have they left for us, eh?" He lifted the cover from each dish, exclaiming in delight over the meat, the crusty bread, the thick wedges of yellow cheese. "A veritable feast!" He lifted eyes that were black in the darkness to hers, and in them she saw the glow of desire and promise ... and again that certain nameless something. "But nothing compared to the *dessert* that awaits. ..."

"Oh yes, dessert—" she repeated with a jaunty lift of her eyebrow. "I believe we'll find something sweet and succulent out on the beach."

He laughed, and opened his arms to her. Swift to take the invitation, Maeve climbed into his lap, reveling in his strength, his embrace, the feel of his manhood beneath her. Already, it was springing to life, prodding the soft flesh of her thighs. He tickled her and she laughed, feeling liberated and free and youthful. How utterly wonderful it was, this newfound ability, this permission she'd given herself, to let go of all the anger and bitterness and hurt, and allow herself to feel something for a man she desired.

"Feed me," he commanded, his eyes glinting.

"Feed yourself, I'm not your damned slave!"

He grinned. "No, but pretend to be, for tonight."

Nestling against him, she drew her dagger and cut the pork into bite-sized pieces, wondering what game he was up to now. But as she stabbed a chunk with the point of her blade, his hand closed around her wrist.

She arched a brow and looked at him.

"With your fingers."

His eyes were narrowed, black with wickedness. She returned his hot stare; then, she pulled the dagger out of the meat, wiped it on the side of the plate, and laid it down. Picking up a piece of pork, she lifted it to his mouth and fed it to him. Desire rippled through her as he licked the juice from her fingers, taking each one into his mouth and sucking it suggestively, slowly, his tongue swirling around each tingling digit.

"You are very *wicked,* my handsome pirate," she purred, throatily, as her blood began to burn once more.

"Nay, madam, I am very *hungry.*" He pulled her thumb from his mouth, his eyes holding hers and making no disguise of just *what* he was hungry for. She felt a rush of longing and sighed as he kissed the inside of her wrist.

"Tell me about your life," she ventured, playfully. "I've told you all about me, yet I know nothing about you but your first name!"

He poured a glass of wine and lifted it to her lips, then broke off a piece of cheese and began to feed her, in turn. His eyes gleamed as he watched her trying to nibble it as a lady might, delicately, prettily, graciously—then laughing, he shoved it in, barely allowing her time to chew and swallow before kissing her with helpless abandon. "Ah, dear madam!" he said, burying his face in the warm curve of her neck, "I cannot get enough of you!"

"Dammit, Gray—" she gasped as his hand found her

breast. "I'm serious! You know about *me* ... Oooh!" She slapped his hand away. "Now tell me about *you!*"

He dipped his fingers in his glass, smeared wine over her nipple, and cupping her breast in his hand, pushed it upward. The nipple popped above the shirt and he closed his mouth around it, suckling greedily.

"You would not like me anymore if I told you about me," he murmured, against the tingling, aching nipple. "By God, you taste good. . . ."

"But I *want* to know about you, Gray—" She moaned as his tongue licked the taut nipple, causing it to tingle and burn and swell with longing. "I want to know when you were born ... *where* you were born ... how many brothers and sisters you have ... what your father and mother are like. . . ."

He lifted his head, his breath feathering against her breast. "I have six sisters and no brothers, my parents live in Surrey, and I was born in Penzance on the fourteenth day of August, in the year of our Lord seventeen hundred and sixty-eight."

And I'm a Knight of the Bath whose head is going to roll, he thought to himself.

"And your father and mother?"

"Good parents. My father ... owns land."

"In Surrey?"

"Aye."

His tongue was circling her breast again. She drove her fingers into his hair, melted against him in one moment, and in the next brought his head up to face her. "What else, Gray? Tell me everything."

"And why do you want me to do that, madam?" he said.

"Because I've changed my mind." She put her hands against the sides of his head and gently pushed him away. Her eyes were glowing, and Gray looked up to see a happy, radiant smile on her hardened face. "You see"—she flushed, looking more like a lady than the Pirate Queen—"I've decided to keep you, and not sell you to Nelson after all."

He went stiff. The blood drained from his heart and pooled thickly in his veins.

"Gray?"

"Why, that is . . . why, that is, uh, wonderful, Majesty."

"You don't sound very happy about it," she said, alarm darkening her voice. "Don't you want to stay here and be my Pirate King, my Gallant Knight?"

Recovering, he leaned forward and kissed her nose, her lips, the corners of her mouth. "Of course I want to stay here with you," he assured her while he cursed himself for the trouble he'd gotten himself into *this* time. Christ, the whole British Navy was probably searching for him and she wanted to *keep* him in this Garden of Eden as if no one else existed.

"I know you're afraid Nelson will be looking for you," she said, "but you're safe here." Her hands cupped the side of his jaw, and her eyes, so hard, so guarded before, were once again full of adoration and affection. "After all, no one knows where the Pirate Queen has her lair, and not even your own Admiral Falconer would know where to find me."

That was for damned sure.

"I will shield you with my reputation, guard you with my life," she vowed, tossing her head and sending her hair flying over one shoulder. "And as for Nelson . . . well, I simply won't go to meet him. You have come to mean too much to me. Besides, he'd probably rather spend his money on his 'dear Lady Hamilton' than on a traitor he'd just as soon hang, don't you think?"

"You are most thoughtful, Majesty."

"Thank you, Gray. No one's ever told me that before, you know." She bent her head, her hair falling down over her eyes, and when she spoke, her voice was uncharacteristically shy and maidenly. "You know, maybe there really *is* a future for us." She played with a soft whorl of his chest hair then looked up, her eyes full of childish hope. At his slight hesitation, she waved her arm and tried to fill in the awkward space with words. "Think of it, Gray!" she cried, her anxious eyes glowing with excitement. "We'll sail the seas together, plundering and pillaging and stealing! We'll become as famous as Calico Jack and Anne Bonney, and sailors the breadth of the Spanish Main will come to fear your name as much as they do mine!"

He was still staring at her, for such a fantasy was of course, an impossibility. Slowly, he said, "Er . . . yes, Majesty. . . . Though I fear my blackened blood is not royal enough for a Pirate Queen."

"Nonsense." She smiled, her teeth flashing in her face, and let her hand drift down to touch him; that part of him had gone temporarily lifeless and now, at her soft caress, began to stir once again. "You are my Gallant Knight," she declared, with a touch of regal hauteur and a defiant lift of her chin. "I have already decided *that!*"

Obviously, she had decided a few other things, as well.

"Gray?"

As much as he would have liked, he could not stay here. And now, with her decision to keep him here on this island, he had to think of a way off of it—and quickly.

His mind had always been at its best when his body was active. Rising to his feet, he scooped her up into his arms and carried her out of the house and down to the beach.

Chapter 11

⌒ᗐ⌒

The night was hot with the sultry kiss of the trades, the breezes scented by bougainvillea, vegetation, and the heady tang of the sea. The aroma of freshly roasted pork lingered near the glowing coals of the bonfire, and out in the bay, moonlight glazed *Kestrel*'s dark hull.

It was a magical night, and Maeve, looking deeply into her pirate's eyes as he carried her down the short path to the beach, was loath to disturb it with words. And if her handsome lover seemed mildly distracted, troubled, well, she would soon entice him out of *that!*

Facing him, she straddled his hips with her thighs and hooked her arms behind his neck. She kissed his face and neck and lips until she felt his arousal pressing against her womanhood. Her skin prickled with desire.

At last, a man who wasn't afraid of her, who was her equal in every way. He was strong, virile, and was everything she ever dreamed of finding in a man, except he wasn't a gallant officer.

But the spell had been fouled, after all. Damned gull shit. What could she expect?

In the darkness, it was hard to see his expression, but she saw the white glint of his teeth, of starlight in his eyes, his hair tumbling and tossing in the wind. She placed her hands against the wide breadth of his chest, feeling his heart thudding against her palm. For such a tall and powerful man, he moved with easy grace and a gait she was well familiar with.

It was the gait of a sailor.

"Don't worry, Gray . . . I told you, Nelson will *never* find you here!" she said, to reassure him.

He said nothing, only lifting a corner of his mouth and letting his gaze rake over her with simmering intent. But something like pain flashed in his dark eyes and quickly disappeared. Heat, desire, and dark promise burned in them once more. She felt his hands locked behind the small of her back, his muscles working beneath the insides of her thighs. With his earring, he could've been a savage buccaneer captain in the manner of Henry Morgan.

But tonight, he was *her* pirate.

"I want ye, wench," he growled, in his best buccaneer's voice. "Here and *now.*"

"Well then, what are you waiting for?" She gave him an equally hot glance, and boldly reached out to touch the probing, velvety head of his arousal.

His mouth closed over hers and as he had done for hours before, Gray claimed her body hungrily, savagely, possessively.

Afterward they lay lazily entwined on the sand. Then, in one swift motion, Gray scooped her up and into his arms, kissing her with hungry abandon.

She heard the gentle splashing of waves foaming against his legs, then his thighs, as he moved through the warm surf and into deeper water.

He was smiling down at her, and it was a cunning, wicked smile.

"Gray, *don't,*" she warned, already guessing his intent.

He chuckled blackly, and she felt the gentle kiss of the sea touching her backside, her ankles, as he went deeper and deeper into the water, never taking his dark eyes off her.

Finally he stopped ... and began to lift her up, up, like a sacrifice to the gods.

"Gray, no!"

He laughed.

"Gray, *no!*"

She shrieked, but he had already tossed her high, laughing in pure delight as she flailed and swore and hit the sea with a resounding splash. Coughing and choking, she thrust downward, trying to find her footing, but the movement only plunged her head under again. Cursing, she broke the surface, found a foothold on a shelf of coral, and slashing her cupped palm over the waves, sprayed him with water.

"Snake!" she cried, as his rich laughter rolled through the night. She sprayed him again. "I'll get you for this, you vile, treacherous rat!"

He folded his arms across his chest. Dark eyes challenged her. "Be my guest, madam."

But his grin was infectious, and even mock anger could not be sustained. Maeve thrust her hand up, shot him an obscene gesture that was challenging of its own accord, and without waiting for his reaction, turned and made a clean, perfect, dolphin dive, allowing him a taunting glimpse of her bare backside before the sea swallowed her up.

Behind her came the splashing thunder of roiling water, and with a swift kick, she angled her body down, down, down, swimming with sure, easy strokes, and unable to see a thing in the darkness. But she knew every finger of coral, every bed of seaweed in this bay; knew them as well as she did every spar and line and gun aboard *Kestrel*. Hands spread before her, her hair streaming sensuously against her spine and backside, she felt her way over sharp ridges of coral and out into deeper water. Then she kicked her legs and angled upward, breaking the surface thirty feet from *Kestrel*'s dark hull.

Treading water and breathing hard, she blinked the salt from her eyes and felt the night wind sighing over her wet hair and face.

Her pirate was nowhere to be seen.

A shiver danced through her, and instinctively, she drew her legs up toward herself, strangely thrilled and excited and nervous all at once. Although she knew he was down there, in the darkness, the idea of his grabbing her legs and pulling her under was unnerving.

She waited.

Nothing.

"Gray?"

Again, nothing. Only the ominous sigh of the breeze making the palms crackle and hiss.

Maeve took a deep breath and dived, swimming back toward the beach. Halfway there she paused just beneath the surface, listening to the underwater sounds. She could hear the muffled thump of the anchor cable against *Kestrel*, the distant, high-pitched clicking of Turlough, and the dreamy, contained rush and swell of the sea.

And nothing else.

Growing nervous, she surfaced.

"Gray?" she called, frantically.

Nothing.

The wind soughed through the trees, and alarm rose in her breast.

"Gray!"

Panicking, she turned and slammed right into his chest.

"Arrrrh, there ye be, my pretty!"

"Damn you, you scared the living *daylights* out of me!"

He roared with laughter and, yanking her up against his chest, crushed her to him. His mouth drove savagely against hers; his tongue forced its way between her teeth, plunged into her mouth, and dueled with her own, swirling, tasting, exploring, conquering.

She moaned, sagging against his hard strength and lost in a rushing flood of erotic sensations . . . Wet skin against wet skin, sealed by the heat of their bodies; waves lapping around her waist; currents teasing her own aroused womanhood; the bottom sand giving away beneath her heels and toes; the cool kiss of the tropical breeze against her tingling, dripping flesh.

He broke the kiss and began nibbling her throat. Her head fell back, offering the pale flesh to his hungry lips, and she felt his broad hands close around her ribs, her waist, her hips. He lifted her high, and instinctively her legs wrapped around his torso and she pulled herself toward him, searching, seeking, wanting.

He laughed in high triumph, hooking an arm behind her nape and tipping her backward until her hair fanned out just beneath the waves like a dark, undulating mermaid's pillow. His gaze raked over her throat, her ripe breasts, bared to the stars like some sacrifice to the gods; she melted beneath that primal gaze, feeling the currents kissing her back, swirling over her belly, and probing her womanhood, now shamelessly bared to the sea's kisses between her open legs. His hand dragged over her breasts, first one, then the other, the hardness of his palm scraping the tender flesh and exciting her nipples to pebbly hardness. He took one, rolled it gently between his fingers until she was sobbing with pleasure; then he was lifting her, his lips against her breasts, kissing, suckling, plundering, until they tingled with the combined sensations evoked by wind and wave, hot mouth and tongue. She gave herself up to the erotic pleasure, her hand anchoring in his wet hair, her blood roaring through her head, her lungs heaving as his fingers drove downward, found her burning womanhood, spread the soft folds underwater, and leisurely, made their entrance.

She gave a throaty sigh, helpless against the building waves of pleasure. "Oh, Gray. . . ."

His fingers probed deeper, his thumb stroking the swollen bud nestled within the soft petals of flesh until she was gasping for air. She tried to drag herself up but his lips were there, pushing her back, his arm like a rock behind her shoulders, the heavy wetness of her hair pulling her head down and back. Ever so slightly he tipped her up, then groaned deep in his throat as her fingers reached for, then closed around, his manhood.

"Sweet Neptune," he gasped, sucking in his breath as she squeezed and stroked him as mercilessly as he had her. He went rigid and pulled her back up, but she only increased the pressure, ringing him with thumb and forefinger until he was groaning, thrusting, gasping.

"Heave to, lass," he ground out, through clenched teeth, "heave to, or by God, you'll have me on a lee shore—"

His grip on her slipped, and he almost dropped her. Heady thrills of desire slashed through her blood like the fiercest of gales; mercilessly, she let her thumb rove over the velvety tip of his shaft until his head fell forward, his harsh breath burned against her shoulder, and in her hand, he began to convulse, to jerk, to throb . . .

"By all that's holy, woman—belay this torture, I beg of you—I . . . can't . . . wait . . . any . . . longer—"

He didn't bother allowing her the pleasure of tantalizing him any further. Shoving forward, he plunged himself deeply into her soft, welcoming recesses, groaning with anguished pleasure and dropping fevered kisses on her neck, her cheek. She felt him stumble beneath her, recover, gain his rhythm, then his pace, as he began to pump savagely, almost angrily, into her, the movements oddly slowed, deliciously thickened, by the dragging pull of tide and seawater and current.

She met each stabbing thrust with blind abandon. Her nails bit into his wet back, her arms clung fiercely to his neck, and still he strained, pumping, slamming, driving himself harder and harder, deeper and deeper, until the gathering waves began to build, to mount, to pulse, to soar, to come together with an explosive, blinding violence.

The force of it rocked him like a ship's broadside even as she closed around him, cried out, and began to climax. He drove into her, wanting only to make it lasting and beautiful for her.

"Gray," she cried, gasping, "Oh, Gray, *now!*"

She lurched unto him, crying out as wave after wave tore through her until at last she lay spent and drained against him, the sea swirling around their still-throbbing flesh. He shut his eyes and held her, lovingly, tenderly, loath to let her go, loath to do what he now knew he must.

Betray her.

For as much as he desperately wanted to, he could not trust her enough to tell her the truth about *himself*. She was, after all, a pirate, and despite his own intuition about where her loyalties would lie, he could not gamble the fate of his country on it.

He had to betray her.

But God help him, was there *any* other way?

"Duty," Nelson had once told him, *"is the great business of a sea officer. All private considerations must give way to it, however painful it is."*

His hand drove upward, tangled in her wet hair and pressed her head against his chest. His heart was hammering, and he wondered if she could sense the inner turmoil there, the angst and the agony, if she could see into his mind and know what he was thinking, plotting, planning—dreading. But no. Her legs tightened around his torso, her arms around his neck, and he felt a gentle, feathery sensation against his nape, then his earlobe.

He shut his eyes, his lips a grim slash of pain.

"You are everything I ever hoped for in a Gallant Knight. You may be a pirate but I would not change anything about you."

Christ, he thought, sick at heart. Why had he ever let himself seduce her, be seduced *by* her? Was he so weak and helpless as all that? So damned *stupid?* And to let himself care for her besides . . .

He stared bleakly out at the dark schooner, thinking himself the most wretched of creatures. *Get it over with, Gray,* he thought. *Get it over with now.*

He couldn't.

But there was Nelson. There was Villeneuve. There was his country.

He had no choice.

She pulled back, her eyes reverent and adoring as she gazed up at him. *Harden up, man.* But doing so was the most difficult thing he'd ever done in his life.

"Do you believe, Gray . . . that we could ever have a future together? That you could ever lo—I mean, have feelings for—a hardened pirate Queen like me?"

He looked at her and forced a smile that tore at the deepest part of his heart. "You mean, love you?"

She looked away afraid and unable to meet his gaze and face a possible rejection. "Aye."

"I could fall in love with you, Maeve," he murmured, steeling himself. " . . . Though I can't say my mistress on Barbados would be very happy about it. . . ."

He caught himself, trailing off as though he hadn't made the mistake on purpose. If he could've spared her, if he could've afforded to take the gamble of confiding the truth to her, if he could've lain down and died—he would have.

But he couldn't. All he could do was wait for his deliberately cruel words to pierce her to the very center of her heart.

Her lips froze against the side of his bearded jaw,

hung there, poised; then, she pulled back as if stunned, as if someone had just slapped her across the face.

"What did you say?"

He felt himself breaking up inside, all of his hopes, his dreams, falling to his feet like a shower of lifeless ashes. She was everything he'd ever wanted; she had trusted him, and now he had to betray her.

And *desert* her.

His throat constricted and the blood ran cold through his veins, sieved through his heart like ice water. *If only he hadn't seduced her, begun to fall in love with her . . . but Christ, she'd said she was taking him to Nelson, he hadn't thought she'd end up wanting to keep him here. . . .*

"Gray—" her voice was a bare whisper. "Did you say what I *think* you just said?"

" 'Twas nothing, madam," he said lamely, and looked away, as though unable to meet those stricken, shocked eyes. "Merely a slip of the tongue. . . ."

"A slip of the tongue?" She stared at him, her face paling to white in the darkness. Already, she was pulling away. Already, the fragile threads of trust and hope had been severed, irretrievably broken. "Is there something you're not *telling* me, Gray?"

He shrugged. "All men keep mistresses," he said, blithely.

"Well, I hope to God you don't *still* intend to keep one after"—smudges of color stained her white cheeks—". . . after this!"

"After what?" he said, with forced innocence.

She stared at him, disbelieving. "After . . . after what we just did. . . ."

"So. What difference does *that* make?"

She flinched as if struck, too dazed by his callousness yet to find the anger he prayed would come, the anger he was depending upon to get him off this damned island and back into the service of his country. "Doesn't what we just did mean *anything* to you?"

"Look, Maeve—"

Her voice rose. "Doesn't it?!"

He heard the waves lapping against the schooner, *her* schooner, and felt more wretched than he'd ever been in his life. The night was suddenly too big, too cold, too empty, and it grew more so as she unfastened her arms from around his neck, slipped down into the water, and began to put distance between them.

"Look, Maeve," he began again. "I'm just a sailor. God knows, I want you, yes, but I"—he steeled himself to utter the cruel words—"I like variety. You understand, surely?"

She shook her head disbelievingly. "I can't believe you're doing this to me. . . ."

Get angry, he thought, desperately. *For God's sake, don't make me hurt you more.* "Doing what? There's nothing wrong with keeping a mistress, most men do. . . . Look, if it'll make you feel better, I'll keep my activities with her a secret—"

"How can you be so vile, so wretched, so cruel? Damn you, I—I *trusted* you!"

He grinned, although the gesture cost him another shred of his heart. "Really, my dear, why are you so vexed? She's just a dalliance—"

"A dalliance? Is that what you think of *me?* A *dalliance?*"

"Now, Maeve, darling—"

"Don't you *now Maeve darling* me!" she cried and swung her open palm against his jaw with all the force in her body.

He stood there and allowed her to slap him, feeling the sting bring a satisfied release from the pain inside. He saw the fire blazing now in her eyes, hot angry fire that burned him to the core.

"Did you feed her with pretty words, too? Did you

worm your way into her bed and play her like a violin and then betray her, too, you slimy bastard? You vicious dog! You deceitful, cunning, filthy *blackguard*—"

"Maeve, you're being unreasonable," he said, grabbing both her wrists. Her knee came up, and if not for the drag of the water, would've damaged him beyond repair. "I can't see what you're getting all upset about; it's perfectly acceptable for a man to keep a mistress—"

"It's not acceptable to *me!*" she raged, tearing free of his grip. "I knew you were too good to be true! I knew you couldn't be what I wanted you to be, what you seemed, no matter *what* I wanted to believe! Why the hell didn't I listen to myself?"

Unexpectedly, her other hand came up and slammed against the side of his jaw hard enough to make him see stars. He staggered and she yanked herself free.

"Bastard!" she cried. "May you rot in hell!"

She struck off, not for the shore as he would've expected but for the schooner, as though it was her only friend, her only comfort. Shaking his dazed head, he dived after her, but she had a head start on him, and moments later was scaling the vessel's side, her hair streaming down her bare back, her legs flashing white in the darkness. He was a scant five feet behind her. Lunging upward, he grabbed the rope ladder and began hauling himself up the side of the schooner, the water rushing down his own naked shoulders, his back, and into the sea.

Her feet pounded hollowly over the deck above him. "Get away from me, you wretched bastard, and get the *hell* off my ship!"

She half dived, half fell down the hatch, just as alarmed voices rang out from the shore.

"Majesty?"

Splashes, curses, lights, shouts, and from the beach, the crack of a pistol, shattering the night.

Gray lunged over the gunwales and onto the deck.

He had no time to survey the double rows of guns, no time to admire the neat readiness in which she kept her vessel, no time to examine this singular little warship from up close, for at that moment his quarry came flying up from the hatch, a blunderbuss in her hands and pointed straight at him.

She fired.

The explosion blew the night apart, brilliant orange-and-blue flames roiling from the lock and a split-second later, the barrel. How she missed him at such close range Gray never knew, and he had not time to ponder it as he dived for cover, landed on his elbows, and crashed heavily against the stout carriage of a cannon. His mind screamed with pain, and then there was nothing but a horde of dark shapes above and around him, and an array of swords, rapiers, knives, and cutlasses all pointed at his heart. He rose up on one elbow, cursing under his breath, and supporting himself with one hand. Someone kicked him in the ribs; someone else slammed a foot into his shoulder and shoved him onto his stomach with enough force to knock the air from his lungs. A bare foot drove between his shoulder blades, and he heard the sounds of a gun being loaded, felt the kiss of its gaping mouth as the Pirate Queen jabbed the blunderbuss hard into his spine.

He let his forehead rest against the deck and shut his eyes, his long lashes brushing the varnished planking.

From above came an ominous click as she drew the weapon to half cock, and the tight, choking sounds of her harsh breathing.

She brought the gun to full cock.

"Don't, Majesty." A voice said quietly. "You'll regret it."

"The only thing I regret, Orla, is—is—that I even l-let this d-d-dog near me."

"It's all right, Majesty," the voice said. He sensed movement and heard someone comforting Maeve. His heart ached. If only *he* could take her into *his* embrace and soothe her, tell her everything; if only—

The blunderbuss was withdrawn. Another foot slammed into his ribs.

"Get up."

Slowly, he did so, acutely aware of his own bare state. His ribs, his back, his elbow ached, but nothing could match the anguish in his heart over what he had done, what he had *had* to do.

A dozen angry women faced him, cutlasses drawn, pistols leveled, eyes fierce. Their bold eyes raked his nakedness and dismissed it with contempt. He saw the small, spritely Irish woman with the elfin face shielding Maeve's bare body from him with a piece of sailcloth.

Then the tall African stepped forward, majestic, fierce, angry. The others gathered behind her, watching her. Her skin was darker than the night, her eyes blazing. She let her gaze roam contemptuously over his nakedness, but he drew himself proudly up, refusing to quail beneath the savagery in her eyes.

"Whatever you did to her," the woman said in a dark, ugly whisper, "believe me, you'll *pay for it.*" She jabbed a pistol into his chest and shoved him roughly toward the bow. "Move," she ordered, with the authority of a general. Gray obeyed, aware of her eyes nailing him between his shoulders; he felt the press of her pistol in the small of his spine and knew she would like nothing better than to blow his kidneys out. Had he gone too far in trying to enrage Her Majesty? Would he pay for this with his *life?*

He walked to the forecastle and when he could go no farther, paused, standing straight and tall and silent.

He did not turn to face them.

"On your knees!"

Eyes straight ahead, he muttered, "Go to hell."

Her booted foot drove into the back of his knees. He crumpled, falling against the windlass and gritting his teeth against the pain. One of the pirates held a cutlass against his throat, and unable to move, he could only lie helpless as they lashed him so tightly to one of the bow chasers that blood rose from his wrists and trickled down his arms. Someone hurled his clothing, picked up from the beach, at him. Then they stood back, and Gray, grimacing in pain, looked up to see the Pirate Queen standing above him.

She had dressed. Splashy-printed trousers, a loose shirt, a leather vest, and a cutlass completed her attire. Her hair was wild, her eyes blazing. She looked *magnificent*. But the look in her eyes was deadly, clearly reflecting the cold hatred and the bitter pain of betrayal.

"Bastard," she snarled.

He waited. Silence all around as she contemplated his fate.

One of the two little Irish sisters tugged at her sleeve. "What are you going to do with him, Majesty?"

"What I *should've* done from the very first, feed him piece by piece to the fish. But I will take him to Nelson and let *him* do the honors."

She spat on him. Then she turned away, calling for the anchor to be weighed and leaving him to his own misery.

Take him to Nelson.

He'd gotten what he wanted. But suddenly it was a hollow triumph, and as the anchor came in and he lay soaking in the brine and seawater the incoming cable brought with it, he could only wonder if such a victory had been worth the price.

Chapter 12

❦

Draped with a blanket, his small fist curled around the miniature that hung slackly from his neck, the exhausted little Admiral lay in his swinging cot, dreaming.

The mighty, thirty-five-hundred-ton *Victory* swung gently beneath him, the tallest of her three masts reaching two hundred feet into the heavens to scrape at the twinkling stars, her massive decks piled tier upon tier above a waterline that lay stories beneath her poop deck. But her Admiral was no longer the debt-plagued, guilt-ridden, haggard hero, hope of a nation and pride of a navy; he was the intrepid, twenty-three-year-old captain of the dashing frigate *Albemarle,* and he still had both his arms, both his eyes, and a terrified new midshipman who was balking at a lieutenant's orders to go aloft.

They were in the North Sea and the lad, thirteen years old and the newest addition to that cheeky group, stood huddled in the shadow of the mainmast, his expression miserable, his mouth a taut slash of terror in a face that was pale with seasickness. He was trying in vain to look brave in front of his peers, but it was a blustery day, with a fast-running sea and a stiff wind to make the twenty-eight-gun frigate jump and lunge like a racehorse. Captain Nelson glanced at the new midshipman, the youngest of his "children," as he liked to call them, and took pity on him.

The poor lad. This one was too tall, even, to huddle.

Cheerfully swinging his spyglass, he walked up to the wretched boy and touched his shoulder. "Such a woeful face, my fine fellow! Might I ask the cause for it?"

The boy's throat worked and he turned frightened blue eyes upon his captain. Tears swam there, but his jaw, too young to even meet a razor, came up and his eye never wavered. "Homesick, sir. And . . . and—"

Admitting fear of going aloft, of course, was not a manly thing to do. And poor little Gray, fresh from the weepy good-byes of six adoring sisters and his parents, in his very first ship on his very first voyage, was trying very hard to act like a man.

Tall, gawky, and all arms and legs, he towered over his captain by at least a head. Nevertheless, Nelson placed his body in front of the wretched boy's and turned him so that his tears would be shielded from the possible malice of the other youths. Gray sniffled and looked up, his face going paler still at the sight of thick, boiling clouds sailing above the snapping pennant at the mast.

"I can't do it, sir," the young voice quavered, "I want to but I'm"—he looked away, his features flushed with shame—"I'm scared."

Nelson smiled. "Well now, my good fellow! I would not ask you to do anything that I wouldn't instantly do myself. What do you say we go up together?" He grinned, pretending that he had only just hit upon this idea of challenging a young recruit to go aloft when in fact it was a method that he often employed, and with unfailing success. "We shall call it a race. Yes, a race! Whoever gets to the top first, wins."

The boy's dark eyes widened. "But sir . . . you're the *captain!* You're not supposed to climb aloft!"

"What I am *supposed* to do, my good man, is my business. Now, do we have a race or do we not?"

The lad stared at him.

"Well?"

The lad gazed up at the tall masts, the bulging sails, the streaming, snapping pennants. "Sir . . . do you think that *pirates*"—he said the word with awe, and a peculiar reverence—"used to go aloft very much?"

An odd question, Nelson thought, taken slightly aback. He pursed his lips and gave the matter some thought. "Indeed, young man, I'm sure they did."

The lad reflected on this for a moment, obviously torn between the challenge his captain had issued and his own fear of those dizzying, swaying heights. The dark blue eyes, determined now, swung to Nelson's once more. "Very well then, sir," he said solemnly. "I will race you. . . . But would you mind very much if we took the mainmast?"

Nelson raised a brow. "The mainmast, my good fellow? And why is that?"

"It's the tallest of the three, sir. If I'm going to go aloft, I should wish to defeat the strongest enemy first. Then, the others will seem insignificant in comparison."

Nelson, infinitely pleased, threw back his head with rare laughter and clapped the boy between his sharp, angular shoulders. "Very well then, Gray, the mainmast it shall be!" He gave his sword to a lieutenant, slung his telescope over his shoulder, and strode to the lee side, his body easily absorbing the roll of the deck. "Ready, young man?"

From the weather shrouds—safer and easier to climb in a stiff wind than the lee shrouds Nelson had discreetly chosen—the lad faced him, pale-faced and terrified but determined to measure up to the proud uniform he wore. "Aye, sir. I am ready."

"Well then, let us be about it!"

Nelson vaulted atop the gunwales and seized the tarred shrouds. Cheers erupted from the deck below, for him, for his determined opponent, and hand over hand he climbed, his watchful, paternal eye on the youth ascending the shrouds, some thirty feet away and directly opposite him. The boy's smart uniform was already streaked with tar, his unruly black hair standing out like wings beneath his hat. They climbed higher, and the wind got stiffer, colder, biting through Nelson's uniform and chilling him to the bone. The boy was still with him. Nelson slowed, pretending to tire, for it would not do to arrive at the maintop before his young protégé. They lost each other behind the great main course, then emerged above its yard; calling encouragement, and now so high above the plunging deck that the steeply angled shrouds were nearly apexed, Nelson glanced down. Sure enough, there was the customary sea of upturned faces, drifting in and out of the shadows of clouds.

He glanced to windward and paused, pretending to wipe nonexistent sweat from his brow. The boy was almost there . . . A few more feet . . .

And then—

"Beat you!" the lad yelled triumphantly, scrambling through the futtocks and appearing in the maintop just above him. Nelson clapped his hat firmly down and tilted his head back, hard-pressed to conceal his own grin of triumph. The youth's face was flushed with pride, and he was breathing hard; but he had conquered his fear and made the climb, and for Nelson, that was all that mattered.

"So you did, young man!" he exclaimed, laughing, and pulled himself up to sit beside his happy charge. "By God, I am only ten years your senior, yet you make me feel like an old man! Huzzah for you, my good fellow, I am thoroughly embarrassed!"

In effect, he was thoroughly *pleased*, and proud.

"Thank you, sir! You were right, there is nothing to it!"

"Indeed, young fellow. How a person must be pitied who fancies there is any danger in making the attempt!"

Moments later, the lad was on his way back to the deck, where he was met by a triumphant circle of grinning peers who clapped him on the back, punched him in the shoulder, and huzzahed him to the sky. . . .

The memory faded, the years folded beneath themselves, and other remembrances drifted into the Admiral's dreaming mind . . . Gray, no longer a tall and gawky midshipman, but a lean young man, glowing with triumph after passing his lieutenant's exam . . . Gray, now in the bright new uniform of a post-captain, bursting with ambition and pride as he escorted Captain Nelson on a tour of his own first command . . . Gray, in trouble over a scandal with an admiral's wife and fighting a duel not with pistols but with cutlasses— cutlasses!—*but sir, they're what* pirates *would've used!* . . . Gray, wounded at St. Vincent . . . Gray, now one of Nelson's famous Band of Brothers, snugging his two-decker alongside a Frenchman and pounding the stuffing out of her as the sun set on the glorious Battle of the Nile. . . .

Memories.

Nelson saw a commodore's flag grace his protégé's mast now, saw him knighted for his bravery at the Nile, saw him transferred to the West Indies Station . . . and hadn't seen him since.

What would he see when the Pirate Queen brought that same man to him?

Horatio Nelson sighed softly in his sleep, his never-resting mind moving as swiftly in his dreams as it did when he was awake . . . to annihilating Napoleon's fleet . . . to retirement at Merton, his home . . . to Emma, dear, beloved Emma! . . . to Horatia, his sweet little daughter . . .

Emma . . .

A hand touched his shoulder and he jerked awake. He looked up and saw the Pirate Queen.

"Good evening, milord."

"By God, how did *you* get in here?!" he cried, bolting up in the cot and shielding himself with the blanket.

"Not by invitation, I can assure you." She moved away, allowing him time to recover, and stood quietly in the shadows, her back toward him. She was dressed pirate-style, in a purple gown clewed up at the hips to permit free movement, and a choker of sharks' teeth ringing her lovely throat. She held a cutlass, and he wondered at the strength this lean woman must possess to wield such a weighty weapon with apparent ease. "Take your time, milord," she said, her voice oddly devoid of spirit. "I will await you in your day cabin."

She sauntered off, quietly, leaving him to stare after her in shock and puzzlement.

"Madam, this is most unseemly!" Thank God he was in his nightshirt. "I do not allow women aboard this vessel; I made a solemn vow to my dear Lady Hamilton that I would not—"

"Milord." She turned then, a stray beam of moonlight from the distant windows slanting across her face. In the dusky gloom he saw that her eyes were haunted with pain, her mouth tight and unsmiling. "I did not come here to try to steal you away from your precious Emma. So please, do not distress yourself. I only bring you your traitor, as promised."

"My traitor? What traitor? . . . Oh, yes, my traitor, *that* traitor!" Fumbling in the gloom, he fastened his breeches, the act taking twice as long as it might have had he two hands instead of one. "And here I thought you had news of *Veal-noove,* you don't, do you? Oh, please, tell me you do, I was a fool, a *fool!* for disregarding your word before; oh, never mind, I will catch up with him and when I do I will thrash him soundly!"

Nelson hurried out into the huge and shadowy dining cabin. "Where is my traitor, madam? I don't see him!"

"Still on my schooner. My second-in-command is having an argument with your officer of the watch about bringing him aboard. Pardon my unseemly intrusion, milord, but I thought I would personally prevail upon *you* to set the matter straight."

"Oh, yes, yes, of course!" Nelson cried, in high excitement and agitation. He threw himself into a chair and tugged his shoes on over his feet, but when he went to don his frock coat, emblazoned with ribbons, orders, and stars, he gave a helpless exclamation of dismay and, peevishly, flung it over the sofa.

Maeve looked at the coat, and with a rather distant look in her eye, murmured, "Surely, a traitor is not deserving of such respectful dress, milord."

"He is not just a—oh, can I tell you? *Can I?* No, never mind, now is not the time and if he wanted you to know, he would have told you, such is not my business and I will not interfere, but oh, my heart, my head, what this does to me! I am in a fever, a turmoil—by God, where is my servant? Damnation, there are some things a one-armed man simply cannot do—"

"Milord?"

He came up short in the middle of his tirade and glared at her. She thought of how he'd been just minutes ago, asleep in his cot, legs drawn up to his chest and his one hand curled around the miniature of Emma Hamilton like a child with a favorite toy. How oddly vulnerable he had looked.

And how sad it was that he, the one man, the *only* man, who'd been able to stop the dreaded Napoleon Bonaparte, couldn't even put on his own coat.

She put out a hand, deliberately touching his severed stump through the empty shirtsleeve. Bleak eyes turned to her, brimming with pride, defiance, anger, and humiliation.

She smiled, for the first time. "I'd be honored, sir, if you would let me assist you."

"I cannot, my dear Lady Hamilton—"

"—would probably be grateful for this small favor to you . . . and *England.*"

He stared at her, fighting an inner battle of conscience and need. Finally, his spine went stiff and wordlessly, he thrust the coat into her hands.

The minute her fingers touched it, Maeve was jolted by an awful, sweeping premonition of violent death. She gasped and dropped the coat as if it had burned her, then, red-faced under the Admiral's piercing, eagle-eyed stare, picked it up off the deck. She was shaking. It was only a coat, a blue coat with white lining and gold lace and decorations of valor. *God, it was the orders, the stars!* that the sniper would see to target the Admiral for death. It was all she could do not to heave the coat out *Victory*'s stern windows and into the sea. Her hands trembling, she held it out while Nelson turned his back to her and slipped his arm into the sleeve, then tossed his proud shoulders to settle the coat snugly in place. Murmuring an embarrassed thank-you under his breath, he stole a guilty glance toward the pastel portrait of Emma Hamilton that hung on the bulkhead.

"My being here," Maeve said, ignoring his long-suffering look as she straightened the tasseled epaulets atop his stiff, erect shoulders, "is merely to return the traitor to you. Surely, your Emma will forgive you my assistance in such a noble matter."

Nelson stared at her, amazed that she had read his mind, astounded at the education and upbringing reflected in her speech. But no. Captain Colin Lord—her *cousin,* by God—had told him all about her, this proud daughter of a New England sea captain and his lovely wife. She was no mere pirate, but a misguided young girl who had run away from home and had likely learned some very harsh lessons in her life.

"I know what you're thinking, milord," she said quietly, "but no, I cannot read minds, only predict the future with occasional frequency."

She smiled then, a sad, lonely smile that was instantly quelled by a tightening of her lips and a quick blinking of her eyes. If her demeanor wasn't so fierce, he would've sworn she was, or had been, crying. He frowned, his brows lowering, as he considered that Gray might be the source of those tears. "Come, milord," she said, tugging at his empty sleeve. "Let's get this unpleasant matter over with. The sooner this bast—I beg your pardon, the sooner this *traitor*—is out of my sight and delivered into your justice, the happier I'll be."

She strode toward the door, her spine stiff with pride, her hair tumbling down her back in tangled glory.

"Wait."

She paused, and he saw her pass a knuckle under one eye, then the other, hastily, in the hope he wouldn't notice. His suspicions burned like acid in his breast and he fixed her with his most penetrating glare. "Has this *traitor* hurt you, madam?"

Her chin jerked up and she gave a defiant, unconvincing hoot of laughter. "Hurt me? No one can hurt me, milord, I passed beyond *that* realm of feeling long ago. Now do you want him or not?"

He guessed that Gray had done something to hurt her, and Nelson, who was well aware of that rogue's philandering ways, had a damned good inkling of just what it had been. His jaw went tight and fuming, he turned, fumbling in his desk. "Payment," he snapped, unable to keep his anger with his former midshipman from his voice, "you must have payment for rendering this service to my country—"

"Keep your money, Admiral. I do not want it."

"No, no, I must insist—"

"Please." She held up her hand. "The only payment I expect is for you to take him off my hands. I hope to God I never set eyes on him again."

She opened the door. A marine stood outside, and he gaped at the sight of her, made as if to grab her arm, and shrank back at the blistering look she gave him. Head high, the Pirate Queen strode past him and out of the cabin, leaving Nelson staring after her with no small degree of dismay and concern.

Damn you, Gray!

Snatching up his hat, the furious little Admiral strode swiftly from the cabin.

Chapter 13

⸻♋♋⸻

Gray stood on the broad quarterdeck of H.M.S. *Victory*, bound at the wrist and watching the schooner melt off into the night with a wistful, calculating look in his dark eye.

He was going to catch hell for this one, that was for damned sure. He was wearing snug black breeches. His hair was wind-tousled and far too long, trailing partway down his back. His feet were bare, his shirt smeared with blood, his jaw cloaked with a rough mat of black stubble, and his ear crucified by a very *piratical-*looking hoop of gold.

It was no way to appear before an admiral, and he instantly set about deflecting the impending attack. Tearing his gaze from the sea, aglitter with waves caught in the glow from *Victory*'s stern lanterns high above, he turned, met Nelson's furious gaze—and grinned.

"So, sir. Are you going to hang me now?"

Nelson's lips thinned out, his eyes flashed, but the quick movement of his throat betrayed his emotion. "You ought to be damned ashamed of yourself!"

"I know."

"You, a King's officer and Knight of the Bath, going about dressed as a goddamned *pirate!* By God, *now* I know why you so desperately wanted the West Indies command, so you could play out your fantasies and pretend you're the scourge of the Spanish Main, am I right?"

"But sir"—Gray's dark face split in an innocent grin and he held his wrists out so that a midshipman, at Nelson's impatient beckoning, could cut him loose—"I *am* the scourge of the Spanish Main. Ask any lady in the Indies and she will tell you so."

Their eyes met. Nelson swallowed, hard. Gray's grin faded. The years fell away, and they were again as they had once been, as they had always been. Gray saw the emotion in Nelson's eyes, emotion he had never been able nor willing to hide, emotion that even here, on the decks of the mighty *Victory* in full view of Hardy, his lieutenants, and several hundred watching men, he was not ashamed to show. His throat worked, and, as though not trusting himself to speak, he reached up, put his hand on Gray's shoulder—and embraced him.

Then he drew back and, turning smartly, beckoned Gray to follow.

The crew watched them go, their famous Admiral and the dark pirate, both radiating the power of command but so drastically different from each other in appearance and manner as to make the crew exchange excited whispers, comments, and speculations. Who was this mysterious stranger brought to them by a comely pirate wench? Who was he that he could address their beloved Admiral as though the two stood on common ground? Who was he that their poor Nelson had nearly wept upon embracing him?

Hundreds of eyes flashed to Captain Hardy, whose face was shadowed from the glow of the deck lanterns by the brim of his hat. Hardy knew. They could tell just by the way he suddenly looked down and scuffed his toe against *Victory*'s deck planking. Then he glanced up and, frowning, barked out an order to trim the main course.

Gray, walking with the easy grace of a man long accustomed to the sea, followed the stiff-backed Admiral down the hatch and to his cabin. He was no stranger to ships-of-the-line, and his eyes glowed as he admired *Victory*'s gleaming paintwork, her neat rows of guns, the detail and workmanship that had gone into every beam, every carving, every turn of wood that made her the formidable machine of war that she was. Magnificently beautiful, the proud first rate was the best the Royal Navy had to offer its most famous admiral, and Gray felt a warm glow of approval on behalf of his friend and mentor.

"*Victory*," Gray said softly, running his fingers over a paneled bulkhead. "It's about time she wore your flag."

Nelson paused outside his cabin. "Yes, and *she* will be the one to carry me to triumph and immortality." He impaled Gray with a penetrating stare that was zealous, determined, and defiant. "Mark me on *that.*"

Gray smiled sadly. "Let us hope, sir, for your sake and our country's that such a fate does not come about too soon."

Nelson shrugged. "I am in debt. My body is a shattered and pitiful carcass. I am racked by guilt, grief, persistent spasms in my chest, and God knows what else. Far better to be done in by a Frenchman's guns than my own poor health. After you, Gray."

Nelson. Ever the fatalist, ever the romantic, still expecting to die in every battle and live forever as the immortal savior of his beloved country. Gray wondered if he still kept his coffin—carved from the mainmast of the French flagship he'd defeated at the Nile—in his cabin. Even now he could remember the morbid delight Nelson had taken in showing off the grim masterpiece to anyone who cared to see it. . . .

But no, as they passed through the palatial dining cabin with its long, mahogany table gleaming beneath the swinging lanterns, its chairs lined neatly around it, Gray didn't see the coffin—though Emma, of course, was in her usual place on the bulkhead. He saw Nelson's eyes flash to the portrait and was happy to know the fire still burned between them.

Gray thought of his last glimpse of *Kestrel*, melting into the darkness, and felt pain washing over his heart.

Nelson waved him toward a chair. "Some champagne perhaps, after your little *excursion?*"

"Rum, sir, if you have it."

"Of course. How could I have forgotten? *Blackbeard*'s favorite drink."

Gray smirked, dropped into a chair just beneath the black, mirrored row of *Victory*'s stern windows, and leaned his head back against the soft padding. *Aah, it felt good just to sit.* With assessing eyes, he watched his friend pour the drinks, and frowned with concern. Nelson's hand was shaking and he did not look well. The Admiral was pale and wan, his cheeks sunken with stress and his respiration marked by a persistent, deep-rooted cough. But there was nothing amiss with his stare, and it was this penetrating eye that he turned on Gray as he handed him his glass and toasted Emma, King, and Country.

Emma, King, and Country. Nelson's three reasons for life, service, going into battle, and, no doubt, for death. No, his friend had not changed at all. A little older, a lot wearier, perhaps a bit calmer, but the same obsessions still drove him. Gray lifted the glass to his lips, let the sweet-harsh liquid burn its way down his throat, and, with an effusive *aaah!* to signify his approval, balanced the glass on his drawn-up knee.

Nelson was staring at him, his eye shrewd, penetrating, questioning, appraising. Gray's answering gaze was casual, patient, relaxed—humorous.

Nelson slammed his glass down atop the table. "Well?"

"Well what, sir?"

"By God, Gray, just what do you have to say for yourself?"

So much for pleasantries and fond reunions, Gray thought, wryly. He draped an arm over the back of the chair. "Say for myself? Well, to start with—damn, it's good to see you again after all these years, sir. You really should come visit more often."

"Hang it, Gray, you know very well what I meant! Here's Bonaparte poised to attack England, *Veal-noove* and the combined fleet romping through the West Indies, and *you're* off carousing with Maeve, the Pirate Queen! You know, you put me in the most distressing position of having to play along with your little game! Do you thing that makes me feel good in *here?*" He pounted his fist to his chest. "Do you think I enjoy having to lie for you? This had better be a damned good story, Gray!"

Gray smiled, looked heavenward, and, spreading a hand over his chest, gave a theatrical sigh. "And here, sir, I thought you'd applaud my cleverness, my shrewdness . . ."

"I will choose whether or not to *applaud* it *after* you explain what you're doing dressed as a pirate—"

"Making a raid upon a Barbados beauty," Gray countered, smoothly.

—"flying a damned *Jolly Roger* from a *King's* ship—"

"A pirate-aspirant must display a suitable flag."

—"and concocting this *ridiculous* story about being a traitor, just to fool Captain Lord's poor cousin!"

Gray sat straight up. "I beg your pardon?"

"Maeve Merrick, Pirate Queen of the Caribbean. Of course, you wouldn't know, would you? Your own flag-captain didn't know and he's been in these waters as long as you've been! Don't look so damned shocked. She and Captain Lord are *cousins.*"

Nelson tightened his mouth, obviously enjoying the fact he had, as usual, the element of surprise.

"Well . . ." Gray raked a hand through the damp, glossy waves of his hair, his thoughts awhirl. *Maeve was Colin's cousin?!* "That is indeed a shock! How did *you,* sir, of all people, learn of such a thing?"

"Captain Lord told me. He recognized her name, and her schooner's, when she crashed in here several nights ago and announced she had a deserter she wanted to sell to me! Seems the girl ran away from home seven years ago and no one's seen her since. Her parents have long given her up for dead—Damn you, Gray, what am I to do with you?"

Given her up for dead? Gray felt the shock hit him squarely in the gut. If they'd given her up for dead, then, contrary to Maeve's beliefs, they *must've* been searching for her! Somehow he had to find her, tell her, take her away from that damned island and set things aright—not only between Maeve and her parents, but Maeve and *himself.*

"Damn it, Gray, I asked you what I'm to do with you!"

Gray was swift to recover. "If I could impose upon you, sir, to have Captain Hardy signal *Triton*—yes, I saw her sailing in consort with you—so that Colin may come collect me? I have some important business to oversee, sir, before I go home on leave."

"How good of you to think of that *now.* A convoy to meet and escort back to England, I believe?"

"Aye, if it has not already left."

"Indeed, it has not. It is anchored at Barbados, where Captain Young of His Majesty's frigate *Cricket* is waiting, and rather anxiously, I might add, for his *commander in chief* to arrive."

"Young is a patient man," Gray said, and absently swirled the rum in his glass. "Besides, what's another day or two, eh?"

Nelson exploded. "Damn it, Gray, must you be so damned *blithe?* Do you know what angst you have caused me these past few days, worrying about you, what absolute *hell* you have put me through? I swear, you have taken ten years off my life! Men of your rank do *not* act out their pirate fantasies and then expect no repercussions from them!"

Gray grinned, embarrassed. "You know then about my . . . um, *acquaintance* with Lady Catherine?"

"I know about Lady Catherine, I know about Mistress Delaney, I know about General Walsingham's wife, I know about the Somersby sisters, and I have a feeling I *know* about Maeve Merrick! And don't look so damned surprised," he added, tartly. "Your faithful Captain Warner was willing to lie through his teeth to protect what reputation you have left, but Captain Lord, bless his soul, is honest to a fault. It distressed him to have to tell me the truth, but tell me he did!"

"Poor Colin. I hope you went easy on the lad."

"By God, Gray, how could you neglect your command when we are in such a state of crisis, of *peril?*"

Gray's teasing humor instantly evaporated. "Sir, I can assure you I have *not* neglected it. I have frigates strategically stationed and a suitable squadron patrolling the Windwards to ensure their safety. Contrary winds, and the fact I was conducting some business with the governor of Jamaica, kept me damnably ignorant of both your *and* Villeneuve's arrival, who, by God, will have a hard time causing any trouble in *my* waters, I can assure you! And as for the women?" He relaxed, grinning once more. "Why, sir, I *am* a sailor . . . with sailorly appetites, I might add. They are nothing but . . . amusements, as I am to them, and they know it as well as I. Things get boring out here in the tropics, as you well know."

"The Pirate Queen did not seem *amused.* I *hope* you

intend to bring that poor girl more happiness than it appears you have already brought her!"

"Have no fear of *that*, milord. Following my business with you, and my fleet, I'll have Colin take me to her island so I can claim her and rectify the situation immediately." He raised his glass and gave a sly grin. "Her days of plundering the Spanish Main are, I can assure you, about to *end*."

"I should damn well hope so," Nelson snapped. "Should the Admiralty in London learn of your *antics*, it'd be disastrous enough, but if you were to involve yourself with a pirate, they'd waste *no* time demanding your resignation regardless of how many laurels your career boasts!"

"All the more reason to put an end to Mer Majesty's piratical pursuits, *now*."

"Well, for *your* sake I wish you luck. I may be going blind, but my sight is not yet so hampered that I missed the very obvious animosity the lady bears you. If I may offer a suggestion, it is that you tell her the truth about who you really are." The feisty little Admiral tightened his lips and shot Gray a condemning look. "A *traitor*," he spit. "I've never heard of anything so damned *preposterous* in my life."

"Well, caution was in order. Had she known my real identity, she might've sold me off to Villeneuve. I was not about to take that risk, so I bluffed her into anger, and bringing me to you. I'm sure that *Monsieur* Villeneuve is a most gracious host, but I've no desire to partake of French hospitality firsthand, thank you."

"Yes, as *always* the dice fell in your favor." The Admiral sipped his champagne, his sharp gaze studying Gray over the bold bridge of his nose. His expression was grudging, perhaps even admiring. "Well, run your command as you wish, Gray, you're more than competent, but in future I beg of you, *please* employ more discretion concerning your piratical *romps*. God help you *and* the Navy should word ever get back to London!"

"Have no fear of that, milord. My men are loyal to a fault and rather enjoy the diversion my er, *antics,* afford them. They would not dare breathe a word of it. But enough of me. You did not put three thousand miles under your keel to seek another bout with malaria, or to pay a mere social call to the commander of the West Indies Station." Tossing down his rum, Gray rose from the chair. He refreshed their glasses and took a seat across from the Admiral, his jaunty insouciance gone, and in its place the focused sharpness that had won him the order of Knight of the Bath, the accolades of his men, the respect of his peers, the position of high command that he now so enjoyed. "We have maybe another hour before my captain arrives? Enough for you to fill me in on what circumstances brought you out of the Mediterranean and across the Atlantic. Pray, let's use it to discuss how we're going to find this French fleet you have chased three thousand miles into *my* waters!"

Their gazes met. The Admiral looked at his companion, so calm, so cool, so utterly at ease with himself and the situation. The confident officer across the table from him had come far since that blustery day he'd been a terrified young midshipman. Nelson sat back, and released a heavy sigh of relief. Then he looked up, and met the steady, challenging gaze of the man who had once been his student.

The man who was now his peer.

Nelson smiled, feeling his troubles dropping away into the wind. "I thought you would never ask."

Chapter 14

Dawn found *Kestrel* on a northerly course, the breeze thrumming through reefed topsails and over spray-flecked decks. Her crew still slept, but Maeve had spent a restless night on deck, watching the miles widen between her little command and the British fleet, now a line of twinkling, distant lights stretching along the horizon. She'd seen the stars go out one by one, and the sky fading from black to indigo to a deep, brooding gray. By the time the sun hauled itself out of the sea in a fiery sphere of blazing crimson, Lord Nelson's mighty force had disappeared from her sight completely.

The Admiral, if he had not done so already, would be rigging the halter from *Victory's* lofty foreyard now, and Gray, she thought sadly, would be standing on deck, waiting for the Articles of War to be read, waiting for the noose to be placed around his neck, *waiting to die.*

She took a deep, shuddering breath and ripped her gaze from the horizon, empty now and bleak as her heart. She felt lonely. Deserted. *Abandoned.* Her teeth bit savagely into her bottom lip. *Do not think of him,* she told herself, and gripped the tiller so hard her fingers went numb. *He was a traitor to his country. He was a traitor to his navy.* She swallowed the lump in her throat. *He was a traitor to you.*

The wind strengthened. She lashed the tiller and

159

strode forward, the mild, salty breeze tearing at her tangled hair and sending it streaming out behind her. She felt it caressing her skin, sending her clothing rippling against flesh that *he* had touched, kissed, loved. She walked faster, as if she could banish the memory, and went forward to haul over the jib. But as her hands closed around the salt-stiff, thrumming line and hauled it tight, her gaze fell upon the sad coil of rope nestled in the nook of the bow, dark with blood that was drying in the fronds of golden hemp.

She shut her eyes, trembling.

Maeve stood there for a moment, torn and miserable. She glanced around, guiltily, assuring herself the deck was still empty; then she ducked into the bow, leaned down, and picked up the bloody rope with which they had bound her pirate lover. Her fingers closed around it, feeling the blood, *his* blood, sticky against her hand.

Anguish tore at her throat. Her fingers bit into the hemp. She raised her arm, pulled it back, and gathered her strength to fling the bloodied rope far off into the sea.

She couldn't do it.

Clenching the rope in her fist, she stormed back to the tiller and stared off over the tossing, brilliant waves.

In another hour Gray—the traitor—would be dead. . . . thanks to her.

She squeezed the rope until the harsh fibers pricked her palm. Then she dropped it beside the tiller and wiped her blood-smeared hand on her hitched-up skirts. The stain was imbedded. She wiped harder, cursing the stain, cursing him, and fighting to keep her emotions in check. She flung her hair over her shoulder and turned to haul in the mainsheet, her lean, muscled arms bringing the boom swinging back to centerline and then arcing out over her head. *Kestrel* tilted upright, then onto the opposite tack as Maeve pushed the tiller over. Spray dashed over the weather bulwarks, streamed in bright, glistening trails down the varnished deck. Maeve turned to follow *Kestrel*'s swirling wake through the lively swells, tracing her course back to the pure, cloudless horizon . . . to the British fleet . . . to *Victory*—

And to Gray.

She shut her eyes. She could see it, even now . . . Lord Nelson, condemning the traitor to death for selling out to Villeneuve . . . Lord Nelson, standing imperiously on the massive quarterdeck of *Victory* as Gray's lifeless body swung to the roll of the ship, his black hair moving in a macabre death dance on the wind . . . Lord Nelson, snapping out the order for the corpse to be cut down and dropped into the sea with curt finality.

No!

Kestrel hit a swell and spray dashed over the gunwale and through the weather shrouds, slapping Maeve's face, trickling down her cheeks, dampening her tangled hair. Her throat constricting, she shut her eyes and ran her tongue over her lips, tasting salt water that, far, far over the horizon, already embraced her Gallant Knight in death.

But no, he was *not* her Knight, he was nothing but a scoundrel, a traitor, a rogue! "I should've listened to myself." She swiped angrily at her eyes with the heel of her hand, her fingers tightening around the tiller until her knuckles threatened to split. "I should've *listened* and not let myself open my heart to him! I wanted a fine and gallant officer for my Knight . . . an *officer,*— like *my father.*

More spray dashed against her face, trickling down her brow, her cheeks, her lips.

"I should've known better than to accept anything less than the real thing!" She picked up the blood-soaked rope and drove her short nails into it, feeling the hemp stabbing painfully into the quicks. "Oh . . . what am I to *do?*"

Go back for him.

But no, it was too late. He would be dead by now, and *she* had killed him.

"Captain?"

Her head jerked up, and she saw Orla, silent, sad-eyed Orla, standing there with a tankard of coffee in her hand. Maeve dropped the bloodstained rope and swiftly kicked it under the binnacle, her face flaming.

"Are you all right?" Orla asked, handing her the coffee.

"Of course I'm all right," Maeve snapped, forcing a smile. "Why the hell shouldn't I be?"

Black eyes met gold. "I'm sorry, Maeve, about the pirate," Orla said quietly.

"Yes, well . . ." Maeve's foot drove against the rope, savagely, desperately, angrily. "He meant nothing to me anyhow, was just a scoundrel like all the rest. By now he's probably naught but a corpse on Nelson's foreyard and good riddance to him!"

She looked down, pretending to study the compass card and blessing the curtain of chestnut hair that fell, swirling about her face. She blinked and a fat tear splashed onto the glass. Angrily, she dashed it away, and, feeling the rope pressing against her toe, finally shoved it brutally beneath the binnacle in a fit of temper.

"Blast it to hell, why did he have to wash up on my shore?!"

Orla watched the proud shoulders crumple in defeat, saw the tears that leaked silently from beneath Maeve's clenched fingers. Quietly, she took the tiller and corrected the schooner's course, then reached out to put her arm around her captain's shoulders, hugging her in friendship and understanding.

"Such things are not always ours to decide, Maeve."

"I killed him, Orla."

Orla bit her lip, her eyes tragic.

"I should have been more forgiving, Orla!"

"You did not cause him to desert the Royal Navy," the other woman gently reminded her. "And if Nelson has executed your pirate, that was *his* decision, not yours."

"I know but—" She shook her head, recovering, and dashing the tears from her eyes. "Oh, blast it all! Put the damned ship about, I'm going back."

"It's probably too late, Maeve."

"I don't bloody well care, I'm going back!"

"*Captain!*"

It was Aisling, racing up from the hatch, barefoot and waving a straw hat.

Maeve spun around. "Hell's teeth, Aisling, you scared the bleeding *devil* out of me—"

"Captain? Are you all right?"

"Of course I'm all right, just a bit of salt spray in my eye, 'tis all!"

"Oh. You look like you've been crying. Not over that stupid pirate, I hope! He's not good enough for you, you know—"

"Aisling, did you have something you wanted to tell me?"

"Tell you? Oh! Yes! I went into your cabin to steal a piece of paper—you don't mind, do you?—and I looked out the windows and guess what I saw?"

But before Maeve could vent her irritable response, Aisling was excitedly pointing to the cluster of islands in the distance, mere splotches of purple and green crowning a turquoise sea. "Look!" The girl thrust a spyglass into her hand, and jumped up and down in excitement. "See? A merchant ship, Captain! Crippled and ripe for the plucking!"

Maeve put the glass to her eye. Distant reefs, no more than purple smudges on a ruffled, blue-green sea, filled the spherical field. Waves paraded toward her, disappeared beneath the bottom edge of the glass. The shoreline of an island hove into view, a glittering expanse of blinding white sand crowned with fringed palm and pine. Beneath her feet, *Kestrel* surged up, surged down—Maeve steadied the glass against the pit of her shoulder and looked to see the fat merchantman Aisling had sighted.

"Well? D'you see it, Captain?"

Oh, she saw it all right. A merchant ship, hove to in the lee of a tiny island, with a black flag of pirate ownership streaming from the only one of its three masts to still remain standing. *El Perro Negro*'s flag, she thought, on a note of savage, reckless malevolence. The merchantman was obviously his prize. But *the Black Dog*'s infamous brig itself was nowhere to be seen, and the big merchantman, conquered, crippled, and shot through with holes, was unguarded and as vulnerable as a sheep that had strayed from its flock and now found itself facing the hunger of a lone and ruthless wolf.

The Pirate Queen's eyes narrowed, and her lips curved in a dark smile. El Perro Negro. Her rival, her enemy, one of the vilest pirates ever to sail the Caribbean; their hatred of each other was mutual and deep, seeded the night Maeve had found his skulking brother raping a helpless young barmaid in a Barbados tavern while a hundred men cheered him on. Her own shouted challenge, a quick fight between cutlasses, and Maeve had run the scoundrel through, inheriting both the barmaid as a crewmember, and the lasting enmity of el Perro Negro.

"You have damned good eyes, girl," she said, slamming the glass back into Aisling's hand just as her crew came running up from below.

"Don't I?" Aisling grinned, her face bright in the sunshine. "Enolia tells me that all the time! Are we going after her, Captain? Are we?!"

"Aye, let's steal her from the bleeding *bastard* before he comes back!" cried Tia.

"Then skewer him to his own gunwales and feed him his guts on a fork!"

Maeve threw back her head and gave a hearty guffaw. But then she thought of Gray—wickedly sinful, darkly handsome—Gray, and the dreams she'd had of plundering the seas with him at her side. What a thrill it would've been to have him with her now. . . .

But no. Gray was dead.

The laughter died abruptly in her breast, to be replaced by a raw, choking ache that manifested in a blind need to fight, to maul, to steal, to *kill*—

"Shall we go after her, Captain?" Aisling prompted.

"Aye, why not?" she muttered, buckling on her sword belt and flinging her ponytail over her shoulder. She drew her cutlass and flexed her arm, letting the blade sing through the air with quick, vicious strokes. "I'm in the mood for a good *fight*. Now, aloft with you, Aisling, and give a holler if you see el Perro Negro's brig returning. We're going in."

Grabbing a pistol, the girl bounded up the shrouds and soon appeared in the crosstrees, a slight figure stamped against the mast, a network of angled lines, and a cerulean sky devoid of cloud.

"Your orders, Captain?" Enolia asked, as the lady pirates ran to their guns and sail stations.

"Run up the flag, and ready about," Maeve commanded, and a moment later, the little schooner was sweeping through the wind, her bowsprit aligning on the crippled merchantman.

El Perro Negro's pirate brig stood under covering of heavy foliage, quite near the merchant ship they had beaten into submission. El Perro Negro watched it *and* the schooner *Kestrel* as she swept down on their helpless prize.

"Ship comin' around the la'b'd island, an' closin' fast. It's the Pirate Queen!"

Hidden as it was behind the pines of the island's headland, and with the blazing sun behind it, there was little chance of *Kestrel*'s sharp-eyed lookouts spotting their brig. But his men had no such encumberances—and had certainly seen *Kestrel* the moment the schooner had burst into view.

Now, in the wake of the lookout's shouted warning, el Perro Negro's crew—a scanty one, what with the fact that half of them had been left aboard the crippled merchantman until they could return with enough men to sail both ships back to port—raced to the rail.

"She's after our merchantman prize, I'll wager," snarled Renaldo, the first mate. He sent a fist smashing against the rail. "The bitch!"

"Well, she ain't going to get it! That whoring slut *owes* me. In fact, I think I'll add her pretty schooner to my collection, as I'm feeling the need to play *admiral* today." Stuffing a fistful of half-cooked chicken into his mouth, el Perro Negro wiped a hand across the back of his lips and belched, dispelling fumes of rum and stomach rot. "Given that we have such an abundance of *almirantes* in these waters lately, that is! Get the tops'ls up, Renaldo, triple shot the guns, and put a fire under your ass, I'm in no mood to tarry, ye hear me?"

The ship hit a jarring swell and from belowdecks came an agonized cry.

"What the hell was that?"

"The merchie's captain," the mate growled, in disgust. "Took a ball in his gut durin' the fight so we brought him off the merchie and stuck him below. Ain't naught but a pup, must be all of twenty summers, by the looks of 'im. But ye know these English—start 'em young, they do."

"Kill him then, and put the son of a bitch out of his misery," el Perro Negro muttered blackly. "That noise is giving me a damned headache!"

Renaldo, dagger in hand, went below, and a moment

later the young English captain's cries of pain crescendoed into a high scream of agony that ended on a gurgling bubble of blood. El Perro Negro smiled. Throat-slitting was Renaldo's specialty. Well, he had his *own* specialty, and it involved *blades* of a far different order.

The trees of the island still shielded the Pirate Queen's ship from his own deck-level eyes, but in a moment they would burst around the headland and surprise would be theirs. In his mind's eye he pictured her schooner, charging down on the merchantman prize, *his* prize, with the wind in her topsails and the spray bursting from her bows. *The Pirate Queen*. Trying to take what was *his*. El Perro Negro spit a wad of phlegm on the deck and ground it in with his shoe. *That* thieving *puta* would get her due today, by God—

"All done, *Capitán*," Renaldo said, joining him once more and wiping the flat of his bloody knife on his trousers.

"Idiota, have Jacky and Pig-Eye throw him overboard! I don't want his carcass fouling my decks, ye hear?"

Moments later, the young man's corpse was hauled topside, blood still dripping from the slashed throat, the gentle eyes open, staring, accusing. El Perro Negro spit on the deck once more and turned away as the body was heaved overboard with all the ceremony of slops into a pig trough.

"Any more *trash* to be disposed of, Renaldo?"

"That's the last of 'em, *Capitán*. And if ye ask *me,* 'tis better off we are for killin' 'em. Should Admiral Falconer get wind of this, our asses would be—"

"I *didn't* ask you, so keep your damned opinions to yourself."

"Aye . . . sir."

"Are the guns ready?"

"Aye, *Capitán*."

"Good. Now heave to, and let's give *Her Majesty*

time to get her claws into our merchie. I want to catch
her by surprise, *off* her ship and on our prize's decks."
Thick lips curved in a black, evil smile. "I never
thought I could use a captured merchant ship as a lure.
But without that schooner under her, the Pirate Queen
doesn't have a chance."

He ran his tongue over his greasy lips in anticipation.
He'd long had an itch to get his hands on that schooner—*and* her notorious lady captain. The latter thought
brought saliva welling into his mouth, and a stiffness to
his groin that only hardened as he watched the schooner's mastheads, their tips just thrusting above the tree-
tops, come to a slow, graceful stop.

Shouts, calls, gunshots, the boom of a cannon—she
would be boarding the prize, now . . .

"Come on, my pretty," el Perro Negro murmured,
reaching down to stroke his swelling penis through his
trousers. He thought of her as he'd last seen her:
Maeve, beautiful, savage, Pirate Queen of the Caribbean, standing proudly at her helm with her hair blowing out around her, her head thrown back, her hands on
her hips and belligerence emanating from every cell in
her body. The memory alone made him ache with lust,
and he shivered in anticipation of her lying beneath
him, beaten, while he pumped and slammed and drove
into her. Soon, he vowed, she'd be warming his own
bed, crying out in passion and pain, *yes, pain,* before he
plunged a knife into her heart and sent her the way of
the dead English *capitán*—

From beyond the trees of the island he heard the
boom of another gun, female shrieks of bloodlust and
challenge, the furious shouts of the handful of men he'd
left to guard the merchantman, and now, the distant ring
of steel against steel as Maeve Merrick and her band of
she-wolves boarded his captured merchantman. The Pirate Queen, apparently, was wasting no time.

"The insolence of the bitch!" Renaldo snarled indignantly. "Doesn't she realize *the Black Dog* wouldn't stray far from 'is prize?"

"Maybe the *bitch* wants to be bred, eh?"

Renaldo's eyes turned sly. "Aye, well they don't call ye the Black Dog for nothin'!"

El Perro Negro threw back his filthy head and laughed. "Aye, and now, I think, it's time for this dog to go a-ruttin'. Ready about, Renaldo, and let's go in."

The Spaniard grinned as the brig fell off into the wind and far beneath him, water began to sing against the hull. And then he reached down, pulled his pistol from its scabbard, loaded it with ball and powder—and waited.

One volley from *Kestrel*'s starboard guns had sent the few men el Perro Negro had left aboard the captured merchantman scurrying for cover, and, in the ensuing melee, the Pirate Queen brought her schooner right up to the crippled merchantman, grappled her ship to it, and, cutlass in hand, led her yelling, whooping, shrieking crew over the side.

The first man came for her as Maeve threw herself over the merchantman's gunwale and onto her deck, and she saw only the black mouth of his pistol before a ball from Enolia's own weapon felled him.

"To me, ladies!" she cried, and whirling, met the next charging shape, a heavy, bearded wretch with sores of disease clinging about his lips.

She thought of nothing but swinging her cutlass ... her father ... revenge upon the fates that had stolen her happiness, and Gray, *yes, Gray,* as she whirled to meet her opponent's savage thrust—

Gray.

The clattering blow sent pain shooting the length of her arm, but she was strong, lithe, able; spinning, she pirouetted, her bare feet light and graceful, the smoke stinging her eyes and burning her nose. The pirate swung for her. She feinted, and sent her own blade chopping viciously into his ribs. Blood sprayed up and out, and he fell, screaming, to the deck. She dived for the next filthy wretch and hacked her sword against his arm as he tried to jerk a pistol up into her face; it exploded near the side of her head, numbing her ears, bits of black powder hitting her cheeks and stinging her eyes.

Gunfire, screams, curses, the stench of sulfur and sweat, spilt blood and the stink of fear. Back and forth her arm swung, blindly, savagely, angrily, the sweat running down her cheeks, the scene fading into a thick and smoky din through which she caught only glimpses . . . of Tia, ramming a boarding pike into a pirate's gut, of Enolia, beating back a huge wretch with a missing ear, of Aisling and Sorcha fighting back-to-back, pistols blazing—A man came for her, his dagger arcing down toward her shoulder, and he fell as a volley from Lucia's blunderbuss caught him in the back. Out of the smoke came another . . . another . . . another. . . .

Gray, oh, Gray. . . . Tears now ran freely down her sooty cheeks, and she didn't care, didn't care any more if she lived or died, didn't give a damn about anything . . . except what she had lost.

"CAPTAIN!"

She whirled, and at the last minute, saw el Perro Negro himself charging through the smoke. Instinctively she spun to meet his savage attack—and felt her feet go out from under her on the bloodied decks.

The Pirate Queen went down, and the last thing she saw before her head cracked against the gunwale was fire, flashing from his pistol. . . .

Then, all went dark.

Chapter 15

Gray had gone off to H.M.S. *Triton* and a long-deserved leave of absence, as the Mediterranean Fleet, baking under the hot Caribbean sun, was threading its way north through the jewellike West Indian islands in a desperate search for the elusive Combined Franco-Spanish fleet. The sea begged tranquillity, but there was no rest for the anxious English Admiral who had crossed an ocean to find—and fight—that missing enemy.

Now Admiral Nelson was pacing his sun-baked quarterdeck, thinking of Emma, the coffin he'd left back in London, and the new battle plan he'd worked up to *annihilate* that fellow *Veal-noove,* when a cry from the masthead broke his obsessed reverie.

"Deck there!"

Captain Hardy stood with the sailing master at the massive, double-spoked wheel. He glanced at Nelson, took off his hat to dab at his sweaty brow, and squinting against the blazing glare, looked aloft. "Report, masthead!"

"Sail closing fast to windward! It's a schooner, sir!"

Snapping his fingers, Nelson called impatiently for the nearest midshipman. He plucked the lad's spyglass from his hand and raised it to his good eye, identifying the little vessel at the same time that Hardy voiced his thoughts.

"It's the Pirate Queen's schooner—by God, what happened to it?"

Cursing the milky film that glazed his sight, Nelson stared hard through the glass until the eye watered in pain and protest. "She's been hit, and hit hard," he said worriedly. "Heave to, Captain Hardy, and prepare to receive her commander."

Moments later, the little schooner was safe in *Victory*'s lee and swallowed up by her massive shadow. Nelson strode to the rail and looked down to the tiny deck far beneath him. He saw shot-torn sail, broken spars, and a mere stump where the topmast had been, not unlike the useless remains of his right arm.

A fair-haired girl scurried out from beneath the shadow of the schooner's torn and flagging mainsail. "Admiral Lord Nelson! Please, you must help us!"

He grabbed a speaking trumpet from Hardy and crawled atop one of *Victory*'s massive cannon so he could lean far out over the nettings. He felt Hardy's steadying hand on his arm, sensed the protective press of his officers surrounding him. But before he could respond, the girl, no more than fifteen summers by the look of her, burst into tears. "Do you have a good surgeon aboard, milord?" she cried, desperately. "Our captain's been hurt and I think . . . I think she's dying!"

VICTORY, JUNE 10TH, 1805, OFF ST. LUCIA
DEAR CAPTAIN AND MRS. MERRICK—

Lord Nelson paused, pen in hand, staring at the white sheet of paper on the desk before him. He brushed his chin with the end of the feather, then jabbed the quill back into the inkwell and began to scribble.

It is my most woeful duty to inform you that your daughter, Maeve, has been seriously injured in

*hand-to-hand combat with a Spanish pirate. Al-
though you may take comfort in the knowledge
that she fought most gallantly, as of this writing
my surgeon is working desperately to save her
life. Should she live, she will of course be de-
tained under the care of the British Navy until my
fleet can return to Europe, where I will personally
ensure that she reaches the safety of England. It
therefore is my wish to—*

He paused, pondering Colin Lord's words. The
young captain had said the girl had run away from
home, that her grieving parents had thought her dead;
what if she recovered, and hated him for his interfer-
ence in matters between herself and her parents? Nelson
shrugged. The boldest measures were always the safest.
He dipped the pen into the inkwell and continued,

*invite you to Merton, my home in Surrey, where
your daughter will be under the care of Lady
Hamilton. I would advise a quick and speedy
journey to England, as I fear your daughter's
time in this world may be a limited one. I am,
most respectfully, Nelson and Brönte.*

Brönte was the name of the dukedom given him by
the grateful King Ferdinand of the Two Sicilies—it still
seemed odd, sometimes, to use it as part of his signa-
ture. Leaving the letter on his desk, Nelson nodded to
the marine who stood guard outside his cabin, and, purposefully made his way down through the decks.

"Afternoon, milord."

"Blessings, sir."

"We'll catch that bugger Villeneuve soon, sir, an'
that's no mistake!"

Nelson nodded in his kind and quiet away, acknowledging the humble greetings of the seamen, who spent their lives packed like sardines on these crowded gun-decks, the sons of England who were all that stood between Britain and Napoleon's tyrannical ambitions. He continued downward. A ship's boy, carrying a pail, passed him, nodded reverently, scurried off into the darkness.

"Easy there, young fellow."

He kept going. He felt the ocean pounding against *Victory's* massive timbers, then there was only muffled, shadowy gloom as he descended down past the water-line and entered the grim domain of the surgeon.

"Dr. Beatty."

"Sir."

"How is your patient?"

"Holding, sir."

Nelson nodded quietly. The girl had been bloody and unconscious when *Victory's* seamen had carried her aboard and down to the surgeon's area, where Dr. Beatty and his mates had spent the last two hours desperately trying to save her young life.

She was only a girl. Nelson clenched his fist in helpless rage. *Just a girl, by God.*

He began to pace, his face anxious as he passed in and out of the dim glow of a lantern. "Is she going to live, Beatty? Tell me, is she going to live?"

"I don't know, milord. The wound itself is not serious, as the ball merely pierced her side and went clean through—but it's the head injury that concerns me most. She hit it when she fell, you know. Granted, she's a game little thing, but one can never tell with these sort of injuries—"

"That is not what I asked you!" Nelson snapped. "Is she going to live?"

"Prayers, milord, would not do her any harm."

Nelson continued to pace. He tried not to look at her, but the soft fall of red-chestnut hair spilling over the table beckoned his eye. She was just a girl who had run away from home on the same day the Battle of the Nile had been fought, a girl who had brought Gray back to him, a girl who had done the navy a greater service than she might ever know, a girl who *deserved to live.*

He went up to her, and stared down at her face, pale with shock, loss of blood, and what he feared was approaching death. He had seen death too many times in his life not to recognize the signs. The shallow, labored breathing. The faint blue tinge to the lips. The pale, ethereal skin that looked more fragile than tissue paper.

The girl's lashes fluttered. He saw a tear welling up at the corner of one closed eye, seeping out from beneath the fringe of dark lashes to begin a halting, rolling path down one pale cheek. Her lips moved. Another tear followed the first, this one tumbling down the opposite cheek.

"Milord . . ." Her voice was the merest whisper, but she knew that he had come, knew that he was there. "Please . . . don't leave me. . . . "

Something caught in the little Admiral's throat. He swallowed hard. Then he reached out to take the girl's hand.

It was dry, callused . . . cold.

Like death.

"Please . . . don't leave me," she repeated. "I don't want to die alone. . . ."

"Damn me if I'll let you," Admiral Lord Nelson snapped, and squeezed her hand.

"I tried . . . tried so hard to . . . survive . . . you'll tell my father, won't you . . . I want him . . . to be proud of me. . . ."

Nelson's mouth tightened. He looked down at the lovely, still face that now, unguarded, looked all of ten years old, the hair, matted with blood, sweeping in damp, sweaty tumbles off her white brow.

Hardy entered, stooping almost double to fit beneath

the gloomy deckhead beams. The Admiral glanced up and bestowed upon his flag-captain his most penetrating glare. He placed the hand he held under the blanket and, gesturing with his hand, led Hardy out of Maeve's hearing range.

"Thomas."

"Sir?"

"There is a letter lying open on my desk. Seal it and put it with the rest of the mail to be delivered at the next landfall we make. And is the *Triton* still within signaling distance?"

"No, sir."

"Then please dispatch our fastest frigate to recall her. Tell Captain Colin Lord to bring his admiral back to me, *immediately.* The girl is dying, and there is only one man who has a prayer of saving her. One man who might convince her that life is worth living. *One man, by God, who has the power to command her to live when I cannot!"*

Hardy's eyes searched the anguished face of the little hero. "Sir?"

But Nelson was gazing down at the still girl beneath him.

"Her pirate," he said softly. "Rear Admiral Sir Graham Falconer."

Chapter 16

H.M.S. *Triton*'s grandest cabin did not belong to its captain, but to another, more powerful man, who outranked not only Colin Lord but the thousands of men in the more than forty ships that made up the Royal Navy's West Indies Fleet.

That man sat in the cabin now, a chart of the Windward Islands spread out before him, the ship's sailing master and captain looking over his shoulder and glancing bleakly between themselves.

On a black snarl, Gray shoved the chart away and sent his fist crashing down on the table. "Bloody hell, that damned island is not even *charted!*" he raged, lunging to his feet and pacing the sunlit chamber with the restless energy of an angry panther. "By my reckoning it's near Barbados. *Barbados!*" He glared at the frightened sailing master. "You mean to tell me you don't know of one miserable, stinking island a stone's throw from Barbados?"

"Sorry, sir. As you can see, it's not on the char—"

"I know it's not on the damned chart!" Gray flung up his hands. "Just get out. Leave me. I wish to be alone."

The poor officer nodded and beat a hasty retreat.

Colin Lord, however, never flinched. "Really, sir," he said calmly, "I'm sure we will find the island."

"As though I have all the time in the world! The convoy's already waiting for us at Barbados, assembled

177

and ready to go. I'm already late; I don't have *time* to go looking for uncharted islands!"

Very carefully, Colin said, "No one said you *have* to, sir."

Gray whirled, eyes blazing. He started to say something, to rebuke his captain for his impudence; then, he sighed and turned away, raking his hand through his hair. Colin did not deserve his anger. The sailing master did not deserve his anger. No one did.

"Forgive me, Colin," he murmured, and strode to the panoramic stern windows as if hoping to glimpse that elusive island. He rested his trembling hands on the brocaded bench seat. "I am not myself."

His gaze moved far out over the blue sea. He saw in his mind's eye, Maeve's lean body beneath him, her eyes beautiful and trusting as he entered her and made her his own. Again, he felt the strange swelling in his heart as she comforted the young Irish girl with motherly love. Again, he felt the tender warmth as she'd confided in him, let down her guard, confessed her fears and hopes. And again, he felt the searing, horrible ache that ripped his chest apart at what he'd had to do in order to facilitate his return to the British Navy—

"If I may speak, sir?"

Gray said nothing, merely looking down as he traced a pattern on the sunlit brocade with his finger.

"You're in love with her . . . aren't you, sir?"

Gray never moved. He felt the sun burning hot against his face, his hands, the wind sweeping through the open windows and playing with his hair. He gazed out to sea once more, and his shoulders settled with something like defeat beneath the glittering epaulets that capped them.

"I don't know, Colin." He looked out at the distant horizon. "Maybe. Hell. Yes, I guess I am. *Christ.*"

The flag-captain's voice was steady, reassuring. "We'll find that island, sir. It may not be on the charts, but surely, *someone* in these waters must know of it. In fact, when we arrive at Barbados—"

The thump of the marine sentry's musket just outside interrupted him. Both officers turned. The door opened, and a young lieutenant stood there, his hat in his hands.

"Mr. Stern's respects, sir, and one of Lord Nelson's frigates is closing fast on us from the north'rd. It's *Amphion.*"

"*Amphion?*" Colin Lord exchanged a puzzled glance with Gray. "Didn't Lord Nelson take the Mediterranean Fleet to Antigua in search of Villeneuve?"

"Aye—but perhaps he has found his nemesis and requests our assistance. . . ."

Colin grabbed his hat. "Excuse me, sir. I must go topside to receive *Amphion*'s captain."

Gray sighed and watched his captain follow the lieutenant out. There was nothing he could do but wait for whatever urgent news *Amphion*'s captain had brought.

And think.

You're in love with her, aren't you, sir?

He smiled.

Yes. I guess that maybe I am.

And then he heard the side party being mustered, the pipes shrilling, footfalls echoing in the tiny corridor just outside his quarters. He sat down at his table, the picture of unruffled calm despite the turmoil that buffeted his heart from all directions. A moment later, the marine sentry was rapping his musket against the deck and announcing Captain Sutton of the frigate *Amphion*.

"I come with grave news, sir, but his lordship wanted you to know." Captain Sutton pulled a sealed missive from his pocket. "It concerns the Pirate Queen. She's been hurt and he thought—"

Gray was on his feet and across the cabin before the startled captain could even hand the missive over. He snatched it from Sutton's hand and hastily scanned Nelson's scribbly words, feeling the blood draining from his face and a chilling tingle lancing his spine.

Colin was there, steady and true and dependable. "Your orders, sir?"

"Put the ship about and lay a course back toward Antigua." Gray crumpled the note and shoved it into his pocket. "*Now*!"

Pain. A dull ache in her head and waves of fire radiating out from her ribs . . . a sensation of metal digging and poking her flesh . . . nothing . . . Admiral Nelson's voice, low and mild and kind, drifting in . . . drifting out . . . pressure of his hand on her wrist. Daddy . . . Nelson . . . *don't leave me, Admiral.* . . . snug pressure around her ribs as a surgeon, yes, he must be a surgeon, bound them tight, tight, tighter . . . the Admiral squeezing her hand . . . *please, milord, don't abandon me!* darkness . . . Daddy—

Gray.

She heard the deep baritone of his voice, now murmuring softly to her, to the Admiral . . . she must be dead, Gray was dead, she *knew* he was dead, Admiral Lord Nelson had hanged him, she had killed him. . . . *Killed him.* . . . She was hot, so hot, sweating . . . feverish . . . movement . . . being lifted up, being carried . . . darkness.

Killed him.

Someone plaiting her hair with gentle, loving fingers. . . . Drifting. Time, passing. Darkness. Voices.

She slitted her eyes and saw a room through a blur. It took too much effort to fully drag her eyes open, so she lay there miserably, sweating in the intense heat and unable to move.

Shadows. Light. Impressions. A quiet room, gentle lantern light, soft pillows under her head, a light sheet over her body. Her head ached. Her ribs hurt, throbbed, pulsed with ripe, piercing pain that impaled her side with every shallow breath. *Don't breathe and it won't hurt.*

"Breathe," a voice commanded. *Gray*'s.

But Gray was dead. She didn't want to breathe. She wanted to sink down, down, down . . . She wanted to give up. She wanted to be with her Knight, her pirate, she wanted to die.

She stopped breathing.

"Breathe, sweetheart." A warm palm cupped her cheek, lips touched her brow. Gray. He wanted her to breathe. He was *ordering* her to breathe, and she hadn't the fight in her to refuse him. Yes, for him, she would breathe. . . . Air swept into her lungs and she whimpered with the searing pain of it. Dizziness swept over her and sweat ran down the soft groove at her temple. She felt sick. Spent. Weak as dishwater.

Breathe.

Oh God, it hurt.

Breathe! the voice commanded, again.

She moved her head, the slightest fraction of an inch, and felt a damp lock of her hair sliding down over her brow, over her eye, dragging the lid shut with it. A hand, broad and strong and tender, was there, brushing it back, the thumb lingering lovingly at her temple, caressing her cheek.

Someone came into the room. She heard footsteps, sensed someone looming over her, peeling back the sheet to check the bandage.

"She may not make it, sir."

"She damn well *will* make it if I have to cross into the hereafter and drag her back!"

Through the slit of her eye she saw shapes and shadows . . . milkiness . . . white. Crisp, clean, white like fresh snow, and buttons, gold ones. Blue fabric. *Naval* blue fabric. The colors and the buttons were fuzzy, blurred, sharpening now into distinct lines and folds and patterns—becoming a coat, like Nelson's.

But the voice was not Nelson's, it was Gray's—and Gray was dead.

"Blast you, is there *nothing* more you can do for her, Ryder?"

"No, Sir Graham. With a head injury, one can never tell the extent of damage until the patient awakens. Nelson's surgeon has already done all that man can do. The rest is up to God."

"Very well then. Kindly leave us."

Maeve lay still, listening to the fading footsteps, the perspiration tumbling down her brow, soaking the sheets beneath her back. She sighed, wishing she had strength to move her head, to fully open her eyes. She saw one of the buttons on Gray's coat. That was all. It was gold, highly polished, with the Royal Navy anchor in raised relief upon it.

Like Nelson's.

"But you're dead," she whispered.

He didn't hear her. She wasn't even sure she heard the words herself or just merely thought them. She tried to move her tongue. It was thick, swollen, dry, filling her mouth. She didn't even have enough saliva to moisten her lips. Her lips parted and then the sofa moved too, as Gray stood up. The button soared heavenward, out of her sight, followed by another, another, another, all gold, all glittering, all with that same anchor on them. Her head rolled on the pillow and through the slit of her eye she saw his immaculate white breeches, the fine, snowy stockings that hugged his calves, a sheathed sword hanging at his hip, peeping out from beneath long, navy blue coattails.

Behind him, the room. No. A ship's cabin. A very *grand* ship's cabin, with a huge cannon snugged into place, rich furniture arranged in a pleasing fashion, and on the bulkheads, woodcuts and gilt-framed portraits of fierce men dressed in clothes that had gone out of fashion long ago, men with savagery in their eyes, men wielding pistols, cutlasses, swords, men who were—

Pirates?

Her head hurt. It was all too much to absorb.

She felt his hand against her cheek, and something hard and slippery touching her lips. A glass. Water. But she couldn't move her mouth. She tried to turn her head on the pillow, but didn't have the strength. Her eyes slitted open again, and she felt her breath whispering against his fingers, smelled his clean, male scent, saw the dark hairs springing up on the back of his hand.

He was sitting on the sofa with her again. He touched her mouth, then dipped his finger into the glass, spreading moisture over her parched lips with the tender caress of a lover.

If she was dead, then she had gone to Paradise.

The water was soothing, his movements slow and painstakingly loving. She heard his voice, above her head, then close to her brow. Felt his lips, touching her forehead.

"You're not going to die, Maeve. You're not going to die, because I am not going to *let* you die. Do you hear me? And if you give up and abandon *me*, so help me God, I shall never forgive you."

Some of the water trickled into her mouth. Her tongue moved, absorbing it with the thirst of a sponge. She felt tears gathering in her eyes, in her heart, and wished he would put his arms around her and tell her she was going to be all right.

I am not going to let *you die.*

He touched her jaw, tilting her head up. She felt the rim of the glass against her lips, and water, no more than a teaspoonful, seeping into her mouth. His thumb, dry and warm, brushed her throat.

"Swallow."

"I can't," she croaked.

"Swallow!"

She tried to turn away but viselike fingers gripped her jaw, forcing it open. Water trickled down her throat and she swallowed, coughed, greedily tried to take more of it—but he held it back, cruelly, not allowing her any more.

A wrenching sob broke past her lips.

She heard the thud of the glass hitting a table, and then he was embracing her, unabashedly, wholeheartedly, making thick, choking noises into her hair. Something cracked inside her; her own tears came flooding out in force, tumbling down her cheeks, soaking his fine clothes. She cried because she lacked the strength to hug him back. She cried because she was dead and so was he. She cried because he cared so much for her whereas she had abandoned *him,* turned him over to Nelson for execution, and she cried because one of those glittering gold buttons was pressing into her cheek and it hurt.

He rocked her, back and forth, back and forth, for a long time, just holding her, just stroking her hair until she quieted. Then he set her back, and she managed to open her eyes. He was looking at her, and never, in anyone's face, had she seen such pure, all-consuming love.

Not since she had been a little girl and the apple of her father's eye, had anyone gazed at her with such tender adoration—and Maeve did not know how to react to it.

"Maeve, sweeting, my love . . . I'm sorry. Everything will be all right. . . . You're safe now. I promise. I'll not let anything happen to you. . . . Ever . . ."

He laid his palm against her wet cheek, cupping it lovingly, tracing its curve, its shape. His gaze was on hers, his eyes dark blue, the exact shade of his coat.

"But you're . . . *dead* . . . *I'm* dead!" And indeed, she must be, because here she was, *dreaming,* with the man she'd sent to his death sitting on the bed with her and looking for all the world like someone straight out of the Royal Navy, not just any *someone* but an *important* someone; complete with rich, tasseled epaulets and stars crowning each shoulder; complete with a medal, not just any medal but the medal of the Nile, hanging from a ribbon around his neck and against that white waistcoat; complete with—

Earring?

"No," he murmured, gently, thumbing her cheek and wiping the tears away. "Not dead." He bent his head, his glossy black hair caught at his nape and trailing down his back—no wonder she could see the earring, but important people in the Royal Navy didn't *wear* earrings, pirates weren't important, traitors were executed, Gray was *dead*—

He must have seen the question in her eyes. He must've read her confusion, for he smiled gently, folded her hand in his, and raised it to his lips.

"I know what you're thinking," he said softly, looking at her from over the top of her knuckles, "but you see, Maeve—I *am* you Gallant Knight after all. I fulfill every blasted one of your criteria."

There had been only one that he hadn't fulfilled, one miserable, wretched one.

For the first time she realized just what that uniform—that gilt-laced uniform, the burst of white lace at his throat, the stiff, high coat collar framing his neck, his jaw—his *clean-shaven* jaw—meant.

"This must be my eternal punishment," she managed to say as she struggled to raise herself. "To see you as the man I always dreamed of having and to not be *alive* to enjoy it."

He pushed her back down and then kissed her hand, pressing his lips to her palm, his gaze never leaving hers.

"Sweetheart, you are alive. I am alive. And since I cannot be the pirate *I* always dreamed of, I fell in love with one instead. I am not a traitor, and in time I will explain it all to you. Trust that I *am* your Gallant Knight. Your officer."

She stared at him, the blood heating her face at his ardent admission.

And then, "Yes, my Knight. And I am Queen Guinevere . . . and Nelson is King Arthur!"

Gray smiled. Her sharp tongue was back—a sure indication that she was going to live to happily torment him.

"Honestly, Maeve," he said gently. "My friends call me Gray. My men address me as Sir Graham. And the rest of the world knows me as"—he smiled a sheepish, charming grin that pushed a dimple into his roguish jaw—"Rear Admiral Sir Graham Falconer, Knight of the Bath and Commander of the Leeward Islands squadron of the Royal Navy's West Indies Station. My flag is hoisted on His Majesty's Ship *Triton,* and we are on our way to Barbados to pick up a convoy of merchant ships to escort back to England, where I shall enjoy a long-deserved leave with you as my wife, if you'll have me, before duty returns me to my post. Maeve?"

Her eyes were slipping shut.

"Maeve?"

But the shock was too much for her.

The Pirate Queen had fainted.

Chapter 17

Admiral Falconer leaned down, slid his arms behind her shoulders, and cupping her lolling head
in the palm of his hand, pulled her gently, tenderly,
up against his chest. Her hair was soft and fragrant,
silky against his newly shaven jaw. Her scent was of
citrus, soap, and the medicinals of the surgeon. She felt
fragile in his arms, vulnerable; resting his cheek atop
her hair, he took a deep, shuddering breath, closed his
eyes, and cursed himself roundly for his rashness in
telling her the truth about who he was.

It was brutally hot in the cabin and the feel of her
molded so intimately against himself did nothing to
cool his blood, either. Her body was a damp, sweat-
drenched furnace that made the folds of her nightshirt
cling to her every curve. Moist heat drove up from her
flesh and set his own to throbbing. But, wrapped in his
cottony nightshirt with her hair caught in a long braid,
she looked more like a little girl than a hardened sea-
queen, and the admiral's surge of lust quickly turned to
a fierce sense of protectiveness that nearly overwhelmed him with the sheer force of it.

God, how he had missed her.

He held her, the sweat running down his brow, his
spine. He should've shed his fancy dress coat and
stripped down to shirt and breeches. But, he'd wanted
to show Maeve he was not a traitor, not a pirate—but
an *admiral*. He'd wanted her to see him wearing his

finest uniform when she awoke. He'd wanted to surprise her.

Instead, he had shocked her into oblivion.

A silly smile crept along his face as he remembered the first time he'd kissed her . . . she'd fainted then, too.

He shut his eyes, kissed her hair, and plucking the damp nightshirt from her spine, locked his arms behind her shoulders. *You should've waited to tell her. . . .*

But no, he'd been so damned eager to prove that he *did* fulfill that final requirement—that of being a gallant officer—he hadn't thought ahead.

Such behavior was highly uncharacteristic of him. He was an admiral, a man who was supposed to display patience, forethought, intuition, and purpose. To think he'd neglected all that he was in his boyish eagerness to prove himself worthy of her affection.

He felt like a wretch.

Well, he would make it up to her. Somehow, some way. He kissed her hair, smoothed the long braid that hung down her back, and touched her side, where he could feel the bandage beneath the thin, damp nightshirt. Although the ball had only nicked a rib and exited without damaging anything vital, the wound had bled with shocking intensity, and his blood went cold at the memory of her still body as he'd carried her off of *Victory* and onto his own flagship.

He shivered, despite the intense heat, thinking how close he'd come to losing her. Once she was his wife, he vowed, all *piratical activity* on her part would come to an abrupt *end*. She could play the Pirate Queen in bed, but beyond that, she would be Lady Falconer. She would have the genteel and elegant life she was born to have, the life that he, as the most senior officer in the Caribbean, could well afford to give her. His arms tightened around her, tenderly, and his eyes closed.

Cradling her head in the curve of his shoulder, he murmured, "I know you will hate me when you awaken, for I have deceived you in a grand way—but this I swear to you, my beloved lady pirate, that I shall have you as my own, my wife.... I love you, you know. I have loved you from the moment I set eyes upon you and I shall love you 'til the day I cease to draw breath. And, damn it, I'll make you believe it!"

He opened his eyes and stared hard out the windows, at the sparkling sea beyond.

"You have suffered much at the hands of others, but by God, you shall never suffer at *mine* again!" he vowed. He buried his face against her hair, overcome by the depth of his feelings for her. "I love you, Maeve—as God is my witness I do. I shall teach you to trust me again. And I shall be all that you ever desired . . . and God strike me dead if ever I allow a single hair of your head to be harmed!"

Just then, the marine sentry outside the door thumped his musket on the deck. "Flag-captain to see you, sir!"

Sighing, Gray let his head fall back against the sofa. Still holding the girl, he stared up at the deckhead, which danced with refracted sunlight. "Come in, Colin."

The door opened and Captain Lord entered, the ship's cat trailing in his wake and rubbing herself affectionately against his ankles. But then, all animals seemed to gravitate toward Colin, a peculiarity Sir Graham had often wondered about. The flag-captain was stripped down to shirt and breeches, and his hat was tucked smartly under his arm. Despite the fact that the fair hair at his temples was dark with sweat, his sunburned brow glistening with moisture, his manner lacked none of its usual aplomb and only his cool gray-amethyst eyes revealed his anxiety.

"How fares my cousin, sir?"

Gray sighed with self-disgust. "She would be better had I kept my mouth shut." He looked up. "I told her the truth and she fainted in my arms," he said sheepishly. "Perhaps I should not have told her *which* admiral I am; the knowledge probably did much to upset her, given my er . . . uh—"

"Reputation, sir?"

"Uh, yes, Colin, that is a good word for it, is it not? But oh, no matter," he said, waving his hand in dismissal of the idea, "my pillaging and plundering days with regard to the *fair sex* are over. I have found my treasure, at last."

Colin hid a grin. His stare, keen despite the deceptive softness of his lavender-gray eyes, settled on his admiral as he held the girl so tenderly in his arms. Sir Graham loved women, yes, but never had Colin seen him treat one with the sort of worshipful devotion he'd bestowed upon Maeve Merrick. He'd made a bed for her on the sofa tucked beside the starboard bulkhead, bathed her sweating skin, and braided her hair to get the hot, heavy mass off her neck. He'd flung open all the stern windows and gone into a rare fit of temper when the tropical breezes had dimmed and the air grew sultry, hot and still. His demands had sent the harassed Dr. Ryder running for the escape of a rum bottle, a midshipman into tears, and the company into hushed and strained eagerness to obey every order relayed through the lieutenants' speaking trumpets. And to top it all off, Sir Graham had had a blazing argument with Maeve's formidable lieutenant, Enolia, over who would get custody of the convalescing Pirate Queen.

Despite the fact the warrior-woman had pulled a sword on him, there was, of course, no arguing with an admiral.

Sir Graham had gotten his way.

Was the philandering admiral finally and truly in love? Well, given Sir Graham's obsession with pirates, Colin was not surprised. It would only stand to reason that he would fall in love with his very own Anne Bonney; God only knows what had happened on that island of hers! Picking up the worshipful cat, Colin turned to go.

"Did you want something, Colin?"

The flag-captain paused. He looked at Sir Graham, sitting on the sofa with the girl held protectively in his arms, and wished that he, too, had someone to love and cherish. . . . But Colin was a private person, and used to keeping his feelings to himself. "Aye, sir. The masthead has just raised Barbados."

"And?"

"We should close with it by nightfall, sir. The convoy is assembled there and waiting for us to escort it home."

"Very well then, Colin. Let us hope, eh? The sooner we're out of the Indies, the better. Escorting a damned convoy of merchant ships back to England is a duty I'd sooner not have to undertake. We shan't dally, though, and will make quick work of getting under way tomorrow. After that . . ."

He trailed off, looking at Colin with a smile in his navy blue eyes.

"After that," the flag-captain finished, quietly, "England."

The two exchanged glances. *England.* How nice it was to be going home again.

It was the unbearable heat that woke her. Perspiration that pasted the nightshirt to her skin. A wall of flesh, hard and solid against her own, suffocating her. She couldn't breathe, she couldn't even *sweat.* She opened her eyes, panting. The body against hers, she realized, belonged to Gray!

No, not Gray, she corrected herself, but *Admiral Falconer*—the most notorious profligate in the entire Caribbean.

"Ah, love, you're awake!"

She pushed hard, feeling sharp pain in her side at the effort. "Dry up and *die.*"

"Would you like a sip of water, dearest? Some lemonade?"

"Only to dump it over your head." She forced her eyes to stay open and glared up at him as he rose to his feet, positioned her against the sofa, and pulled up a chair. The sunlight gleamed against the gold tasseled epaulets on each shoulder; to think she'd felt *guilty* over sending him to his *"death"!* "I don't want a damned thing from you, you deceitful, wretched, conniving, *bastard.* You tricked me. You made me look like a fool—"

"The lemonade would probably be better, I think. Here, love, sit up. I have some all poured and ready for you."

"I—"

He pressed a glass to her lips. He was smiling, his dark eyes twinkling, but she felt the determination, the strength, in the hand he held against her jaw, forcing her head in one place when she would've turned away just to spite him.

She was no match for it.

"Now Maeve, sweetheart, do not be difficult," he chided, tipping the glass, still holding her jaw so she couldn't turn away, and watching her like a hawk to make sure she drank. "I dosed it with plenty of sugar. You'll find it nice and sweet and tangy, just like you."

"Leave me alone, you—you *snake.*" Glaring at him from above the rim of the glass, she shut her mouth, refusing to swallow, and the lemonade ran down her chin, her throat, and onto her sweat-drenched nightshirt.

The navy eyes narrowed. *"Drink."*

Such a sudden change of manner caught Maeve completely off guard and she drank.

The admiral was smiling again.

He made her finish the glass. Every last, tarnal drop

of it, until there were only a few pale shreds of lemon on the bottom. Her stomach felt as though it would explode, her bladder to burst. She swallowed the last mouthful and her eyes slipped shut. Her head fell back against the pillows he'd propped at the arm of the sofa. "You're a miserable wretch," she choked out, too weak to even wipe the tangy drops of juice from her chin.

He set the glass down, dipped a cloth in a bowl of water, and gently dabbed the lemonade from her parted lips. "I know."

"And I think you're a vile son of a bitch."

He wiped her chin, his touch achingly gentle. "I know that too."

His tenderness frightened her, made her feel vulnerable and helpless and defensive. She recoiled inside, from him, from the feelings he evoked in her, for such feelings were those had by other women. Sissified, simpering, *weak* women.

"I'll see you dead," she vowed, on a note of bitter fury.

"Someday, perhaps. But not now." He dragged the cool cloth over her neck, her throat, the soft swell of her breasts, refreshing it with water and wiping up the spilt lemonade. "Maybe in thirty, forty years or so . . . depending on which one of us outlives the other."

God, she was too tired, too weak, to fight with him. Her eyes fell shut and she lay there, lacking the strength to even clench her fists in fury as the cloth moved soothingly over her hot skin. "Where is my ship . . . my crew?"

"Your schooner is in company with us, sailing just to leeward under a fine press of sail. As for those vicious she-wolves you call a crew, they are all safe, so do not distress yourself. 'Twas only by their quick thinking that you even lived to wonder about them, for it was their idea to bring you to Nelson."

"Why Nelson?"

"He has a surgeon." The cloth moved over her mouth, and the navy eyes above it were gentle, concerned. "You, on the other hand, did not."

"What of that *pig*, el Perro Negro?"

The admiral grinned at the venom in her voice. "Your crew wished to kill him, of course, but decided instead to save him for your—*mercy*, I believe they called it. Not that he shall ever see it, of course. As we speak the Spaniard is locked below, deep in the hold, where he shall remain until I can bring him to England, trial, and probable execution."

"Probable?" She tried to sit up, her jaw falling open, only to have him push her gently back down. "You let that *bastard* live, after taking an English merchantman?"

"Aye, but he also professes to have a French letter of marque, issued by Villeneuve himself, which means that *I* have no honorable choice but to treat him as a prisoner of war. Have no fear, dear madam. I doubt he'll be able to produce such a paper, and you shall probably see him swing, yet."

"I'll slit his damned throat!"

"No, you will not."

"Don't you dare think to tell *me* what to do, you wretched pile of offal, you stinking son of a—"

"Your mouth cries for a good bar of soap, madam. Please refrain from such blue language, as I do not like it."

"I don't give a bloody *damn* what you do or don't like, you bastard!"

Refusing to be goaded, he dropped the cloth into the bowl of water and leaned forward, his eyes hard, intent, determined. "I said, *enough.*"

She set her lips and glared mutely up at him.

"I am going to marry you, you know," he announced, in the same tone he might've used to proclaim the state of the weather. But beneath it was a tough note of steel, a steadiness of purpose that was not to be questioned. "You shall be Lady Falconer. There is no use fighting it, Maeve."

"I'll fight you 'til the day I die."

"No. You'll fight me until you learn to trust me. And trust me you will, as God is my witness."

"*You*, of all people, are the last person on earth I'd *ever* trust!"

He pulled his chair so close to the sofa that his knees pushed against the cushion and made it buckle beneath her body. Leaning forward, he rested his elbows on his knees, put his chin on the heels of his hands and looked at her, studying her, his face just inches from her own. She shut her eyes to block that handsome visage out, wishing she could block *him* out as well. "I know you're furious with me for deceiving you," he said gently, and she felt him brush his knuckles against her cheek. "And, I'll allow that you have every right to be. Shall I even try to defend my actions? No. Let it be said, though, that I am as devoted to my country as Nelson is, and I acted as I saw fit."

"I don't recall asking for your explanation *or* your apologies."

"Could I have trusted you? Could I be sure you wouldn't have turned me over to Villeneuve instead?" He went on as though she hadn't spoken, a habit she found intensely infuriating. "Surely, even *you* will agree that the French would have liked nothing better than to have a powerful British admiral fall into their hands."

"An admiral," she spit, twisting her head on the pillow so she wasn't tempted to look into that rakish, handsome face. "A bloody *admiral*. Just my luck, isn't it? I didn't wish for anything more than a captain; hell, I would've even taken a lowly lieutenant, and what do I end up with? The highest-ranking officer in the Indies, a bloody *admiral*."

He chuckled softly. "One must take what one can

get, Majesty." He clapped a hand to his chest in a gesture of dramatic eloquence. "I am an admiral. *Your* admiral. And I, dear sovereign, am at your command."

"My command is for you to get the hell out of my life. I've heard all the stories about you! You're a rake and a libertine! You're a wenching womanizer with a reputation from here to Jamaica!"

"That was before I met you, love. Please calm down before you upset yourself."

"But you're too *young* to be an admiral!"

"Why thank you. How nice to know that at thirty-six, I am still considered 'young.' " He gave a charming, dimpled grin that made her heart flutter in her breast. "Suffice it to say that I'm considered to be a very good commander. My promotions came swiftly. More lemonade, my dear?"

"No. Nothing from you." She clenched her fists, confused and frightened by his light manner, the blatant love and affection in his indigo eyes—but no, it was all an act, surely, all an act, to further humiliate her and strip her of pride. *"Your behavior is not that of an admiral!"* she raged, as though shouting the words would make them believable. "Admirals aren't supposed to go about with gold earrings and pirate clothes and carrying cutlasses instead of dress swords. Admirals aren't supposed to associate with pirate queens and seduce women when they're trying to weave spells to net Gallant Knights. Admirals aren't supposed to submit to rough treatment without complaint at the hands of a crew of pirate women—"

"I love rough treatment. Especially at the hands of pirate *queens.*"

"Just get out, Gray! Or are you Sir Graham now? Admiral Falconer? Just get the bloody hell out, so I can think, so I can fathom my situation, so I can—I can—" She took a deep breath and exploded, "Christ, *so I can*

*take a damned PEE without you hovering over me like
a bloody nurse!"*

"Dearest, you should have told me you have bodily
functions you are anxious to address."

"GET OUT!"

"Really, Maeve, you need attendance. I shall not suffer you to stand by yourself. You hit your head when
you fell, and therefore may be quite unsteady on your
feet." He pushed back the chair and stood, his face
grave. "Here, allow me to help you."

"I BEG your pardon!"

"I absolutely forbid you to get out of that bed unless
I help you." Before she could protest further, he slid his
arms beneath her hot and sweaty back and lifted her up
off the sofa. Pain lanced her side, waves of nausea assailed her, and a fresh tide of sweat broke out along the
length of her spine. Weakly, she clutched at his lapels,
her cheek falling against the fancy gold lace, the cool
medal of the Nile that lay against the crisp, white-
ruffled folds of his neckcloth.

"Put me down."

"But you have bodily functions to address, my dear."

"For God's sake, *Gray,* I have my pride," she wailed.
"Can't you understand that?"

He stood, holding her, appearing to think for a moment. Then he carried her across the cabin and stopped
before a fancy commode. It concealed a porcelain
chamber pot and this, he pulled out using his foot.
Then, he carefully eased her down until her feet, bare
beneath the hem of his nightshirt, rested on the cool
floor.

"Go ahead."

She looked up at him with miserable abjectness; then
she bent her head and bit down savagely on her lip. "I
can't . . . not with you standing here."

"I shall turn my head."

"Please," she pleaded. "I'd rather you leave."

"I cannot."

He pulled her up by the wrists. Humiliation and despair burned behind her eyes. The worst of it was, he was right; she was so weak she couldn't have supported herself in a squatting position for all the money in the world. "Don't touch me," she snarled, hanging from his grasp and leaning her cheek against the inside of her elbow. "Don't help me. Just get the hell away from me and leave me to myself!"

She hung there, shaking, sweating, running hot and cold and trying valiantly not to be sick, not to faint, not to show weakness, not to let him help her in any way, shape or form. She twisted in his grip and kicked him in the shin, hard, and reluctantly, he let her go. Immediately, the floor rushed up to meet her, and he caught her before she would've fallen.

"You see, dearest, I cannot leave you alone for a moment."

"Go away," she cried, wanting to die. "For God's sake, just leave me alone. . . ."

He set her down in a chair. Her chin fell to rest on her chest, and great tears of helplessness and fury flowed down her sweating cheeks and dropped into her lap. She put her hands over her face and sobbed bitterly, her hair lying in a thick braid over one shoulder, her wet shirt swallowing up her body.

The admiral stood looking down at her chestnut hair, her shaking shoulders. Then he knelt down before her so that his eyes were on a level with hers. He reached up, put his fingers beneath her jaw, and slowly lifted her chin until the anguished golden eyes met his.

Her misery nearly broke his heart. "Maeve, dear love," he said gently. "I have seen many things in this lifetime, and I shall see many more before I exit it. I will not be shocked by the necessity of a very seriously injured young woman having to relieve herself. But should my presence disturb you so very much, I will send for one of your crew to be your nursemaid. However, I warn you that your *Kestrel* is a good cable's length to leeward of my flagship, and it would take a fair amount of time before she could be up with us. If you can wait that long, then by all means, do so. If you cannot, then pray, take my hand and let me support you. I promise you, that on my honor I shall not look."

"Bloody right you won't look, because I won't do it!"

"Take my hand."

"I won't do it, do you hear me? I WON'T DO IT!"

He put his hands beneath her arms, pulled her up, grasped her wrist, kicked the chamber pot against her feet and, true to his word, turned to look out the window, beginning to whistle a British sailor's tune she recognized as "Hearts of Oak."

Humiliation and mortification burned through her that she was incapable of performing even this simple task by herself. Yet there was no recourse. Dizzy, nauseous, and faint, she was helpless and at his mercy, and he knew it. The tears came faster, harder, burning twin rivers of shame and anguish down her cheeks.

The whistling became humming, loud, annoying, obnoxious.

Maeve eyed the chamber pot at her feet and sniffled loudly. Oh God, why didn't he think beforehand to send one of the girls to attend her, why did he insist on putting her through this embarrassment, this humiliation—

The humming burst into downright singing, the volume loud enough to be heard two decks above, if not in the main top itself.

"We ne'r see our foes, but we wish them to stay! They ne'r see us, but they wish us away! If they run, why, we'll follow, and run them ashore, for if they won't fight us, we cannot do more! Hearts of oak, are our ships, jolly tars, are our men! We always are ready, steady boys steady, we'll fight and we'll conquer, again, and again! Da dum da dum da dum da dum, da dum, da da da!"

He had a rich, deep baritone voice, and he knew how to use it. To drown out all thoughts. To drown out other voices. To drown out sounds that she didn't want him to hear, *to drown out sounds he* knew *she didn't want him to hear—*

And suddenly she realized why he'd taken to singing so lustily, so loudly—so she could do what she must without suffering the embarrassment of him hearing her do it.

Maeve held up the hem of her nightgown, and did what she had to do.

And when she had finished, she squeezed his hand and without pausing in his singing, the admiral swept her up into his arms, kissed her cheek, and deposited her back onto the sofa. He peeled off the sodden nightshirt, and with an almost clinical detachment for the womanly charms so blatantly revealed to his gaze, put her in a new one that was dry and clean and comfortable. And then he kissed her again, straightened her braid over one small shoulder, and stood gazing down at her, his eyes fond, admiring, soft.

"No matter what you think," he said gently, and took her hand, "I love you. Now, always, and forevermore. Nothing you may say or do will sway my affections, for they are as constant as the swing of the tides, the rise of the moon and stars." The dark navy eyes gazed down at her with gentle affection, quiet adoration. "I love you, Maeve."

He raised her hand to his lips, kissed it, and replaced it tenderly at her side. And then he stood, just looking down at her, while a fond smile curled his mouth.

"Now, go to sleep." He strode to the door, pausing only to point a finger at her in warning. "And that's an order."

Chapter 18

El Perro Negro, locked in a small, choking hold deep in the bowels of H.M.S. *Triton* with the six surviving members of his bloodthirsty gang, woke at about the same time the Pirate Queen, several decks above him, did.

He might have slept forever and died in his own blood, had Pig-Eye's ministrations—encouraged more by a sense of fear of his leader rather than any remote affection—not penetrated his unconscious haze.

"Capitán!" There, the voice again, drifting into his swimming senses, and a slow awareness of pressure ringing his arm as someone drew a bandage tight. Ah, yes, he remembered, now. The merchantman . . . the schooner . . . a savage fight between pistols and cut-lasses '. . . and the black African, charging out of the smoke and cutting him down as he'd emptied his pistol into her *puta* of a captain. At least he'd had the satis-faction of seeing the disbelief on the Pirate Queen's face, extinguished by that one savage blast, before his own world had gone dark. . . .

He hoped she rotted in hell, the whoring bitch! Curs-ing, he clawed himself up through sheets of pain and opened his eyes.

"Ah, *Capitán*, you are awake! Thank God!"

It was Pig-Eye, his face barely discernible in the thick gloom. *"Idiota!"* el Perro Negro snarled, for with consciousness came a deep, searing agony in his left arm that clawed all the way up and into his shoulder. "Why didn't you just let me be, you stupid *shit?!*" But even as he sat up, tugging at the too-tight bandage the faithful wretch had made from strips of his own shirt, he realized he was in a grave situation and his survival instincts, honed by years of running from the law, took over. Shoving Pig-Eye brutally aside, he pulled himself to his feet, stumbled over a sprawled, groaning body, kicked it in fury, and groped desperately at the seams of a shut and locked door.

"It is no use, *Capitán,*" Pig-Eye said, dejectedly. "We have already tried to escape. *El almirante* is no fool. Not only is the door bolted shut, but he has placed a marine guard outside to make sure we . . . behave. There is no way out."

"What do you mean, there's no way out? What the hell are you talking about?!"

"We're prisoners, *Capitán,*" he said, nervously. "After you shot the Pirate Queen, her crew snatched her up, fled back to the schooner, and loosed a broadside into us that killed most of our crew. We may be fine fighters, but we are only flesh and blood—no match for a cannon shot. Next thing we knew, they'd overpowered those of us who were left and dragged us off to Nelson—"

"Nelson?!" El Perro Negro snared Pig-Eye's filthy collar and yanked him savagely forward, nearly snapping the man's neck. *"We're on Nelson's ship?* You damned fools, why didn't you tell me!"

Pig-Eye shrank back, his eyes white in the darkness, the sweaty stench of his terror ripe and hot against a background of other, fouler smells—bilge water, rat shit, damp wood, and closer, the stink of vomit and blood. "I did not say we are aboard Nelson's ship, *Capitán,*" he gasped, trembling. "We are on the ship of *el almirante,* aye, but *this* admiral is not Nelson—"

"Which admiral is it, then?!" he roared, heaving Pig-

Eye backward. He heard the man hit a bulkhead and fall on a cry of pain.

Frightened silence. And then:

"Sir Graham Falconer."

El Perro Negro went stiff. He stood frozen, fear creeping up his spine like a glacier sliding out of the north. Sick bile welled up in his gut and a high, coppery taste filled his mouth. He slammed a fist into the bulkhead and dragged a hand over his face, smearing sudden, cold sweat over skin that had gone dry and waxy. *Falconer.* The English admiral would make short work of him, especially after he'd so ruthlessly taken the merchantman that had been destined for the convoy Sir Graham would be escorting back to England. Not to mention the fact he'd killed its crew, including the young *capitán.* But yet—

But yet, he was still *alive.*

Why?

Jacky, seeming to read his mind, spoke from the darkness of a corner. "You can thank Renaldo for the fact we've been spared, *Capitán.* He told *el almirante* we hold a letter of marque from the French Admiral Villeneuve back on our brig, right, Renaldo?"

The sprawled figure that el Perro Negro had kicked earlier, rolled into an upright position. "Aye . . . and the son of a bitch believed me, too."

El Perro Negro let out his breath on a shaky sigh, and released a short, hysterical burst of laughter. "Well, well, Renaldo, you never fail to surprise me." He moved to the mate, reached down, and hauled him roughly to his feet. "Perhaps you have bought us some time, after all."

"I've bought nothin'," Renaldo said, bitterly. He rubbed at the spot in his ribs where his captain had kicked him. "Once Falconer learns we ain't got no letter of marque, and thus, ain't entitled to any rights as prisoners of war, he'll hang us for sure."

"Not if I can help it," el Perro Negro said softly, and moving back through the darkness, sat down on the damp floor amidst his little circle of followers. "For you see, my good *piratas*, I have a plan. I have already killed an English *capitán;* why not an English *almirante* as well? After all, we have nothing to lose. We shall bide our time—and then, we'll act. And when we do . . ."

"Yes?" they cried, excitedly.

"And when we do, escape and freedom shall be ours. Now listen. . . . "

It was sunset, and the clouds were on fire above a molten sea. Barbados, dark against the blazing sky, was speared on *Triton*'s thrusting bowsprit and growing larger by the minute, and Nelson's fleet had fallen beneath the horizon several hours past. Now, a fine wind had sprung up to huff itself into *Triton*'s huge courses and royals, spread to catch every hint of the breeze that had been stingy and soft for most of the day.

The quarterdeck of any warship is the domain of its commanding officer, and even the captain trod that sacred place lightly when it was occupied by an admiral. Tonight was no exception, and the brilliant sunset found Sir Graham pacing thoughtfully back and forth, quite alone, quite preoccupied, his tactical mind mulling over pursuit, strategies, the chase—*conquest.*

Maeve.

His rank make his as far removed from his men as a king from the common people, and those on watch regarded him with no small degree of awe and respect as they went about their work. What military secrets, what thoughts that could potentially shape history, went through the mind of a man as highly placed as their dark admiral? From the seamen hauling on braces to bring the huge ship onto the opposite tack, to Captain Colin Lord himself—who had a better idea than most just what his admiral was thinking about—nearly eight hundred sailors watched him and wondered. . . .

Indeed, Sir Graham's brow was relaxed, his step slow and thoughtful, his eyes pensive, his manner quiet. But behind the calmness of his facade the admiral's tactical mind was hard at work. He made another turn, hands behind his back, head bent, walking forward, walking aft, walking forward. . . .

Thinking.

He paused only to stare thoughtfully at the little schooner *Kestrel,* keeping station just to windward of the mighty battleship. Then he looked to the north, where Nelson had taken the Mediterranean Fleet.

Two admirals, both on a desperate chase. One after a Frenchman's fleet—and the other, after a Pirate Queen's heart.

"Sir Graham!" the voice outside the flag-captain's door announced.

Colin Lord was making a notation in his log when the unexpected thump of Sergeant Maitland's musket against the deck outside jarred him from his thoughts. Taken off guard by his admiral's unannounced visit, he leapt to his feet and snapped off a stiff salute.

"Be easy, Colin, this is nothing official," Gray said mildly, putting his hand on the younger man's arm. "May I come in? There is something I should like to discuss with you."

"By all means, sir. Pray, please do." The flag-captain gestured to a chair, brushed a wrinkle from his shirt, called for a servant to bring tea, and led the way to his fine mahogany table, the surface of which glowed warmly beneath the lantern that swung from the beams overhead. The log lay open on his desk and he snapped it shut, his habitual neatness evident even in this small action. "With the wind as it is, we'll anchor in Barbados by midnight, Sir Graham. The master assures me

that we should be on our way out of the Indies with the
convoy by tomorrow afternoon at the latest—"

Sir Graham nodded, and moved with easy grace
across the cabin. He settled himself in a chair, deliberately affecting a relaxed pose, one arm lying across the
chair's back, legs crossed, and a pensive look about his
dark face. Then he spotted the ship's cat, sprawled lazily in the sun streaming through the stern windows; he
bared his teeth and made a face, the cat fled, and the
admiral burst out laughing.

"Kitty, kitty, kitty!" Sir Graham coaxed, scowling
playfully at the cat, who now glared at him from beneath the safety of Colin's desk. A loud, angry hiss met
his summons, and, again, the admiral's rich, booming
laughter filled the cabin.

The servant, looking harried, brought a silver tray in
and set it down before the two officers. Colin picked up
the teapot. "Cream and sugar, sir?"

"No, just rum."

"Just rum, Martin. As the admiral likes it."

The servant returned with plates and a fine lemon
cake frosted with sugar. Colin poured the admiral's tea
and, lifting a steaming cup to his lips, eyed him with
wariness.

And then he saw the thoughtful crease in Sir Graham's brow, the determined but preoccupied look in his
eye, and knew.

The Pirate Queen.

"Colin, my lad . . ." the admiral began, and the flag-
captain braced himself.

"Sir?"

Sir Graham took his time about it. He sipped his
rum-laced tea, pushed the crumbs around on his plate,
fixed Colin with his dark stare. "I have a scenario for
you."

Colin set down his tea. *Here we go,* he thought.

The admiral looked out the opened stern windows

and thoughtfully tugged at his earring. "If," he said
slowly, his gaze distant, preoccupied, "you were to find
yourself in say, a small frigate, confronted by a squadron of enemy ships-of-the-line, and, given that just
one—one, mind you!—of the ships that said squadron
was protecting—we shall make it a merchantman, for
the purpose of this discussion—was rich enough to enable you to live out the rest of your life in relative
happiness—given this situation, Colin, would you let
that mighty fleet and its rich merchantman alone, or
would you attack and risk all, even though the odds
were surely against you?"

Colin looked at him, wondering what his shrewd superior was leading up to. That it was a test, he had no
doubt—the admiral often engaged such methods to
keep him sharp, to teach him, to prepare him for his
own promotion to flag rank some day—but Colin knew
that this was more than that. And he would've wagered
the lace from his coat and both epaulets off his shoulders that Rear Admiral Sir Graham Falconer was *not*
talking about ships. . . .

"Well?"

Colin answered carefully. "Why, I would attack and
risk everything, sir . . . of course."

"Of course. You are an Englishman, after all."

"As are you—sir."

"Very good. Point established. Now tell me, my dear
Colin, how, given this situation, you would go about
defeating this formidable enemy whose guns are run
out, this enemy who is determined not to let you get
close enough to board and take him?"

"Every vessel has a vulnerable area, sir," Colin said,
moving his chair back slightly so the poor, harassed cat
could jump into his lap. He stroked the feline's back,
choosing his words with care and precision. "As you
well know, both bow and stern have comparatively insignificant firepower and are therefore quite vulnerable

to attack. Or, one may consider the structural weaknesses of a particular design, or vulnerable areas provided by nature herself, such as at the waterline, or below it if one happens to be to windward of a ship that is heeled hard over on her beam."

The admiral smiled, his dark eyes gleaming.

"And where, Captain, would those weaknesses be in a mighty warship? How would you go about quelling *her* into submission . . . without damaging her timbers or sacrificing one jot of her spirit?"

The admiral was watching him intently, too intently. Carefully, Colin said, "I would range around her stern, sir, out of the reach of her big guns and broadsides, where she would be most defenseless. I would rake her, cripple her steering by taking out her rudder, and then, once having annoyed and distracted her thus, I would fall off, and try to get in another shot, perhaps in her bows. . . ."

"And if that method was to fail, Colin?"

"We are considering that surrender to the enemy is not to be considered?"

The admiral smiled. "It is not even an option."

"Well, then, I say there is no other recourse, sir, but to confuse her, get to windward of her, grapple . . . and board her"—Colin smiled sheepishly and pinkened like a young lad—"in the smoke. Works every time . . . *sir.*"

Sir Graham finished his rum-laced tea and set the cup down on the table. "Very good, Captain. I am delighted to see that our great minds think alike." He grinned, his eyes alight with the anticipation of challenge, his jaw dimpling boyishly. Then he rose to his feet, and still smiling, strode for the door.

"Sir?"

The admiral paused, arching one black brow.

Colin flushed. "Good luck."

The bastard. *Bastard!*

Maeve awoke to suffocating heat, the glow of a lantern over her head, and a single, perfect red rose on the pillow beside her.

Angrily, she reached out, picked up the blossom, and crushed it in her fist. A heartbeat of regret paused her actions, and she sadly caressed the velvet petals. Then she flung the crumpled flower to the deck flooring.

She was too weak to hurl anything bigger than a flower in her fit of temper, too weak to get out of bed to *find* something to hurl, too weak to do anything but burn with humiliation as she remembered him helping her attend to that most mortifying bodily function. Color flooded her face and she put her hands over her eyes, ashamed, embarrassed. He could've left her to her own devices, but no, he had insisted on supporting her. At least he'd had the consideration to preserve her dignity by trying to drown out the sound of the act!

But still, nothing could make up for what he had done to her, the vile wretch! To think that he had allowed her to believe he was a *traitor,* of all things. He, Admiral Falconer, one of the most renowned flag officers in the British navy and surely, the worst libertine to hit the West Indies since—since *Blackbeard.* To think she had lain with such a rake, given away her heart . . . the *bastard!* He must think her a damned easy conquest. How he must be laughing! And Nelson! He was no better, a slinking dog in the guise of a hero, a wretched, insufferable little peacock totally undeserving of his laurels, his titles, her respect. It was a cruel betrayal, an ugly realization, and she felt sick. *Nelson.* She couldn't even trust *him,* the gallant, honorable Nelson!

Her curses pierced the stillness of the spacious cabin. *Men!* She hated them all, trusted none of them, and after this she'd never trust another again, for they were all nothing but a pack of slimy, heartless, arrogant *bastards!*

She couldn't, *wouldn't,* stay here. She couldn't face him after what they had *done* together on her island. She couldn't look him in the eye and know he was probably thinking of what she'd looked like naked, what he'd done to her, and oh God, what she'd done to *him.* And no way in Satan's hell would she further suffer the mortification of his ministering to her wounds.

"I'd rather *die* first," she said bitterly, and clutching the side of the sofa, dragged herself to an upright, sitting position. She swayed dizzily, and felt the snug press of a bandage around her waist. Christ, no wonder she was so hot, no wonder she couldn't breathe—and what the devil was this wet garment that had tangled itself around her body?

In horror, she gazed down at the sleeves that ended several inches beyond her fingers, the seemingly yards of excess material that had twined and bunched and wrapped itself around her torso, and realized she was not in her own clothes, but a soft, fine nightshirt that belonged to Sir Graham himself.

Cursing with impotent fury, she plucked at the fabric, pulling it away from her damp skin. Even that simple exertion tired her, sickened her, brought dizziness to her head and illness to her stomach. Hellfire and damnation take the blighty devil! Had he stripped her clothes away as she'd lain senseless? Touched her body, invaded her person, taken liberties that she would never let him take again?

Blast him! Her strength was failing her, but with every gasping breath her resolve mounted. Her body screaming in pain, in protest, the Pirate Queen pulled herself up and stumbled across the cabin. Nausea rose in her throat and sheer will alone kept her from vomiting. The cabin spun about her, the paintings of the long-dead pirates with it, and she made a wild dive toward the bulkhead, where an ancient cutlass rested beneath a portrait of Sir Henry Morgan, the undisputed

King of the Spanish Main nearly a century and a half before—

She missed, her nails gouging into the wood, her fingers hitting the sword and knocking it from its precarious perch. It struck her heavily on the shoulder and Maeve fell with it, feeling the wound open beneath the bandage as she hit the deck, where she lay cursing with fury, pain, and the refusal to admit defeat. The sword lay several feet away, just out of reach; she dragged herself across the deck, pulling her body with her arms, pushing herself with her feet, the nightshirt tangling around her body, suffocating her. The sword, just out of reach, was now in her hand . . . oh God, could she lift it?

Desperate, groping fingers closed around the ancient hilt and possessively pulled the heavy blade across the carpet, inch by torturous inch.

"I'll make you pay, Admiral Sir Graham *Falconer* . . . so help me God, you'll pay . . . no one makes the Pirate Queen look like a fool . . . damn your eyes"— gasping, she pulled the sword up and under her breast and fell atop it, her brow touching the floor, her lips kissing the old metal—" . . . damn your *eyes,* you *bastard.* . . . " She lay there, panting, her eyes clenched against her reeling vision, her lips against the cool steel, her arms folded beneath her, the sweat racing down her face and her heaving sides to soak the bandage around her waist. But there was more than just sweat running beneath that bandage, she *knew* there was more than just sweat running—

I'm bleeding, she thought, raising her head and swallowing against the bile that rose in her throat. Fear rose within her but she beat it back. *Must get out of here . . . away from him.* She raised herself on trembling arms. Her hair hung in a mussed braid over her shoulder, her face dripped sweat, and beneath her, the sword caught her tormented reflection.

Thick, ugly warmth spread from her waist, and panic rose with every quickening beat of her heart.

I'm bleeding. Dear God, I'm bleeding to death. She shut her eyes, wrapped her fingers, cold now, shaking, around the grip of the sword. It felt alien, too big, too much for her to grasp, let alone lift, and now the blood was running fiercely from her side, thick warm rivers of it seeping through her bandage, and she knew that the damp nightshirt wrapped around her waist was dark with a rich, blooming stain of crimson.

Somebody, help me. . . . She wrapped her fist around the sword, clutching it like a lifeline. Dizzily, she raised her head once more.

The Pirate Queen finally gained her knees, fell, and on her elbows, began to drag herself back across the deck flooring to the dining cabin. The door was only ten—twenty?—feet away, but she knew she would never reach it. *Try, Maeve. You can do it. . . .* She paused, pushed the sword ahead of her across the carpet, followed it, cursed, cried, bled.

Oh God, help me . . . I just need to reach the door . . . just help me get to the door, God, that's all I ask—

It opened and the admiral walked in.

"Maeve!"

He saw a trail of blood, and Maeve, his beloved Maeve, wrapped in his nightshirt like a little child and lying helplessly on the floor, head drooping, forearms digging into the carpet, pulling herself along by her elbows and leaving a slick ribbon of crimson in her wake.

He dived forward, caught her as she collapsed, and swept her up into his arms. Without breaking stride he pounded from the cabin, nearly knocking the sentry outside over, and raced down companionways, through deck after darkened deck, in his blind haste to reach the surgeon.

Chapter 19

"She'll be fine, Sir Graham," the surgeon said, as he bound Maeve's ribs with a fresh bandage by the light of the swinging lantern above. He worked swiftly, for the admiral was pacing frantically, beside himself with worry, as Her Majesty's blazing glare, hot enough to blister the skin off a seaman's hands, followed him back and forth and the surgeon was not anxious to be caught between the broadsides of the two of them. In fact, the sooner he could finish his task, the sooner he could get to the bottle of rum hidden beneath the bench in the corner—

"Well, thank God for *that*," the admiral exclaimed. He took the girl's hand, his thumb caressing her palm before raising it to his lips. Her eyes flashing, she opened her mouth to deliver a scathing rebuke that the admiral effectively cut off: "I daresay, she has taken a decade off my life with the amount of worrying I've done about her. Do be careful there, man. She's to be my wife, you know."

"Like hell I am," Maeve snarled.

"She'll not bleed anymore, I trust?"

"She may, sir," the surgeon replied, working faster now, as nervous sweat began to stream from his brow, "but not to worry. Wounds of this nature often do, especially under exertions that you, young lady, should not be engaging in. My orders to you—"

"The devil take your bloody *orders!*"

"I'll hear you out, man," the admiral commanded, irritably. "She'll answer to me."

"I don't answer to *traitors."*

"You were saying, Doctor?" Sir Graham prompted, a muscle ticking in his jaw.

The surgeon's hands were fluttering, his heart racing. "My orders to *you,* Captain Merrick, are complete bed rest for the next several days. Sir Graham, a bit of air would not do her any harm either; perhaps you could have your captain rig an awning on the poop deck to shade her from the sun so that she may sit out—"

"Yes, by all means, I will have that attended to immediately."

"And I would advise no exercise yet. And no exerting yourself, madam."

"I want to return to my ship."

"She will not exert herself, Doctor, you have *my* word on that—"

"I want my crew."

"And also, Sir Graham, please make sure the wound is kept clean and dry—"

"I want my blasted freedom!"

"Watch your mouth," the admiral chided mildly. "You're in mixed company, my dear, and the good doctor deserves some respect."

"The doctor and *you* can all go straight to hell where I hope your balls burn off and your—"

"Really, Doctor, should it be wrapped so tightly? I don't think she can breathe."

"She can breathe."

"Can you breathe, dearest?"

"—cocks smolder away into ashes! I hope you all rot in *hell* forever, do you hear me? I hope—"

"Yes, Doctor, I fear she can breathe very well. Wrap it tighter, if you please."

"Ouch!" Maeve gasped, feeling the pressure.

"Not that tight, damn you!" Sir Graham snapped.

"Ease up there, yes, that's better. Is that better, my love?"

"I'm not your *love,* you blackguard."

"Is that better *my love?*" he repeated, firmly.

"Yes," she bit out, from between clenched teeth.

"Very well then. A fine job, Doctor. I must remember you in my report tonight. Oh, bother, I hate reports. I shall recommend it to Captain Lord, he doesn't mind paperwork in the least. Should've been a lawyer, damn his eyes. Maeve? Maeve, sweetheart, can you sit up now? No, your shirt covers you, no need to blush, here, take my hand—"

She tried to jerk away from him.

"Maeve, dear, I said, *give me your hand.*"

"I'll give you a knife to the gut, you wretched bastard. Get the hell out of my life; just go away and leave me alone."

"Women!" he exclaimed, with a smile that drove a boyish dimple into his jaw. Black lashes, almost feminine in their thickness and length, swept down to conceal the twinkle in his eyes. "Really, Doctor, why do they insist upon giving us such a devil of a time? I've instructed the cook to prepare something light and nourishing for you, and he also makes devilishly good lemonade. Why, we'll have you back on your feet in no time, if I do say so myself."

"Aye, that we will, Sir Graham," Dr. Ryder said hurriedly, sweating harder now, and obviously ill at ease in the presence of one so highly ranked as Admiral Falconer.

"You've done a splendid job, as always, Ryder. Huzzahs to you, she looks as right as rain. Ready, love? No, don't even *try* to stand up, I won't allow it. Has anyone ever told you how lovely you look in braids? So innocent and sweet; no, don't scowl, it doesn't become you at all! Up we go!"

"Got her, Sir Graham?"

"Of course I have her, you fool," the admiral said, but good-naturedly. Above Maeve's head, he shot the surgeon a wink, then kicked the door open with his foot. "Damned comely burden, if I do say so myself. Hold that door for me now, will you, Doctor? Yes, thank you. You're a fine man, Ryder, a fine man. Splendid work!"

"Thank you, sir," the surgeon said, beaming.

"Pray, go reward yourself man, you deserve it. In fact, Ryder, why don't you have an extra tot from that bottle you've got hidden beneath the bench? Rum, is it not? I say, 'twas Morgan's favorite beverage!"

The surgeon blanched. "B-but sir, how did you know that I . . ."

But Sir Graham had already swept out of the room, leaving the surgeon gaping in disbelief, for surely, the admiral could not have known he had that bottle hidden there!

He remembered Captains Lord's warning, spoken so many times:

Never underestimate Sir Graham.

One of these days, he'd remember there was more than just charm and good looks to the keen and discerning admiral in charge of the Royal Navy's West Indies Station.

And so, he feared, would the Pirate Queen.

Humming as though he were a common seaman on his way to grog, Sir Graham carried her up through the decks, his shirt smeared with her blood, the waves of his black hair caught in the gleam of swinging lanterns as they passed beneath them. She saw the fury in the tightness about his mouth, felt it in the tenseness of his arms beneath her back. "You scared me, Maeve. I know I hurt you but believe me that I would cut off my right arm before I would hurt you again." She saw him swallow hard as he silently strode toward his cabin.

Then his voice turned light and teasing. "Maeve, Maeve," he chided, "pray, what am I to do with you? Do you want to end up killing yourself, for God's sake?!"

"I'd prefer to end up killing *you* but I can't lift the sword yet."

"Ah, I've no doubt that you will try once you have regained your strength. Evening, Lieutenant Pearson, carry on, carry on!" He paused beside a bulkhead and without warning, exploded, *"But so help me God, Maeve, if I catch you with so much as a FOOT out of bed against doctor's orders again, I'll personally blister your damned hide, do I make myself clear?!"*

The breath burst from her lungs on a loud guffaw—

"Hang it, woman, *do I make myself clear?!*"

She met his blazing eyes, smiled malevolently, and spat, *"Very."*

He stared at her for a long moment; then he sighed and to her surprise, crushed her fiercely to his chest, burying his face against her hair and tightening his arms so hard about her that she couldn't draw breath. "I love you," he murmured, his body shaking beneath and around her. "By all that's holy and all that's not, I love you." He held her for a long, long moment, then raised his head and said hoarsely, "Don't *ever* do that to me again."

Then, as though the outburst had never happened, he relaxed his death grip on her and resumed his brisk pace.

She was too stunned by his unguarded display of emotion to remark upon it, and instead, maintained a sullen silence as he carried her up through the hatch to the next deck. A myriad array of feelings tore through her, not the least of which was guilt. She swallowed hard. His behavior when she'd awakened to find him hovering anxiously over the surgeon, alternately pacing, slamming his fist against a bulkhead, inquiring after her prognosis, declaring his love for her in one breath and damning himself in the next for having left her alone— could not have been more genuine.

Don't let yourself be fooled, she told herself. *He'll only hurt you. Betray you.* She tightened her arms protectively to her heart. *Abandon you. He's a* rake *for God's sake!*

A very handsome rake. And in that glittering admiral's uniform—

She shut her eyes, feeling the heat of his body against her own, his muscles moving smoothly beneath her as though she weighed no more than his hat and coat.

"I love you, Maeve."

"Yes? Well I love you, too. About as much as I do el Perro Negro."

"Maeve, that hurts. I know you've good reason for your feelings. I'm strong enough to handle them, so if you're trying to get a reaction out of me, I fear you must work harder. When you're strong again we can fight all you want."

She tilted her head back to stare up at him. "How can you be so *nice* to me after what I did to you?!"

"Pray, what did you do to me?"

She thought of the bloodstained hemp aboard *Kestrel* with which they had bound his wrists, the dank cell they'd kept him in, the cruel treatment he had endured at their hands. Embarrassment washed through her, deep and biting and sharp.

"Maeve?"

She was too ashamed to even answer. "Never mind."

"Oh, you must be referring to my, er, *captivity* while on your island? Your ship? Dear Lady, do not trouble yourself over *that;* it was indeed an adventure. Why, 'tis not every day that an admiral who wishes he was born a pirate gets to be captured and held prisoner by a whole gang of them! Indeed, it will be something to tell our children about."

"Tell *your* children about," she corrected him.

"Oh, no, Majesty. You will marry me. I vow it."

"Over my dead body."

As usual, he continued on as though he hadn't heard her. "We'll have fine, strong sons, and daughters as lovely as you. You'll have to give up your piratical rovings, of course—I'll have no wife of *mine* risking her neck by sailing the seas as a pirate, no matter how charming I might find the vision!—but oh, think of what children we shall have; why, I hope they get your hair, have I ever told you how beautiful it is? I had a most wonderful time braiding it. Come to think of it, I'll wager that the formidable Anne Bonney's was of a similar shade—"

"I *want* to go back to my ship, *Gray.*"

"However, her beauty and fire would not have held a candle to yours. I am the lucky one, am I not? My God, I can't wait to get you to England, and show you off to my sisters, my family, my peers, my friends at Portsmouth. . . . How they shall envy me!"

"I—*want*"—she ground out through clenched teeth—"to go back to my *ship.*"

"No doubt you do, and then you'd be away from me and leading me a merry chase. Ah, yes, where was I? England. We're going there, you know. The Admiralty has granted me some leave time and so I will be escorting a fleet of merchant ships back there with me. They can use all the protection they can get, what with the damned French running around loose. And Nelson, he is in awe of you. Do you realize how much favor you have won with him for your bravery, for returning me to him, and, of course, for telling him where the French had *really* gone? He was most impressed, dear lady, *most* impressed; why, he has invited us both to his home, Merton, upon our arrival in England, where he wishes you to make the acquaintance of his dear Lady Hamilton. You will like her, Maeve, she is a true sailor's woman, full of bawdy humor and ribald fun, a real gem if I do say so myself."

"I don't want to meet Lady Hamilton, I don't want to go to England, I don't want to suffer your intolerable company another blasted minute; I JUST WANT MY SHIP!"

They had arrived at the door of Sir Graham's quarters, where a scarlet-coated marine, assigned to guard the life of the most valuable man in the fleet, snapped rigidly to attention.

"Evening, Sergeant Handley," Gray said brightly. "Breeze is getting up, I fear!"

The guard, staring straight ahead, did not shift his gaze, did not crack a smile, did not move anything except his lips. "Sir."

"We shall have a blow by daylight, eh, Sergeant?"

Maeve's temper exploded. "Furthermore," she raged, "I will *not* marry you and spend my days as a bored and breeding *landlubber*—"

The admiral clapped his hand over her mouth. She bit him. He never flinched, only grinning and pushing his palm harder against her teeth to smother her snarls of fury.

The marine's gaze moved, briefly, to take in the struggling girl in Sir Graham's arms, and he caught the gleam in the admiral's eye. He stared again over Sir Graham's shoulder. "Er, yes, sir. If I, uh, do say so myself."

"Pay it no heed, I shall set storm sails to ride it out. Carry on, Handley!"

The admiral pushed open the door of his cabin and kicked it shut behind him.

"I have no intention of being your Lady Falconer," Maeve exploded, the moment he released her mouth. He carried her through the dining cabin and past the paneled bulkheads with their pirate paintings and crossed cutlasses. "I have *no* intention of giving up the sea, my ship, or my *life,* so I wish to hell you'd quit telling everyone otherwise. Furthermore, I will not stay near or with you one moment longer than I have to and I'll never help the British Navy again, because you're all a bunch of arrogant blackguards with no thought for anyone else and nothing but betrayal and conquest in your foul hearts. I hate you, I hate your navy, and I hate Nelson!"

"Maeve!" He halted, looking properly shocked, but whether it was an act or not, she could not tell.

"What?"

"How could you hate Lord Nelson? Whatever has he done to you to make you say such harsh things about him?"

"He lied to me," she said, sullenly.

"Did he, now?"

"Well"—she faltered, suddenly ashamed—"he went along with *your* lies!"

"Pray, with enthusiasm or annoyance? I should think it the latter, as we had a bit of a tiff about that, he and I, and it was *my* impression that his lordship was not at all happy about having to play along with my game."

"I'll bloody bet."

"Indeed, dear heart, he was not. Took me quite to task, and it was only after I assured him of my intent to marry you that he left off."

"I will *not* marry you, d'you hear me? I—will—not—marry you. *Period.*"

"So anyhow," he continued, once again ignoring her outburst, "I think you're being terribly unfair to poor Lord Nelson." Still holding her in the curve of his arm, he bent to tidy the pillows on the sofa. "After all, you have *him* to thank for your life. If not for his quick thinking—and that of your crew, I might add—you would be dead. Now, where would that put you, if you were dead? I cannot bear the thought of it! And to think that milord even allowed you aboard the *Victory*—he does not allow women aboard his ship, you know, does not suffer himself even to touch one unless she answers to the name 'Emma Hamilton.' More jealous than a school-lad, that one, and she no better besides! But oh, it suits them. A better-matched couple I've yet to imagine, although I must admit that you and I will have a fine go of it once the squalls leave off."

He talked too much. And yet Maeve sensed it was not chatter, but merely a buffer, a way of glossing over some shrewd intent, some hidden motive, a way of lulling an adversary into letting down his—or *her*—guard. Falconer was no fool. She had already seen the swift direction his thoughts could take, the sudden turn of his temper, the rapier-sharp intellect behind the navy blue (and what a damned *appropriate* color) eyes. He knew how to put a person off guard, then slam in for the kill.

She must be on her toes. He was shrewd, this admiral.

She must be more shrewd.

"So really, Maeve, I beg of you, do not harbor such anger toward poor Nelson; he did all in his power to help you. He is a kind man, blameless, much loved by his sailors, his officers, the fleet, and everyone who knows him." Lowering himself to the sofa, he settled her across his lap, cradled her shoulders within the curve of his arm, drew the sheet up over her breasts, and smoothed the fringy end of her braid. His touch aroused a hot wash of desire in her blood and she bit her lip, hard, hoping the pain would distract her.

"Furthermore," he said, lifting a glass of lemonade to her lips and tilting her head forward so she wouldn't choke, "he is very anxious about your health, and I'm really the only one to deserve the heat of your anger—"

"Fine, dammit! I forgive him, all right? I FORGIVE HIM!"

"Good. Now that *that's* settled, I should like to rebraid your hair and then strike a bargain with you," he continued, not missing a beat. He turned her onto her side and she felt his fingers smoothing the hair back from her temples, sliding along the length of the thick plait. Mutinously, she stared at the windows directly across from her, then the grinning countenance of Henry Morgan. The admiral's knee was hard beneath her cheek, but not uncomfortable; his hands were sliding through her hair now, gently loosing the tresses from their mussed-up braid. She shut her eyes. It felt good. If this was how he gained his victories, no wonder he was an admiral at such a young age.

"You are enthralled by officers; I, by pirates," he murmured, from above her head. "What say you and I share bedtime stories? You tell me a story about pirates, I'll tell you one about my adventures as an officer. Do you wish to go first?"

"No."

"Very well, then. Allow me. . . ." And as she closed her eyes and allowed him to brush out her thick tresses, her anger faded to wariness, her wariness to acceptance, her acceptance to exhaustion. His voice faded in and out, and she knew only the feel of his hands, gently tugging and pulling on her hair, slowly plaiting it in a long, thick braid. He took his time about it, apparently enjoying the act as much as she did, telling her about the ships he'd captained, the places he'd gone, the thrill of having the King knight him for his bravery at the Battle of the Nile as one of Nelson's "Band of Brothers." He told her about his sisters—all six of them—and how much he loved them, he told her about his home in England, he told her about his Cornish ancestors from Penzance—"pirates, Maeve! I had *pirates* in my background!"—and his own since-boyhood obsession with the buccaneers who'd carved a bloody, romantic path through the Spanish Main nearly two centuries ago. . . .

The braid was finished, and now there was just his fingers, gently stroking her cheek. "Am I boring you, love? Are you comfortable?"

She lifted eyelids that felt like fishing weights. "Huh?"

"I said, are you comfortable?"

Comfortable . . . She was more than comfortable, though she'd never admit it. She felt . . . *safe* within the admiral's protection. Cherished.

Loved.

It was frightening, letting go and allowing herself to feel such things normally reserved for weak and insipid people. She fought against them. Felt herself losing the battle.

Allow it, Maeve.

"Aye," she murmured. "I'm . . . comfortable."

"Well then, I think that is all for tonight's bedtime stories. You will sleep now."

"I don't want to sleep."

"Oh, but you will, there was laudanum in that lemonade you've been drinking. But have no fear, sweeting, I shan't leave you until it takes effect."

"You're . . . despicable." She dragged open her eyes, trying to be angry with him for this latest manipulation, but it was hard to summon fury when he was being so damnably *nice,* so damnably *caring,* so damnably *gallant.*

He eased himself out from under her and with tender care, dragged the sheet up to her chin. His fingers brushed her shoulders as he tucked her in, his lips grazed her temple. *Stay,* she wanted to say. *Don't leave me.* But her eyes slipped shut before her heart could betray her, and she lacked the strength to force them back open.

Her lips moved against the pillow. "And where are you going, *Admiral?* . . . Don't *you* ever sleep?"

She sensed him kneeling down beside her, felt his breath on her cheek as he lovingly absorbed every detail of her face and smoothed the wispy hair that had come loose from the braid back from her temple. "Sleep? Not when my lovely Queen is under my protection. I am an officer, Majesty, and I have my sworn duty."

An officer. Guarding the lives of those he loved.

"I love you, Maeve," he said softly, and kissed her.

She sank, down through warm, comforting darkness, his words following her, wrapping around her, infiltrating her last coherent thought before sleep claimed her.

I love you.

Chapter 20

"You did *what*, sir?!"

"Now Hardy, don't give me that look; I only did as I saw fit. Besides, I'll answer to any ill consequences that come out of it."

"Does Sir Graham know you wrote this letter to her parents?!"

"Of course not, this is no one's business but my own. And I don't want his flag-captain to know of my meddling, either—the fellow *is* the girl's cousin, you know, and of course *she* cannot know, because what if her parents really *don't* show up? No, no, they shall come, I am sure of it, Hardy. No parents would abandon their daughter like that, and besides, didn't Captain Lord himself say they think her dead?" Lord Nelson waved his hand, fussily dismissing the matter and snatching up a telescope from the rack. He strode to the side, climbed up onto a cannon, and pushed the long instrument through the shrouds to balance it. "Now I don't wish to hear any more on the subject, Thomas! Just get me to Antigua, where I hope, no, *pray!* to receive word of my friend *Veal-noove*. Oh, the thought of returning to England empty-handed does not bear thinking about!"

"The nation will still love you, sir."

"Will it, Hardy? *Will* it? Oh, if I fail to find the enemy—oh, Hardy, pray *God* we receive word at Antigua!"

Raising the telescope to his good eye, the Admiral trained it on the dark sea, as though he could summon his nemesis from the waves themselves.

But it was empty, and even Lord Nelson could not know that the panicky Villeneuve had already received word of his pursuit and, against Napoleon Bonaparte's orders, was fleeing the Caribbean as fast as the wind could take him.

Miles away from Antigua, Sir Graham Falconer's fleet was also preparing to leave the Caribbean.

The convoy that he was taking back to England with him was—as it had been for a week—waiting at Barbados when H.M.S. *Triton* had finally arrived and dropped anchor there several hours after sunset. Now, the following morning, 130 merchant ships of every size, shape, and degree of seaworthiness were hastily preparing to get under way. From the massive 1200- and 800-ton Indiamen and three-masted ships down to the brigantines, barkentines, schooners, and sloops, the convoy made an impressive sight beneath a pale morning sky smeared with haze. Three smart and dashing frigates from Sir Graham's fleet of warships, commanded by equally smart and dashing young captains vying with each other to impress him with their prowess, cruised between the merchant ships like sheepdogs rounding up a flock, and towering protectively over the entire armada of fighting and merchant ships alike, her gunports open to catch every lazy bit of breeze, was the powerful flagship of Sir Graham himself, H.M.S *Triton*.

For some, the young flag-captain Colin Lord, the homesick men of the fleet, and the dark admiral himself, the several-hour stop at Barbados to pick up the convoy was far too long. Most of them had not seen their beloved Britain for years, and were impatient to gaze upon those misty shores once more.

Their course was already plotted. They would use the

westerlies, turning their prows northward, swinging in a long, gentle curve parallel to the North American coast, before crossing the Atlantic and going on to England. Sir Graham anticipated no trouble—though he, like most navy men, detested the laggardness of the merchant ships and the characteristic sloppiness and disregard for sailing efficiency that their captains were noted for.

Now, with most of the convoy safely clear of Barbados and a lieutenant waiting to carry his dispatches off the ship, Gray was still below, finishing up official business. He hated writing, and his penmanship—a long, sloping scrawl that looked like waves parading before a storm—reflected it. Indeed, he was the only one who could read it, but then, there was a reason that admirals were afforded a secretary and several clerks—to do the pen-pushing for them.

His secretary, Shoesmith, looked up, his eyes very pedantic behind his tiny spectacles. "Will that be all, sir?"

"No, one more memorandum, Shoesmith." Sir Graham had been walking back and forth, thinking on his feet, dictating his wishes aloud for the past two hours. Since arriving in Barbados last night, he'd dictated a letter of farewell to the governor of Barbados, settled a dispute between two of his captains, answered a request from a commander on Antigua for additional marine support, dispatched two frigates to investigate reports of French harassment of fisherman off one of the Leewards, declined an invitation to dine with the premier planter on Barbados, declined another to attend a ball given by a Lady Sarah Wanderley, responded to another flag officer's request for supporting warships, made a report to the Admiralty in London, ordered some flowering plants and a dozen roses to be brought aboard his flagship, and sent a polite note to Lady Catherine terminating their brief, but fiery affair.

An average day in his life as an admiral. Thank God he was going home for a while after two years of continuous Caribbean service.

He dictated one last memorandum giving final instructions to the senior captain he'd be leaving behind and dismissed the loyal Shoesmith. After seeing his dispatches delivered to the waiting lieutenant, he donned his coat and hat and, nursing a headache brought on by the series of mundane matters he'd had to spend his morning engaged in, went topside.

A blazing sun beat down upon him. The convoy was still filing out of the harbor to the tune of foc's'le chanteys and fiddles, the shouted commands of captains and lieutenants alike; capstans heaved and groaned, men sweated, anchors were catted, and crews waved to the people—boatloads of fruit merchants and prostitutes, lavishly dressed ladies and dapper gentlemen lined the shore.

Someone coughed, and the officers on the quarterdeck snapped to rigid attention at Gray's appearance.

"Sir!"

He found Colin near the helm, anxiously watching each ship make her laborious way out of the anchorage and into open sea. The young flag-captain looked up and touched his hat. "Any change in formation, sir?"

"No, Captain Lord," Gray responded, formally. "If we can keep this miserable lot in something of a rectangle, with our three frigates ahead, astern, and on the wings of it, I shall be most happy. A devilishly impossible wish, of course, but see what you can do."

"Aye, sir."

"Signal the frigates *Harleigh* and *Cricket* that I shall want them ahead and to windward of the weathermost column of the convoy, so they can quickly run down to wherever they may be needed. Damn this sun, it's hot!"

"And the little *Kestrel,* sir?"

"Eh?"

"The Pirate Queen's schooner. . . . I'm sorry. You

wouldn't know. She sent one of the Irish girls to me an hour ago and volunteered the ship for our use. *Kestrel* is to accompany us back to England. I—uh, already gave them a copy of the signal book."

"Surely, you're not serious."

Colin shrugged and looked at him patiently.

"Very well then. If they want to play navy, signal them to run up British colors. Whose idea was this, anyhow? I cannot, for the life of me, imagine Maeve allowing the crew of that little toy to assist *me* in any way."

"With all due respect, sir, then perhaps you should ask her. She and the two Irish girls are on the poop deck, er, watching you."

"Is that so, now?" Sir Graham grinned and drew himself up like a rooster thrown amidst a flock of hens. "And who's commanding the schooner?"

"Her lieutenant, sir. I tried to explain to my cousin that this is *not* how the navy operates, but . . ."

The admiral shook his head. Now that the paperwork was out of the way, his headache fading, and most of the convoy clear of the harbor, he could afford to feel obliging and tolerant. "No, it's not, but I will make an exception in the interest of . . . amusing her. Especially since she's a convalescent and quite unhappy about it. Advise that she-viper she left in command of the schooner to station herself just to windward of Captain Warner's *Harleigh,* where she might find a use for herself in acting as lookout. That ought to keep her out of trouble, harm's way, *and* my hair."

Colin nodded formally and kept his eye on Sir Graham, looking resplendent, capable, and yes, annoyed, as he watched a brigantine struggling to set her mainsail.

The admiral rolled his eyes and turned away from the sight. "I would like to see topsails up shortly, if you please."

"Aye, sir." Colin turned and stiffly barked out the order. "Topmen aloft!"

"Topmen aloft!" the first lieutenant repeated, through his speaking trumpet, and moments later, a swarm of men were leaping up the shrouds and streaming out along the yards. Gray, his hands behind his back, nodded in quiet approval as bright curves of sail came spilling down, arcing to the wind, thundering with eager power and anticipation.

Forward, the anchor cable was vertical and taut, the lieutenant there turning to signal to Captain Lord that the mighty ship was ready to show her heels to Barbados.

"They're watching you, sir."

"Really, now?" His face instantly brightening, the admiral turned aft to face the poop deck, swept off his fancy gold-laced hat, and saluted the Pirate Queen.

Beneath the awning, Her Majesty—wearing the admiral's long nightshirt and wrapped in a light blanket—sat in a chair flanked by two of her ladies-in-waiting, Aisling and Sorcha.

"The Admiral just saluted you, Majesty."

"He can go to hell."

"He's very nice, Majesty. Do you know what he did?"

"No, and I don't care."

"You should care, Majesty, after all, he *did* send that note over to *Kestrel* inviting us aboard to keep you company."

"How magnanimous of him."

"So, do you want to know what else he did?"

Maeve yanked her straw hat down so she could gaze at Sir Graham without his taking note of her perusal. But he had caught her stare, and even from this distance she could see his smile, the devilish glint in his eye. "No. And I don't *want* to know."

Obviously, Aisling was determined that she *would*

know, whether she wanted to or not. "He sent over a
shipment of pistols and gunpowder to Enolia and Orla.
And he gave me this—" She angled her head to the side
and showed her very annoyed captain the mermaid
charm that rested on a rope of serpentine gold around
her neck. "Isn't it pretty? He gave Sorcha one too.
Show the captain *yours,* Sorcha."

"Mine's a seahorse."

"Lovely," Maeve said, acidly.

"And he was worried about how few people we have
to crew *Kestrel,* so he had Captain Lord send over some
seamen under the command of a lieutenant with a front
tooth missing. Is he *really* your cousin, Majesty?! He's
so *handsome!*"

"Sorcha's in love with Captain Lord! I saw the looks
she was giving him!"

"And you're sweet on that toothless lieutenant, Aisling."

"Am not."

"Are too."

"Am not!"

"Are too!"

Sir Graham was grinning, looking her way.

"Stop it, both of you," Maeve said, irritably.

"I think you should be nicer to Sir Graham, Majesty," Aisling declared, and sat down on the deck beside Maeve's chair. "After all, he *did* give you these
roses."

"And that pretty dress."

"And that poem on your breakfast tray."

"I think he wrote it himself. He did, didn't he, Ash?"

"Oh, he must have. We should ask the flag-captain.
You should ask the flag-captain, Sorcha, since you're so
in love with him."

"Am not!"

"Are too!"

Maeve was getting a headache. "Leave Captain Lord alone; he's busy getting his ship under way."

"Sir Graham says we're going to England. El Perro Negro's going to go on trial there, but I'll bet Sir Graham hangs him all the same. At least I hope he does!"

Maeve said nothing, for she had plans of attending to the Spaniard's disposal herself.

'I've never been to England, have you, Majesty?"

"No. And I have no *desire* to go to England. If that bloody arrogant man wasn't forcing me to stay on this ship, I wouldn't have had to *volunteer Kestrel's* service. I'll be damned if I go *anywhere* without my crew."

Above, wind thundered in sails that waited impatiently to be sheeted home. Instinctively, Maeve glanced up at the mizzenmast, where a white flag emblazoned with a red cross streamed proudly in the wind. Aisling followed her gaze. "I've never seen so many flags in my life. What does *that* one mean, Majesty?"

"That an admiral is aboard this ship."

"Why's it white?"

"Because Sir Graham is an Admiral of the White."

"What's that mean?"

"The Royal Navy is divided into three squadrons, blue, red, and white. Don't ask me any more because I don't know and I don't *care* to know."

"So, you mean that when the admiral is aboard his personal flag goes up? What if he goes aboard another ship?"

"Aisling—"

"The English have flags for everything, don't they? And speaking of England, Majesty, why don't you want to go there? Just think, all those princes and kings and lords and ladies—"

"Because *he's* going to be there."

"He told us he's going to marry you. You'll be Lady Falconer! Doesn't that sound grand?"

"It sounds vile," Maeve muttered, and shut her eyes.

"But *why*, Majesty? Think of what a fairy-tale life that will be!"

"Playing host to a bunch of gossiping naval wives, attending stupid balls, dressing in restrictive clothes and watching my husband go off to sail the seas while *I'm* forced to stay home and breed babies is not my idea of a damned fairy tale! Now leave me alone, I've got a headache."

The girls giggled and turned back to stare at Sir Graham and the handsome young Captain Lord, their youthful chatter drifting in and out of Maeve's attention. From beneath the shadow of her hat, she watched the activities on the quarterdeck, saw the two officers striding back and forth in quiet conversation. In their fine blue-and-white uniforms and cocked hats, they looked tall, competent, and handsome, and despite herself, a thrill shot through her at the thought of the admiral, *her* admiral, being in command of all these ships and sailors—and *these* were just the ones she could see. Sir Graham also commanded a fleet of over forty battleships and frigates, most of which would remain here in the West Indies during his leave of absence. To think that their every movement, every action, was done in direct accordance to his orders, his wishes. . . .

Stop it, Maeve.

She put her hands over her eyes and bent her head.

"Majesty? Are you all right?"

"No," she murmured, and sagged forward, even as dizziness and darkness swept in and the Vision seized her. . . .

Guns crashing around and about them, ships fading in and out of the smoke, cannons booming, men dying, masts falling across shattered decks, into the sea, musketfire—open sea, run, run, run, get Nelson and bring him back!

"Maeve?"

Hurry, find Nelson and bring him back!

"Maeve!"

Confused and blinking, she opened her eyes and saw Barbados moving away from them, blue sea around them, and Sir Graham kneeling down before her, his hand on her wrist, his fingers beneath her jaw, his eyes dark, concerned, anxious, *afraid*. He was breathing hard, and Maeve guessed he had run all the way from the quarterdeck, where even now, her cousin had turned to watch them with stiff attention.

"Are you all right?!"

"I'm fine," she said, shakily. "Just ... a Dream."

"Get her some water," the admiral commanded, and the girls ran off to obey.

He tilted her head up and looked into her eyes. "What did you see, sweeting?"

Her eyes were huge and frightened. "Enough that I can tell you *not* to make this journey. A sea fight. Death, gunfire, the French fleet—"

"The French *fleet?*" The admiral laughed and waved his hand in dismissal. "Yes, yes, of course, dear. There's nothing to worry about."

"Gray, I'm *telling* you—"

"Dearest heart," he said patiently, "what you no doubt *saw* was Nelson finally catching up to Villenueve's fleet and drubbing the hell out of it. That's what *I* think. And you know what else I think? That you've been far too long out in this heat. I shall bring you down to the quarterdeck and set you beneath the shadow of the poop deck; 'tis much cooler there, and I can keep a better eye upon you."

"Gray, you *must* believe me!"

He paused and his face grew serious. "Maeve, I don't doubt that what you saw seemed real but I can't change our fleet's charted course, or Nelson's, based on a Vision. I'm sorry. I can only proceed as planned and hope that God will be with us."

An hour later, they were well clear of Barbados and

the fleet—130 merchantmen guarded by three frigates and the mighty ship-of-the-line H.M.S. *Triton*—was heading steadily north-northeastward, baking beneath a blazing sun, driving along under set stuns'ls, and happily oblivious to the fate that the Pirate Queen of the Caribbean had seen for them.

Chapter 21

Plan I—Plying the Enemy with Flowers and Gifts—was not working.

Plan II—Bringing Aboard the Enemy's Crew—seemed to be failing miserably.

It was time to put Plan III—Enticing the Enemy Out of Port—into action.

As soon as Barbados was well astern of them, the convoy herded into a barely manageable pack of lumbering vessels, Sir Graham left the deck to Captain Lord, went below, and summoned the two Irish sisters, Aisling and Sorcha, to his quarters. Turning on every ounce of his considerable charm, the suave, handsome admiral plied them with lemonade, cookies . . . and feigned despair.

"You're so nice to invite Sorcha and me aboard, Sir Graham!" piped young Aisling, happily munching a cookie. She, like her sister, was dressed in shirt and trousers, with a dirk at her waist and her hair scattered in a bright cloud about her shoulders. "We've never seen a mighty ship of the line get under way! Even Her Majesty was in awe, and it takes a *lot* to awe *her,* right, Sorcha?"

"Huh?"

Aisling kicked her sister under the table. Sorcha was gaping at Sir Graham in his handsome uniform, her eyes starstruck.

"I *said,* even Queen Maeve was in awe!"

"Oh, yes. . . ."

Sir Graham walked to the window, very aware of two worshipful pairs of young eyes on his back. He knew well how to make himself noticed; he knew well how to draw a lady's eye, and with this in mind—and despite the heat—he had purposely and cunningly exchanged his seagoing frock coat for his finest full-dress uniform. The dark blue coat was carefully brushed, with bright gold bars of lace at sleeve and lapel, more lace at collar, cuffs, and pockets, and the epaulets with the single star winking proudly from each shoulder; the waistcoat and breeches were snowy white, and a black cocked hat was framed with even more gold trim. Uniforms—especially full-dress ones usually reserved for formal occasions—were a sure bet for winning female hearts and with this in mind, the admiral turned just so, knowing that the sunlight would—*move a little more to starboard, Gray*—he heard one of the girls gasp—*yes, that's it*—touch upon the gold fringe of his epaulets with blinding brilliance. With a private, wicked smile, he struck a deliberate pose, relaxed yet commanding all at once; and then, affecting a great sigh, he stared out at the flagship's swirling wake, placed his hands on the sill, and murmured, "Queen Maeve. I fear that my efforts to soften her are failing miserably, ladies."

"Keep trying, Sir Graham. She'll come around."

"But how the devil am I to win her? You two must help me more," he mused, deliberately drawing them into his plans. "Tell me . . . what is her favorite meal?"

"New England fare. Boiled."

"With apple pie for dessert."

Sir Graham reached up to rub at his handsome jaw. "Apple pie. . . . Very well then, I shall see that my cook prepares some tonight."

"Do you want to know her favorite color, too?" Aisling prompted, slyly.

"By all means."

"Blue."

"Damn," he said, frowning, "and here I have been sending her *red* roses—"

"Roses don't come in blue, sir."

"Indeed, they do not. Dear me, that *does* present a dilemma . . . I shall have to see what can be done to make up for it."

"She likes sharks, too."

"And ale."

The admiral was still standing at the windows, the hilt of his sword barely showing above the fine scabbard of black leather at his left hip. He was resplendent, glittering, like a handsome, gallant prince, and the intended effect was not lost on the girls, who stared at him in awe, their eyes wide, the cookies temporarily forgotten.

His deep voice broke the spell. "So, what do you suggest I do, ladies?"

He stared out to sea, knowing very well what he would do. But he wanted to involve these two youngsters, win them over to his side. *Draw the enemy in. Drag them over to your camp, until their commander finds herself alone and unsupported . . . vulnerable.*

"Do? Um . . . I don't know. Sorcha, give me another cookie."

"Get it yourself!"

The admiral turned. "Perhaps if I invite her to dine with me tonight," he mused, tapping his chin in contemplation. He moved away from the windows, poured himself a glass of lemonade, dosed it with rum and allowed a pensive expression to steal over his face. "Tell me, ladies, has she had any . . . er, suitors, since this Frenchman she once loved?"

"A few," Aisling piped up, "but she didn't care for any of them. Said none of them were as fine and good as her papa, so she sent them packing."

"I see." He took a sip of his lemonade. "And what is her papa like?"

"We never met him, Sir Graham. Orla has, though. She said he was very gallant, right Sorcha?"

"And very handsome."

"Smart, too."

"Just like you, Admiral."

He heard the quick thump of a heel hitting flesh. "Ouch! That hurt, Ash!"

"You're not supposed to say things like that in front of a person, don't you have any tact?"

"More than *you!*"

Suppressing a grin, Sir Graham began a slow, thoughtful walk, back and forth in front of his windows. "Tell me, then," he said carefully, "more about what she thinks her father did to her."

"You mean, why she ran away from home?"

The admiral paused, angled his head, and bestowed upon them his most devastating grin. "Aye."

"But I don't think she'd like that, Sir Graham. . . ."

"Ladies," he said smoothly, and picked up a cookie, "do you want me to win the heart of Her Majesty or"—he took a bite—"do you want me to fail?"

"Oh no, Sir Graham!" they cried, in chorus. "We would like nothing more than to see you win her heart, and her to become Lady Falconer and live in fine, grand style—"

The admiral munched his cookie, loudly. Crumbs broke off and fell, speckling his jaw, his lips, his neckcloth, the front of his coat. He made no attempt to wipe them away. Instead, he took another bite, his absurdly long lashes sweeping down to mask the expression in his eyes, apparently unaware of the total mess he was making of his fine appearance. The girls giggled and exchanged swift glances, thinking him amazingly boyish, youthful, endearing . . . one of them.

A partner in crime.

He reached for another cookie. "Very well, then. I shall ask her myself. Perhaps over dinner."

"Oh, yes, Sir Graham! You must ask her to dine with you!"

He turned, clasped his hands behind his back, and gazed out the windows, hiding his grin. "And," he mused, "what do you two ladies think I should wear for such a . . . *formal* occasion?"

Again, he knew very well what he would wear, to tempt the heart of this distrustful Queen who pined for a fine and gallant officer. . . .

"Oh, Sir Graham, you *must* wear that uniform you're in now!"

"Aye, Her Majesty won't be able to take her eyes off you!"

He turned, and put his arm out in front of him, pretending to examine the handsome laced bars at his cuff. "Really, now? You don't think all this splendor is a bit . . . much?"

"Oh, no. Not at all. Her Majesty has always adored men in uniforms. She loves sea officers, you know."

He frowned.

"But don't worry, she didn't fall in love with any of them, and she loves *you,* Admiral! She just won't admit it to herself because she's too mad at you for deceiving her. But her temper'll blow itself out, you just watch!"

He smiled faintly, looking at his sleeve and pretending to be engrossed in studying the fine lace. "Next," he murmured, evasively, "you'll be suggesting I wear my Order of the Bath. . . ."

"That's right! You're a *real* knight, aren't you?!"

"Of course he's a knight, you idiot!" Aisling chided. "Why do you think he's called *Sir* Graham?"

The admiral executed a courtly, elegant bow that elicited excited squeals from both girls. "Yes, ladies, I *am* a knight. The king bestowed the Order on me following my actions at the Nile." He gave them a secretive, wicked look from beneath his long lashes. "Surely, now, you'll not suggest that I don my Order, too?"

"You mean you have it *with* you?"

"Oh, Admiral, yes, I think you should *definitely* wear your Order!" Aisling cried.

"Well, I—"

"Please, Sir Graham?"

"Pleeease?!"

He shrugged, the deliberately dropped hint succeeding as he knew it would. "Very well then. I will wear it . . . if you think it will do any good."

"Where is it?"

"In my wardrobe," he said, pretending indifference.

The two scurried to his wardrobe, oohing and aahing over each glittering uniform, each snowy-white shirt, until they found what they were looking for.

"Oh, my! Sorcha, look at this!" Reverently, Aisling lifted it out, and carried the Order and its red sash across the cabin as though they were the Crown Jewels. Gray bowed his head, and Aisling carefully slipped the broad scarlet sash over his right shoulder, watching Sorcha from beneath his long lashes as she reached out to touch the elaborate, star-shaped badge that was the Order itself.

"You look grand," she whispered, her eyes huge. "Her Majesty will be completely undone."

"You think so, now?" He turned his head, looked at the brilliant red sash that made such a resplendent contrast against the gold bullion of his epaulets, the dark navy blue of his coat. "I'm nearly at my wits' end, trying to devise a way to win your captain's heart . . ."

"Well, first let us make you presentable."

"Eh?"

"Cookie crumbs, Sir Graham," Sorcha said, blushing and giggling.

"Yes, yes. Of course." He raised his chin, allowing the girls to brush the crumbs from his neckcloth, then stood back to survey himself in the mirror. He straightened his neckcloth, touched his clean-shaven jaw. His men were going to think he'd completely lost his mind. Such a full rig was reserved for the most formal of occasions, interviews with high-ranking superiors, and audiences with royalty.

Royalty.

A twisted smile curved his mouth, and the dimple appeared in his chin.

"You look grand, Sir Graham," Aisling said, clasping her hands in front of her.

He turned, and bestowed upon them his most winning smile. "Grand enough to pay court to the Pirate Queen of the Caribbean?"

"Grand enough to *marry* her, Sir Graham! Now, let's get you on deck so she can see you."

He had gone. Thank God.

The effort of keeping Sir Graham at bay—and her heart protectively locked up—was growing too wearisome for one who fought Spanish pirates, Death, and the admiral's affections all in the space of a few short days. Maeve pulled off the straw hat, closed her eyes, leaned her head back against the chair, and felt the smooth, easy movements of the mighty warship beneath her, a warship that dwarfed her own tiny *Kestrel* many times over, a warship that was a floating battery of firepower and majesty and brutal, smashing force. The gentle winds tickled the thick hair lying against her damp neck; sunlight bounced off the sea, warming the backs of her eyelids, creating dancing patterns of stars and speckles, warming the side of her cheek as her head lolled to one side.

Maeve drifted, drowsing and healing and dreaming ... of her father ... of Gray the pirate....

Of Sir Graham the admiral.

A shadow fell across her, and she opened her eyes, blinking.

It was he.

"Go away," she murmured.

He knelt down, and put a flower under her nose. She turned away. He tickled her under the chin with it. She wanted to swear at him. "Stop it."

"Will you accept it?"

"No."

"Please?"

"No."

"Majesty . . . it's just a poor, innocent flower. To think that its very existence, its very life, was ordained so that it could be presented to you . . . that its very life was cut short so that it could bring a smile of delight to your lovely lips—and now, you don't want it." He put his hand to his heart and affected a hurt look. "Dear God, if I were that flower I would be sorely crushed, and go to my death drowning in tears of bitterness and rejection and hurt and *abandonment—*"

"Oh, give me the blasted thing!" she cried, and snatching it away from him, held it protectively against her breast.

Sir Graham smiled, his eyes twinkling.

"Why do you torment me so?" she muttered, looking away.

But he noticed that she clutched the stem of the rose as though it were a lifeline.

"Because I love you."

"I don't *want* you to love me."

"I cannot help my feelings, Maeve."

She moved her head and looked at him. Her eyes widened as she noticed his resplendent attire, then narrowed in suspicion. Sparks ignited the catlike golden depths and she met his eyes. "So, why the glittering uniform, Admiral? Expecting somebody *important?*"

"Very."

She made a sound of derision.

"Actually," he said, squatting down so that he was on her level, "I've come to ask you to dine with me. Is that an unreasonable request?"

"Yes."

"Very well, then. Consider it an order."

"Order refused."

"Oh, Maeve. You hurt my feelings, truly you do."

"And you annoy *mine*," she said, trying not to look at him, for he was far too handsome, too *dangerously handsome*. A man of contrasts, he was dark hair and swarthy skin against white grin and snowy small-clothes; he was all that represented good in the resplendent uniform and all that represented wickedness in the gleam of his eye and the piratical earring. Damn him! Was this another calculated attempt to win her over?

Gray saw her indecision, the anger fading, and pressed his advantage. "I confess that I've been interrogating your crew. I managed to learn what your favorite dish is. Really, Maeve, my poor cook went to such pains to prepare it for you."

She set her jaw.

"Surely, you cannot keep up this pretense of anger forever, can you? My hull is tough enough to handle your wrath, but my poor cook . . . think of *his* feelings, Maeve."

She shut her eyes. *"Why do you do this to me?"*

"Because I love you."

He saw her throat moving, a muscle tensing in her jaw. "But I am . . . unlovable."

"I love you," he repeated, firmly.

Her fingers tightened around the stem of the rose. She bent her head ad clutched the blossom to her breast, as though it was the only thing she dared to trust.

Sir Graham reached out and gently, lovingly, tipped her chin back up. Her eyes were miserable, her face wretched with pain. A tendril of hair had come loose from her braid; he cleared it off her cheek, and tenderly smoothed the soft skin with his thumb. "Will you dine with me, Maeve?" He smiled gently. "It would make me very happy."

Her nod was barely perceptible, a mere jerk of her head before she turned her face away, unwilling to let him see how much his kindness was affecting her. He scooped her up. And then, her bare feet dangling, her hot, weak body wrapped safely in his arms, the Gallant Knight carried her belowdecks and into his cabin.

Chapter 22

⌒◯◯⌒

Sir Graham strode toward the spacious, grand cabins that were his floating headquarters, nodded to the rigid-backed sentry posted just outside (who still managed to keep his eyes straight ahead), kicked the door shut behind him, and carried the Pirate Queen aft into his day cabin.

"My lady," he said, and belatedly Maeve realized her arms had been locked in a death grip around his neck. Embarrassed, angry with herself for this small victory she'd allowed him, she let go, and, with a charming grin, he gently, carefully, lowered her into a chair of polished mahogany.

It was then that she saw the table, all set and ready for a meal.

The tablecloth was blue. The napkins were blue. The lovely porcelain plate in front of her was an Oriental design of white and blue. The flowers that made up the centerpiece were purplish blue, the vase they reposed in—blue.

Sir Graham grinned at her, and she saw a devilish, wicked gleam in his blue eyes before his long lashes swept down to hide it. "You are pleased, Majesty?"

"What the hell is all this . . . *blue?*"

"The Irish sisters told me it is your favorite color before I sent them back to *Kestrel,* which, as you'll see if you glance out those windows yonder, is keeping station just off to windward."

247

She bit her lip, trying not to respond to the earnest look in his eye, the eagerness in his teasing grin. *Don't let him know that he's gotten inside your defenses,* she thought, and looked down at her hands, clenched tightly in her lap, so that he wouldn't see the fleeting smile she was helpless to prevent. "You ... try too hard," she said finally.

"Am I succeeding?" He picked her up, chair and all, and set her closer to the table.

Maeve grabbed the table's edge to steady herself. Then she looked away as he strode around the table to take his own seat. Her eyes hopeless, she stared out the huge, sweeping windows at the broad expanse of the sea.

It was blue.

"Am I, dearest? Pray, tell me that I am and I shall be the happiest man alive."

Color swept over her face, ripe, frustrated, hot. She looked down, wishing he would stop this relentless pursuit, yet praying that he would not, wishing she could only dare to open up, to believe in him, to *trust* him. It was getting too blasted hard to fight him, to fight *herself.*

"Maybe ... maybe just a little," she allowed, her tone defensive, angry.

"Ah, splendid! I daresay, there is hope for me yet! Shall we eat, then?"

She shrugged, glanced at him for the briefest of instances, and then back out the window. She could just see *Kestrel,* driving along with a stiff breeze filling her fore and main, her lee rail buried in washy foam.

The admiral seated himself across from her and, as though by magic, two servants hustled in, carrying steaming platters and covered dishes. The service was finest silver, the wine goblets of crystal, and it occurred to her that he must be a terribly wealthy man—or, in debt up to his epaulets. She glanced up at him. He was watching her, as fixedly as a wolf that has cornered its prey and waited for the final kill.

"Comfortable, dearest?"

"Quite," she muttered, and looked away.

He lifted the cover from a dish and said smoothly, "I am holding a conference in my cabin tonight with my officers and the captains of my frigates. You are, of course, invited to join us."

"*Why?*" she asked, guardedly.

He looked up, smiling patiently. "Because I consider you to be one of my captains, too. Especially as I have commandeered your little *Kestrel* and employed her in scout duty."

"I am not in your navy," she declared, rising.

"No matter. Your ship is, at the moment. Sit down."

"Does everything you say have to be an *order?*"

"No. Consider it an invitation, if you wish."

She set her jaw, suddenly regretting her offer to let him use *Kestrel.* So much for her own ploy to keep her crew out of trouble and her ship close by.

The servants set the last platter down on the table and quickly left. An uncomfortable silence ensued. Maeve glanced out the window at *Kestrel;* she glanced at the bulkhead beyond Sir Graham, and found herself looking into the savagely grinning countenance of Sir Henry Morgan, Pirate King; she looked down at her plate, back up, and her gaze collided with the admiral's.

His eyes gleaming, he lifted the cover from a dish. "Some chicken, my dear?"

Without waiting for an answer, he reached across the table, picked up her plate, and piled several tender slabs of choice white meat on her plate.

"I'm sorry," he said. "Do you prefer white meat or dark?"

"White."

He nodded in self-satisfaction and plucked the cover off another dish. "Some potatoes?" He spooned some onto her plate, then uncovered another dish. "Turnips? Ah, what have we here . . . carrots. Will you have some, dearest?"

"Please."

"And what is this—ah, cornbread!"

Maeve's head jerked up. "Cornbread?"

"Yes. I thought it suitably . . . New Englandish." Again, that swift, disarming grin, that wicked sparkle of challenge and amusement in his eyes. "I thought you'd find it . . . agreeable."

She stared down at her plate as he set it before her. Steam wafted up, tickling her nose and moistening her cheeks. The food, so carefully arranged on her plate by Sir Graham himself, blurred, wavered, rippled.

Cornbread.

Like home. . . .

She picked up her fork, felt pressure on her wrist, and looked down to see his tanned fingers resting lightly atop her hand.

"Maeve?" he said, tenderly.

She jerked her hand away. "You did this on purpose!" she accused, hotly.

"Did what?"

"Had this meal made up so it would remind me of home. You . . . you *knew.*"

"I would be a liar to claim otherwise," he said softly, and reached across the table to take her hand once more. This time she did not jerk away. He tried to draw her hand to his lips, but the distance between them was too great; and so he stood, tall, resplendent and handsome, and leaning over her hand, bestowed a single, loving kiss atop her knuckles.

Maeve shuddered, and bit her lip to keep it from trembling. And then the admiral slowly released her hand, regained his seat, and sat gazing at her from across the table, across the steaming plates, across the tray of yellow cornbread.

She didn't like the way he was looking at her. Assessing her. Gauging his success, looking for a chink in her armor. He gazed at her for a long time and she stared back at him, her own eyes challenging, angry.

And then he made a fierce face at her, took up his knife as though it was a pirate's dagger, and baring his teeth in a manner meant to be threatening, growled, "Aaaaargh! Eat yer dinner, matey, before I carve out yer liver and feed it to the sharks."

She stared at him, her jaw falling open.

He stared back, the corners of his mouth twitching, his face deceptively little-boy innocent. "What?"

"You're . . . deranged," she murmured.

"No, merely hungry. For you. Hurry up and get better so we can make savage, uninhibited love."

Maeve couldn't help it. She laughed, a coarse, full, hooting guffaw that she quelled with a palm slammed quickly across her mouth.

The admiral laughed with her.

She looked up and their gazes met. Swift color flooded her cheeks. And then the servant was back, handing a bottle to the admiral, and something was gurgling in her mug, something fizzing and dark, and brown. Ale. She watched it foaming up to the rim, her gaze traveling up the admiral's fine hand as he poured, past his decorated sleeve, up his arm to his shoulder, his stand-up collar, his earring—his face.

He was looking at her. Grinning.

The beer foamed over the top of the mug and with a start, he jerked back.

"Dear me, look what I've done! Majesty, I swear, you have me consistently backing my topsails."

She laughed again, for he really did look quite ridiculous, all a-splendor in that magnificent uniform with the red sash of knighthood across his shoulder, the table laid as though for a nobleman's dinner, everything perfect and splendid—

—and ale moving across the tablecloth in a rapidly spreading stain.

She plucked her napkin from her lap and began to sop it up.

"Oh, no, allow me."

"I can do it."

"Yes, but *I* spilled it."

"No, really—"

His hand closed over hers, warm and strong. "Maeve."

He left it there for a moment longer than necessary, then let her go. She grabbed her fork and began nervously to push her food around on her plate.

The admiral didn't move. "You're very beautiful, you know."

She pushed the food faster.

"I've always loved red hair. It indicates a woman of fire and spirit. I wonder if you might allow me to brush it out for you, later?"

"I don't think so."

"Why not?"

"Because I don't want you to."

"That's not a very good reason." He buttered a piece of cornbread. "Give me a better one."

"It's good enough for me."

"But not for *me,* and I'm admiral here."

"I don't give a damn if you're an admiral or King George, you're *not* touching my hair again."

He smiled at her, took a bite of his cornbread, chewed, swallowed, and dabbed with gentlemanly grace at his lips. Then he carefully folded his napkin, put it beside his plate, rested both elbows on the table, and leaned toward her, looming, powerful, threatening, heart-devastatingly handsome. "Maeve."

She drew back, away from him.

"I will not hurt you. Ever again. I will never give you reason not to trust me, ever again. What must I do

to win you back to me, dearest? What must I do to re-
gain that magical love we so briefly shared, to win your
hand in marriage?"

She flung her fork down and leapt to her feet, jerking
her hand out of his grasp. "There is nothing you can
do, do you hear me? *Nothing!* My heart is my own, *has*
been my own for seven years, and shall be my own for
the rest of my life! You don't understand that, do you?
And as for marriage—hah! You fantasize about making
love to a pirate queen but did you every stop to consider the consequences of *marrying* one?! That's just
what your king needs, to have the wife of one of his admirals sailing the Spanish Main as a modern-day Anne
Bonney! Never stopped to think about how *that* would
go over, did you?" Her voice turned bitter. "Just as *I*
never thought about how utterly whimsical *my* fantasy
was of marrying an *officer."*

"As my wife you would no longer *need* to be a pirate."

"Do not think I will ever give up the sea, Gray!
Don't think it *for a damned minute!* I worked too
damned hard for all that I am, to give it up for you or
any man! And I've learned my lesson, the hard way,
about *trust!"*

He put down his fork. "But Maeve, I am different—"

"You, *different?!* You, the worst of the lot. The notorious Admiral Falconer! Ha, you think you can have
any woman you want but I tell you, you shall not have
me, not now, not tomorrow, not ever again! You ask me
to trust you! Why the bloody hell *should* I? Do you
think I was born yesterday? Do you think I haven't
heard the stories about you, and your string of para-
mours stretching from Jamaica to Tobago? Your *doings*
are a shame to your navy! How poor Nelson must blush
for you!"

She expected anger, fury, a reaction. What she got

was just one of his wicked, dimpled smiles and a thoughtful tugging at his chin.

"Well ..." he murmured, on an expulsion of breath.

"Is that all you have to say? *Well?!*"

"What would you wish me to say? To deny my reputation would make me a liar. I will not lie to you. I have ... sampled the charms of many women. But!"—he raised his hand, staying her angry words— "that only makes me all the more sure I have found the one I want to marry. I never realized what it meant to *love* a woman until I met you. Yes, there have been many women in my life, but none of them were the woman of my dreams."

"And neither am I." Maeve rose to her feet. "I'm merely your *fantasy,* nothing more!"

"Oh, you're more than that, Maeve," he countered smoothly.

She stood frozen, her hands gripping the back of her chair, her eyes blazing with anger and defiance. But he merely picked up his fork and knife again and began to eat. "To begin with, you're a piratess. In case you haven't noticed, I have a certain fondness for pirates."

"I wouldn't have *guessed,"* she said acidly.

"Secondly"—he pushed a small mound of carrots onto his fork—"I happen to admire you. For your spirit, your courage, your seafaring ability, and ... your tenderness. For the reputation you've managed to carve out here in the West Indies, which, I'm delighted to discover, has no bearing in truth at all."

"My *reputation?"*

"Aye." He lifted the fork to his mouth, chewed, wiped his lips. "Do you think I would've waited so long to find you had I known you were anything *but* the sour-toothed, wretched old hag of questionable sexual preferences that legend had it you were?"

"What?!"

"So you see," he said, mildly, and raised his glass to her, "one cannot always place stock in a *reputation.*"

Stunned, she sat back down in her chair, her fingers clutching her napkin. Sour-toothed hag? Questionable sexual preferences?! "What about *your* reputation, then? Are you saying that yours is false, too?"

"On the contrary." He looked up and gave her his wicked, charming grin. "I'm every bit the blackhearted rake you've heard that I am. I eat ladies' hearts for supper and spit them out in the morning. More cornbread, my dear?"

"No!"

"Very well, then. Where was I? Ah yes, your attributes. Number one, you're a pirate queen. Number two, you're fiery and spirited and a true seafarer. Number three, you're dangerous and beautiful, in a savage, exciting sort of way. Number four, you are leading me as merry a chase as Villeneuve is Nelson. Number five, and most importantly, I find myself in love with you. My most demanding task, at the moment, is making you see the truth of that."

"I see nothing but clever manipulations enacted by a master manipulator!"

Very softly, he asked, "Do you love *me,* Maeve?"

His unexpected and sudden switch from blithe insouciance to studied focus caught her off guard. She sat there, her mouth slack, the napkin growing warm in her hands and now, twisted into a ball in her lap. "I—"

He smiled, gently. "Do you?"

She raised her chin and looked him straight in the eye. "There is a difference, Sir Graham, between love and *trust.*"

"Do you love me then, Maeve?" he repeated, softly.

"I . . . I don't know what I feel for you." She picked up her napkin and slammed it down on the table, rising to her feet at the same time and thinking only of escape before she could admit something she'd later regret.

"But it doesn't matter, because I don't *trust* you and never will! You deceived me, Gray, you made me look foolish in front of my crew, you made me the laughing-stock of your navy and God knows who else, you made me feel like an idiot for falling for your stupid story about being a *traitor,* and now you expect me to trust you?"

"Do you love me, Maeve?"

She turned away, clenching her fists at her sides.

"Do you?"

Whirling, she yelled, *"Yes, damn you!"*

"There now. That wasn't so hard to admit. Now that we have *that* cleared up, please sit down and finish your dinner."

She stared at him, amazed, appalled, shocked. He was eating, just as calmly as before, looking down at his plate with those ridiculously long black lashes veiling his eyes, lying against his cheeks. He glanced up, stopped chewing for a moment, glanced pointedly at her chair, her plate, and inclined his head to indicate that she should sit down.

Maeve sat. Or rather, fell into the chair. Now that she'd said it, admitted it, she felt foolish, ridiculous—conquered. It was not a comfortable feeling, and she shot back to her feet, feeling trapped and humiliated.

"Sit down."

"Stop telling me what to do, I hate it!"

"Sit down."

She sat glaring at him, wanting to bolt.

He glanced up, grinning. "I *am* your Gallant Knight, you know."

She looked away, her mouth severe and hard, her hands fisted in her lap.

"Your heart has been sorely wounded, Maeve." She heard the scrape of his chair as he pushed it back and came around the table toward her. She felt his presence behind her, felt his hands touching her hair, then resting lightly upon her shoulders. It was a gentle touch, a possessive, protective one, and beneath the weight of it she melted inside. His thumbs grazed her nape, eliciting an involuntary shudder; his breath was warm against the crown of her head as he leaned down and kissed her temple.

"I love you, Maeve."

She clenched her hands together fiercely, her nails biting into her palms.

"I love you so much I would give my life for you."

Her fists buried themselves in the folds of the blanket, and the nightshirt just beneath.

"I love you so much I would marry you tonight, if I could. But I shall wait, because I would have your father's consent on the union."

"My father," she snarled bitterly, "has washed his hands of me. Disowned me. Forsaken me as his daughter. *Abandoned* me."

"Your father," he responded, his voice deep and soft just above her head, "has, for the past seven years, believed you to be dead."

Gray, standing above her, felt every muscle in her body go rigid.

"D-dead?" Slowly, she twisted around in the chair to face him, all chalky face and chestnut hair and a lost-child look that drove a fierce urge to protect her, to shield her, into his heart. "What do you mean, he thinks I'm . . . dead?"

"Your cousin Colin realized who you were the day you burst into Lord Nelson's cabin the first time," he said softly. "He told Nelson, and Nelson told me, and now, I'm telling you." He gazed deeply into her eyes, and stroked her cheek. "Your father did not abandon you, dearest. He thinks you are dead."

"You lie!"

"No, Maeve. I do not."

She went very, very still. Her eyes fell shut, and her body began to tremble violently. "Oh . . . my God. . . ."

He said nothing, merely stood beside her, being there for her, at this moment of horrendous discovery.

"You mean . . . you mean, all these years I've thought he'd disowned me, when all the time he thought I was *dead?*" She looked up, stunned, her face frighteningly pale. "But why? *Why?* Why would he think that?"

"According to Colin, your father went after you as soon as he discovered you had run away from home, Maeve. He got as far as Florida, where he was told by some Bahamian fishermen, and then, the captain of a French merchantman, that a topsail schooner had wrecked on the reefs on one of the Keys." He took her hand. "The schooner answered *Kestrel's* description, Maeve."

"And he *believed* that?!"

"Apparently not. He searched for weeks for you. And returned home brokenhearted. I am not a father, but I can well imagine his grief, and his denial of the fact, that his headstrong young daughter had met her end because of a silly argument over what he, in his love, thought was best for her. Perhaps he went on denying her death—but since he never heard from her, ever again, he must've had no choice but to accept the apparent truth. How awful it must've been for him, and your family, to bear."

"Oh, my God," Maeve whispered. "Oh, my *God.* . . . To think that all these years . . . to think I believed the worst of him—I—" She put her head in her hands, then shot to her feet and stumbled dazedly to the windows. "I'm so *ashamed.* . . ."

He moved behind her, turned her to face him, and pulled her against him, holding her safely against his chest and resting his cheek on her hair. Her braid hung down her back and he let his hand smooth the ropy length.

"To think that he, too, probably watched the shore every day in the futile hope that *I* would return, to think he probably stood on the beach every single night, every *awful, single night,* staring at the horizon and wishing he could turn back the clock and change things. Oh, God"—she felt him hugging her close, and didn't pull away—"Oh, *God,* what am I to do. . . ."

"You'll do, dearest, what your heart tells you to do."

"But it's been seven years, Gray, *seven bloody YEARS!*"

"In the scope of eternity, that is but the blink of an eye."

"I know, but I'm—I'm so *ashamed!*"

He held her protectively against his heart. "Whatever you do, Maeve, I love you, I will stand beside you, I swear to God that I *will not abandon you,* do you hear me? I will not aban—"

A musket thumped outside, angry voices sounded, and the door opened just enough to admit Colin Lord's fair head. His face was crimson with embarrassment, his eyes anxious. "Admiral, sir, forgive me, but there's a lady here to see you. I told her that you would not wish to—"

"Pooh on what you told me, Captain-dear," came a feminine voice, and the woman shoved past both Colin and the marine sentry and strode brazenly into the cabin. She stopped, her lip curling with contempt at the sight of the admiral and the chestnut-haired girl who'd gone stiff in his arms. Maeve stared back. The woman's lips were awfully red. Her face, awfully fair. And then she gave a slow, sultry smile and driving her hand into her pinned-up hair, sent it tumbling down her back in a sleek fall of liquid ebony.

"Well, well, Sir Graham," she said, her voice a study in practiced, husky sexuality. "I see you've found yourself another *trollop* with whom to amuse yourself. What, weren't my attractions *hot* enough for you?"

Maeve stared, in shock, in horror, in devastating dismay. She turned, speechless, and looked up into Gray's face.

But the admiral had turned a ghastly white, and beads of sweat were dappling his forehead. He did not look well. He did not look well at all.

The woman smiled. "Surprise, surprise . . . *Gray*. I see you're just eating dinner. Mind if I join you?"

"Cat," he said shakily, and raked a hand through his dark hair. "I th-thought you were . . . on Barbados."

Chapter 23

"**B**arbados?" The woman strode forward, plucked Gray's mug from the table, sipped from it, and put it down. "Oh, darling, you of *all* people should know how positively *bored* I am with the tropics, and it's been *so* many years since I've sampled the delights of London. I thought I would take passage on one of the merchantmen that Papa's sending home with your convoy. 'Twas an easy matter to just have a boat bring me across. After all, I'm still waiting for a dangerous pirate to whisk me off in the middle of the night. Oh, don't look so shocked, Gray! Did you really think I'd let you sail back to England without me?"

The admiral made a choking noise and motioned for Colin and the sentry to leave.

Maeve had gone numb with shock. For a brief, hollow moment she was unable to feel anything; then, like a savage blow the pain slammed into her gut, her soul, into every cell in her body, stealing her breath away, caving the ribs in on her heart, and causing bitter, ugly bile to fill her throat.

She thrust herself out of his arms and stared up into his ashen face. "Gray—who is this *female?*"

"L-L . . . Lady Catherine Fairfield," he managed, his eyes confused, stunned. He looked lost, and, for the first time since she'd known him, a prisoner of a situation rather than master of it.

So, this was the mistress on Barbados.

"Look, Maeve, I know what you're thinking, but this is not what it seems—"

"Indeed, Gray," the woman said silkily, with a pointed, insulting glance at Maeve, "I should hope it *isn't.* And who is this . . . chit? Your latest *toy?"*

"She's no *chit,* Catherine, she's to be my wi—"

Maeve jerked free of his grasp, drew the blanket about her as though it was a monarch's robe, and glared at the other woman. "I am Captain Merrick, Pirate Queen of the Caribbean, and if you do not watch your tongue, I'll make you pay for your insolence with *blood."*

Lady Catherine smiled. "How charming. Your newest kitten has claws, Gray."

"Really, Catherine, this is not the time or place for this—this *discussion—"*

"What, would you prefer to have it in more *pleasurable* surroundings, my handsome admiral? I seem to recall you have a penchant for creative positioning within the confines of such unlikely surfaces as tables, hammocks, and overstuffed chairs. I'm sure something can be *arranged."* She turned disdaining eyes on Maeve. "Pirate Queen, eh? Fancy that. From the stories I've heard about you, I would've thought you were much . . . older."

"As you so obviously are?" Maeve asked softly, and saw her barb hit home. The woman colored with rage, but Maeve—trying in vain not to explode in rising fury, trying desperately to play the *queen* and not the *pirate*—merely lifted her chin and with suitable hauteur, drawled, "Forgive me, but I'd forgotten what the tropical sun can do to a lady's face. Yours, I'm afraid, seems to have suffered the worst for it."

"Why, you vicious, coarse little *bitch!"*

Maeve turned, ignoring her. "Excuse me, Sir Graham. I have affairs to attend to on deck, if you don't mind. Please, do not let me keep you from your business with this . . . commoner."

"How dare you insult me so, you brazen little hussy!"

Maeve strode up to the other woman, paused in front of her and stared at her for a long, tense moment. Then, fast as lightning, she raised her hand as if to slap her face. The *lady* flinched. Maeve laughed in satisfaction and lowered her hand.

And with that, she walked to the door, stiff-backed and proud, fiery and beautiful and every inch the Pirate Queen of the Caribbean. She heard the admiral's sharp intake of breath, the angry exchange between him and that—that *woman*, felt the hem of the nightshirt brushing her calves with every step she took, and fought the darkness that threatened to bring her down as she walked across a deck that was suddenly like ice beneath her feet.

Keep walking.

"Maeve!" he shouted, from just behind her.

She clamped her jaws together, hard, so she could not give in to the fierce urge to turn and scream out her anguish at this man who had deceived and betrayed her yet again, for so-help-her-God, the last time, the *very last time*. He did not love her. He never had. He only wanted her because she was a piratess, a *toy,* as his pretty slut had called her. Part of the fantasy, another piratical item to add to his collection.

She pushed open the door.

"Maeve."

Finally she turned and faced him, chin high, mouth white with fury, eyes glittering. She did not know what to expect when she looked into his face, but it was not the utter terror and desperation she found there. "Aye, Sir Graham?" she said, her voice dangerously calm.

"Don't—don't go." His eyes were imploring, begging her to understand. *"Please."*

She gave a soft, serene, totally sweet smile that nearly cracked her face and her composure along with it. Out of the corner of her eye she saw Lady Catherine's swift grin of triumph, for now she would have the admiral all to herself.

"Really, Gray," Maeve said, gripping the door latch so hard it nearly broke off in her hand. Pain radiated up her wrist, her arm, with the force it took to retain her composure, and she moved her body in front of the door so neither could see how white her knuckles must surely be. "Where indeed would I go? Your ship may be huge, but it is, after all, finite. Please"—she gave an imperious wave of her hand—"carry on with your little doxy. When you have put her back in proper temper you will find me topside, where you may attempt to do the same with *me.*"

He moved forward, as though to stop her, as though he didn't quite trust her; he stole a swift glance at the sultry Lady Catherine; then he sighed heavily, swore beneath his breath, and raked his hair back, the movement causing the late-afternoon sun to burst in brilliant shards of light against the golden tassels of his epaulets.

But suddenly they didn't look so grand anymore, and neither did that splendid uniform his shoulders filled so magnificently.

Head high, Maeve strode out the door . . . past the marine . . . through the passageway, up the hatch, and out onto the broad quarterdeck. Beyond the nettings, she saw the convoy moving along under clouds of sail. Colin Lord was gazing off to larboard, a telescope to his eye, his fair hair standing out from beneath his cocked hat in the wind; a lieutenant touched his elbow and the flag-captain spun around as she passed, staring at her first with shock, then alarm.

"Good afternoon, *cousin,*" Maeve purred, and strode purposefully past him and up the steep ladder to the poop deck. Her strength rapidly failing her, she moved across and up its long, empty expanse, focusing on the beckoning trio of high, mounted stern lanterns and the wispy clouds that framed them, and didn't stop until she reached the flag locker and the taffrail, where there was nothing beyond her but blue sky, the broad, glorious expanse of the sea—

—and *Kestrel.*

"Maeve!" her cousin shouted. *"Stop her!"*

The Pirate Queen threw off the blanket, climbed up onto the taffrail, and swayed there for a brief moment, the wind whipping the admiral's nightshirt around her body, tearing strands of hair from her braid; then she took a deep breath and threw herself outward, the wind screaming in her ears now, shrieking, the sea coming faster, faster, faster, to swallow her up with a horrific, bone-slamming crash that burst every stitch in her bandaged side and left her stunned and senseless in the water. She lay there for a moment, dazed, the waves breaking over her head, her body beginning to sink down, down, down . . . then she heard the cries of alarm from the flagship's decks some two stories above, the desperate shrieks of the bosun's calls, and was roused by the thought of pursuit.

With the last of her strength, Maeve raised her arm to summon *Kestrel,* but it was a wasted motion, for already the little schooner was changing tack and sweeping in to rescue her drowning captain.

Chapter 24

"**P**repare to heave to, Mr. Pearson!" Racing to the side, a horrified Captain Colin Lord watched the lone figure floundering in the waves, the schooner sweeping in to her rescue. "Brail up courses, t'gallants and royals, and back the main tops'l! Lively now, for God's sake!"

Pipes shrilled, sailors ran to their stations, the helm was put down, and the mammoth *Triton* swung into the wind with a protest of shaking rigging and groaning timbers just as Sir Graham came pounding up the hatch to the quarterdeck. His young flag-lieutenant, John Stern, caught his arm, and ran with him toward the nettings, gesturing madly. "There, sir! Just to starboard!"

Gray reached the side in time to see Maeve being pulled out of the sea by her crew. His eyes widened and he stared forward, his mouth opening with disbelief. She'd jumped. The fool girl had *actually jumped*—

Paralyzed with shock, he gripped the shrouds and watched her climbing up the schooner's side, his now-transparent nightshirt clinging wetly to her body, her hair a dark rope streaming down her back—and a stain of crimson blossoming just above her hip with alarming speed.

"Bloody hell, she's *bleeding!*" he roared, the sight shocking him into action. He spun around, nearly colliding with his flag-captain, his flag-lieutenant, the first lieutenant, and a little midshipman who looked as though he was about to pee in his breeches. "Damn your eyes, Colin, *how the hell could you simply let her walk off the flagship?!*"

Little Midshipman Jones dived in recklessly to save his captain. "It w-was m-m-my fault, s-sir," he said bravely, trembling as his admiral's furious stare swung on him. "I saw her h-h-h-heading toward the p-poop deck and didn't tell the c-c-captain soon enough—"

"No, Mr. Jones, it was *my* fault," Colin said soberly, standing stiffly at attention and refusing to let his officers take the blame. Composed and proper, he dauntlessly met the admiral's glare. "I saw her too, but must confess I was too shocked to react as quickly as I might have had the circumstances been different."

"No, Captain," First Lieutenant Pearson declared, "*I* should take the blame, I was nearest the ladder and didn't move to stop her—"

"Damn your eyes, damn *all of your eyes!*" Gray raged. "It was *my* fault and *I'll* take the goddamned blame for it!" He fisted his hands into knots of helpless fury and let loose such a foul string of sailor language that the very air seemed to smoke. "She's escaped me, who the bloody hell cares how, it's the damned *why* of the matter, I was so close, so *damned* close to winning her trust . . ." He trailed off, spun around to watch the schooner, and bent his brow to his hand, feeling the weighty, nervous silence of the officers behind him.

"Mr. Jones," he heard Colin say quietly. "See to it that the admiral's barge is made ready, if you please. I suspect he may need it directly."

Lady Catherine . . . Gray's deceit . . . her father, not abandoning her after all, but thinking her dead all these years—

It was too much.

Panting, winded, her wet hair streaming around her shoulders and down her back, Maeve hauled herself

over the rail with the help of her horrified crewwomen.
"Up topsl's," she gasped, nearly collapsing in their
arms, "and hurry!"

"Captain! Oh, look, your *side*—"

"I'm fine, for God's sake; it's nothing but a few burst
stitches!" Gripping their hands she swung onto the
deck, the familiarity of her own ship infusing her with
a sudden burst of life and energy. This was *her* command, the one place in the world that was a safe refuge,
a trusted haven, *home*. Already she could feel the
schooner's spirit surging into her soul, that quick thrill
of heady exaltation, and utter invincibility. The admiral
would never catch her now; not in that massive and
mighty flagship, not in a million years, not *ever,* damn
his lying, blackhearted, wench-loving soul!

"Captain!"

She whirled, neatly catching the cutlass Aisling
tossed to her, the weight of it nearly bringing her down.
Tia threw a light jacket over her for the sake of modesty and, trailed by the two Irish girls, Maeve ran toward the tiller, feeling the blood oozing from her side
but knowing she had no time to worry about it now. He
would send someone after her, she *knew* he would send
someone after her, if only to save his rotten pride, if
only to prove his *ownership* over this latest addition to
his pirate collection, if only to make her life hell—

Orla was at the helm, her eyes dark and condemning.

"Maeve—"

"Not now, Orla, just get me away from that suffering
bastard, and the sooner the better! I hope I never set
eyes on that *worm* again!"

"Worm, Captain?" Sorcha cried, her eyes widening
in horror at the bloodstained nightshirt just visible beneath Maeve's jacket. Already her sister was running to
get fresh bandages. "Whatever has poor Sir Graham
done now?"

Maeve exploded. *"Poor Sir Graham* flaunted his

mistress right under my nose, that's what he did! I hope
he rots in hell, the bastard, the wretch, the slimy, two-
timing, bucket of bilge-rotted"—she screwed up her
face and screamed the last word out from the very
depths of her throat—"*SCU-U-U-U-UM!*"

Orla merely set her lips and staring past *Kestrel*'s
plunging jibboom, said quietly, "Your orders, Captain?"

Maeve bent her head to her palm, wanting to kill,
wanting to scream, wanting—

"Trim for beam reach, I think—yes, yes, a beam
reach, a bloody, blasted beam reach, and set the
t'gallants too!"

"I think you're being hasty," Sorcha said smugly as
she drew a knife, sliced through Maeve's soaked shirt,
and, with the help of her sister, began rebandaging
Maeve's side. "The admiral loves you."

Maeve's head jerked up. "Well darling, here's a lesson for you: men like the *admiral* don't know how to
love. Love me. Ha. He's a slinking slimy dog, just like
the rest of his kind! He doesn't love me; the only thing
he loves is gratifying the itch between his legs! He'll
not leave his precious mistress for me, he'll send someone else, and then, only because he's obsessed with pirates and *I'm* a pirate and the most interesting addition
to his *COLLECTION!* Blast it, don't you understand,
don't any of you *understand?* If he was my Gallant
Knight, he wouldn't relegate his dirty work to a subor-
dinate, he'd *damn well come for me himself!*"

Enolia was standing at the rail with a glass to her
eye.

"He is."

Her sides heaving, Maeve came up short. *"What did
you say?!"*

Enolia lowered the glass and looked at Maeve. "I
said he is."

The blood drained from Maeve's face. She turned

and stared dumbly at one of the starboard guns, unable
to speak, her lips going gray with shock.

"Captain? You all right?"

Relief. And then fear, guilt, elation, and anger all
bubbled up in her breast. She grabbed a telescope from
Aisling and pressed it to her eye, the wind whipping
loose strands of wet hair around her neck and making
it sting her cheeks. Sure enough, she could see the frantic activity even from here; officers gesturing wildly,
seamen running down the gangways, a boat being
swayed out, a frigate—*oh God, he was summoning the
frigate* Harleigh, *the fastest ship he had!*—charging
down toward the big flagship—

Trembling, she dropped the glass.

"He's coming after you, isn't he?" Aisling taunted.

"Of course he's coming after her," Sorcha cried, with
a look of triumph on her face. "He's her Gallant
Knight. Do you think he's just going to let her *go?*"

Shrieking with delight, both girls ran to the rail,
jumped atop the guns, and, waving their arms and cupping their hands over their mouths, began yelling at the
very top of their lungs.

"Come on, Sir Graham! Come get her!"

In a daze, Maeve pressed a hand to her rebandaged
side and stared out over the frothy sea. She felt the
strength and intensity of the admiral's determination
even from here—and saw the white flag with the red
cross dropping from *Triton*'s mizzen and shooting to
the top of the frigate *Harleigh*'s.

"He's aboard the frigate, Captain!"

"Here he comes!"

Maeve shut her eyes, ripped her braid apart, and
stumbled to the weather rail, seized by a dumb urge to
laugh, to cry, to sit down and curl herself into a little
ball where she could hide from herself, hide from the
truth of what Gray was doing: coming for her whether
she wanted him to or not. She gripped the shrouds in

both hands and looked down, where the blue, frothing mirror of the sea threw her words back at her. "You're not *supposed* to come after me, Gray," she whispered, closing her eyes against her whipping hair as the schooner smashed through the swells and spray licked her cheeks. "You were supposed to stay with her. . . ."

"Come ON, Sir Graham! Yippee! Look, Ash, there's the admiral himself. Hello, Admiral! Yoo-hoo, Sir Gra—ham!"

"Damn you, Gray," she murmured, "I'll never doubt you again. . . ."

She got up, crossed the short distance to the helm, and pressing her hand to her throbbing side, stood beside Orla. Together they watched *Harleigh,* neither saying a word, as beneath them the brave *Kestrel* leapt and plunged through the waves in a race she could never win.

"I give up, Orla," Maeve whispered, on a bleak little laugh. Her heart was now pounding, pulsing, echoing in her ears, and thrilling tingles shot through her at the sight of that glorious English frigate, charging forward and piling on every stitch of sail she carried. "I just—plain—*give up.* . . ."

"Shall we heave to and let the admiral close the distance, then?" Orla asked, her eyes grave as she peered at the new bandage just visible beneath Maeve's coat. Already, fresh blood was soaking through it.

Maeve's head snapped around so fast her hair took a full two seconds to follow. "What're you, *insane?!* Heave to, and fail Sir Graham's expectations of me? Heave to, and let him down? No way in bloody HELL, Orla, will I heave to! Merricks do not give up! Pirate Queens do not give up! The chase is not over yet, for WE have *Kestrel,* my father's ship, the most famous vessel in the American Revolution, the swiftest schooner afloat, a living legend—"

BOOM! Smoke burst from the frigate's bows in a

plume of gray, and the ball threw a waterspout as high as *Kestrel*'s mainsail boom.

The Irish sisters howled with delight. "He's firing on us!"

Clutching the old coat around her like a shield and laughing with sudden, sheer exultation, the Pirate Queen leapt atop the old gun her mother had long ago dubbed *Freedom*. The cannon's hot iron surface nearly burned the calluses off her soles and, brandishing her sword, she yelled:

"Come and get me, Sir Bloody Graham Falconer! You want me so damned much? Hah! If you can catch me, I'm *yours!*"

Orla's voice, urgent and quick: "Captain?"

"Come on Sir Graham! I dare you! Come on, Admiral, show me what you're made of!"

"Captain!"

The desperate urgency in Orla's voice lanced her exultation, and whirling, she followed her friend's arm, nearly tumbling from the gun. "Strange sail off the starboard bows," Orla murmured. *"Far* off the starboard bows. Look."

Maeve grabbed a telescope and nearly slammed it into her eye—one ship, two ships, frigates, and several miles beyond them, cloaked in drifting haze, huge, massive shapes, rippling flags, a fleet the size and might to rival if not surpass Nelson's—

"Holy bloody HELL!" she cried, dropping the telescope. "We've stumbled onto the combined Franco-Spanish fleet! *It's Villeneuve!*"

Chapter 25

"**R**eady about!" Maeve cried, desperately.

"But Captain, you said—"

"To hell with what I said, that's the French fleet out there and Sir Graham must be warned!"

But even as the Pirate Queen clutched the edges of the coat around her wet body and ran to the side, even as *Kestrel* swung herself neatly through the wind, even as a low chorus of awed disbelief rose from the crew around her, Maeve knew the admiral had seen it, too. A mighty, invincible line of twenty battleships and seven frigates stretching from one end of the horizon to the other, buried in haze, barely discernible, the might and strength of Napoleon Bonaparte's Combined Franco-Spanish fleet—

"Go below and change, Captain."

"Orla, there's no time!"

"Go below, Captain—if he sees you all bloodied, he won't go, he'll not do what he must to save his convoy, his ships, *himself!*"

"But—"

"Go, Maeve!" Orla cried, her eyes filling with tears. *"For God's sake, go!"*

Maeve shot one look at the oncoming English frigate and fled down the hatch. With Aisling hot on her heels she burst into her cabin, flung open her wardrobe, hurled clothes over her shoulder until she found the purple satin gown.

273

"Captain, hurry, *hurry!*"

"Aisling, these buttons, I can't do them, I can't reach them—"

Quick, fluttering fingers, rebandaging Maeve's wound, hooking the buttons, her hair catching in them, *damn, damn!*

"Oh, do hurry, Aisling, *hurry!*" she cried.

"Just go, Captain!" Aisling shoved her toward the door, and together the two raced topside. Orla had the schooner close-hauled, and wind and spray hit them in the face; they reached the rail just as Gray's frigate met them, came about, and, paralleling their course, plunged through the sea alongside them.

"Maeve!" It was him, *him!* standing on the quarter-deck with *Harleigh*'s company assembled behind him, his feet planted against the desperate plunge of the ship—

She leaned over the rail, one hand thrust toward him as though she could reach across the waves and touch him. "Gray, forgive me, I was rash, oh please forgive me—"

"Maeve, *listen to me!*" The two ships were running neck and neck now, the frigate a savage, dashing warrior, the schooner a pert little predator, so close they could've grappled, the crews staring at each other across the short, rushing space.

He stood between two cannons, the wind blowing his hair out from under his hat and whipping it across his cheeks, and she knew then that she had been wrong about him, *wrong!*—that he loved her and her alone. In his face, in his words, in the desperation of his stance, she saw the truth. "You must listen to me!" He cupped his hands over his mouth to be heard over the roar of wind and sea. "Can you hear me?"

"Yes!"

The sea thundered at the bows, spray drove over the rail, the wind keened, and far off in the distance, one of the scouting frigates of the enemy fleet was detaching itself from the others, turning its bowsprit toward them—

The admiral spared it one glance, grabbed a speaking trumpet, and shouted, "You must carry word back to Nelson! He has the fleet! *The fate of a nation depends upon your obeying my command,* do you understand me, Maeve, *obeying my command!*" He tore the speaking trumpet from his lips, flung it aside, and across the wind-whipped gulf that separated them, yelled, "The fate of a nation depends on your finding *Nelson!* Go to Antigua and bring him back!"

Miles to windward, the French scout set her topgallants and another, just beyond it, left the line of battleships to follow suit. Another . . . And another . . .

"No!" Maeve cried, planting her feet and clawing her whipping hair out of her eyes. "I won't leave you, Gray! Damn it, I *won't abandon you!"*

"GO FIND NELSON AND BRING HIM BACK!"

Love. Honor. And *obey.* She didn't have a choice here and so she gave orders to her crew to steer for Antigua.

Gray had already yelled something to *Harleigh's* captain, and then the English frigate was showing her copper as she bore off to carry the admiral back to his flagship. Already flags were going up *Harleigh's* halyards, sending Sir Graham's urgent instructions to Captain Lord aboard the mighty *Triton;* already he had made up his mind what course of action he would take. He had one battleship and three frigates against the might of Villeneuve's fleet, nothing more, nothing less, and the meaning of the Vision she'd had upon leaving Barbados—the blood, the death, the sea fight—was suddenly clear in all its ghastly horror.

He would die—honorably, gallantly—*like an officer.*

And there wasn't a damned thing she could do about it.

Maeve saw the convoy beginning to disperse in compliance with Sir Graham's signals, already breaking apart and fleeing to leeward while the massive *Triton* and the remaining two English frigates, *Cricket* and *Chatham*, piled on sail and, beating against the wind, drove forward to meet their admiral aboard *Harleigh*.

"Captain," she heard Enolia saying, "if we don't get ourselves out of here now . . . we never will. One broadside from those Frenchies and we're done for."

Not trusting herself to speak, Maeve nodded her head in a quick, jerky motion, her gaze fastened on the diminishing shape of *Harleigh* as she ran down to meet the oncoming *Triton, Cricket,* and *Chatham. Harleigh* was stern-on to them, giant pillars of sail rising gloriously skyward. Signals were bursting at her halyards, answered by equally rapid acknowledgments from the mighty flagship.

She curled her fingers around the rail. *Don't abandon me, Gray . . . please, don't abandon me.*

She raised a telescope and put it to her eye. A single, commanding figure had strode to *Harleigh*'s taffrail, there to stand rigid and alone, invincible, magnificent and dauntless. Gray, the officer. Gray, the admiral. Gray, the one and only prayer the convoy—and maybe even England—had.

Her gaze met the admiral's across the rapidly widening sea. Tears choked her throat, and Maeve saw him cup his hands to his mouth a final time. The wind snatched away his words, but she already heard them in her heart.

I love you.

From the gundecks above came the roll of drums calling the crew to action, the squeal of trucks and deep, rumbling thunder as the big cannons were dragged up to their ports; barked commands from the officers; pounding footsteps just overhead, yells of encouragement, blasphemous oaths, and cheers and shouts of excitement.

Aboard H.M.S. *Triton,* el Perro Negro and his companions waited for the organized confusion to cover their escape from the hold.

Tricking the young marine guard into opening the door, they killed him with a blow from the stock of his own musket, tossed his body into the hold, and escaped into the depths of the flagship.

And in the desperate race to get the mighty ship ready for battle, no one noticed.

Aboard *Harleigh,* Sir Graham stood on the quarterdeck with its commander, Captain Ben Warner, and watched the French frigates—seven of them, all told—closing the distance aft.

Thank God Maeve had gotten safely away. . . .

"Shall I wear ship and fight, sir?" Warner smashed his fist into his palm, his blue eyes glowing. "Please sir, let me at them, I'll bloody their noses good—"

"In good time, Captain, all in good time," Sir Graham murmured, resting the heel of his hand atop his sword hilt. "We must dally for a bit, buy time so the convoy can get out of the area."

"Your orders then, sir?"

"Clear for action and beat to quarters."

To the ominous beat of a marine's drum, the British frigate prepared for battle as men ran to their stations. The guns were run out, shot was carried up from below, and the lieutenants barked orders through speaking trumpets.

"Look lively there, look lively!"

"Get a move on, damn your eyes!"

Aft, the leading French ship fired her bow chaser, and a ball raised a harmless waterspout in *Harleigh*'s wake as the enemy gunner tried to find the range. *Harleigh*'s crew sent up a chorus of jeers, raising their fists in challenge and defiance. Some yelled obscene threats, others roared with derision, all looked toward the admiral whose command they would obey, even if it might mean their deaths before this day was over.

"I daresay, Warner, your people have spunk!" Gray said, with boyish delight.

The French frigate fired again.

"Poor Nelson," the admiral mused, watching the enemy ship closing the distance. "Imagine, Captain Warner! Here he's chased this very fleet nearly thirty-five hundred miles across the Atlantic and *we* are the ones who shall get to fight it! What Nelson wouldn't give to be in my shoes right now. . . ."

"Sir?"

The admiral grinned and wagged a finger. "But mark me, I'd not trade places with him for the world!"

Thunder rolled again from the French frigate, and another ball splashed into the sea a hundred feet off the starboard quarter. The next shot might be a hit.

"Take in your t'gallants, Captain Warner, and allow the enemy to catch up. At this rate they'll spot the convoy before it is safely over the horizon. And please, do not look so woeful! You'll get your chance to fight today, I can assure you. And now, while we are waiting for Captain Lord to collect me, it is time to put my plan for confusing and confounding the enemy into effect. Where is my flag-lieutenant? Ah, there you are, Mr. Stern!"

The young officer clapped his hat to his head and tearing his gaze from the enemy frigates and the immense fleet beyond, turned and walked briskly across the deck. He was terrified; Gray could see it in his eyes, in his stance, in the color of his skin.

"Muster your signals party, Mr. Stern, and be quick about it," the admiral said. "I have a horrific number of messages I will be making directly, is that understood?"

"Aye, sir."

"Very well then, Lieutenant. Now, come with me."

Already, midshipmen were scurrying from the lockers with armloads of colorful flags. Gray joined them, noting their nervousness that he, their admiral, was in their midst. "Are you ready, my young lads?"

"Aye, sir!" they cried in chorus.

He crossed his arms, tugged at his earring and angled his head to one side as though lost in thought. "The first signal I should like to make," he said pensively, "is to *Triton*, to be repeated to the convoy beyond. And make haste, Mr. Stern, as you must warm up for the work you shall soon have to perform for me!"

"Aye, sir!"

"To the convoy: *continue sailing with all haste for England.* With any luck, they'll be safely away before Villeneuve sees them, but if not, I doubt he will be fool enough to chase after them and thus weaken his own strength as a massed fighting unit. Make the signal directly, Lieutenant, we haven't all day, you know!"

The signals were hauled skyward, bursting from *Harleigh*'s masts, clawing at the wind. Puffs of smoke plumed from the leading French frigate, a half mile away now and closing fast. Another ball plowed the sea, twenty feet beyond *Harleigh*'s taffrail. Seconds later, the sharp report echoed across the waves.

"My second signal. Make to Captain Lord in *Triton*: *Prepare for battle and make more sail.*"

Sir Graham watched the French frigate running out her bow chaser. "The third. Make to our frigates *Chatham* and *Cricket. Prepare for battle and take station to windward of* Triton."

The Frenchman fired again. The ball hit just aft of *Harleigh*'s rudder.

More flags darted skyward, the little midshipman trying desperately to keep the pages of his signals book from fluttering in the wind. He glanced at his admiral, that man so far removed from his own lowly rank that he might have been a god, and found Sir Graham smiling at him.

The admiral winked. "Cheer up, Mr. Marshall, I have not even *begun* to work you yet!"

"Signal from *Triton*, sir! *Acknowledged!*"

Out of the corner of his eye, Gray saw Captain Warner fidgeting with impatience.

"Signal from *Chatham*, sir! *Acknowledged!*"

The admiral gave a barely perceptible nod. And then he saw the pile of signal flags lying on the deck, the flag-lieutenant and the midshipman standing ready, an anxious marine positioned nearby, and Captain Warner regarding him anxiously. He saw nearly three hundred men all watching him, wondering what he would do, how he would get them out of this, their eyes nervous, confident, trusting.

"Cricket acknowledged, sir!"

And then he gazed up at the halyards on each side of the ship, the fathoms and fathoms of ropes and flags, the party of loyal men, all anxious and ready to convey his barrage of signals to an unsuspecting fleet.

Another half hour and *Triton* would reach him. Another ten minutes and he estimated the convoy would be well out of sight of Villeneuve's fleet. Another minute, maybe two, and *Harleigh* would be trading fire with the first of the enemy frigates.

"Are you ready, Lieutenant Stern?"

"Aye sir, as ready as I'll ever be!"

"Very well, then, let us proceed. And do ensure that my messages can be viewed from every angle. I wish the French to see them as clearly as my own ships can."

He put his hands behind his back, and when he looked at Lieutenant Stern, his eyes were gleaming with wicked humor, his mouth curving in a smile and his jaw dimpling with delight. "My first signal is general and to the Fleet: *All hands prepare for divine worship.*"

"Uh—all hands prepare for divine worship, sir?"

"Just make the signal, boy, and be quick about it!"

Aboard the frigate *Cricket*, an excitable lieutenant with nineteen years behind him seized his captain's arm and pointed wildly. "Signals from Sir Graham aboard *Harleigh*, sir! Look!"

Captain Roger Young grabbed his telescope. Quick-thinking and competent, he'd had his ship cleared for action before he'd even received his admiral's signal and now, sweating, bare-backed gun crews stared up from their huge cannon and as one swung to look at the signals bursting from the frigate *Harleigh*.

"What the devil?" the captain said.

"Can you make them out, sir?"

"Of course not, lieutenant, they are all mumbo jumbo to me! Midshipman Beauregard! Yes, you with the damned French name! Can you make out that signal the admiral is flying?"

The little midshipman opened his signals book, pushing through the spray-damp pages to look up the meaning of each flag. Bracing his legs against the leaping deck beneath him, he slowly began to spell out the message. "It"—shaking his head, he turned bleak and confused eyes upon his captain—"it makes no sense, sir!"

"Read it!"

The boy puckered his brow, his high-pitched and still-girlish voice laboring over the message: "Signal from *flag*. It says"—he looked up at his captain, confused—*"All—hands—make—ready—for—divine—worship."*

"What?"

Thunder cleaved the air as the French frigates opened fire upon *Harleigh*.

"It says, 'All hands make ready for divine worship,' sir—"

"Damn you, I know what you said, surely it must be some mistake!"

"No, sir, it's in the book—"

Another gun boomed from the French ship, raising a burst of spray off *Cricket*'s quarter, and Captain Young clenched his fists as he willed more speed from his vessel.

"Look, sir, another signal!"

"Read it, Mr. Beauregard!"

"*Prepare—to—*" he hunched his shoulders, screwed up his face, stuck his neck out—"this can't be right!—*take—on stores.* And another—*B—L—A—C—K—* What? *Blackbeard Forever?* Sir, what does that mean, 'Blackbeard Forever?' Wait, another! It's an easy one, number 2045 . . . but it doesn't make any sense!"

"READ IT!"

Beyond *Harleigh,* the leading French frigate hove to, suspicious and obviously confused by the barrage of signals breaking from the British ship's ensigns.

The boy screwed up his face and looked at his captain, his expression stating his opinion that Rear Admiral Sir Graham Falconer had clearly lost his mind. "It says, *Can you spare an anchor-stock?*"

But Captain Young was staring past him, his eyes intense, hard; the next signal was already at *Harleigh*'s masts, equally ridiculous, equally nonsensical, fluttering in beautiful bursts of color for all the world to see. And as the second of the French frigates hove to and stood off, Captain Young figured out just what his admiral was about.

He was buying time. For himself, his frigates, the convoy—for all of them.

"Bonaparte's *blood!*" he swore, laughing, and then, to the poor little midshipman, "make signal to *Harleigh,* Mr. Starkey. *Acknowledge!*"

He glanced aft, but the massive flagship *Triton* was already overtaking him, a fortress of checkerboard sides and hungry guns rising straight up out of the sea, crowned by acres of sail and strung with an array of brightly colored flags streaming gaily in the wind as she charged forward to collect her admiral.

On the deck of his own flagship, Admiral Villeneuve, in command of the Combined Franco-Spanish forces, trained his glass on the distant British frigate and the mighty ship-of-the-line that was beating to windward to meet up with her. Sweat dappled his aristocratic upper lip, and apprehension clawed at his gut. *Sacré bleu!* He didn't like this, didn't like it one bit.

He lowered the glass. "All those signals . . . whatever do they mean?"

"Je ne sais pas, sir," his flag-captain responded. "But were I to hazard a guess, I would say that English frigate is calling for assistance, maybe, to that fleet whose sails we can just see over the horizon?"

"I am confused. I must know what those signals mean!"

The captain gave a shrug. Between the emperor's threats, insults, and orders, the deplorable state of the Combined Franco-Spanish Fleet, the constant confrontations with his officers, the Spaniards, and that most bone-chilling fear of all—the fear of the dreaded English Admiral Nelson, the clever, cunning, fierce Admiral Nelson who would never rest until he had run them down at last—Villeneuve had lost his nerve.

The alarming news that his English nemesis was *not* looking for them in Egypt as he'd been led to believe—but had chased them clear across the Atlantic—had sent Villeneuve fleeing the West Indies in blatant disobedience of the Emperor's orders that they remain there to wait for reinforcements.

Napoleon would *not* be happy. . . .

"That British battleship and its three meager frigates will pose us no threat, sir," the French flag-captain assured his panicky admiral. "Our seven frigates will make short work of them. And as for Nelson, you have eluded him once again—I know what you are thinking, sir, that that frigate is summoning *his* assistance, but surely, the English admiral is still foolishly searching for you in the Indies—"

Villeneuve swung on his captain. "Surely, you don't think that is *Nelson* that frigate is signaling to, do you?!"

"Oh, no, sir, surely not! Besides, if those sails out there were Nelson's fleet, you know as well as I do that he'd be running *toward,* not away from us—"

Villeneuve was falling apart. "Well, I'm not taking any chances! *Mon Dieu, Capitaine,* don't just stand there! Signal our frigates to attack immediately, and for one of Gravina's battleships to go with them in case that Englishman is too much for them!"

"And us, sir?"

"Continue on our present course for Europe!"

H.M.S. *Triton* and the frigate *Harleigh* reached each other at last.

To the wild cheers of seven hundred men, Rear Admiral Sir Graham Falconer clambered up the sides of his flagship, saluted the quarterdeck, and shook hands with Captain Colin Lord. Then, the two senior officers of the fleet strode briskly to the helm, where they watched the big Spanish battleship detach herself from the Franco-Spanish fleet and turn her huge bows toward them.

"Ready for a pell-mell battle, Captain Lord?"

"Aye, sir. You'll not find my men lacking this day!"

"Yes, well, we'll show those French buggers yet, eh, Colin?" The admiral clapped a hand across his flag-captain's shoulders to encourage him in the face of the terrible odds. "Besides, I have a strategy that cannot fail. Now, raise the flag, Captain Lord."

"*The* flag, sir?" he asked, shocked.

"Yes, Colin, *the* flag."

"Sir, may I remind you that if we are defeated and taken prisoner while flying *that* flag, we shall all be deprived the rights and protection of prisoners of war—"

"I know that, Captain Lord, but I do not intend to suffer defeat, and I damn well won't surrender! There will *be* no prisoners, do you understand? *No prisoners!* So hoist that flag and be quick about it!"

Moments later the flag broke to the wind. It was a flag no respectable admiral would *ever* carry, a flag no Royal Navy vessel would ever possess, a flag that the Admiralty back in London might well have executed Sir Graham for flying, a flag that even the French would have no trouble understanding.

It was a flag that *all* of them knew well.

The piratical flag of the Jolly Roger.

Chapter 26

VICTORY, JUNE 13TH, 1805

MY DEAR LADY HAMILTON,

I have learned the French fleet passed to leeward of Antigua on Saturday last, standing to the Northward and no doubt steering for Europe. My opinion is firm that something has made them resolve to leave these islands and proceed directly for Europe, but at least I leave the Indies knowing Britain's holdings here are secure. As you may believe, my dearest, beloved angel, *your Nelson is very sad at not having got at the Enemy here, but I shall hound them all the way back to Europe where I hope to bring them to glorious battle at last and* annihilate *them. Then, my beloved, I shall return to you crowned with glory, and the only reward I ask will be my dear Emma's love. Oh, if not for the wrong information given me by that damned Brereton, I would have been at them days ago, and your own dear Nelson would have been forever* immortalized—

"Sir?"

Nelson was just putting the third emphatic bold line beneath *angel* and *forever immortalized* when the lieutenant's words jolted him back to awareness. "Mr. Pasco!"

"I'm sorry, sir, I didn't mean to give you a start—"

"No, no, Mr. Pasco, it is *my* fault for not having

286

heard your arrival. Pray, what is it?" Reddening a bit, he curled his arm around the letter, hiding his words from the young lieutenant with all the guilty protectiveness of an adolescent in love.

"The captain's respects, sir, and the masthead has just sighted the Pirate Queen's schooner closing rapidly to windward. She seems to be in utmost haste, sir."

"The *Pirate Queen?* Whatever is *she* doing here, she is supposed to be with Sir Graham . . ." Trailing off, Nelson jumped to his feet, blanching as his swift mind put two and two together. "Oh, dear God—Falconer . . . the convoy—*Villeneuve!*"

Flinging down his pen, the Admiral grabbed his hat and charged out of the cabin.

Dawn.

The sky was bleak and gray, with low-hanging clouds dragging behind the darkness of night. The ocean was still, tense, expectant, the swells filing endlessly past, lifting up the debris—broken spars and splinters of wood, ragged cordage, and pieces of shot-torn sail—that littered the lonely patch of sea and dropping it into each successive trough.

Silence, and the haunted sighs of the wind.

A battered British frigate lay in the lee of a noble leviathan whose mizzen still flew the proud colors of a rear admiral. Where there had been three frigates, there was now only one, and some thousand feet below them the wreck of the *Chatham,* and those who had died with her, made her final anchorage on the bed of the Atlantic.

The other, *Harleigh,* had been dispatched to catch up to the unprotected convoy.

Deep in *Triton*'s innards, the orlop was as dark as the long night had been, with only the meager glare of swinging lanterns to illuminate that dismal space that had not seen daylight since the great ship was built.

The smell of blood, sickly and sweet, stained the air. The deck planking was drenched with it. Vomit and excrement and suffering made a choking stench strong enough to make one's eyes water. But the surgeon and his mates had had no respite since *Triton* had engaged the mighty Spanish *San Rafael* and now, twelve hours after the battle, Dr. Ryder moved like a sleepwalker, his apron crusted with dried blood, his eyes dazed, his movements mechanical, his sweat-damp hair clinging to his brow.

It was a wonder they were all even here at all, and not lying dead on the decks, sunk, or worse, chained as prisoners of war in the hold of one of the enemy's ships.

And they could thank their admiral, Sir Graham Falconer, for *that*.

Ryder thought of how, his Bible in hand, Sir Graham had solemnly recited the Twenty-third Psalm in his clear baritone as the bodies—sewn in sailcloth and weighted by cannonballs—had awaited that final journey to the bottom. Ryder knew the solemn ceremony would soon be repeated; already, sad shapes lay beneath sheets of canvas, waiting to be sewn into their canvas coffins. Less fortunate men lay groaning in pain in the gloom around them, some babbling in delirium or screaming in agony as a limb was removed or a splinter cut out, while others merely lay on the deck propped against the bulkhead, their eyes staring into space as if they were already dead.

One of the survivors was set a bit away from the rest, still and unconscious now after the agonies he had suffered earlier. Ryder's eyes went bleak that the fates had laid waste to such a fine young officer as Captain Colin Lord. It was always ones like him that God took; the finest, the most promising, the cream of the crop, the *best*.

He heard footsteps approaching and his mouth

curved in a sad smile. Well, if God wanted Captain
Lord, he was in for one hell of a fight.

The admiral paused to comfort a ship's boy who had
lost a finger and was sobbing brokenly for his mother.
And then, his face solemn and the ship's cat struggling
in the crook of his arm, he walked slowly to where his
flag-captain lay, and knelt down beside him.

"Colin."

Out of the corner of his eye, the surgeon saw Sir
Graham set the little animal carefully down against the
flag-captain's ribs, then reach out to take the still hand
in his own.

"He'll not hear you, sir," Ryder said quietly, watching as the cat flattened itself protectively against Captain Lord's side. "I dosed him up good with rum before
I set the leg. He has a remarkably low tolerance for alcohol and will be out of it for a while, I'm afraid."

"It is better that way." Sir Graham looked up, his
dark eyes troubled, anguished. "I should like to have
him moved to my quarters, Ryder. This is no place for
him to—"

To die, he'd been about to say.

"Pardon me, sir, but the captain extracted from me a
promise to leave him here. He didn't want to desert his
men, sir."

"Of course," Sir Graham said, in complete understanding, "but he extracted no such promise from *me.* I
am his admiral and I want him moved to my cabin as
soon as possible, is that clear?" He reached out, curved
his arm beneath Captain Lord's neck, and lifting the
fair and lolling head, adjusted the crumpled and bloodstained coat that served as a pillow. It was the young
officer's own, the tassels of one sad epaulet lying
against his cheek. With paternal tenderness, the admiral
smoothed the damp hair away from the young man's
brow.

"Will the leg be saved, Ryder?"

"I don't know, sir. I did all I could for him, but the ball did break it in three places ... shattered it, in fact. At the very best, he'll have a limp. At the very worst—"

"Never mind, Ryder, I do not wish to hear the *very worst.*"

"Aye sir." He looked at the admiral's shoulders, slumped with fatigue and grief, yet still proudly reassuring beneath the bright epaulets that crowned them. Aye, it was a sad thing about the young flag-captain, but didn't Sir Graham realize or care that his actions had saved a whole *convoy?* Didn't he realize or care that he had met, and beaten, nearly impossible odds?

That he had outsmarted Villeneuve and a Spanish admiral besides?

Apparently not.

"What is the dead count up to, Ryder?"

"Thirty-three, sir," the surgeon answered. "Not including the master's mate. I don't expect him to last the day."

Sir Graham nodded wearily. He pulled the sheet up to Captain Lord's chin and dragged himself to his feet. Gray's eyes were tragic, his face stubbly with new beard, his shirt, so fine and bright before the battle, now torn and smudged with soot. He looked nothing like an admiral, yet he looked *everything* like one. For a moment, he stared blankly at the ship's timbers, started to rake a hand through his dark tresses, and let his arm drop to his side.

"Sir?"

"Carry on, Ryder. Summon me if my captain's condition worsens—"

"Sir Graham!"

The admiral glanced up as a midshipman burst into the room, his cheeks flushed with having run down several decks to reach this hellish hole. The boy snapped off a hasty salute and blurted, "Lieutenant Pearson's respects, sir, and there's something he thinks you should come topside to see!"

Gray looked at the pile of covered bodies and felt the last of his spirit draining out of him.

Villeneuve.

He took a deep, bracing sigh. "My compliments to the lieutenant, Mr. Fay, and I will be up shortly."

The midshipman fled the room. Gray stood for a moment, steadying himself for the inevitable sight, knowing already that Villeneuve had discovered his ruse and returned to finish the job. He looked at Colin, shattered beyond repair; he looked at the dead and the dying, who would never fight again; he thought of Maeve, and her heartwarming refusal to leave him in those last moments before he had sent his ships to attack the enemy. But even the possibility of hope where *she* was concerned failed to rouse his spirits, and he despaired of being able to muster the confident optimism he knew he must summon, if only for the sake of his men. Their captain was down, out of action, and in all likelihood crippled for life; they had lost a frigate, had lost a lot of good men, and now, with Villeneuve coming back to sweep up the pieces . . .

He nodded to Ryder, picked up his hat, and trudged up through the hatch to the next deck, too dispirited to notice that with each level it got brighter and brighter, the darkness falling away behind and beneath him, the sunlight probing through, weak at first, now getting stronger, stronger, stronger—

Cheering.

He heard it, at first just as a dull, muffled din, now an unmistakable roar bursting from a thousand raw throats throughout his tiny collection of ships.

The admiral hauled himself up the last hatch, out onto a quarterdeck blazing with sunlight—and stopped in his tracks.

Their backs to him, seven hundred wildly cheering

men lined the rail, the hammock nettings, the shrouds, the yards, standing atop cannon and out on the cat-heads. Some were throwing their hats to the sky, others dancing with excitement, and in the shadow of the mainmast a little ship's boy was weeping openly.

Someone turned, saw him, and a hundred sailors cleared away to make a path for their admiral as he stepped up to the hammock nettings.

"There, sir," Lieutenant Stern said, hoarsely, and handed him a telescope. "Look."

Gray raised the glass to his eye. He looked far to the west and saw it, even as the cheering grew so loud his head rang, even as the realization of what he was seeing made his eyes begin to water with strain and emotion. For there, hull up on the horizon was a ship, a huge, dauntless, mighty ship, with an invincible fleet spread out around her in a glorious array of power and majesty and strength.

Nelson.

And *Victory.*

And there, leading them—a tiny, mothlike speck nearly dwarfed by the magnificence of that formidable array—was *Kestrel.*

Chapter 27

A sailor through and through, Maeve refused the bosun's chair and, looping her skirts up and over one arm so they wouldn't tangle in her legs, scrambled up *Triton*'s side the minute Lord Nelson returned to the *Victory*.

She'd waited all morning for Gray's business with Nelson to conclude so she could go to him, impatiently pacing *Kestrel*'s deck and watching the sun blaze down to scorch the deck planking until the rigging oozed tar and the very guns baked and sizzled in the heat. Now, as she scaled the massive wall of the big warship's tumblehome, she tried not to look at the angry gouges the French and Spanish shot had struck in the wood, tried not to envision her beloved admiral, standing unprotected on the quarterdeck as H.M.S. *Triton* had sailed into battle—and tried not to think about what awaited her in the moments ahead. He would refuse to see her, she *knew* he would refuse to see her.

True, he had called out his love for her moments before she departed in search of Nelson, but that had been a desperate moment. Guilt ground her heart. She was miserable thinking how she had mistrusted him, how she had *deserted* him when *that woman* came into the cabin. She was sure that in the time since they had last seen each other he had realized that in his life he needed a woman who loved him unconditionally, who trusted him, who would be a proper admiral's wife . . . not a damned Pirate Queen.

She almost turned back.

Almost.

Don't repeat the mistake that you made with your family with Gray. Don't run and hide and allow yourself to believe the worst. Confront him. Let him explain to you about that woman. Trust him. Believe him. Give him the benefit of the doubt, give him a chance, go to him and give him your love.

Then she was through the entry port and a moment later, standing on the warship's broad quarterdeck, and there *was* no turning back.

A lieutenant, his hat tucked under his arm, had stepped forward to receive her. He was a round-cheeked redhead with an equally round belly, and he blushed like a schoolboy at sight of her. With her trim shape wrapped in a gown of satin, purple enough to please any monarch, fragile gold earrings kissing her shoulders, a straw hat atop her head and her long chestnut tresses caught by a dark purple ribbon, she looked sweet, soft, and feminine—

—as long as one discounted the choker of sharks' teeth around her neck, the cutlass in her hand, and the wicked, gleaming dagger strapped to a bejewelled belt about her waist.

"Please don't ogle, Lieutenant, it makes me damned uncomfortable!"

"Sorry, ma'am, it's just that—well, we don't have ladies aboard very often, you see, and . . ."—he flushed and gulped, staring at her bare feet—"well, you look quite fetching, ma'm, and, uh, well . . ."

"Never mind me," she snapped, looking about her. "Where is your admiral?"

"Sir Graham is in his cabin with the flag-captain, Miss Merrick."

"*Captain* Merrick."

"Yes, of course, forgive me, *Captain* Merrick, sorry, ma'am—"

"Or you may call me 'Majesty.' But since I am here as the commander of a ship, I would prefer 'Captain.' "

She saw several men smirking and elbowing each other at the young officer's obvious discomfort. "Oh, yes, ma'am, I mean Majesty, do forgive me, I meant to say Captain—"

"Oh for God's sake, Lieutenant! If you cannot manage any of that, simply 'Maeve' will do! Now where are your senior officers?"

"Captain Lord is ... has been seriously wounded, ma'am." The lieutenant looked down at the deck. "The admiral is with him now."

"Oh ..." Maeve murmured, suddenly feeling very small. Then her head snapped up, her eyes flashed, and she was the Pirate Queen once more. "Well, what are you waiting for? Take me to them, immediately."

The lieutenant looked around as though for orders, but he was the most senior officer present.

"I said, *now*, lieutenant!"

"Yes, ma'am. Of—of course."

She tucked her hand in his elbow, straightened her spine, and head high, allowed him to lead her aft.

He's going to reject me, he's going to send me away, I know he will. He's had too much time to think and realize that I've done nothing to make him respect me enough to love me—

She thought of Nelson as his bargemen had rowed him back to *Victory* not fifteen minutes ago, how he'd looked up and waved his hat at her, his melancholy little face breaking into a smile of reassurance as though he knew of her fears and trepidation.

I ought not to have come.

All too soon, they were standing at the door of Gray's cabin. A marine, sober-faced and severe, stood just outside. "Admiral's not seeing anyone," he growled, staring straight ahead.

"He will see *me!*" Maeve snapped before she could falter, and pushing past him, shoved open the door, closed it in his face, and strode into the cabin, blinking away the sunspots.

Stillness. Thick, cloying quiet. No movement, no sound, *nothing*. Only the gentle wash of the sea around the great ship's rudder, far, far below her.

"Gray?"

After the blazingly bright sunlight, it took a moment for her eyes to adjust to the comparative gloom of the cabin. She saw her cousin, sprawled on the same sofa she had used and looking about as close to death as a person could get without stepping over into the hereafter. She saw a cat nestled against his blanketed feet, its jaws open in an angry, threatening hiss at her. She saw a roll of bandages on a table beside him, a half-empty glass of brandy, the bottle, and there—the admiral himself.

Asleep.

She froze, torn between an absurd and cowardly urge to flee before he could waken—and going to him.

He was slumped over the table, his brow resting on his forearm, his black hair streaming down his back, his sleeves pushed up to the elbows in a futile attempt to escape the heat. His fine naval coat lay over the back of a chair, his hat on the table beside his arm. A stack of papers was spread out around him, and a pen lay in his relaxed fingers, dribbling ink all over the reports and dispatches he'd been working on when exhaustion had finally done him in.

There was fatigue in the lines of his face. A cut on the back of his hand. Blood on the edge of his cuff.

"Gray," she said softly, and tiptoeing forward, stood over him. Time stopped. The world went away. Holding her breath, she slowly, hesitantly, reached out, her fingers coming to within an inch of his shoulder before halting in uncertainty.

The Pirate Queen swallowed, hard, overcome by emotions she couldn't name or recognize.

She hadn't thought a mighty admiral could look vulnerable, but this one did. She hadn't thought a man who commanded a fleet of battleships and the lives of thousands of sailors could look so defenseless, but he did. She didn't think the sight of her Knight in such a state would rouse such a magnitude of love and fierce protectiveness in her breast—but it did.

For a long moment, she stood there, listening to the soft sounds of his breathing and holding this special, private moment next to her heart. Sir Graham, alone. Sir Graham, defenseless. Sir Graham, vulnerable.

Sir Graham—*hers.*

A half-finished report lay beneath his wrist, three paragraphs of the worst handwriting she'd ever seen in her life sprawled across the page before the words faded off into a black dribble of ink. Her brows snapped together in indignation. Why didn't he employ his secretary, his clerks, to write the blasted thing? He was an *admiral,* for God's sake, with a whole staff of personal servants to attend to such menial matters!

And then she saw that it was no report at all, but a letter—a letter to *her,* full of the outpourings of his heart, an apology about the *woman,* and declarations of the utter, infinite magnitude of his love for her.

A thick knot of emotion lodged in her throat. Never would she doubt this wonderful man again. She sucked her lips between her teeth, carefully slid the paper out from under his wrist, took the pen from his lax fingers—and on a deep, poised breath, touched his shoulder.

He jerked awake, blinking, his eyes momentarily unfocused and confused. *"Maeve?"* He stared up at her, but Maeve glanced at Colin and put her finger to her lips. "Don't worry, he'll never hear us. I got him foxed so he could get some relief from the pain . . . Good God, am I *seeing* things?"

Touch me, Gray. Hold me. Comfort me. I need you.

"Of course you aren't seeing things," she snapped, tossing her head and retreating behind the safety of her customary bluster. She picked up his hat with the point of her cutlass and flung it at him, her eyes flashing. "You're a damned fool, Gray!"

He stared at her in bewilderment, clutching the hat to his chest.

"And I'm a bigger one," she added, sullenly. She bent her head, examining the wire grip of her cutlass, suddenly unable to meet that dark stare. "I'm sorry for taking off on you like that."

He didn't move, and she wondered if he was allowing this awkward silence on purpose so she would have no choice but to fill it with something. *Anything.*

The tactics of an admiral. She was becoming wise to them.

Her head snapped up. "I had to come back, you know. After all, you *are* my Gallant Knight." Then, she slammed the cutlass against the top rung of an empty chair, the resounding crash echoing through the cabin. *"But I'll tolerate no more long-lost lovers on your part, is that understood?!"*

Guiltily, she glanced at Colin, but her cousin remained still and unmoving. As for Gray, he was looking slowly, pointedly, at the sword buried in the rung of his chair, his brow lifted in silent amusement.

Maeve immediately saw her predicament. "Oh, shit." She tried to pull the heavy blade free of the wood, but it was stuck fast. She gripped the hilt of the blade and tried to jerk it up and down—to no avail. Sweat dampened her brow and her face went a deep, blazing red. "Oh, *shit!*"

He rubbed his chin, as though trying to mask a grin. "Need some help, Majesty?"

"You laugh and I'll ram this thing up your—"

"Uh, uh, uh, Maeve, that's no way for a monarch to talk."

"You think it's funny, do you?" She put her bare foot against the seat of the chair, gripped the cutlass, and yanked with all her might, her skirts jerking with every erratic, furious lunge. "Bloody *hell!* Son of a—"

"Here." He put the hat down on the table. Then he stood up, tall and handsome, his head nearly touching the deckhead above and a wicked smile lighting his face. "Allow me."

"I can do it, damn you!"

He merely lifted a skeptical brow, used his body to push hers aside, raised the chair high over his head— and slammed it down on the deck with a crash that sent pieces of wood flying and the cutlass clattering from the chair rung. Then he bent down, picked up the heavy blade, and on a flourishing bow, presented it to her with all the chivalry that he, a gallant Knight of the Bath, could muster.

"Your sword, Majesty."

He was grinning, that dimpled, wolfish grin she'd come to know so well. Humiliated, she glanced at the still-motionless form of Colin Lord, and snatched the cutlass away from him.

"Thanks."

"You're quite welcome."

"I'll . . . replace the chair."

"There is no need."

"No, I insist."

"I said"—a faint smile of admiration and approval curved his mouth as he studied her ladylike garb— "there is no need. There are other ways of paying me that would suffice just as well." The smile grew slow, lazy, hot. "Better, in fact."

He stepped forward.

She stepped backward.

He moved closer.

She puffed out her chest and forced herself to stay put.

Then, very slowly, the admiral reached out, took the cutlass from her suddenly boneless hand, and laid it carefully, deliberately, across the table beside his hat. His hands closed around her elbows, traveled up her arms, and, as he drew her into his embrace she felt her defenses crumbling, her body melting, her heart flying. "Oh, Gray," she murmured, and went into his arms with all the desperate gratitude of a lost child who has suddenly been found.

He kissed her deeply, his hand catching in her hair, his arm a steel band around her waist. She drove upward, clinging to him, her tongue mating with his, her heart wanting to weep with gratitude that he had been spared. Finally she drew back, her eyes misty.

"Leaving you to fight Villeneuve was the hardest thing I have ever done. I thought I'd never see you again. I thought you wouldn't have a chance against all those ships—"

He set her back to stare down into her eyes, his expression ripe with humor. "Come now, dear lady," he said softly. "Do you have as little faith in my abilities as all that?"

"For God's sake, Gray, I heard all about what you did; you could've been killed!" she said, angrily.

"And *you* could've left me to my fate." His thumbs smoothed her hair from her temples, and his eyes went soft and dark with wonder. "And yet . . ."

"And yet, what?"

"You came back to me," he said softly.

"Aye, well I"—she looked down so he wouldn't see how red her face must surely be—"I realized I was acting rashly about that—that *woman.*"

"You acted as you thought best."

Her head snapped up, her eyes blazing with challenge. "You don't think I behaved like a damned fool, then?"

"Oh, on the contrary, Majesty." He smiled, and dropped a kiss on her brow. "But I love you anyhow."

A soft sigh ensued from behind her, and she gasped and spun around, remembering Colin's presence.

"Have no fear, love. As I told you, my captain is dead to the world and will not eavesdrop on us, I can assure you." The admiral's easy humor seemed to fade like an expelled breath, and at her request to know what had happened to her cousin he gave a great, weary sigh and gazed bleakly at the still form on the sofa. "Another casualty of war, I'm afraid, caught by a ball from a French cannon. His leg is shattered and so, I fear, is his career in the navy. He may well end up as a cripple—even if he *does* live."

"Why wouldn't he live?" she asked, frowning and following his gaze.

"If gangrene sets in, the leg will have to come off. But let's not talk of so gloomy an affair. We survived the engagement, thanks to a trick up this old dog's sleeve, and as for young Colin—well, he's made of stern stuff indeed." He gave a brave smile, though she knew the fate of "young Colin" was very much on his mind. "He'll recover—or I'll thrash him to within an inch of his life, the pup!"

Maeve swallowed hard, her heart aching for him. He was like his mentor, Nelson. Kind and concerned and always putting the fate of his men before himself. "I could send Aisling and Sorcha across to nurse him," she offered, slowly. "Perhaps they could read to him, clean the wound, keep his spirits up. . . ."

"Oh no, they're far too young; I could never allow it."

"Young, but not entirely innocent. His would not be

the first male thigh they have seen. And besides, they'll be together"—she paused at the stubborn look on his face—"for God's sake, Gray, there's only so much one overworked surgeon can do! He has a far better chance of survival with my girls nursing him."

But the admiral was cocking his head, narrowing his eyes and looking at her speculatively. "And just why do you care so very much, eh?"

"What?"

"I know he's your cousin and all that, but you barely know him."

She caught her breath, feeling like a thief who's been suddenly found out. "I . . . I don't know." She drew her mouth tight, not willing to examine these feelings of tenderness and compassion for another. "I just do, all right?"

His eyes darkened, and he took her face in his hands. "Maeve, darling, sweetheart, *love.* You try so hard to hide that gentle heart of yours beneath bluster and ferocity. But inside, you are a warm and compassionate soul, full of generosity, concern and caring, with so much love to give—"

Panicking, she drew back, feeling suddenly threatened, vulnerable, *scared.* "Surely you're talking about some *other* woman you know," she said defensively.

"Maeve?"

She sighed and shut her eyes, her shoulders drooping with defeat.

"Please sit down," he said quietly. "Don't abandon *me.* I could use a friend right now. It gets lonely sometimes, being the lone man at the top of the ladder."

Don't abandon me. Nothing he might've said could've affected her more. That simple, unashamed plea, that honest admission that he didn't want to be alone— obviously the admiral had no such fears as *she* did about laying bare his heart, his feelings. Reluctantly she sat, pressed her palms together, and tried to avoid those dark, steady eyes.

He knows. Damn his hide, he knows I'm scared, knows me for what I am, knows that aye, maybe I really do care, and now he'll be able to use that against me if he so wishes—

He poured two glasses of rum, sat down, and pushed one across the table to her. "Do you have any idea how I felt when I saw your little schooner leading the might of the Mediterranean Fleet back to me this morning?"

She glanced at the door, her heart beginning to slam within her breast.

"Trust," he said gently, and she felt the warmth of his dark gaze upon her, "works both ways. You could have forsaken your promise to me and simply gone back to your island without ever summoning Lord Nelson. You could have abandoned *me,* but you didn't. And I *trusted* that you wouldn't. I trusted you so much that I kept my two ships sitting here in the middle of the damned ocean waiting for you, because I *knew* you'd return— and I didn't want you to come back and find me gone. I didn't want you to think that *I* had abandoned you, when it might seem that everyone else in your young life has done just that."

The room grew very silent. From somewhere above, came the shrill of a bosun's pipes. A long moment passed; then, he reached across the table to lay his knuckles against her cheek. She shut her eyes and caught his hand with her own, pressing her cheek against his palm and wishing for more than just a simple touch, wishing he would carry her away and make the world cease to exist, cease to matter. *Hold me, Gray. Love me. . . .*

"I never loved Catherine," he said softly. "I never had any intention of keeping her, or any other woman, as a mistress, because once I met you, Maeve, all other women ceased to exist for me. I lied to you about keeping a mistress, but only to trick you into taking me to Nelson. Forgive me love—I could think of no other way at the time, and didn't know you well enough to trust you not to bring me to Villeneuve instead." He pulled his hand from her grasp and rising, came around the table to put his hands on her shoulders and tilt her head up so that she had no choice but to look at him. "I love you, Maeve. Nothing can change that. *I love you,* and shall not be happy until you are my wife."

His wife. The words should have thrilled her; instead they brought a bleak despair to her heart, for *his wife* was something she could never be.

"You still want to marry me," she said flatly.

"Of course I still want to marry you." He pulled the hat from her head, tossed it to the table, ran his hands through her long, silky ponytail. "Nothing has changed."

He was right. Nothing *had* changed. She was still the Pirate Queen of the Caribbean. Pirate queens didn't desert their ships, their crews, the lives they'd built for themselves to take a reckless gamble on a man's love. And pirate queens didn't marry admirals.

Not if they intended to *remain* pirate queens.

She bent her head, picking at a hangnail on her thumb while he planted a kiss against her nape. "Gray," she said slowly, "I don't think we *can* get married."

"Don't be silly, love, of course we can get married."

"No. We can't."

His lips found the sensitive spot behind her ear. "And whyever not, sweeting?" he said, cheerfully.

"Because your career as a naval officer would never survive the reality of having a wife who's out roving the Spanish Main."

He looked amused and, straightening up, ruffled her hair affectionately before tearing the bright purple ribbon from her nape. Then his lips came down against hers and she moaned softly as his tongue explored the recesses of her mouth. "Ah, Maeve," he murmured, reluctantly breaking the kiss. "Any roving you do after we are wed will take place in our marriage bed."

"No, Gray," she said firmly, savoring the taste of him on her lips. "I intend to remain in my present capacity as the Pirate Queen."

"Don't be ridiculous, dear. There is no reason for you to carry on as you are. I can give you everything you need—lovely clothes, servants, and maids; grand parties, balls, and soirees. You will entertain dignitaries, diplomats, and naval officers, take tea with members of your own fair sex instead of crossing swords with criminals, killers, and rogues. By God, never again will you have to steal just to feed yourself, fight just to defend your honor! I will take care of you, Maeve. I will love you. As my wife you shall enjoy the life you *deserve* to have, one of grandeur, society, and status."

"But that is not the life I *want.*"

He drew back, hurt. "What do you mean? Isn't that what every woman wants?"

"It is not what *I* want. And I am not 'every woman.' "

"Well, what *do* you want, then?" He twisted the purple ribbon in his hands, looking bewildered, confused, lost. "Ask, Maeve, and you shall have it."

"My freedom. My ship. My life, to live as I see fit. Please understand, Gray. It's not that I don't love you . . . it's that I'm scared of becoming an admiral's wife. I won't fit in. I have obligations—to my girls, my ship—" Her voice grew desperate. "Please say you understand."

"As my wife, you won't *need* a ship."

"No. I *do* need my ship—"

"For God's sake, Maeve, I won't have my *wife* sailing the Caribbean as the modern-day incarnation of Anne Bonney!"

She leapt to her feet. "I thought you LIKED Anne Bonney!"

"Aye, but I damn well wouldn't marry the woman!"

"Oh, I understand, now," she cried, grabbing her hat and slamming it down atop her head. "It's only the fantasy, isn't it? Well, my gallant admiral, it's about time you learn to distinguish the difference between reality and fantasy. I am a pirate. Understand?" She jabbed her finger into his chest. "*Pirate.* I steal, plunder, and fight as well if not better than any man! I curse and drink and toast my skin in the sun! I'd never do as an admiral's wife, because I would embarrass you in front of those people you'd want me to impress!"

"No, Maeve, you would make me *proud,* d'you hear me, *PROUD!*"

"*I am a pirate!*"

"I wouldn't care if you're a bloody gutter rat; *I love you, dammit!*"

Their breathing echoed harshly through the cabin. She tore the purple ribbon from his hand and, turning her back on him, stuffed it down her bodice with quick, angry jabs. Outside, the sea washed around the rudder and from the sofa came the flag-captain's soft breathing.

She stared at the wall, trying in vain to control her emotions.

"Fine." His voice was flat and toneless from behind her. "I guess we can't get married, then."

"Aye." She picked up her hat, swallowing hard. "Guess not."

"For God's sake, Maeve!"

She spun around, eyes blazing. "Don't 'For God's sake' me! I've fought hard to get where I am and now you're asking me to give it all up! For what? Fancy balls, a life of bored leisure, and 'Lady' in front of my name? *Your* name? I'll not grow fat and lazy entertaining a bunch of stuffy hussies who'll only sneer at me and whisper about me behind their backs! I'll not desert, nay *abandon,* those who depend upon me for leadership, their next meal, their very existence! They're my *family* now, Gray, the only family I have! I cannot desert them! I learned my lesson the hard way, seven years ago, when I gave up everything I had for the sake of a man's *love,* and I'll never do it again!"

"Maeve!"

"Never!"

She slammed her hat down atop her head, stormed across the room, tore open the door—

And came face-to-face with el Perro Negro.

Chapter 28

Maeve didn't even have time for a startled scream. Her hand went for the knife at her waist even as el Perro Negro's fist crashed into her jaw and rocked her head back on her neck. White lights exploded in her brain and she fought to maintain consciousness, knowing even as she felt herself falling, sinking, fading, that she . . . could . . . not. . . .

Her eyes rolled up and with a little sigh, the Pirate Queen sagged bonelessly into el Perro Negro's clutches, as he snared her with one grimy arm before she hit the deck. Holding her with his arm beneath her ribs, he grabbed her hair, yanked her head back to expose her throat, and thrust the flat of his knife against the pale flesh.

He looked up—and saw the admiral facing him from behind the black mouth of a pistol.

El Perro Negro smiled. "Drop the gun, Admiral."

The dark eyes burned with murderous fury. "So help me God, if you so much as scratch her, you'll not live to see the light of morning."

"I said, *drop it*. Or the *puta* dies."

Gray never flinched, though his hand was sweating around the pistol's grip. How the pirates had escaped he didn't know, but all seven of them filled the doorway and there was no room for heroic measures. Beyond, he could see the faithful marine sentry, sprawled on the deck with his throat cut and gushing blood. On the deck directly above, he could hear two lieutenants, obviously unaware of what was happening, calmly discussing the weather. He looked into the desperate black eyes of el Perro Negro . . . at Maeve, hanging senseless under his arm, her glorious hair framing a face as white as death . . . thought of Colin, defenseless behind him and now, starting to stir—

"Kill her."

"Belay, damn you!" Cursing, he lowered the pistol, tossed it to the table on a snarl of disgust, and stood helplessly as el Perro Negro threw Maeve roughly against one of his cohorts. Then the pirate stepped behind Gray, looped his filthy arm around his neck, and held the knife to his throat.

"Pig-Eye! Gimme the *almirante*'s pistol."

Gray's dark stare bored into the eyes of the pirate who held Maeve. *If you so much as breathe on her, I'll kill you,* he silently vowed, and saw the man's face go pale in understanding. Then el Perro Negro had his gun and was holding it to his temple.

"One wrong move, Admiral, and I'll splatter the fleet's intelligence all over these pretty decks, ye hear?"

Gray didn't answer.

"You hear me, *Almirante?!*" the pirate shrieked, jabbing the mouth of the pistol against his skull.

"You'll not get away with this," Gray said softly, dangerously, his gaze still threatening the pirate who had Maeve.

El Perro Negro's laughter was high, desperate, hysterical, the stench of his unwashed body—and the fear that reeked from his every pore—pungent and acrid. "No, *Almirante,* I *will* get away with it! For I will take you, *king of the sea,* as hostage to ensure my escape from this ship. You think I'm *estupido,* fool enough to believe I'll get a fair trial back in England? Baah! You English *peegs* are all vile, wretched bastards and I'll

not take my chances— Tie up that *puta,* Renaldo, good
and tight. And hurry up, I don't have all day!"

"Ye ain't takin' 'er with us, *Capitán?*"

"I don't have time, *idiota!* I have the *almirante;* he
is all the insurance we need! Now, *move!*"

Maeve . . . Maeve, wake up . . . please, wake up. . . .

Splitting pain cleaved her skull and she moaned in
nausea, in agony, with every gentle roll of the deck beneath her. Something hard and unforgiving lay beneath
her cheek, and she tried to move her arm . . .
couldn't. . . .

"Maeve . . . help me."

The voice was real . . . the accent, English . . . not
Gray's.

She opened her eyes and saw her cousin Colin lying
on the deck not five feet away from her. He was on his
stomach, his bright hair falling over his sweating brow,
his gentle eyes glazed, and half of the bedding trailing
behind him and connecting him to the sofa. Stupidly,
she thought he was supposed to be in bed and started to
scold him. . . . Belatedly, she realized she, too, was lying on the deck. Memories slammed back into her aching head. She surged to her feet, only to lose her
balance and fall, painfully, back to the deck.

"Colin, the admiral—"

"I know," he whispered, his voice tight with agony.
"I heard most of it. They have him topside, Maeve.
I—I tried to go for help . . . can't get any farther with
this leg, God knows I tried—" .

"They'll kill him, Colin! They've tied me up; you've
got to help me get loose!"

"—God knows, I tried . . . you've got to save him."

"Dammit, Colin, you're *drunk!*"

"Yes, I daresay . . . drunk . . . Got to save Sir Graham."

Desperately, she managed to get to her feet, even as she noticed the deck above was deathly still and quiet.

"Colin, *help me!*"

He shook his head, and she saw a flash of sobriety in his eyes; she squatted down before him, thrusting her bound hands directly in his face. "Colin—my knife! It's in my belt, you've got to cut me loose!"

"Drunk . . . Maeve . . . might cut you . . . can't."

"For God's sake, Colin, we're talking about Gray's *life!" Damn you Gray for getting him so bloody soused he can't even think straight!* "Colin—my knife. *Please.*"

She felt him pulling the thick, deadly blade from her belt, bit her lip as he began to saw, slowly, too slowly, at her bound wrists. "Bloody *HELL* Colin, hurry up!"

"Hold still, almost there . . . hurry, Maeve . . . they'll kill him—"

She felt the last thread break free just as Colin sank back beneath the haze of pain and alcohol. On a little cry, she grabbed up the knife, stumbled once, twice, and fled the cabin, leaving the flag-captain passed out on the black-and-white-checkered deck.

"One more stupid move and your commander in chief *dies!*" el Perro Negro snarled, holding the pistol against Sir Graham's head and daring *Triton*'s crew to try any more foolish heroics in an attempt to rescue him.

El Perro Negro was not taking any chances. He felt the animal fury emanating from his hostage, the raw power in his body, the quiet rage in his stance. But the *almirante* had remained dangerously silent as they'd forced him up through the hatch and onto the quarter-deck, and that was somehow worse than anything he could've said, done, or threatened—for el Perro Negro had no idea what clever plan was going on behind those dark eyes, and that alone was enough to bring fear tingling up his spine.

That there *was* a plan, he had no doubt. El Perro Negro had been in the Caribbean long enough to know that Sir Graham Falconer was not a man to trifle with.

Now, standing on the deck beside him, he glanced up into the *almirante*'s swarthy face—and found those dark, cold eyes regarding him.

The *almirante* smiled, and the pirate felt the ripe sweat of fear and desperation beneath his armpits. *I will kill you,* those dangerous, enigmatic eyes seemed to say. *You just see if I don't.*

He would too, el Perro Negro knew. The English admiral would not forgive him for his treatment of the *puta.*

Nor for the insult to his flagship's crew.

He looked away, making sure the pistol was snugly against his hostage's skull. As they'd forced the *almirante* topside, one of the young midshipmen had come running to his aid, only to be felled by a shot from Renaldo's musket. A lieutenant had then pulled his own pistol—and on a sharp command from the *almirante,* angrily sheathed it. Only then had *Triton*'s crew—some seven hundred of them, el Perro Negro figured—gone silent, terrified to make a move for fear he would kill their commander in chief.

Obviously, he thought in satisfaction, they held their *almirante* in high regard indeed.

Darkness was falling, and fast. There was no time to waste. Forcing several of *Triton*'s unwilling sailors to help them, el Perro Negro's men were already preparing to swing out one of the flagship's lug-sailed launches on tackles rigged to the great ship's fore and main yards. With it, they could make a clean escape into the darkness and be away before any of the other ships, or even Nelson, aboard *Victory* a cable's length away, knew what they were about. El Perro Negro's only regret was that he didn't have time to bring that *puta* the Pirate Queen along with him. How he would enjoy slamming his own *blade* into her over and over again before he killed her.

As for the *almirante*—

Once they were well clear of the big flagship, he'd have no use for his valuable hostage. One bullet to the head and the Royal Navy wouldn't, either.

"Hurry up, you damned fools!" he snarled.

High above, he heard the yards creaking as they took the weight of the launch. He tilted his head back to look—

And Sir Graham made his move.

A vicious elbow jab to the pirate's ribs, a swift uppercut to his jaw; the pistol flew from el Perro Negro's stunned grasp, and with the desperation of the damned, he dived for it at the same time his hostage did. His body hit the *almirante*'s, bringing them both heavily to the deck, and snatching up the pistol, the pirate thrust it between the dark and challenging eyes of the man beneath him.

His eyes wild, el Perro Negro screamed, "I'll blow your brains out for that, you *estupido*—"

A voice, deadly with purpose, came from behind him.

"I believe that prize is *mine.*"

Turning, el Perro Negro lunged to his feet. He saw a beautiful woman in purple, the flash of metal through the air—and then, nothing.

Gasping and twitching, he was dead before he even hit the deck, the Pirate Queen's dagger buried in his throat.

Chapter 29

◦───୨◎୧───◦

Stunned, shocked, speechless, Gray lay on his back and stared up at the woman who stood triumphantly atop a cannon fifteen feet away.

For a long, terrible moment, everything was still.

And then, chaos.

Officers running to his assistance. A pack of angry seamen leaping on the other pirates. A short scuffle, a lieutenant shouting wildly for order—

—and Maeve.

There she stood, still atop the long black breech of the cannon, her hair blowing wildly about her face, her head high, proud, defiant.

Their gazes collided, hers glittering with relief and love, his blank with appalled shock.

She jumped down from the cannon and walked toward him with the regal hauteur of a queen.

He watched her coming. He didn't move, though a score of hands were reaching down to help him up. Couldn't speak. Not yet. Again, he saw that vicious dagger scything through the air, true as an arrow. Again he saw the look of high triumph on Maeve's beautiful, angry face as the blade caught the pirate in the throat. Again, he heard el Perro Negro's strangled gasp, the sounds of his choking and dying on his own blood.

And now he saw Maeve standing directly above him, while his officers and seamen stared at her in awe and shock.

"Excuse me," she said, smiling sweetly, and they respectfully moved aside so that she could reach down to help him up.

He looked up at that slender arm, that feminine hand that had thrown the knife with such skilled and savage accuracy, those golden tiger eyes that shone with love only for him. He saw the knife, arcing through the air once more, saw her standing there on that cannon, never blinking an eye over the fact she had just brutally killed a man—

And felt sick.

He could not touch that hand. He got to his feet, shakily. Seeing the knife, flying through the air. Again . . . and again.

"Sir Graham, are you all right?"

Heard her words, echoing over and over in his mind. *Well, my gallant admiral, it's about time you learned the difference between reality and fantasy . . . I am a pirate.*

Dear God, he'd just learned the difference. He had thought her piratical antics charming, titillating, and on the whole, harmless. *Fantasy.* But to have seen her hurl a dagger into el Perro Negro's throat and gloat over the fact she'd just killed a man. . . .

Reality.

I am a pirate.

"Sir Graham!" It was Lieutenant Stern, desperately gripping his elbow. "Sir, I repeat, are you all right?"

Maeve's hand was still stretched toward him. He felt, rather than saw, her expression go from triumph to bewilderment to hurt as he ignored that graceful hand and moved past her. Lieutenant Stern tried to take his arm. Gray waved him off, raked his fingers through his hair and moved toward the hatch.

He shook off offers of help, felt himself nodding woodenly to anxious inquiries over his welfare . . . saw again the knife arcing through the air.

He felt her eyes on his back.

"Gray!"

He could not look at her.

"Gray!" she cried, pitifully.

But the admiral kept walking, and did not look back.

Stunned, Maeve stood on the dark quarterdeck, the wind blowing her skirts around her bare legs, her hair about her face. She heard the excited talk of the men around her, dumbly accepted their gushing praise, their gratitude for saving their admiral—and stared at the hatch where he had gone.

One of the little midshipmen was babbling excitedly in her ear but she never heard him. A smartly dressed lieutenant was offering to get her something to drink, but she only shook her head, staring at that spot in the deck where Gray had disappeared, and feeling the raw agony of rejection welling up in the very pit of her soul.

She had seen it in his eyes. Horror and shame—that she had thrown the dagger, that she had reveled in the killing, that she hadn't fainted dead away as a proper *admiral's woman* might have, should have, would have, done. Was she supposed to just stand there screaming while el Perro Negro blew out the brains of the man she loved? No, she had taken matters into her own hands when his own crew could not, and saved her admiral's life.

And he had rejected her.

Out of the corner of her eye, she saw the seamen lifting el Perro Negro's bloody corpse and heaving it over the side, the red-haired Lieutenant Pearson directing the crew to rig halters to the foreyard for immediate execution of the remaining pirates.

I didn't do anything wrong, Gray. I merely saved your life, and I would do it again in a moment. She swallowed hard against the sudden burning in her throat, thanking God for the darkness that concealed her misery. *I'd do it again in a moment, because, dammit, I love you.*

She stared hard at that darkened hatch for a moment longer and then, her back stiff with pride, moved away, feeling the great deck moving beneath her feet, the sea wind clawing at her hair. At the nettings, she stood and looked out over the darkening sea. Where her heart had been there was a great, empty vat, full of despair and grief.

He had turned away. Just as her parents would have done had *they* seen her hurl a dagger and cut down a man. Gray would never want her now, it was clear. Just as her parents wouldn't if they could see what their headstrong daughter had become after seven years of fighting for survival and supremacy in a Caribbean that showed no favors to anyone.

"Hello, Father. Hello, Mother"—she was a grown woman now, and "Daddy" and "Mama" would no longer do—*"I'm sorry you thought I was dead all these years but I've been busy roving, pillaging, stealing, and oh, yes, killing. Don't look so shocked, it's only been in self-defense or to save the lives of those I hold dear . . . Mama? Daddy! No, wait! Wait. . .*

She saw them turning away in rejection and disgust, refusing to accept this ugly, savage monster that had once been their daughter.

Turning away—as Gray had done.

Her heart was cracking and going to pieces, the wind lashing her hair across her face. She saw a boat putting out from *Victory,* and knew she couldn't bear the condemnation on Nelson's face, either.

I am what I am, she thought, proudly, defiantly. *So damn them all to hell.*

Her head high, she called for Lieutenant Pearson, and asked him to fire the two guns that would bring *Kestrel* back for her.

* * *

Morning came and with it the sounds of footsteps on the deck above her head scrubbing and scouring the sand and night's spume away.

Maeve opened her eyes and lay staring up at the deckhead while her little ship came awake around her. As it was every morning, her first thought was of her father, who had once slept in this very same bed. She wondered what he was doing now. What her mother was doing now. If they missed her.

And then she thought of Gray, and his cold rejection of her.

Sitting up in bed, she put her aching jaw in her hands, her hair spilling into her eyes. Then, she raked the thick tresses back, swung her legs out of bed, stumbled to her washbasin, and began to dress.

She put on the necklace of sharks' teeth. She donned baggy breeches, a loose silk shirt, a dark green vest of patterned brocade. Her dagger was gone, still buried in el Perro Negro's throat; lamenting its loss, she found another to replace it and, on a note of sullen defiance, jammed it into the scabbard on her belt.

She was just ready to go topside and order her ship to be put about and sailed back to her island, when there was a knock on the door.

"Captain? You awake?"

"Aye," she grunted, miserably.

The door opened to admit young Aisling, with Sorcha right behind her. Between them they carried a tray, a pot of coffee, and breakfast—hot oatmeal, a piece of fruit, and a mug of stiff, bitter ale.

On the empty plate was a folded note.

"If it's from the admiral, I don't want it," Maeve said.

"Oh, it's from the Admiral all right!" Aisling chirped, and despite herself, Maeve felt a quick flutter of hope within her breast.

"Give it to me, then."

"You sure?"

"Dammit, just give it to me!"

She grabbed the note, broke the seal, and saw a paragraph of stilted, crabbed writing that was nearly as bad as Gray's.

My dear Captain Merrick, the note began.

Nelson. She lowered the note in disappointment. *Wrong admiral.*

"His lordship had a midshipman send it over just as soon as it got light out, Captain! What's it say?"

"Yes, read it! Read it!"

She turned away, unable to look at the blistering words she knew she would find. He would condemn her, she knew he would, and somehow that hurt just as much as Gray's reaction had—for Lord Nelson, like her parents, like Gray—was all that was good, all that was heroic, all that was honorable and just—all that she, the Pirate Queen of the Caribbean, was not and could never be.

Trembling, she brought the note up, and her gaze fell to the choppy, left-handed scrawl. *My dear Captain Merrick,* she read again, *it is with the deepest sense of gratitude and relief that I send you this note to thank you for once again coming to the aid of the Royal Navy. You acted with calmness, skill, and valour, and had you not thought quickly and calmly during the attempted murder of Sir Graham Falconer, I fear that our service, and our Country, would have lamented the loss of one of its finest officers.*

"Forever in your debt, Nelson and Brönte," she trailed off.

"What's it say, Captain? What's it say?"

Dazedly, she handed them the note. "Read it yourself," she said quietly, and strode from the cabin.

In another, nearby ship, Sir Graham also lay in his lonely bed, thinking, as the sun rose over a silver sea and suffused it with the colors of dawn.

It wasn't really much of a bed, but rather a swinging box, suspended from a pole and enclosed with curtains lovingly embroidered by his little sister. Closed off as he was from that beautiful sunrise, his main cabin, and the rest of the ship, Sir Graham was alone with nothing but his thoughts.

He heard his servants bustling about in the dining cabin just beyond his sleeping quarters, laying out his breakfast, his uniform, and hot water for shaving. He heard footsteps just above his head as Colin's servants, or maybe even Dr. Ryder, looked in on the flag-captain, who had been moved back to his own cabin after showing marked signs of improvement.

Maeve.

No sooner had she departed for *Kestrel* than Nelson himself had come aboard H.M.S. *Triton,* having seen the commotion and heard pistol shots from his own ship. And no sooner had the little hero gleaned the details of what had happened than he was singing Her Majesty's praises—and slamming a blistering broadside of anger into Gray's disbelieving ears.

"You damned *fool,* she saved your life, by God!" Nelson had raged, furiously working the stump of his arm through his sleeve. "Is this how you show your *gratitude?*"

Gray flung his arm over his eyes, wishing he could block all of it out. The killing. Last night's executions. Maeve. Nelson's harsh anger. But damn it, Nelson hadn't seen the woman *he* loved kill a man in cold blood, and delight in the doing!

He tore the hangings aside and crawled from the cot. The smell of hot coffee and sizzling pork assailed him, making him feel sick. Beneath his feet the deck was cool and damp, and he dreaded the thought of going topside and seeing, in the light of day, the place where his beloved had hacked down a man and then looked at

him like a cat expecting a word of praise for laying a
dead and gutted mouse at its owner's doorstep.

There would be blood there. The stains might never
come out.

*It is time you learned the difference between fantasy
and reality.*

He reached up, raked a hand through his hair, caught
his thumb on the gold earring—and nearly ripped it out
on a wave of disgust.

Suddenly, there was nothing remotely alluring about
pirates.

Nothing at all.

On a futile hope that a similar, forgiving note might
come from the man she loved, the Pirate Queen decided
to remain with the British Fleet for another hour and no
more. She went on deck and, as though to defy Sir Graham's distaste for her prowess at the sport, engaged in
a savage sword fight with Enolia that nearly killed the
both of them. Then, trembling and exhausted, she collapsed in the shade of the gunwale and sullenly nursed
a mug of cool ale.

Nothing.

She took out her dagger and pared her fingernails.

And still, no message came.

That was it, then. To hell with him. She got to her
feet, slammed the mug atop the binnacle, and stormed
to the tiller.

Orla met her along the way, her eyes worried.

"Put the ship about, we're going back to the island,"
Maeve snarled.

"But Maeve—"

"I said, *put the ship about!*" she shouted, and after a
hesitant, mutinous pause, her friend went forward, calling for assistance to raise *Kestrel*'s foresail.

All along the deck, she saw her crew staring at her as
though she'd taken leave of her senses.

Maeve spun around and went to the tiller, drumming her fingers on the smooth wood in angry impatience. Up went the big foresail, and she felt her heart breaking with every inch the long, swinging gaff crawled. Sail spilled to the wind, shook itself out, thundered and fluttered in the early morning sunshine. Shadows swung to and fro over the deck with every swing of the great assembly of spar and canvas.

Still, no boats putting out from H.M.S. *Triton,* no alarmed figure appearing on the quarterdeck, no signal, nothing.

She felt raw, wrenching pain clawing at her chest.

"Put up the main," she ordered curtly, and as her crew ran to the halliards and began to haul up the throat and peak, she couldn't help glancing over at the H.M.S. *Triton.*

Movement.

A flag, rising up the mast . . . another . . . another.

"Captain! Sir Graham is signaling!"

"Sir Graham can go to bloody hell and rot there 'til his balls turn black."

"We have to get the signal book Captain Lord issued us so we can see what he's saying!" Aisling cried, grabbing her sister and racing below.

More flags soared up the great warship's masts.

"Hurry up, damn you!" Maeve shouted to her hesitant crew.

She stared back at *Triton*—and saw a gun port opening along that massive, towering side. The black snout of a cannon crawled out into the sunshine, its hungry mouth trained on *Kestrel*—

"Just who the bleeding *hell* does he think he is?!" she snarled, even as another port opened, and yet, another. She turned just as the Irish girls came running forward, the signal book in their hand. "Give me that damned thing!"

And there, the last flag, fluttering angrily from the big man-of-war's mast.

She flipped through the pages, noting the meaning of each flag even as another gun poked out of the warship's sides . . . and another.

And closed the book with a furious snap.

"What's he saying, Captain? What's he saying?!"

She stared at the big ship, the colorful array of flags waving in the wind.

"He says," she muttered, on a dark little laugh, "that if I so much as even *think* of sailing off, he'll blow us out of the water."

"Oh, Captain, surely he wouldn't do *that!*"

But Maeve remembered the admiral's shocked and stricken face when she'd saved him from el Perro Negro . . . and wasn't so sure.

Chapter 30

I t had been seven days since they'd caught up with the merchant convoy, two weeks since Sir Graham had ordered *Kestrel* to remain with his fleet, and a half hour since Sir Graham had joined Colin Lord for dinner in the flag-captain's cabin.

The atmosphere between them was strained and tense, for with every league the fleet, the convoy, and Gray's few warships drew closer to Europe, with every league the little schooner *Kestrel* hovered mutinously at its fringes, with every league of sun and rain and wind and salt they put behind them, Sir Graham's normally jovial mood had evaporated into a dark and simmering silence that no one—with the exception of Nelson and Colin—dared to disturb.

Courageous to a fault, diligent in his pursuit of every detail, possessive of a keen maritime acumen, and guided by an unflappable sense of fairness, duty, and insight, Colin was by no means stupid, and should have known better than to broach the subject of Maeve Merrick. Yet Gray saw it coming; it was there in Colin's eyes, in the faint puckering of his fair brows, in the way he was fidgeting and shifting the pillow beneath his thigh to take the weight off his leg.

Gray picked up his napkin and dabbed at his lips. "Leg bothering you, Colin?"

"Not really, sir. It's a bit itchy beneath the cast, but otherwise, healing quite nicely, I think."

"Good. I'd hate like hell for anything to happen to you. You've been the best damned flag-captain I've ever had."

The young captain's cheeks colored, and gratitude lit his eyes. "Thank you, sir." Distractedly, he pushed a piece of roast beef around on his plate, making a dollop of gravy in its center. "Though sometimes, I wish I'd chosen a different career . . . something that preserves life, rather than destroys it. Forgive me, sir, but I've seen enough of death and killing to last a lifetime, I'm afraid."

Death and killing. "Aye, so have I," Gray drawled, and glared out the window, where he could just see the distant shape of *Kestrel* hugging the horizon, as if poised for flight. He had no doubt she would've been long gone, if not for the fact he'd ordered his frigates to keep an eye on the little pirate schooner and fire on her if she tried to escape.

The flag-captain finally looked up at Gray. "If I may speak, sir?"

Gray raised his wineglass—he was no longer drinking rum—sipped it, and motioned impatiently. "Be my guest."

"Well, I've been thinking, sir, about that time you came to me and asked, in a roundabout way, the best way to, er, go after the heart of the Pirate Queen. . . ."

The admiral's fist tightened around the stem of the glass.

Colin, unflappable and unfazed, ignored the sudden tenseness, merely pushing the beef around and around on his plate. "Well, forgive my bluntness, sir, but I think you're behaving very hypocritically."

Gray's glass slammed down on the table so hard it shattered into a thousand pieces. Wine went everywhere, and servants came running.

"Damn you, I'll have you watch what you say to me!"

Colin lifted his head, regarding him steadily. "I merely speak the truth, sir, as I see it."

The admiral glared at him, bristling with anger, his shoulders very stiff beneath the proud epaulets.

Colin did not back down. "You loved her when she would not have you, when you thought her nothing but a little girl playing at being a pirate queen. She was a source of amusement to you, a . . . fantasy."

Sir Graham's swarthy countenance went dark with fury.

"Forgive me, sir, but you've put this ship in peril with your orders to fly pirate flags, your unconventional habits, and your expectations that my crew and I turn a blind eye to your doings. We have done so, sir, because you are a fine commander and we have nothing but respect for you. But I cannot respect a man who conducts his behavior under a double standard."

The admiral lunged to his feet on a snarl of fury. "You'll watch your damned tongue, *Captain Lord!*"

The young captain put down his fork, placing it just so beside his plate, and looked calmly up at his commanding officer. "Sir, if I may ask you a question. . . ."

A muscle jumped along the admiral's jaw, and Colin saw his hand fisting with suppressed fury. "Out with it," he bit out, through clenched teeth.

"If it had been *I* who'd thrown that dagger and saved you from el Perro Negro's bullet, would you have rejected me as you have her?"

Gentle eyes of lavender met angry ones of dark fire. Sunlight drifted through the stern windows, struck gold in Colin's hair, glanced off the tassels of Gray's epaulets.

"I repeat, sir, would you?"

The admiral's nostrils flared. "You are a *man,* by God!"

"So?"

"That's bloody different!"

"I take that to mean it is permissible for me to defend those I love, even if it means killing someone, just because I am a man? That if I were a woman and had just saved the life of a high-ranking officer, it would be less than heroic? Sir, you cannot sit there across from me and tell me that if the situation were reversed, and Maeve's life had been the one in peril, you would not have done the same as *she* did. You cannot, for that matter, tell me you did not want to kill el Perro Negro yourself when you saw him strike her unconscious, and, I daresay, you *would* have killed him if only the opportunity had afforded itself."

"That's a damned stupid question, *of course I would have!*"

"Precisely my point, sir," Colin said, returning his attention to the beef.

Gray merely stared at him, helpless against the younger man's logic. Angry because he had no defense against it. Feeling his temper rising ... rising ...

The flag-captain continued in his calm, infuriating way. "You may think she should be soft and feminine, pampered and sweet, a *lady* in the accepted sense of the word, but she is what she is, sir, and acted with those qualities that, in a man, would have been applauded as heroic. Courageous." The gentle eyes looked up at Gray, silently condemning. "I'm sorry, sir. But I think you are unfair to reject the woman you love just because she defended that which *she* held most dear."

The admiral's fist crashed down on the table. "You think it's unfair, do you?!" he roared.

"Aye, sir. I do."

They stared at each other, neither willing to give ground—and, for a brief, terrible moment, Colin thought his superior was going to strike him. Then, Sir Graham's chest rose on a great, shaky sigh, and he sat heavily down in his chair to glare sullenly out the stern window.

"Sir?"

"You're a damned cunning bastard," the admiral growled, and without another word, attacked his own supper.

An hour later, Gray—embarrassed, angry, and determined—called for his barge, signaled for *Kestrel* to close with the flagship, and, wearing his best uniform, decided to make peace with the Pirate Queen.

His officers saluted him as he strode grimly past them, but he knew the gossip would be flying the moment he left the flagship. And as the barge cut through the heavy swells, the spray drenching his fine uniform and soaking the smart, handpicked crew, he saw their grinning faces exchange silent comments, saw their amused gazes flickering between the little schooner and their dark and angry admiral.

"Row, damn you!" he roared, and gripped the gunwale so hard it nearly broke off in his hand.

The schooner's black side loomed before, then above him. High above his head, her two masts thrust toward the sky. Gray waited for the barge to hook onto the little ship's main chains and, grasping the ladder that Aisling and Sorcha tossed eagerly over the side to him, began to climb.

He was halfway up the schooner's side when he happened to glance up and saw the bell-like mouth of a blunderbuss staring him in the face.

"Halt right there, Admiral," came Maeve's low, angry voice. "Or so help me God, I'll shoot."

Gray merely set his jaw and on a dark smile, continued climbing.

"I'm warning you, Gray!"

Beneath him, he heard one of the barge crew gasp in alarm . . . another, choking back an amused snigger.

"Dammit, Gray, don't make me hurt you!"

He reached up, seized the cold metal of the weapon,

and with one savage jerk, yanked it from her hand and flung it into the sea.

And kept climbing.

Up he came, his hat now level with the schooner's gunwale, his progress never faltering.

A cutlass thrust itself before his nose. "I mean it, Gray!"

Never pausing, he knocked it aside and began to haul himself up and over the gunwale. She tried to step on his fingers as he reached for a hold. He grabbed her trim ankle. She pulled her knife on him. He snared her wrist and threw the weapon aside. She screamed every curse she knew at him.

And he pulled her into his arms and kissed her, to the wild cheers of her own traitorous crew.

Small fists beat at his chest. Her bare foot slammed down on his shoe. Her angry protests vibrated against his mouth, and her knee came up on a vicious swing to connect with his groin.

Gasping, he doubled over in agony, his hat tumbling from his head and his vision going black around the edges.

"Admiral!" Aisling and Sorcha caught him as he fell, their hands beneath his elbows. "Admiral! You all right?"

He stumbled to his feet, shook his head to clear it, and recovered in time to see Maeve's stiff, silk-clad back just disappearing down the hatch.

"I'm fine," he ground out and, pausing only long enough to retrieve his hat and slam it back down on his head, went after her.

The fierce Enolia tried to bar his way with her cutlass, but he kicked it aside and kept walking. Down the hatch he went, after Maeve. He strode right up to the door of her cabin, seized the latch, and yanked.

Locked.

"Open the door, Maeve."

"Rot in hell, you wretch!"

"Open the goddamned door, Maeve."

"I said, go to—"

He raised his foot, drew back, and with all his strength, kicked the latch. Once, twice—and then it burst apart under the force of his blows, the door crashed open, and he was in the cabin and striding angrily across the tiny space.

He saw her, facing him with her back against the bulkhead, her breasts thrusting against her shirt and her face white with rage. She was holding a pistol, pointing it at him. Her hands were shaking. Her throat was working. He went right up to her, seized her collar, yanked her forward, and drew her up to within an inch of his face.

"I have one thing to say to you," he shouted, holding her so close that her breath touched his cheeks, "and one thing only—"

"Say it!" she screamed.

He smiled, his teeth flashing white in his swarthy face. "I love you."

And then his head bent and he claimed her lips with his own.

She melted beneath the sheer force of the kiss, the fury and love and desperation with which he drove his mouth down against hers. The pistol fell from her hand, but she never heard it hit the deck. He forced her backward, crushing her between his hard body and the bulkhead. His tongue plunged into her mouth, and she smelled salt water in his clothes, tasted it on his lips. Gasping, she tore her lips from his. "Bloody hell, Gray, how dare you think you can just come in here and—"

Her tirade was effectively cut off by his mouth slamming down on hers once more. He kissed her with an almost brutal desperation, robbing the very breath from her body, the strength from her legs, the resolve from her will. She could not resist him. Had never been able to—

She came up, dazed and gasping, her eyes glazed with desire.

"I'll dare anything I damn well please," he ground out, his dark face just inches from her own. He reached up, tore the hat from his head, the sword belt from his waist, and flung both to the deck. "Tell me you love me, Maeve."

"I—"

"Tell me!"

"Aye, I love you, but I'll not marry you! I'm a bloody *pirate,* remember? A vile, despicable, thieving, *murdering* pi—"

His lips came down against hers yet again. Struggling, Maeve felt his tongue stabbing into the warm recesses of her mouth, his hot breath burning her cheeks. It was no use fighting him. It was no use fighting how she felt about him. Sighing, she sagged against him, even as his hands caught the collar of her shirt and, with one savage yank, ripped the blousy garment from her body. Her breasts filled his hands and she moaned as he tore his mouth from hers and left a hot path of kisses simmering the length of her neck, capturing first one nipple and sucking hungrily on the hard bud, then the other, until she was writhing with delight and despair.

"Dammit, Gray . . . I cannot resist you. . . . You cannot resist me. . . . Does it have to *be* this way?"

He bent his head, licking, tasting, suckling, her breasts, while all the while his hand strayed lower until it found the hot core of her womanhood and made her writhe with the pressure he exerted there. Her knees felt liquid, but she was able to hold her balance, pinned as she was between him and the bulkhead. Dark spots swam before her eyes. His hand drove beneath her waistband, yanking the trousers down and off; she felt his fingers sliding inside of her, and on a half sob of anger and defeat, sank down against his hand.

"No Maeve, it *doesn't* have to be this way," he muttered, against the damp hair at her temple. "Two people who love each other ought to be together. Not fighting each other."

He stepped back and caught her as she fell. She felt herself being hoisted up in his arms, but he never made it to the bunk. Halfway across the cabin he set her feet down, tore off his coat, laid her down atop it, and kissed her until she couldn't see straight, think straight, even remember her name. His body covered hers, seeking, driving, wanting. Her hands clawed impatiently at his shirt, found the damp skin just beneath, then downward, the flap of his breeches. His mouth drove against hers and his body crushed her, forcing her head and spine against the deck. But she never felt the pain, never felt anything but the boiling cauldron that was her blood, the stiffened arousal that reared against her hand.

The climb was short, fast, hard, and brilliant. He drove himself into her, and took her with a savage intensity that nearly impaled her to the deck upon which she lay. And when it was over, she lay bathed in sweat and the ashes of her anger, clasping his body fiercely to her heart. His breathing was harsh and fast above her; his curses, soft and angry. He reached up, and gliding his hand into her hair, stroked it gently, over and over again.

"I can't believe I just did that," he muttered. "I feel like a bloody animal. God, Maeve, tell me I didn't hurt you."

"You didn't."

He raised himself up, taking his weight on his forearms so as not to crush her. He was silent for a moment and then he asked, "Can you forgive me, Maeve?"

"There is nothing to forgive you for, Gray," she said,

with a little smile. "You have made love to me. Never apologize for *that.*"

"No, no, you don't understand." He dropped tender kisses on her brow, her cheeks. "I turned away from you after you killed el Perro Negro. After you'd saved my life, for God's sake. I was wrong, Maeve. Wrong to expect you to behave like a fainthearted bit of fluff, wrong to be angry with you for showing the bold courage that first attracted me to you. Here you defended me, saved my life, and how did I thank you? By turning away." His voice was anguished. "I feel like a vile, undeserving *wretch.*"

"You are." She grinned at his helpless look, then reached up to touch her finger to his nose. "But I forgive you, Gray."

"Do you, Maeve? Do you, honestly—"

"I *forgive* you, Gray," she said again, kissing him.

"Then you will give up your life as a pirate and marry me?"

"I wish I could, but I can't."

"For God's sake, Maeve—"

"Gray, I told you, I have *obligations.*"

He stared down at her for a long, frustrated moment; then, his eyes went black with hopelessness and he lunged to his feet, leaving her lying there on the floor with his coat beneath her back. He buttoned his breeches. Picked up his sword belt. Retrieved his hat.

"Gray, please, you don't understand!"

He shook his head. "Belay it, Maeve, I don't want to hear it. I offer you everything I have, and still you throw it back in my face. Go find some thieving scoundrel like the one you just disposed of, if that's what you want. Because you sure as hell don't want an officer, despite whatever rubbish you once told me about *Gallant Knights.*"

"But why must you *marry* me?" She got up, hugging her arms to skin that was suddenly cold where he had earlier touched it. She felt empty inside, scared. "Must you own me, Gray? Can't we just be lovers?"

He spun around, his eyes blazing with blue fire. "I wish to marry you, Maeve, because I'm an honorable man! I wish to marry you because you are everything I ever wanted in a woman! It has nothing to do with *ownership,* I wish to marry you because, dammit, *I love you!"*

He snatched his coat up from the deck, and donned it with angry, jerky movements that nearly tore the lining out of the sleeves. Maeve caught her lip between her teeth to keep it from trembling, to keep herself from saying the words she longed to say, that he longed to hear.

But then she thought of her family of pirates she would be deserting, and the words just wouldn't come out.

"Good day, madam," the admiral said coldly, and turning on his heel, strode swiftly from the cabin.

"Really, Falconer, you are the *last* man I would expect to have trouble getting a lady to marry you!"

The two admirals walked *Victory*'s stately quarter-deck, working off their suppers and listening to the band playing "Hearts of Oak." They were a familiar sight, Sir Graham munching a cookie and staring glumly off at *Kestrel,* Nelson fretting with his empty sleeve and staring anxiously out to sea. Tonight, like every night for the past week, they were together, commiserating over their mutual misery.

For Nelson, the likelihood of catching up with his panicky nemesis Villeneuve grew more and more remote as the British forces neared Europe. His face was pale and haggard, and he was in desperate need of rest. His nights were hellish, and he managed no more than two hours of sleep before violent coughing spells woke him; then, huddled in his coat against the damp night

air, he would go up on the lonely quarterdeck and stare
dismally out to sea.

His thoughts were sadly transparent. He had crossed
the ocean in search of an enemy, and failed to find and
destroy him. He had let England down. He would no
longer be a hero. Villeneuve was still loose, and probably safely back in some French or Spanish port by
now. But the threat of invasion still remained, and Nelson could not sleep, could not eat, could not think of
anything but his frantic desire to *annihilate* the enemy
fleet—and the brilliant new plan he was working out
for doing just that.

"You think it amusing, do you?" Gray was saying.
"The one woman in the world I have ever truly loved,
and she won't have me." He stared off at the distant
schooner. "By God, sir, I don't know what else to do to
convince her of my love for her."

Poor Falconer, Nelson thought. He would not have a
practicing pirate for a wife, and she would not have an
admiral for a husband. Two stubborn people, neither
willing to make compromises . . . a fine mess, the two
of them were in!

"Persist in your chase, Gray, and I daresay you'll be
up with her soon enough!"

"No. She refuses to give up her life as a pirate."

"And it is unthinkable, of course, for you, as an admiral, to marry one."

"I don't know what to do, dammit."

"She'll come around."

"I don't think so."

"For God's sake, Falconer, the girl's in love with
you! If only you could have seen the state she was in
when she came to me with the news you'd found the
enemy fleet."

Gray perked up, ever so slightly. "Really?"

"Aye, really." Nelson smiled with remembrance.
" 'Twas quite affecting, if I do say so myself."

Victory hit a swell, and spray hissed along the great hull. Nelson thought of the letter he'd sent the girl's parents when she'd lain so close to death, and wondered idly if he should mention it to Gray. But maybe some matters were better left alone.

"Well, she still refuses to marry me. You'd think that any woman would want the life I can give her, but no. Not Maeve. She refuses to exchange her life as a she-wolf for one of comparative dullness, boredom, and wealth."

"Sarcasm does not become you, Gray."

"No? Well, I have been chasing her as ardently as you have the French with the same fruitless results!"

Nelson sighed, stopped, and looked the younger man straight in the eye. "Let me tell you a little story about the French, Gray. . . ."

Just off *Victory*'s weather quarter, *Triton* awaited her admiral's return. Framed in the space between bowsprit and forecourse, Gray could just see *Kestrel*, a lone speck on the horizon.

Maeve, he thought, bleakly. *What will it* take*?*

"For two years I blockaded the enemy at Toulon," Nelson was saying. Then, irritably: "Damn you, Falconer, are you listening to me?"

"Why yes, sir, of course—"

Nelson pursed his lips and made a noise of impatience. "For two years," he said again, "I blockaded the enemy at Toulon. Call me impatient, but I was not happy keeping them bottled up, safely in port. *I wanted them to come out so I could fight them.*"

Gray looked at his friend. Nelson was staring out to sea, his sharp face in profile, his bold nose as straight and true as the tiller of a sailboat.

"And?" he prompted in mild annoyance, wondering what Nelson was getting at.

"And so I devised a scheme to tempt them out."

The setting sun turned the sea to molten gold. Nelson

stared at the fiery orb, his poor, abused eye beginning
to water helplessly. "The French admiral was like a
mouse playing bo-peep at the edge of her hole, creeping
out to see what I was up to, darting back in, tormenting
me, teasing me—" He paused, seized by a spell of
coughing, then he turned to Gray, his eye penetrating
and fierce. *"And I knew that as long as I hovered near
her hole, that mouse would never come out.* So you
know what I did? I shall tell you! I took my fleet out
to sea, and in so doing, I *tempted the mouse out of the
hole!*

"Veal-noove," Nelson declared, wagging his finger
before Gray's nose, "may have escaped me at Toulon,
but when I catch up with him—*as indeed I will!*—I
shall pounce, I shall destroy, I shall *annihilate* him!
And to that end, Falconer, it is time for me to tell you
about my plan, my plan to defeat him and any hopes
that devil Bonaparte has of invading England. Now
come with me, and I will explain it to you!"

With Nelson leading the way, they strode beneath the
poop deck—and it was there, in the gloomy shadows
that Nelson revealed the true magnitude of his genius.

"Now pay attention," he snapped.

Snatching up a pencil, the little Admiral flipped over
a chart and drew a line of ships while Gray leaned over
his shoulder, watching with growing attentiveness.
"The British navy," Nelson said, sketching madly, "has
always put its ships in a line alongside that of the enemy, the victor being determined by whichever side has
the superior force of guns. But I am devising a *new*
plan, Gray, a singular, brilliant plan which *cannot fail.*

"This is *Veal-noove's* fleet"—Nelson dashed off a
line of wedges representing ships—"all sailing in the
traditional line-of-battle formation. And these"—he
penciled in three short columns, all spearheading toward the long enemy line on a right-angled collision
course—"are *my* ships. I will break the line, Falconer.

I will smash it in three places and thus overwhelm them! Do you understand, Gray? Tempt the mouse out of the hole, then divide and conquer! It is the only way . . . *and it—can—not—fail!"*

He slammed the pencil down and looked up, his eyes penetrating, fiery.

"You are . . . brilliant, sir."

"I said, *do you understand,* Gray?!"

Gray met that intent stare. "Yes, sir," he said softly. "I understand *indeed."*

A plan to tempt the mouse out of the hole. A plan to *divide and conquer.*

Not a French fleet—but a Pirate Queen's heart.

"Very well then," Nelson snapped, but his eyes were gleaming. He smiled, faintly. "Now get back to your ship, Falconer, and be about it!"

Maeve's first glimpse of England was one she would never forget, a distant sighting of wind and surf-beaten rock stretching away into a long coast swallowed up by morning mist. Clutching the rail, she choked back the seasickness that had been hers for the last week, and stared bleakly off into the fog.

She had never been seasick a day in her life.

And she knew that her nausea was not *mal de mer.*

Now, as the convoy and the little squadron that accompanied it beat its way up-channel—the two frigates that had survived the battle on station to windward, *Triton* lumbering along with the rear admiral's flag fluttering in and out of the mist at her mizzen, and Lord Nelson's *Victory,* minus the Mediterranean Fleet, which had been left at Gibraltar, in the van—Maeve could only view her future with dread and uncertainty.

"Gray," she whispered, as the cool mist drifted across the deck and touched her face. She thought of him the last time she'd seen him, when he'd broken down the door to her cabin and in a towering rage, forced her to listen to him.

Forced her to love him.

No, she thought on a little smile. *Not forced. . . .* He would never have to *force* her to do *that. . . .*

But then her smile faded, for he'd left her after that stormy scene—and she hadn't seen him since.

Night after night she'd lain in her bunk aboard *Kestrel,* burning with desire for him, staring out at the lights of the mighty *Triton* and pining for him with a desperation that burned a hole in her heart. Night after night she cried herself to sleep, wishing she dared trust him enough to give up her hard-won life of independence. And day after day a boat had put off from *Triton,* carrying a cheeky midshipman with a packet of sealed dispatches for her. Except they weren't dispatches at all, but ardent declarations of love and devotion written in the admiral's atrociously unreadable hand.

And then, unexplainably, the letters had stopped coming.

Just like that.

Now, the only contact she had with the flagship was a daily exchange of signals—signals that advised where *Kestrel* should be positioned, signals that conveyed the admiral's annoyance when she strayed too far from the Fleet, signals that spelled out friendly invitations to Aisling and Sorcha to have dinner with him and his flag-captain, Colin Lord.

You've got to tell him, Maeve.

No. She couldn't. She couldn't even tell her *crew,* whose loyalties she no longer trusted.

Would your life as an admiral's wife be as bad as all that? He said you could go to sea with him. He said you could always stay near him. He said you could have all the freedom you wanted. His only wish is that you give up the pirating. And given that he's an admi-

*ral, that's really not such an unreasonable request . . .
is it?*

"I *can't!*" she whispered.

Why not?

"Because . . . I don't *know* any other life! Because
I'm scared, dammit!"

She saw the mist drifting around his flagship, making
the great man-of-war look like a ghost vessel in the dim
gray light. *Kestrel* surged on a swell, and again she felt
the nausea curling in her belly, and with it the terror . . .
the joy .. and the realization that she was soon going to
have to make a decision.

If not for herself, then for the tiny life that grew
within her.

*Do you want his baby to grow up to a life of thiev-
ing, piracy, and killing, only to die some day at the end
of a noose? Or do you want it to have the things that
you once had . . . two loving parents . . . a belly that is
always full . . . a fine education, a safe home, and a
solid understanding of decency, morals, and guidance?*

A father.

*Doesn't that innocent little life deserve more than
what you alone can give it?*

Her hand strayed protectively to her belly.

Doesn't it?

She could smell the land now, the fishy stench of a
harbor, the smoke from chimneys, the ripe scent of
grass and vegetation. *A father.* She thought of her own,
who had once served this country and later fought
against it, and wondered if he had once glimpsed these
very shores, strode the very streets she would soon
walk. She thought of the little schooner that had carried
her here, which had once fought against Britain's fleet
and now sailed in company with not one, but two English admirals. To have British colors flying from her
gaff didn't seem right—but yet, it *was.* It was poignant,

strangely ironic, almost as though *Kestrel* had come home.

The mist parted and she had a clear view of Sir Graham's huge two-decker. There was a cluster of officers gathered on her quarterdeck, and it was all Maeve could do not to raise her glass and try to find *him* in its circular field.

Oh, Daddy. I wish you were here . . . I don't know what to do.

Marry him, of course. You love him, don't you?

She hugged her arms to herself and bent her head, torn, scared, and never feeling so alone in her life . . . while forward, *Kestrel*'s little jibboom thrust through the mists, steady and true as an arrow.

Aisling and Sorcha had come aboard *Triton* the previous evening with the declaration that they wanted to make cookies for Colin Lord, and had ended up staying the night—safe, of course, in a lieutenant's cabin under the grumbling protection of Sergeant Handley after the culinary deed was done. Now, Gray wished that his heart wasn't so damned soft with regard to letting them stay, for his belly was sick with an overindulgence of the cookies and he was nursing a headache of thundering proportions.

So much for drawing the "enemy" into his own camp, he thought wryly. He had all of them eating out of his hand except Her Majesty herself.

He glared off across the misty water at the schooner as *Triton* entered the Spithead anchorage, fired her guns in salute to the port admiral, turned into the wind and let her massive anchor splash down into the sea.

He turned to his flag-lieutenant. "Mr. Stern, make a signal to *Kestrel,* would you? Tell Captain Merrick, *repair to* Flag *immediately*. I wish to see her before I'm called to pay my respects to the port admiral."

"Aye, sir."

Gray caught the arm of a midshipman as the boy hustled past in the lieutenant's wake. "Mr. Hayes!"

"Sir!"

"Go and ready my barge. And be quick about it."

Off to starboard, he heard twin splashes as the frigates *Cricket* and *Harleigh* dropped anchor nearby.

"*Kestrel* not acknowledging, sir."

Gray swore beneath his breath. It was bad enough his own lust for the Pirate Queen had kept him up every night with an arousal as hard as his sword hilt. It was bad enough that he could think of nothing to prove the depth of his love for her. And it was bad enough he'd been forcing himself to stay away from her when he wanted nothing more than to storm aboard that damned schooner, love her until she couldn't see straight, and carry her off as his bride.

But no. His *à la Nelson* plan of tempting the mouse out of the hole seemed to be failing miserably.

"Fire a gun and get her attention," he snapped.

His order was promptly carried out. "She's still not acknowledging, sir."

Nelson's words came back to him. *Divide and conquer.*

He stared at the little schooner. Then he yanked his hat down over his brow and calling for his barge, strode to the rail.

His patience had reached its end.

Chapter 31

"The *admiral's* here, Captain!"

"Thank you, Orla. Please show him in."

The Pirate Queen went to the stern windows and leaned out over the water, her hands shaking. She had known it would come down to this, yes, even *hoped* it would come to this, after her blatant refusal to answer his summons—

The door crashed open and Sir Graham stood there in full uniform, magnificent in his fury, his eyes blazing.

He strode forward, slammed his hat down on the table and roared, "By God Maeve, I don't know what the bloody devil you're up to but I can assure you I'll tolerate no disobedience from any ship under my command! I *ordered* you to come aboard the *Flag* and you blatantly ignored my summons!"

Head high, the Pirate Queen merely shot him a scathing glance and moved gracefully across the cabin, her green satin gown whispering on the deck behind her, a shaft of stray sunlight gilding her lovely profile. She was haughty, poised, aloof, the choker of sharks' teeth emphasizing the elegant grace of her neck, her hair piled atop her head and anchored there by a tiara of pearls. She looked every inch a queen. She looked every inch a warrior preparing for battle. She looked every inch a lady.

She turned and met his black glower. "Sir Graham."

Reining in his temper, he folded his arms and leaned

343

against the door, watching her and wondering what game she was playing now, what pretense she was up to, what she was trying to prove—and what she was really trying to say but *couldn't*.

"Let me clear a few things up for you." She lifted her chin, trying to look down her nose as any good queen should, but his height made that a bit difficult. "I am not part of your navy. I fly your flag as a *courtesy* to you, and do not forget it. Therefore, you cannot *order* me to do anything."

He smiled, and looked at her through the long sweep of his lashes. "Of course. I had forgotten."

She turned away, her nose rising once more, her voice lofty with challenge. "Furthermore, I have decided to weigh anchor. I don't like the looks of this place, am sick of your high-handed ways, and am leaving on the evening tide."

"Oh, really?"

She faltered, her aloof composure shaken by his casual acceptance of her impending departure. "Yes, that's what I said. I'm *leaving*, Gray—"

"I heard what you said, dearest, and you're not going anywhere as long as your ship is still a part of my squadron. Which, at the moment, it is. Sit down."

"I beg to *remind* you that you are speaking to the *captain* of this ship—"

"And I beg to remind *you* that I am your admiral and you'll obey *my* command."

She drew herself up, eyes flashing. "How dare—"

"I—am—your—admiral." His tone was low and dangerous. "Is that understood?"

They stared at each other, he commanding, unbending, secure in his power and authority, she glaring at him and refusing to back down. Her mouth began to tremble and he saw her suck her lips between her teeth; then, on a hoot of laughter, she threw herself in a chair and tilted her face to look up at him. "Oh, Gray. I love it when you get angry."

"Look, Maeve—"

She made a flippant gesture with her hand and shook her head. "Don't try to stop me, dear darling Admiral. I'm leaving. Tomorrow. After I replenish supplies. I've made up my mind and nothing you can say or do will sway me. Besides, what is there for me here in England? Your snobbish peers will never take to a sun-burned woman who sails and curses and fights with a sword."

He merely leaned against the door with his arms crossed and one hand idly tugging at his earring, watching her, as Nelson's words echoed through his mind. . . .

Tempt the mouse out of the hole.

"They'll never take to someone who *kills,*" she goaded.

He refused to rise to the bait. "So, you really have to leave then, eh?"

She rose and began to walk around the cabin once more, her words no longer controlled and detached, but coming out in hurried little bursts, as though she was about to lose her studied composure and wanted to get them out while she still could. "Yes, I have to go. You see, I left unfinished business back on my island. I need to take care of my dolphin. Water my flowers. Weed my garden. . . ."

She shot him a challenging glance, her head high, her eyes unnaturally bright.

"I need to paint my dock. Make sure my island's safe. See about getting a new set of topsails for *Kestrel. . . .*"

"Like hell you do," he said softly.

She glanced away, and in that fleeting moment, Gray knew his intuition had been right. The hauteur, the pride, the cool detachment—it was an act, just as he'd suspected. He knew women. He knew *her.* And he saw the longing in her face, the desperate plea for him not to leave her, not to *abandon* her—

He sighed, and very gently asked, "What do you *really* want, Maeve?"

She raised her head and looked at him. Her eyes were huge, and he saw her throat working as she bravely tried to contain her emotion.

"What I really want is—oh, God, this is difficult for me to admit, to say—"

He walked forward, took her hands in his own, squeezed them tightly. "Trust me."

"I—"

"Trust me."

She drew a deep, tremulous sigh, raised her head, and met his patient gaze. Her hands tightened around his, and he bent down to tenderly kiss her lips.

"What I really want, Gray, is . . . to spend the rest of my life with you, the only man that I have ever truly loved and trusted, the only man who has been patient and tactical and determined enough to pierce the armor, to understand and love me for who I am. What I want is the courage to shed that armor . . . to put the draw-bridge of my castle down so that it won't be such a cold and empty house of stone." She looked up at him, her eyes desperate. "What I really want is the courage to trust not only you, but others, with all my heart, with the knowledge that they won't condemn me for the hard and savage woman that I am, and because of . . . certain unexpected things in my life right now—"

"Maeve, dearest," he said softly, and set her back so he could look into her eyes. He tipped her chin up, bent his brow to hers. "I am not going anywhere. You can begin by trusting me on *that.*"

He smiled at her.

Hesitantly, she smiled back.

She took a deep, quivery breath. "What I want, Gray, is the courage to confront my parents . . . despite the fact they may not forgive me. It's hard for me to admit that I'm afraid—I mean, I'm a pirate queen, pirate queens aren't supposed to be afraid—but I am. I'm more than afraid, I'm terrified."

"It's alright to be afraid, Maeve."

"No, it's not. I'll bet *you*'re never afraid."

"On the contrary." He gave her a lopsided, dimpled smile, and slowly shook his head. "Fear and the courage to admit it are part of being human."

"So you *are* afraid of some things, then?"

"Hell, yes. I'm afraid of losing friends I love to war and battle. I'm afraid of going aloft in high winds. I'm afraid my sisters will meet rogues like me. And—"

She looked up at him, her eyes huge.

"—I'm afraid of failing to convince the woman in my arms how very much I love and adore her . . . and that she will leave me and we will never again find happiness in our lives." He smiled, gently, and touched his brow to hers. "No, I'm more than afraid," he said, repeating the words she had used. "I'm *terrified.*"

"Oh, Gray . . ."

She went into his arms, her heart so swollen and heavy that she didn't think her breast could contain it. He held her for a long moment, then he picked her up, shut the door behind them, and carried her to the cushioned bench seat beneath the stern windows, where he set her down as gently as if she were his mother's finest china. He bent his head and claimed her lips. His mouth lingered on hers, savoring the taste of her. His kiss was achingly sweet. He pulled a pin loose and watched the chestnut locks tumble against her throat; another, and a glorious fall of hair slipped over her brow. Reaching out, he pulled the tiara free, smoothed her hair back, and kissed her again.

"I *know* how much you love me," she whispered. "And . . . I hope you know how much I love you."

"Say you'll marry me, Maeve."

"Oh, Gray, don't ask that . . . not now."

"I will continue to ask until I receive the response I seek," he said, brushing her cheek with the back of his hand. "Don't think I give up as easily as all that."

"There are . . . obstacles."

"Yes, but together, we can overcome them. There are solutions. Ways around things. *Trust me,* Maeve."

"I can't marry an admiral, I'm a pirate!"

"So retire. You don't *need* to be a pirate. We've been through this before, love."

"I can't give up my ship!"

"I never said you had to. I merely said I'd not stand to have you engage in piracy. Period."

"What about my crew?"

"Give them your plantation house."

"But where would we live?"

"Barbados."

"All the time?"

"When we are not at sea."

"We?"

"We."

"Gray, I'm pregnant."

He froze, his hand in midair, his face looking like a thunderbolt had just driven out of the sky and struck him. His mouth slowly fell open, and he stared at her as though he'd never seen her before.

"What did you say?"

"I'm"—she gave a faint, frightened little smile—"going to have a baby."

He made a noise that sounded a bit like a sob, a bit like laughter—then his face broke into a radiant grin, and sweeping her up in his arms, he threw back his head and gave a great whoop of joy that had to have been heard by every ship in the anchorage. "By God, my prayers are answered, now you'll *have* to marry me! Oh, glory, glory, *glory* is mine!"

"Gray, a baby alone would not be enough to make me marry you."

The laughter died in his throat, and his face began to darken with fury. "I'll tell you right now, Maeve, I'll not have my child brought up as a damned pi—"

She cut off his tirade with a hand across his mouth. "I'd have to love you, besides"—she let her hand fall, and gazed into his eyes—"which . . . I do."

Slowly, she let her hand fall from his lips. He remained very still, as though not daring to breathe.

"Gray . . . I will marry you, providing you let me keep my ship. I learned how to sail aboard her—she was built by my father you know—and someday, I want *our* child to learn the ways of the sea as I did, on her deck, at her helm. I . . . I suppose I could give up the pirating, too. Yes, I'm sure I can give that up, I think." She frowned, and fire glittered in her eyes. "But this I tell you, Gray, that I shall guard the lives of those I love, 'and if ever I see anyone—do you hear me— *anyone,* seeking to harm one hair of your or my baby's head, I will do as I did with el Perro Negro, and if you don't like that, you can just eat worms!"

"Eat *worms?*"

Her nose came up with queenly hauteur and she looked away. "I am trying to refine my language as befitting the wife of an admiral."

He sucked his lips between his teeth so he wouldn't laugh. "Really, *Majesty,* you needn't go to such extremes."

"No?"

"No."

"All right then," she said prettily, "eat shit."

He gave a deep hoot of laughter, and saw an answering sparkle of humor in her eyes. And then she laughed too, that harsh, guffawing bellow that reminded him of gale winds and rain squalls, blustery sunshine and ringing cutlasses. He took her into his arms and hugged her fiercely.

"Ah, dearest, we must set a date," he said, into her hair. "A very *early* date, given your delicate condition!"

"Aye," she said, tonelessly, her laughter dying away.

Alarmed, he pulled back and stared into her face. "What is it, dearest?" he asked gently, cupping her cheeks in his broad hands and lifting her face to his.

"Nothing," she said, with a little shrug, and tried to look away.

"Maeve—I will permit . . . ah . . . I mean there should be no secrets between us."

She gave a little smile at his sheepish look, but her eyes were unnaturally glassy behind the dark fringe of her lashes. "It's just that . . . well, I just sort of wish"— she glanced hopelessly out the stern windows, trying to hide the emotion in her eyes—"well, here I've finally found my Gallant Knight and am going to marry him, and my own father won't be here to give me away at my wedding. . . ."

He watched her throat working, her chin coming up as though to deny her own pain, and his heart ached for her. "If you write him now, Maeve," he said gently, "your family could be here in a little over two months."

"No, Gray. I can't write. They still think I'm dead."

"Of course they do, love. That is why you must write them."

"I *can't,* Gray." She looked up at him, her eyes brimming with pain and fear and despair. "Don't you understand? I can't, because"—she looked down, suddenly finding her thumbnail of great interest—"I can't bring myself to tell them what I've become. Better that my father remember me as his innocent little daughter, not . . . the woman I now am. Better that he go on thinking that I'm dead."

"No, Maeve. That is *never* better."

"Don't force me, Gray. *Please.*"

He said nothing, only looking at her with his heart in his eyes.

"My parents are decent people," she continued, still picking at her thumb. "If they knew of the things I have done . . ." She flung her hands away from themselves. "Gray, please understand, I can't go through any more rejection, I just can't!"

He watched helplessly as she sat on the bench seat at the stern windows and looked at him, her eyes desperate, pleading, bright with unshed tears.

"You understand, don't you, Gray?"

He sat next to her and smiled gently, curving an arm around her shoulders and hugging her sad body fiercely to his. "Of course I do, dearest. In time, you will put the demons to rest. But if I may add my own thoughts to the matter, I should think your parents would be quite proud of you for surviving as well as you have . . . and, very, very excited that they will be gaining not only a daughter, but a grandchild as well."

She swallowed hard and looked away.

"Furthermore," he said softly, "I cannot imagine *any* parents preferring their beloved little girl to be dead over her having become a lady pirate."

She looked up at him, her tears perilously close. "Gray, please. I don't want to discuss this anymore. It hurts. I don't want to hurt. Not now. Someday, maybe, I'll write them, but not now."

Long moments went by. She leaned into the comforting curve of his arm, wishing she were braver than she was.

"Would you rather talk about setting a date then, love?"

She looked over at him, sitting beside her, his legs swinging and purposely bumping hers, his eyes full of teasing confidence, and in that moment she loved him more than she had ever loved anyone, anything, in the entire span of her life.

"Oh, Gray—" She reached up to touch the golden tassels of one of his epaulets. "You're not angry with me, are you?"

He was still gazing at her, his eyes twinkling. "Naaaah."

"I don't know what you see in me; I'm a coward, really, I am. And I have behaved abominably. If you *are* angry with me, you have every right to be. . . ."

"Now, why on earth would you think I'm angry with you?"

"You've been avoiding me."

"Have I, now?"

"Don't play innocent. You were ignoring me. Pretending I didn't exist. Inviting Aisling and Sorcha to your ship but purposely excluding me. You even stopped sending those . . . those love letters."

"I do everything for a reason." He leaned over and kissed her ear. "You should know that by now. As you can see my plan has landed the prize did it not . . . right in my lap!"

"Aye, it surely did," she admitted, grudgingly. Then she grinned and playfully pushed him away, his good-natured teasing driving away the gloom brought on by thoughts of her family. "You're a real blackguard, know that, Gray? Sometimes I hate the fact you're so . . . *tactical.*"

"Do you? I can be a pirate, then, if you like."

He pulled her back, his tongue slipping out to circle the inner folds of her ear.

A heated shiver ran down her spine. "You *are* a pirate in the true sense of the word. And now you are trying to rob me of my sense just as you have stolen my heart. I love you."

"Ah, how I have longed to hear *those* words again!"

Trembling, she shut her eyes as his lips moved down the sensitive skin behind her ear. "Know what I wish, Gray?"

His legs bumped against hers. "What?"

She gave him a girlishly shy smile. "That's you'd make love to me, right here and now, in broad daylight."

"Oh no, the baby—"

"The baby will be fine. And *I* want to be ravished by an admiral."

He grinned hard enough to raise his dimple. "So, my lady pirate has her own fantasies, eh?"

"Blast it, Gray, don't make me beg!"

"As if I could." His dark eyes glinted. "Well then, dearest, let's indulge your fantasy."

Almost shyly, she rose up on her knees and faced him, looking lush, rumpled, and lovely; she put her arms around him, kissed each tasseled epaulet with its silver star of rank, kissed the medal of the Nile that hung from around his neck. Then she slid the coat from his shoulders, gently pushing it back and away and down, and kissed him through his shirt.

"I wonder," he said jokingly, his eyes twinkling, "if you would still love me if I were anything but an admiral."

"I loved you when I thought you were a traitorous spy, I loved you when I thought you were a thieving freebooter, I loved you even when I thought I hated you. Don't laugh, that makes perfect sense! Besides, how do I know you don't love *me* just because I am—I mean, *was*—a pirate?"

His dark gaze roved down the front of her gown, raising the heat of her blood, and he chuckled softly. "You have me there, my lady. Guess you're just going to have to *trust*, eh?"

Trust. He'd taught her much about *that.* If only she dared to do the same where her family was concerned. . . .

She slid off the cushions and stood before him in the V of his legs. The evidence of his desire for her was all too visible beneath the white breeches. Trembling with anticipation, Maeve turned her back to him, allowing him to unfasten her gown, and sighing with pleasure at the warm, gentle brush of his hands against her skin. She felt him clearing the hair from her neck, fumbling with the clasp of the sharks'-tooth necklace. It slipped free, and he held it up, looking at it, as though it symbolized all the defenses that she had carried with her for so long.

"You know," he said thoughtfully, "I've always had a fantasy of making love to Anne Bonney. But I'll bet she wasn't half the pirate queen you are, Maeve."

"And I," said she, "have always had a fantasy of some gallant sea captain coming along to sweep me off my feet. But I find that admirals are far more exciting."

"You'd damn well better. Because if I ever catch you turning those tiger eyes on anyone but me, I'll have you strung up to the yardarm so fast you won't know what hit you!"

"And if *I* ever catch *you* flirting with anyone but me, I'll make you *eat* this necklace of mine and God bless the consequences!"

He laughed, a hearty, deep, baritone sound of sheer delight. "Ah, Maeve . . . How I love you!"

Facing him, she put her hands on his thighs and gazed into his eyes, her knees pressed against the bench seat and her belly just inches from that rigid tumescence. "And I love *you*, Gray. I'm sorry I've made your life . . . difficult."

"Difficult? You have made it a veritable hell! But it has been quite an adventure. I would not have had it otherwise."

She grinned, thinking of *other* kinds of adventures, and playfully dragged a finger across his thigh.

"Well?" he said, arching a dark brow.

"Well, what?"

"I don't bite."

"Oh. I was waiting for *you* to make the first move."

"I have. Your gown is conveniently unfastened. Or had you not noticed?"

She looked up and stuck out her tongue at him.

"Do that again and I'll forget I'm trying to adhere to decorum."

"Decorum?"

"Aye, Majesty. We're aboard *your* ship. I was waiting for you to initiate this . . . this *cruise.*"

"And here I thought you were going to play pirate and plunder me," she said, prettily. He laughed, and she pushed her hands beneath his shirt, spreading her palms over the taut muscles of a chest that was perfectly suited to the span of broad, capable shoulders upon which so many decisions had rested, so many lives had depended.

She stepped back, away from him, and allowed him to undress her until she stood before him in only her chemise, and then, not even that, her hair streaming over her shoulders and down over her breasts. Very gently, he reached out and pushed the silky masses back over her shoulders, baring her lithe body to his admiring gaze.

"Beautiful," he murmured, watching the dusky peaks harden with desire as she stood before him. And then he put his hand on her still-flat belly, and smiled with wonder and awe. "And to think that a life grows within you . . . a child. My child. *Our* child. . . ."

Hot color crept up her neck. Her breathing grew shallow and the hard nipples seemed to jut toward him, beckoning him. She looked down at his groin, swollen beneath the confinement of the breeches, and felt a desperate, aching need deep in her womb. "Gray . . . stop delaying. I swear, you won't hurt anything by making love to me."

He smiled faintly, just enough to raise crinkles at the corners of his eyes. He laid his hand between her breasts, letting their warmth envelop his fingers as her heartbeat thumped beneath his palm. Then he spread his hand, his thumb gently touching, stroking, caressing, one tightened bud.

She looked down, saw his swelling tumescence. "Does it hurt, Gray?" she said, playfully.

"Does what hurt?" He followed her gaze for the briefest of moments. "Oh, that? It's fair to killing me. But again"—he gave a wicked grin—"I'm a patient man."

Her fingers crept toward his groin, traveling slowly up his hard thighs. She heard his own breathing begin to quicken. "Shall I *test* that patience, Admiral?"

"Ah, love . . . you can test anything you like." He fondled her breasts, cupping them in his hands, bending his head to drop kisses on each pouty crest. "But do keep in mind that I intend to test *your* patience as well, Majesty."

She felt him tickling, then licking, her nipples; she felt the slick, warm, wetness of his mouth, the gentle nip of his teeth, the feathery heat of his breath, the hard warmth of his hands, cupping each soft mound and pushing it up so that he could taste the sweet buds that capped it. The combination of sensations was wildly erotic, and he knew it; she had a feeling that her admiral knew a lot of things about her, about women, and that this playful contest to see who could hold out the longest was one she could never win.

Oh, Gray, if I could marry you this morning, I would. . . .

Her fingers crept the final inch to his arousal, hot and throbbing beneath the breeches.

"You're determined, aren't you?" he murmured, his breath hot against her breast.

"I will win, Sir Graham. I'll have you on your knees and begging for mercy within the next five minutes."

"We shall see about *that,* love. And I will have you as my Lady Falconer before the month is out."

She didn't answer. His arm circled the small of her back, and his hand moved down the curve of her bottom, caressing it. Her breasts tingled, flared with fire, and she moaned a little as he grasped a lock of her hair, rubbing the silky tress over first one wet nipple, then the other. She began to burn inside, down below, and of their own accord her hips thrust toward him, seeking him, seeking his love.

Her naked thigh encountered his breeches. The sensation of her own soft flesh meeting coarse fabric was wildly erotic, and she began to doubt her own boastful words. The admiral knew what he was about. Even now, his hand was moving up her leg, dragging a path of fire with it, moving back down again . . . up. She began to pulse with need, with want, and a fierce desire to push him backward onto the soft cushions and have her way with him.

But no. She had made a vow, and she would stretch his so-called *patience* to its very limits. Her fingers found the buttons of his drop front, slid them through their holes, and she sighed as his arousal—hot and full and hard with desire—spilled into her hands.

The admiral groaned.

She cupped him between her palms and began to rub. Hard.

"Maeve . . ."

She felt wicked, powerful, *alive.* His head drooped, his brow fell against her shoulder, and a moment later his teeth had caught the petal-soft lobe of her ear, nibbling it, licking it, as his hands, hot with need, dragged up and over her bare bottom.

She laughed huskily. This was going to be one hell of a close contest.

Breathing hard now, she tugged his shirt up and over his head, letting her fingernails rove up the tapering waist, the darkly tanned shoulders until her fingers came to rest dead center on his chest. She let her other hand drop, down, down, down, until her fingers ringed his hot and swollen arousal.

His heartbeat thudded beneath her palm. His manhood gave an impatient jerk. His dark eyes watched hers, wickedly inviting, intensely pleased, beneath the lengthy fringe of his lashes. "Still think you're going to win, Majesty?"

She gave a slow, confident, cat's smile. "I *know* I'm going to win, Admiral."

And then, her gaze still locked defiantly with his, she pushed him gently, forcefully, back, until his very tense body lay angled across the cushions, arms crossed behind his head, black hair spilling over his wrists and framing his swarthy face, the sunlight gilding his handsome body. His legs were loose and spread, his feet dangling several inches from the floor, and there, conveniently placed, was that which would make him lose this contest of patience.

She stood between his legs and cupping that swollen organ, let her thumbs rove over the engorged tip. With her other hand, she dragged her nails over the lightly furred flesh of his inner thigh. She watched his face, saw his eyes drift up, then shut, the sweat breaking out on his brow and beading the top of his lip. Oh, this was costing him. And costing him dearly. Back and forth she moved her thumb, slowly increasing the pressure until slickness eased her sweet toil; up and down she dragged her nails over his flesh, until his head rolled to one side, his thighs tightened around her lower hips, and a helpless groan escaped his parted lips. Then she relented, tracing feathery fingertips over him and gazing intently into his face. The dark lashes draped his cheeks now, and he turned his face against his wrist, where veins and tendons stood out in high relief.

"I want you, Maeve," he managed, hoarsely, his lips barely moving. "So help me God, I do. . . ."

She sank down, and took him gently into her mouth. His whole body went stiff and he sucked in his breath on a strangled gasp. She circled him with her lips, with her tongue, pulled him deeply into her mouth. She heard him cursing softly, felt his hands driving into her hair; but still he did not break, did not allow himself release. Such control, such fortitude!—where, she wondered, was the admiral's mind that he was able to exhibit such mastery over his own virile body?

She cupped his sacs in her hands, lightly stroking him, still lightly dragging her nails over the inside of his thighs while she loved him with her tongue, her mouth, her lips. His curses changed to groans, his groans back to curses, and his hold on her hair grew almost painful.

Even an admiral could not hold out forever.

"Sweet God above, Maeve—"

She suckled him, harder.

"Maeve, please," he said hoarsely, and she tasted the first sweet drops upon her tongue, "I . . . am only . . . a man—"

She lifted her head, saw his face pressed against the curve of his wrist, the dark lashes lying against his cheeks and a lock of his hair fluttering near his mouth with every burst of his labored breath. Slowly, she stood up and looked down at him; he turned his head and his eyes drifted open, the navy depths glazed with desire.

Huskily, wickedly, she asked, "Do I win this test of patience, then, Admiral?"

He focused on her. And smiled. It was a slow, spreading, wicked, deadly smile.

"No."

She climbed up beside him, covering him with her hair and feeling the thick masses caught between them as his arm went around her neck and drew her down atop him. She felt the hard length of his body against hers, his arousal stabbing against the soft, dampening curls of her womanhood, the damp heat of his chest beneath her breasts; then his tongue plunged into her mouth, plundering it greedily, savagely.

He broke the kiss and rolled over, pinning her beneath him, his arms twin pillars on either side of her head and his manhood already poised at the junction of her thighs. Anchoring a hand in her hair, he kissed her lips, her face, her throat, and lowered himself down to her. She felt every bone in her body turn to water. He probed her moist entrance, sank into her, and began the timeless motion of love.

She was lost. She knew it even as his mouth came down atop hers, ruthlessly plundering its depths; she knew it even as his strokes grew slow, strong, smooth, deep, perfectly controlled, and perfectly orchestrated; she knew it even as he put his weight on one arm and with the other hand, reached down to rub and enflame her hot entrance at the same time he was sliding in and out of her.

"Oh, Gray. . . ."

There had never been any contest. Faster and faster he moved, taking her with him on a spiraling, breathless climb to the clouds. His fingers had found the hard bud of her desire now, his manhood the deepest caverns of her body. Her breath came in short, hard pants and gasps, and she felt her release building, climbing, peaking—

"Gray! Take me *now,* I beg of you!"

With a last, driving shudder, he impaled her to the very hilt of himself. She arced up to meet him, crying out and feeling his hot seed pulsing within her. She clung to him, aching with love and joy and relief. And when it was over, and the admiral lay in her arms, belonging to her and no one but her, she thought of what it might be like to be married to him, and making wild, uninhibited love like this for the rest of her life.

"I guess you win," she murmured, against the salty skin of his shoulder.

She felt his lips curve in a smile against her throat, the brush of his lashes tickling her skin. "Aye. But next time . . . I may not. Indeed, I should hope I lose. 'Twill be a sweet defeat."

He held her for a long time, keeping his weight on his arms so as not to crush her. Then he raised himself up on one elbow, idly playing with a chestnut curl. "Maeve."

"Sir Graham?"

"Want to steal off and get married, tonight?"

She reached out and touched the dimple in his jaw, the arching black brows, the plane of his cheek. Sighing, she looked into his eyes, determined but twinkling behind his lashes, and mischievously shook her head. "We can't, and you know it."

"When, then?"

"I don't know. I'll give you my answer tomorrow. Tonight—tonight, I think I'd prefer to have another contest of patience."

"Dammit Maeve!"

And then, as she squealed in delight, he went about ravishing her once more, and this time it was indeed the admiral who lost the contest.

Chapter 32

He was the scourge of London.

No pirate who'd ever swung a cutlass this side of Jamaica had ever looked more formidable. Dressed in a billowing white shirt and skintight breeches, with a patch over one eye and a kerchief around his throat, Sir Graham Falconer, Knight of the Bath, Rear Admiral of the White, savior of the season's richest convoy, and now, fresh from a long and stuffy meeting with his crusty old superiors at the Admiralty in London, stared up at the open window of Maeve's hotel room, two stories above his head.

He held a grappling iron in one hand, its long rope in the other, and a gleaming dagger between his teeth. God help him if anyone saw him engaging in such ghastly behavior. But hell, if *this* little performance didn't convince Her Majesty of the lengths he would go to to have her, then he feared nothing would!

He was sick of waiting.

And he was beginning to find he wasn't such a patient man after all, not where *she* was concerned.

Her crew had remained in Portsmouth with *Kestrel*, but for the sake of appearances, Orla had checked into a room with Maeve, and he had taken a neighboring one. It was not an arrangement he intended to keep. Oh, hell no. He had no intention of sleeping alone.

Just as he had no intention of allowing her to dally anymore with regard to setting a date for their wedding. She'd damn well give him a date tonight—or, he'd carry her off to *Triton* and have his own flag-captain marry them, and amen to *that!*

Aaaaarrrh, me pretty!, he thought with sudden, reckless glee, warming to his role and beginning to thoroughly enjoy himself. "I shall have ye, yet!"

He looked up at the square of golden light directly above him. A shadow passed before the window. Good. She was still awake. . . .

And now, for the proposal to outdo all marriage proposals . . . *pirate style.*

A noise sounded behind him. He whirled, but it was only a cat, staring at him in fright.

He removed the knife, and bared his teeth, making the face he used on Colin's pet.

The animal hissed, and skittered away. He laughed. Then, narrowing his eyes in concentration, he put the knife between his teeth once more, tightened his hand around the rope, and began to swing the grappling iron in a wide, powerful circle, focusing on the sill two stories above.

One last circle, and he let the grapple go.

Chunk! The iron claw found purchase and he froze, waiting to be discovered.

Nothing.

He let out his breath, relaxing, grinning, rubbing his hands together in anticipation of snaring his prize. "Aaaargh," he growled happily, rolling the words around his teeth as he figured Blackbeard must've done, "ye'll not escape me now, wench!" He pulled on the rope, testing it. That was all he needed, to begin climbing and have the damned thing let go to send him crashing to the street! But no, the grapple was solid, strong, tightly in place.

With a last wary glance behind him, he pulled himself up and began to climb, the knife clenched between his teeth, cutlass at his side, hair trailing down his back, powerful arms and bare feet pulling and pushing him up the thick rope.

I'll have ye yet, woman, he growled, reveling in the role of marauding pirate.

Higher and higher he went. Heights did not bother him; he was, after all, the most fearsome freebooter ever to sail the Spanish Main, the most dangerous pirate ever to stalk the streets of London. Adjusting his eye patch and sheathing his dagger, he paused just beneath the windowsill, breathing hard, grinning fiercely, and wondering how to best make his surprise entry. Then, in a single movement, he pulled himself cleanly up and through the window, and drawing his cutlass, leapt into the room with a savage, bloodcurdling yell.

"Aaaarrrrrrghhhhhh!"

"Eeeeeaaaaaaaaaaaaah!!!!"

An elderly woman, in slippers and nightgown.

"SHIT!" Gray cried, and bolted for the door.

"Thief! Intruder! Somebody, *help!*"

Cutlass in hand, he tore frantically down the hall, the old woman's screams echoing in the corridor behind him. *How could he have chosen the wrong room?!* He tripped, nearly fell, cut himself on the blade of the sword, and finding speed, darted away from an opening door, when he heard more calls and shouts ringing out behind him.

And as he charged around the corner he saw two flag officers just entering the hotel dining room, wearing cocked hats and epaulets on their shoulders—

He feinted to the right, charging down a carpeted corridor—

"There he is! Thief! Somebody, stop him, *thief!*"

Behind him he heard pounding feet, knew the two admirals had seen him and were in hot pursuit.

Bloody hell, where was Maeve's room?!

He charged around another corner, running as fast as his bare feet would take him, shirt billowing, hair flying out behind him. There, thank God, thank God, thank *God!*, her door—

"Maeve, open up!"

"Gray, darling? Is that you?"

"For God's sake, Maeve, open the goddamned door, *now!*"

"Now Gray, that's no way to talk to *royalty—*"

He pounded savagely against the door, nearly holing the elegant wood. "Jesus, Maeve, *OPEN THE GODDAMNED DOOR!*"

He heard more people running toward him. The old woman in her nightgown, hotel personnel, maids, clerks, a nobleman in elegant silk—*Oh, God, not the Marquis of Anderleigh*—"I say, Sir *Graham,* is that *you?*"—and then the two flag officers, not just *any* flag officers, but Lords Hood and Barham, both admirals and the latter, the most senior man in the entire bloody *navy,* from whose office Gray had just come not an hour before—now striding with tight-lipped authority around the corner.

He slammed his fist against the door a final time. "Maeve, for the love of God, *open the door!*"

"SIR GRAHAM!" Lord Barham's voice thundered through the hall. "What in *GOD'S NAME* are you *DOING?!*"

Silence. He fell back, plastering his spine against the door, a pirate with a patch over his eye, a cutlass in his hand, his shirt open to his navel, and their shocked eyes upon him, while the crowd gaped and stared and gathered and smirked.

The door opened and he fell, prostrate, at the Pirate Queen's feet.

"Maeve! *Say you'll marry me!*"

Chapter 33

Several hours after Maeve Merrick agreed to marry Rear Admiral Sir Graham Falconer, a post chaise carrying one Captain Henry Blackwood arrived at Nelson's home, Merton, with the news that Villeneuve was holed up in the Spanish port of Cádiz with more than thirty ships-of-the-line. And so began the last stage of events, all rushing toward that final decisive battle that the Admiral, in those last weeks of his long-suffering life, knew was coming.

In the Channel, and in the French and Spanish ports of the Atlantic seaboard, great fleets stood poised for the final confrontation while Europe stood waiting. . . .

Off of the Spanish port of Cádiz, where Villeneuve's forces had fled for refuge, the bored and frustrated blockading fleet under the British Admiral Cuthbert Collingwood complained bitterly about their dour old "Cuddie's" puritanical ways: "For charity's sake, send us Lord Nelson, oh ye men of power!" wrote one of the desperate captains, in a letter home to his wife.

And in England, while anxiously waiting to go aboard *Victory* for the last time, Lord Nelson paid his bills with his dwindling resources, put his affairs in order, and spent his time playing with his little daughter. On one of his trips to London he stopped to pay a somber visit to an old friend, fashioned from the mainmast of the French flagship *L'Orient* which he had defeated at the Battle of the Nile, and now, waiting patiently for

that time when the two of them would be together forever. That old friend had traveled many miles with him;
now, it rested safely in the care of one Mr. Peddieson.

"Get it properly engraved for me," Nelson joked to
Peddieson, "for I shall probably need it upon my return."

That old friend was his coffin.

At Falconer House, things were in a state of high excitement as the family's only son, the days of his own
leave numbered before he returned to his West Indies
command, eagerly awaited his marriage to the Pirate
Queen, to be held at Nelson's home, Merton.

Gray's happiness over that upcoming event was
heightened by an urgent message sent to him by Lord
Nelson, but he did not tell his Pirate Queen the surpris-
ing contents of the Admiral's note. For Sir Graham
knew that his lady must conquer her demons herself—
and as her wedding day dawned, she did.

She got up that morning, dressed, and long before the
house awoke and Gray's six little sisters sought her out
for tales of piracy on the high seas, tiptoed quietly from
her bedroom and down the great staircase . . . across
plush carpeting and marbled floors . . . past the statues
and busts and paintings of ancestors that lined the
walls, until she saw the half-open door to the study.

It called to her. It was now or never. She could not
live with the pain anymore.

She paused only once on her way to that room and
all the fears she would confront there, and that was to
stop, as she always did, beneath the magnificent portrait
that dominated the wall just outside the door. It was a
glorious portrait, stretching from the height of her waist
to the tall ceiling, of a pirate standing before a dark and
roiling sea with storm clouds gathering behind him like
a great, unholy halo. His hair was black, magnificent,
wild; his eyes were bold, his stance, godlike and com-

manding. He leaned on a cutlass, wore a flowing shirt of white silk, and jackboots that reached to his knees. Behind him was a fleet of ships, *his* ships, and the elaborate nameplate affixed to the painting's gilt frame read, *Rear Admiral Sir Graham Falconer, K.B.*

Maeve tilted her head back, stepped forward, and kissed the only part of that magnificent portrait she could reach: his boots.

Leave it to her Knight to be painted as a pirate, when any admiral worth his salt wouldn't dare be portrayed in anything but his uniform.

She touched the portrait one final time, as though the courage of the man himself could reach her. But he had gone to London last night to meet with the Admiralty, then on to Merton to see Nelson, and she had yet to hear the hoofbeats signifying his return.

"Gray," she whispered, staring into the dark, commanding eyes, "how I wish you were here, right now. I need you. I'm afraid. But I must do this thing that has to be done . . . and I must do it alone."

She was trembling. She heard the sounds of the big house, amplified by the intense quiet; the ticking of a clock somewhere down the hall, various creaks and settlings of aged wood, and outside, the crow of a rooster. Sunlight, weak and orange, slanted through the tall windows, angling toward the door of the study as though directing her to do what needed to be done.

What difference did it make, now? She was getting married today. She should've written the letter to her family months ago, when she'd first learned they *hadn't* deserted her, after all. Now, it was too late.

Do it, Maeve.

But even as her heart tried to retreat behind the walls it had hidden behind for seven long years, she knew there was no turning back. She had been affected these last three weeks by watching Gray's family revel in the love they had for each other. It was time to put the demons behind her, to face the truth.

"I love you, Gray," she whispered to that magnificent man in the portrait, and indeed, she did. For if her admiral had not taught her about vulnerability, open hearts, love and courage and trust, she would never have been contemplating what she was about to do.

Head high, the Pirate Queen pushed open the door to the study and saw the sunlight, like a beacon from God, touching nothing in the room but the carved oak desk beneath the window. She closed the door behind her and walked across the room, pulled out the chair, and sat down.

Around her, the silence pressed.

She looked at the quill pens laid out on the desk. The inkwell. The sheets of blank paper, set there as though awaiting the outpourings of her heart.

Stop delaying.

She picked up a quill, running her fingers over the soft feather. Her heart thundered in her breast. Slowly, she pulled one of the pieces of paper toward her.

Far down the hall the clock chimed the hour, reminding her that time was trickling by, bringing back memories of her beloved Grandpa Ephraim and the obsession he'd had for timepieces.

What are you waiting for, Maeve? Do it.

Once again, she picked up the quill in her trembling hand, bit her lip, and began to write. . . .

DEAR MAMA AND DADDY,

As I write this, the sun is coming up and I am in England. I think you should know I'm getting married today—

She paused, reading over her words. They seemed cold. Impersonal. With a little sob, she snatched up the paper, wadded it into a ball, flung it to the floor and tried again.

DEAR MAMA AND DADDY,

This is your daughter, Maeve. I know you think I'm dead, but—

No. That was even worse. Frustrated, Maeve crumpled up the letter, shot to her feet, bolted for the door, and paused, her lungs heaving and the tears choking the back of her throat. She stood there, watching the orange sunlight getting stronger, brighter, whiter, hotter. She touched the door and thought of the portrait just outside. She could flee this room and no one would ever know but her; or she could stay and confront her worst fears. She looked back at the desk, the pen lying across that stack of paper, the chair pushed aside and waiting for her to come back to it, and made her decision.

Fisting her hands at her sides, she slowly went back to the desk, sat down, and weeping quietly, began to write once more.

DEAR DADDY AND MAMA,

I don't know how to begin a letter, and I especially don't know how to begin this one. It's awfully hard to write a letter of apology after seven years of believing the worst about somebody, especially when it's your own family, but I am forcing myself to do it and if this letter never reaches you at least I will have made a start. . . .

She bit her lip, her teeth bringing the blood to the surface as the pen gathered speed and her thoughts began to pour out upon the page. . . .

The most singular set of circumstances have occurred in my life to bring about my writing to you at last, not the least of which is my meeting a wonderful man who has shown me what it means to love, to trust, and to be willing to take chances. Were it not for him, I would not be writing this letter; were it not for him, I would still be nursing my anger and bitterness and broken heart in the Caribbean, where I've made my home these past seven years. Now, I realize that all the time I was nursing my broken heart, you were both nursing yours. Oh, Daddy, oh, Mama, how can you ever forgive me? How can you ...?

The tears were flowing now, uninhibited by barriers of distrust and fear, racing down her cheeks and beginning to spatter upon her wrist. Her arm. The paper on which she wrote. She did not see them. She did not hear the harsh sounds of her own breathing anymore, her sobs, the sound of the dogs barking outside, the thump of feet on the floor of an upstairs bedroom, nor see the sun pulling itself up through the clouds in a magnificent dawn of beauty and glory and hope.

Mama, Daddy, I am so very ashamed of myself, for believing you have turned away from me. How can I apologize for that belief? I'm crying as I write this; I'm crying for all the lost years, all the sadness and grief and hurt and pain, the misunderstandings, the fact that I ran away from home and never came back. I'm crying because I love you, never stopped loving you, will always love you whether you can find it in your hearts to forgive me or not, crying because I'm getting married today and—

She paused, her chest heaving in great, convulsing bursts of grief—

and you shall not be here to see it . . .

She pulled back, sobbing wretchedly, and was about to crumple the letter in her fist when a warm hand closed over her own.

She looked up, the tears streaming down her face and splashing onto the back of his hand. Her hand. The letter itself, blurred and smudged with her tears of grief.

"Leave it be," he commanded, quietly.

"I can't do it, Gray, I can't send this, it's stained and they won't be able to even *read* it—"

"Leave it," he said again, softly.

She shot to her feet, her hand still pinned beneath his. "I'm a coward, really I am, I should never even have thought I had the courage to do this—"

"You *do* have the courage, and you have done it." He moved around to join her behind the desk, taking care not to read what she had written. He made her sit back down in the chair, and kneeling down so that he was on a level with her, looked steadily in her eyes. "Maeve," he said gently.

She looked up at him, miserable, wretched.

"Leave it be," he said. "And let the tear stains remain. Nothing else could stand as proof of your love for your family as they can."

He was right, of course. The admiral was always right. She lunged out of the chair and buried herself in his arms, crying bitterly, feeling his hands stroking her hair and soothing her. He held her for a long time, and then he gently set her back, gazing lovingly into her eyes and thumbing away the wetness upon her cheeks.

Then he stood, tall, dark and splendidly handsome, and gave her an encouraging smile. "Finish your letter,

Maeve," was all he said, and, turning on his heel, left the room.

"They'll not come. Dear God, what have I done, I know they wrote to say they would be here, but they won't come, I know they won't come, it's already late, late! And they have not come—"

"Nelson," she said soothingly, "it's six o'clock in the morning. Not everyone rises as early as you!"

"They won't come, and here I've already told Falconer they would, dear God, what if he's told *her*? Oh, Emma, I should never have told him, I should never have written that damned letter in the first place, I should never have interfered; this, if nothing else, shall be the death of me, the very death of me!"

He was so distraught he hadn't shaved, hadn't even washed his face yet this morning, his dear, sad, suffering little face that she loved so much. And how could he? How could he, with only one arm?

She took his hand, sat him down in a chair, filled a basin, and lovingly did that intimate task for him, trying to remain cheerful and brave despite the knowledge that he would soon be leaving her once again to lead the British fleet against the might of Bonaparte's navy.

"It's early yet," she said again, dipping the washcloth in the bowl. She kissed his scarred brow, touched his lid, the eye beneath still bold, still penetrating, despite the fact he could barely see out of it. With love and tenderness, she washed his face, taking care to keep the soapy cloth away from his eyes, touching the lips that were now pinched tight in a perpetual frown of worry and despair. "Besides, the wedding ain't 'til this afternoon. For all you know, their carriage might've broken down, a horse thrown a shoe; why, they might even 'ave gotten lost!"

"They said they'd be here *yesterday,* Emma!"

"And so did the girl's cousins, but *they* 'aven't arrived yet either. And you, of all people, know that Admiral Sir Christian Lord is as true as the shot from a carronade. 'E'll be 'ere. *They* will be 'ere. Now sit still, would you? All this fidgeting of yours'll make me slip and get soap in your eye."

He reached up, caught her hand, pressed it to his lips, and on a resigned breath, murmured, "Emma, dear, sweet, Emma . . . what would I do without you?"

"You'd get on just fine," she joked, "for you are Nelson. Now be still—we 'ave much to do before Sir Graham and 'is bride-to-be arrive!"

She laughed, but in her heart were tears and sorrow and misery, for soon he would depart for the *Victory* at Portsmouth, and she had the strangest, most awful feeling that he wasn't coming back.

Merton Place was a lovely, sprawling property just southwest of London proper, complete with a little river affectionately renamed the Nile in honor of its owner's famous victory, a pond filled with pike, grassy sloping lawns bordered by shrubbery, and a gravel drive that grumbled and crunched beneath the wheels of their carriage as the lathered steeds pulled up before the stone steps.

"Here we are," Sir Graham said cheerfully, and waited while the footman opened the door. "Now stop looking so sad, my love. You are getting married today and I shall think you don't want me after all!"

Maeve nodded, and tried to smile. She had finished the letter to her parents. She had posted it. Several weeks from now, they would be reading it.

Oh, if only she'd written it months ago. If only her family could be here today, on this happiest, yet saddest, day of her life. . . .

The door to the big house opened and a woman rushed across the dewy lawn, the morning sunlight gilding her voluminous, cream-colored gown. Maeve put her hand on Gray's sleeve and allowed him to help her out of the carriage.

"Why, what took you so long?" Lady Hamilton grabbed Sir Graham, clasped him in her arms, kissed him unashamedly and affectionately on the cheek, and, without skipping a beat, turned and embraced Maeve too, her emotions as naked and guileless as were those of Nelson himself. "Come, come, let me look at you, this woman milord has told me was the only one who knew where the French 'ad gone, this woman who's done so much for our glorious an' gallant navy! Oh, you're lovely, beautiful, so exotic, an' you're going to make our friend Gray here very 'appy, very 'appy indeed! Are y' nervous, love? Are y' scared? 'Ere, let me take your things, and do come inside, we're just ready to sit down to breakfast and you simply *must* join us!"

Emma's inelegant and unaffected voice was that of a country woman, loud and bawdy and full of fun and life. Maeve stared at her, momentarily taken aback by the sheer force of her personality. This was the woman whose charm and sensuality had won Nelson away from his cold wife, the woman who had been friend and confidante to the queen of Naples, the woman whose doings, past and present, had the gossipy tongues of all England wagging—the woman whose portrait hung in Lord Nelson's cabin, around Lord Nelson's neck, in every room of Lord Nelson's kind and generous heart.

"It is a pleasure to meet you, Lady Hamilton."

"And it's a pleasure to meet *you,* an' please, you must call me Emma! Come, come, we 'ave much to do before the guests start arriving! Really Gray, you're such a rascal, why didn't you bring the poor dear yesterday? We 'ad room, you know we 'ad room, and you 'ave always been welcome at Merton!"

Gray merely shrugged, smiling distractedly and gazing at the two women; one tall and slim and honed with muscle, the other effusive and matronly and as stout as a flagship. Both had chestnut hair, both were faultlessly beautiful—and both were sailor's women, which in the end, of course, assured him they would get along famously.

Emma was shamelessly hugging the very stiff Maeve to her ample bosom. "Come, come, let's go inside," she cried. "Milord 'as told me all about 'ow you saved Sir Graham! Such courage! Such valor!" She clapped a hand dramatically to her heart. "No wonder our dear Sir Graham is so taken with you!"

With her two guests on either arm, Emma hustled them back toward the house, chattering all the way and hollering for Nelson. He, just coming around the side of the house, met them on the lawn; at first, Maeve didn't recognize the Admiral, for he was dressed as a civilian, in black gaiters, green breeches, a somber black coat, and a little tricorn hat, to which was attached a small, lime-colored visor to shade his good eye from the sun. He carried a walking stick in his hand, and his melancholy face was a study in anxiety, despair, and, as he saw Gray, relief.

"Gray," he said, in that severe tone reserved for use by admirals, generals, and the like, "I must talk to you. *Now.*"

"Is there something amiss?"

Nelson jerked his head, indicating the garden, where servants were busily setting up tables and chairs for the afternoon ceremony. "I hope not. Can you come? Oh dear, forgive me, you must have some breakfast first—"

"No, no, that can wait," Gray said, concerned at Nelson's obvious distress. He looked at Maeve, but Emma was already folding her in the circle of her arm and drawing her away.

"Go on, the two of you!" she said, waving her hand. "Perhaps you can reassure our Nelson that *everything will be fine.* And you, Maeve? Come with me, we 'ave much to do before the guests arrive. . . ."

* * *

An hour later Maeve, sitting stiffly in a chair at Lady Hamilton's mirrored dressing table while Emma attempted to make elegance of her hair, heard the crunch of gravel outside and knew the first guests had arrived. Emma's mother, a kind, earthy woman who called herself Mrs. Cadogan, hurried downstairs to meet them, while her daughter ran to the window and drew the curtains aside.

She gasped in delight, the sunlight picking out the classic beauty of her profile. "Oh, dear me! Admiral Hood is here, and Captain 'ardy, and there, Lord Barham himself! Now who is that naval officer with 'im? Nelson, I must find Nelson and ask him, but wait, there's another carriage, and a very 'andsome young man getting out of it—'e's blond, on crutches—do you know anyone of that description, love?—'e's a real looker, 'e is!"

"That would be my cousin," she murmured, staring woodenly at the dressing table. "Colin."

Lady Hamilton never noticed the sadness of Maeve's tone, the tears that threatened her golden eyes. "Oh, yes, of course! The Colin I've heard so much about, a pity about 'is leg. . . . Look, another carriage and another . . . and there's Gray's family. And good 'eavens, would you just look at that, there must be a whole passel of young women out there, and they're dressed most fiercely, if I do say so myself! Why, one of 'em is even 'olding a *cutlass!*"

"That would be my crew," Maeve said tonelessly.

"Oh, just think, in a few short hours you'll be Lady Falconer!"

She looked down at her hands. "Yes, Lady Hamilton."

"Emma, you must call me Emma. Oh look, they're putting the flowers on the tables now, you really should come see this, love! And wait 'til you taste the champagne. Milord sent to town for the finest of it; indeed, 'e is most anxious to see that you and your admiral 'ave the most memorable of days!"

"Lord Nelson is the kindest man I have ever met."

Emma turned and hurried forward with a gasp of dismay. "Why lovey—you're crying! Whatever's wrong?" Gentle hands grasped her shoulders. "Why, this should be the 'appiest day of your life! You're about to wed the most eligible officer in the King's navy! An admiral at his age; that is unheard of! You 'ave a whole life of 'appiness before you! Fine children, fine relations, the very *finest* of husbands—"

"*I do not have my family.*" Maeve's throat worked against the tears, and she stared defeatedly down at her trembling hands. "And there is nothing, nothing, I would've wanted more for this day than to . . . to . . . to have my father here to give me away. . . ."

"But your cousin, Admiral Lord," Emma said slowly. " 'E'll do the honors?"

"I have never set eyes upon Admiral Lord in my life. I do not know him and besides, it is his wife Deirdre who is my cousin, not him. I don't know her either, and I barely know their son, Colin. . . . and oh, I just want my D-D"—she bent her head to her hands and burst into tears—"*Daddy.* . . ."

Emma stepped forward, and maternally, impulsively, hugged the stricken girl to her bosom. Outside, she heard carriages in the drive, greetings as guests recognized each other, female voices, the guffaws of sailors, Nelson's high laughter as he showed off little Horatia to an admiring crowd who would never know she was his own daughter.

There wasn't much time left and now she, too, began to feel the anxiety that Nelson had been unable to quell. But what could she do? What could any of them do?

"Don't cry, m'love," she said, feeling helpless for one of the first times in her life. "Don't cry . . .

everything'll be all right, you just wait and see. . . .
Please, don't cry. . . ."

But Maeve was still weeping as, nearly two hours
later, Emma and her mother straightened the folds of
her gown, placed the tiara atop her upswept tresses, and
led her downstairs, to where the man she had never
met, the celebrated Admiral Christian Lord, waited solemnly to take her hand and lead her to the husband who
awaited her in the garden outside.

In later years, her memory of those last few moments
were fuzzy and dreamlike; she remembered tucking a
small dagger into her bodice when Lady Hamilton
wasn't looking; she remembered looking up at the tall
man whose elbow rested beneath her gloved hand and
seeing the face of a stranger; she remembered thinking
he looked stern and distinguished, with good looks un-
dimmed by the years and an aura of authority he wore
as easily as the gold epaulets upon his broad shoulders;
she remembered thinking he was nothing like the mirthful and merry soul her daddy had been, and blinking
back a fresh wave of tears as she raised her chin, commanded every ounce of courage and strength and pride
she had, and allowed him to lead her outside into the
bright sunlight.

The band was playing. She could hear it, even from
here, and above it, the sound of voices, laughter, gaiety,
merriment . . . sounds that abruptly ceased as Admiral
Christian Lord escorted her across the lawn and to the
gardens, where the guests had formed into two groups
on either side of a flowered path.

Faces.

All turned expectantly toward her.

As she passed them, she saw Aisling and Sorcha,
barely restrained by Enolia and both waving madly in a
gleeful attempt to be recognized by the lady of the day;
she smiled tremulously, her feet moving of their own

accord, her fingers tightening over a muscled arm that was alien and unfamiliar to her beneath her soft, satin gloves.

Faces.

She saw the squire and his wife—Gray's parents—and all six of his sisters, each dark head covered by a colorful hat, each face bright and excited.

Faces.

She saw people she didn't know, people she did. Orla, and *Kestrel*'s rowdy crew; Colin, leaning heavily on his crutches, standing beside a lovely woman with curly black hair and a strange, Celtic crucifix about her neck—that would be Deirdre, his mother and Maeve's own cousin; Mrs. Cadogan, one of Nelson's sisters, and Emma, rushing to the head of the line and weeping with joy; a cluster of unknown sea officers, their wives in lovely gowns and parasols to shield their complexions from the sun . . .

Faces.

And there, at the end of the path, at the end of the crowd, Lord Nelson—aglitter with every star and decoration and order he owned, his neck draped with medals, his hat plumed by a brilliant diamond aigrette—standing triumphantly beside the minister and the man who would soon be her husband.

Sir Graham was in his best uniform. The one that had never seen sea service, but was reserved for only the most honored of occasions, the gold buttons and lace and epaulets blindingly bright in the sun, the medal of the Nile around his neck, the broad red sash of knighthood across his right shoulder. His hands were clasped behind his back; a sailor he was, even here, and he was smiling, his eyes radiant with love as he caught sight of her and watched her move slowly down the path, toward him.

Gray . . . .

Her feet continued to move, but her stare was on

Nelson. Why was the Admiral looking so smug? So satisfied? So very proud of himself?

And then Sir Graham was gazing beyond her shoulder, nodding ever so slightly; beside her, Christian Lord stopped, stepped away from her, and with a deferential bow, relinquished her unto the care of another.

The voice came to her, moving across time, across memory, across pain and fear and anguish and hope. . . .

"Faith, lassie, did you really think you could steal my schooner and get away with it? Did you really think I wouldn't show up to give my daughter away at her own wedding? Good God, what the *devil* is this world coming to?!"

She froze, not daring to breathe, to hope, to think; she felt his arm sliding under her gloved hand, heard his melodious Irish voice echoing through her ears and every joyous cell in her awakening body; she blinked once, twice, and slowly, looked up—into a face she hadn't seen in seven long years and thought never to see again.

A handsome face framed in chestnut hair gone gray at the temples; a youthful face, lit by a mirthful grin and Irish eyes now filling with tears of joy and love; a beloved face, a cherished face, that of the one man whose love and forgiveness meant more to her than anyone else's in the whole, entire world.

Her father.

"Dadd-e-e-e-e-e!" she cried, and threw herself into his embrace.

And as he swung her around and around, she saw beyond him, gathered in a circle and now rushing forward, her family. Mama. Uncle Matt. Aunt Eveleen. Her sisters and brothers and yes, even old Grandpa Ephraim, swinging a pocket watch and grinning that great, yellow-toothed old grin she remembered so well.

The tears streamed down her cheeks. Her family converged upon her, hugging her, kissing her, sobbing over her. And even as she wondered how they could've known she was in England, even as she wondered how they could've known to find her here, her gaze fell upon the frail figure of Lord Nelson, standing a bit apart from the others and smiling a faint, satisfied smile.

Their eyes met. And in that brief, wonderful moment of revelation, Maeve knew the truth.

Gray had given her back the ability to trust.

The little Admiral had given her back her family.

After seven long years, the Merricks were united at last.

I commit my life to Him who made me.
—NELSON

Epilogue

Friday night at half past ten, drove from dear, dear Merton, where I left all which I hold dear in this world, to go to serve my King and Country. May the great God, whom I adore, enable me to fulfil the expectations of my country; and if it is His good pleasure that I should return, my thanks will never cease being offered up to the throne of His mercy. If it is His good Providence to cut short my days upon earth, I bow with the greatest submission, relying that He will protect those dear to me that I may leave behind. His will be done. Amen, amen, amen.

The post chaise rumbled through the night, carrying Lord Nelson south, away from Emma and Horatia and the home he loved so much.

He thought of Emma, sobbing and nearly collapsing at the table yesterday; he thought of the tearful, final farewells at dinner, and little Horatia as he'd knelt at her bedside in the darkness and prayed for her; four times he'd gone back to look at his sleeping daughter, before finally striding out the front door, down the steps, and into the waiting chaise, where a young stablehand had stood holding the door for him. "Be a good boy 'til I come back again," Nelson had said fondly as he'd climbed in, and then, the lights of Merton had faded away into darkness. . . .

The prayer had been in his mind for days. At a break

384

in the journey at a coaching-inn, he had copied it into his diary. And as the miles fell behind him he stared out into the night, thinking of the enemy at Cádiz, of his plan for defeating them, of his waiting coffin and glory and the words of a gypsy he'd once met, long ago. . . .

I can see no farther than the year 1805 for you. . . .

Thinking. . . .

Of his own premonitions, his fears, a visionary orb of white light that had come to him long ago when he'd been a despairing teenager, remaining to guide him his entire life—and of his last farewell to the Pirate Queen, who had embraced him with tears streaming down her cheeks as a bewildered Sir Graham stood helplessly nearby. . . .

You can see the future, Maeve—what do you see for me? Will I beat the French? Oh, tell me, will I?

And she, faltering, her eyes filling with tears before she'd looked away. . . . *You, milord . . . will fulfill your own destiny. . . .*

Through the night the chaise went. On through the sleeping countryside, past woods and fields and darkened houses, on to the Hampshire coast, where morning light glowed upon the chalky bluffs and the scent of the sea filled the air, on across Portsea Island and finally, to Portsmouth—where the noble *Victory* stood in quiet readiness for the greatest admiral her country had ever known.

The sally port was choked with crowds, all pushing and shoving, all anxiously waiting just to get a glimpse of him as, after lunching at The George, Lord Nelson left England for the last time. He tried to avoid them, but in the end it was no use, and as he walked toward the beach in his jaunty, rolling, seaman's gait, the people came rushing through the narrow streets of Portsmouth after him in a tumultuous flood of adoring humanity. He—this little man they regarded as their savior, this little man who symbolized England, this little man upon whose shoulders the hope and fate of their country depended—was going off to fight their war, to save them from the dreaded Napoleon Bonaparte, and they were determined to send him off in a fine display of love and emotion. Hands reached out to grasp his, seeking to touch his greatness; people knelt in his path, praying for him, for a victory; some were crying in great keening wails, others wept quietly, all followed him as he headed for the beach.

Across Southsea Common he went, the vast multitudes trailing in his wake, sobbing, screaming, crying his name—*Nelson! Nelson! God bless you, Lord Nelson!*—already he could see his barge, waiting for him, the soldiers having to fight to clear a path through the throngs so that he could get to it. There was an officer, sitting solemnly in the sternsheets, and the barge crew, their oars raised smartly.

And beyond, *Victory*—waiting.

He descended the sixteen steps of the wharf, the frenzied clamor of thousands of people ringing in his ears. The barge swayed beneath him as he stepped down into it, acknowledging Hardy's salute and taking his place beside him. The clamor rose to a deafening thunder, and, as the oarsmen pushed off from shore, separated itself into three distinct and mighty cheers that shook the very clouds in the sky above.

God bless Lord Nelson! God bless Lord Nelson! God bless Lord Nelson!

Misty-eyed and overwhelmed, he took off his hat and waved it to the crowds. "I had their huzzahs before," he murmured softly to Hardy. "I have their hearts now."

And in that vast, swelling crowd, the new Lady Falconer stood with her own admiral and the family that Nelson had given back to her. She thought of her last tearful good-bye to the brave hero and the shining future that awaited her as Gray's wife. Through the din she heard her husband talking to her father, felt the press and breath and heat and life of thousands of bodies around her—but in those last, melancholy moments everything faded and it was just she and the little Admiral. She watched the oars rising and falling in precision as the barge, diminishing now in size, moved toward the ship that would carry him to Cádiz ... to the British Fleet ... to battle ... to glory—

And, she knew—to Eternity.

Good-bye. . . . she thought, her eyes blurring with tears. *And thank you.*

Author's Note

"*My* last thought shall be fixed on thee, yes my last sigh *shall go to my own dear, incomparable Emma. I see nothing terrible in death but leaving thee.*"

On the 21st of October, 1805, Horatio, Lord Nelson—after more than two years of waiting, planning, and praying—finally brought the British and Combined Franco-Spanish fleets to battle off the Spanish port of Cádiz.

He never doubted a glorious victory. The Battle of Trafalgar, as it came to be called, won Britain a supremacy over the seas that was to last for the next one hundred years. Ending forever the threat of Napoleonic invasion, the triumph was darkened only by the loss of Nelson himself, who, at the height of the battle, was hit by a French sniper who spotted the gleaming medals of his coat as the Admiral and his flag-captain, Hardy, calmly paced *Victory*'s shot-torn quarterdeck.

He died three hours later, after receiving word of a complete and overwhelming victory.

Avon Romances—
the best in exceptional authors and unforgettable novels!

If you enjoyed this book, take advantage of this special offer.
Subscribe now and get a

FREE
Historical
Romance

No Obligation (a $4.50 value)

Each month the editors of True Value select the four *very best* novels from America's leading publishers of romantic fiction. Preview them in your home *Free* for 10 days. With the first four books you receive, we'll send you a FREE book as our introductory gift. No Obligation!

If for any reason you decide not to keep them, just return them and owe nothing. If you like them as much as we think you will, you'll pay just $4.00 each and save at *least* $.50 each off the cover price. (Your savings are *guaranteed* to be at least $2.00 each month.) There is NO postage and handling – or other hidden charges. There are no minimum number of books to buy and you may cancel at any time.

Send in the Coupon Below

To get your FREE historical romance fill out the coupon below and mail it today. As soon as we receive it we'll send you your FREE Book along with your first month's selections.

- -